About

Melanie Milburne re... seventeen in between... After completing a M... decided to write a n... romance author was b... for the Australian Childhood Foundation, a keen dog lover and trainer, and enjoys long walks in the Tasmanian bush. In 2015 Melanie won the HOLT Medallion, a prestigious award honouring outstanding literary talent.

Yahrah St. John is the author of forty-one published books and and won an award from RT Book Reviews for *A Chance With You*. She earned a Bachelor of Arts degree in English from Northwestern University. A member of Romance Writers of America, St John is an avid reader, enjoys cooking, travelling and adventure sports, but her true passion is writing. Visit yahrahstjohn.com

Cara Colter shares her home in beautiful British Columbia, Canada, with her husband of more than thirty years, an ancient, crabby cat and several horses. She has three grown children and two grandsons.

Tempted by the Tycoon

Tempted by the Tycoon
Forbidden
Attraction

MELANIE MILBURNE

YAHRAH ST. JOHN

CARA COLTER

MILLS & BOON

TYCOON'S FORBIDDEN CINDERELLA

MELANIE MILBURNE

To my dear friend Julie Greenwood.

We have been friends since the seventh grade, and
I can't imagine how different life would be if
I hadn't met you.

I have so many fun memories of us horse riding
and sitting in the mulberry tree at my parents'
farm with purple-stained fingers and mouths.

You are one of a kind.

Love always. Xxxx

CHAPTER ONE

AUDREY EYED HER mother's wedding invitation as if it were a cockroach next to her breakfast teacup and toast plate. 'I would do anything to get out of this wedding party and I mean *anything*.'

Rosie, her flatmate, slipped into the seat opposite and pinched a slice of toast off Audrey's plate and began munching. 'Three times a bridesmaid, huh? Go you.'

Audrey sighed. 'Yes, well, being a bridesmaid three times would be bad enough but they're my mother's marriages and all to Harlan Fox. I thought she'd learned her lesson by now.'

'I guess that does complicate things a bit…' Rosie twisted her mouth in a *glad-it's-you-and-not-me* manner.

'I don't know why my mother hasn't learnt from her past two mistakes.' Audrey stirred her tea until it created a whirlpool similar to the one she was feeling in her stomach. 'Who marries the same man *three* times? I can't bear another one of my mother's marriages. I can't bear another one of my mother's divorces. None of them were civilised and private. They were nasty and hor-

ribly public.' Her teaspoon fell against the saucer with
a clatter. 'That's the problem with having a soap opera
star for a parent. Nothing they do ever escapes public
attention. Nothing. Good or bad or just plain dead embarrassing, it's all splashed over the gossip magazines
and the net for millions to read.'

'Yeah, I kind of figured that after that spread about
your mother's affair with one of the young cameramen
on set,' Rosie said. 'Amazing she has a daughter of
twenty-five and yet she can still pull guys like a bar-
man pulls beers.'

'Yes, well, if that wasn't bad enough, Harlan Fox is
even more famous than my mother.' Audrey frowned
and pushed her cup and saucer away as if it had mor-
tally offended her. 'What can she possibly see in an
aging rock star of a heavy metal band?'

'Maybe it's because Harlan and his band mates are in
the process of reforming to go back on the tour?' Rosie
had clearly been reading the gossip pages rather avidly.

Audrey rolled her eyes. 'A process somewhat stalled
by the fact that two of its members are still in rehab for
drug and alcohol issues.'

Rosie licked a droplet of raspberry jam off her finger
and asked, 'Is Harlan's hot-looking son Lucien going to
be best man again?'

Audrey sprang up from the table as if her chair had
suddenly exploded. The mere mention of Lucien Fox's
name was enough to make her grind her teeth until her
molars rolled over and begged for mercy. She scooped
her teacup off the table and poured the contents in the
sink, wishing she were throwing it in Lucien's impos-

sibly handsome face. 'Yes.' She spat out the word like a lemon pip.

'Funny how you two have never hit it off,' Rosie said. 'I mean, you'd think you'd have heaps in common. You've both lived in the shadow of a celebrity parent. And you've been step-siblings on and off for the last... how long's it been now?'

Audrey turned from the sink and gripped the back of the chair. 'Six years. But it's not going to happen again. No way. This wedding is *not* going to go ahead.'

Rosie's eyebrows lifted until they met her fringe. 'What? You think you can talk them out of it?'

Audrey released her stranglehold on the chair and picked up her phone from the table and checked for messages. Still no answer from her mother. Damn it. 'I'm going to track Mum and Harlan down and give them a stern talking-to. I'll resort to blackmail if I have to. I have to stop them marrying. I *have* to.'

Rosie frowned. 'Track them down? Why? Have they gone into hiding or something?'

'They've both turned off their phones. Their publicists apparently have no idea where they've gone.'

'But you do?'

She drummed her fingers on the back of her phone. 'No, but I have a hunch and I'm going to start there.'

'Have you asked Lucien where he thinks they might be or are you still not talking since the last divorce? How many years ago was that again?' Rosie asked.

'Three,' Audrey said. 'For the last six years my mother and Harlan have been hooking up, getting hitched and then divorcing in a hate fest that makes headlines around the world. I'm over it. I'm not going to let it happen again. They can hook up if they want to but another marriage is out. O.U.T. Out.'

Rosie shifted her lips from side to side as if observing an unusual creature in captivity. 'Wow. You really have a thing about weddings, don't you? Don't you want to get married one day?'

'No. I do not.' Audrey knew she sounded like a starchy old spinster from a nineteenth-century novel but she was beyond caring. She hated weddings. Capital H hated them. She felt like throwing up when she saw a white dress. Maybe she wouldn't hate weddings so much if she hadn't been dragged to so many of her mother's. Before Harlan Fox, Sibella Merrington had had three husbands and not one of them had been Audrey's father. Audrey had no idea who her father was and apparently neither did her mother, although Sibella had narrowed it down to three men.

What was it with her mother and the number three?

'You didn't answer my question,' Rosie said. 'Are you talking to Lucien again or not?'

'Not.'

'Maybe you should reconsider,' Rosie said. 'You never know, he might prove to be an ally in your mission to stop his dad and your mum getting married.'

Audrey snorted. 'The day I speak again to that arrogant, stuck-up jerk will be the day hell turns into an ice factory.'

'Why do you hate him so much? What's he ever done to you?'

Audrey turned and snatched her coat off the hook

behind the door and shrugged it on, pulling her hair out of the collar. She faced her flatmate. 'I don't want to talk about it. I just hate him, that's all.'

Rosie's brows shot up again like skyrockets and she leaned forward in her chair, eyes sparkling with intrigue. 'Did he try it on with you?'

Audrey's cheeks were suddenly feeling so hot she could have cooked another round of toast on them. No way was she going to confess it was *she* who had done the 'trying it on' and been rejected.

Mortifyingly, embarrassingly, ego-crushingly rejected.

Not once but two times. Once when she was eighteen and again when she was twenty-one, both times at her mother's wedding reception to his father. Another good reason to prevent such a marriage occurring again.

No more wedding receptions.

No more champagne.

No more gauche flirting with Lucien Fox.

Oh, God, why, why, *why* had she tried to kiss him? She had been planning to peck him on the cheek to show how sophisticated and cool she was about their respective parents getting married. But somehow her lips had moved. Or maybe his had moved. What did it matter whose had moved? Their mouths had almost touched. It was the closest a man's mouth had ever been to hers.

But he had jerked away as if she had poison on her lips.

The same thing happened at their parents' next wedding. Audrey had been determined to act as if nothing could faze her. She was going to act as if the previous

almost-kiss had never happened. To show him it hadn't
had any impact on her at all. But after a few cham-
pagnes to give her the courage to get on the dance floor,
she'd breezed past Lucien and hadn't been able to stop
herself from giving him a spontaneous little air kiss.
Her mouth had aimed for the air between his cheek and
hers but someone bumped her from behind and she had
fallen against him. She'd grabbed at the front of his shirt
to stop herself from falling. He'd put his hands on her
hips to steady her.

And for a moment…an infinitesimal moment when
the noise of the reception faded away and it felt they
were completely and utterly alone…she'd thought he
was going to kiss her. So she'd…

Oh, God, she hated thinking about it even now…

She'd leaned up on tiptoe, closed her eyes and waited
for him to kiss her. And waited. And waited.

But of course he hadn't.

Even though Audrey had been tipsy on both occasions, and a part of her knew Lucien had done the hon-
ourable thing by rejecting her clumsy advances, another
part of her—the female, insecure part—wondered if
any man would ever be attracted to her. Would any
man ever want to kiss her, much less make love to her?
She was twenty-five and still a virgin. She hadn't been
on a date since she was a teenager. Not that she hadn't
been asked a few times but she'd always declined because she could never tell if guys wanted to go out with
her for the right reason. Her first date at the age of sixteen had been a disaster—an ego-smashing disaster she
would do anything to avoid repeating. She'd only been

asked out because of who her mother was. It had nothing to do with *her* whether the boy liked her or not. It was about her celebrity mother.

It was *always* about her celebrity mother.

Audrey picked up her keys and the overnight bag she'd packed earlier. 'I'm heading out of town for the weekend.'

Rosie's eyes twinkled like they belonged on a Christmas tree. 'Am I allowed to know where you're going or is it a state secret?'

It wasn't that Audrey didn't trust her flatmate, but even Rosie with her down-to-earth nature could at times be a little star-struck by Audrey's mother. 'Sorry, Rosie. I have to keep the press out of this if I can. With Mum and Harlan in hiding, the first person the paps will come looking for is me.'

Please, God, not again. The press had followed her relentlessly after her mother had gone to ground. At Audrey's flat. She'd stayed for three weeks and had taken three overdoses, not serious enough for hospitalisation but serious enough for Audrey to want to prevent another marriage between her mother and the hard-partying Harlan Fox.

'What about Lucien?'

'What about Lucien?' Even saying his name made Audrey's spine tighten and her scalp prickle as if a thousand ants were tugging on the roots of her hair.

'What if Lucien wants to know where you are?'

'He won't. Anyway, he's got my number.'

Not that he'd ever used it in the last three years. Or the last six. But then, why would he? She was hardly his type. His type was tall and blonde and sophisticated, women who didn't drink too much champagne when they were feeling nervous or insecure and out of their depth.

'Gosh, how lucky are you to be on Lucien Fox's speed dial.' Rosie's expression had gone all dreamy. 'I wish I had his number. I don't suppose you'd—?'

Audrey shook her head. 'It'd be a waste of time if I did. He doesn't date boring homespun girls like us. He only dates size zero supermodels.'

Rosie sighed. 'Yeah, like that one he's been dating now for weeks and weeks—Viviana Prestonward.'

Something slipped in Audrey's stomach. 'H-has he?' Her voice came out scratchy and she cleared her throat. 'I mean, yes, yes, I know.'

'Viviana's amazingly beautiful.' Rosie's expression became one part wistful, three parts envious. 'I saw a picture of them at a charity ball last month. Everyone's saying they're about to become engaged. Some girls have all the luck. They get the best looks and the best guys.'

'I wouldn't call Lucien Fox a prize catch.' Audrey couldn't keep the bitter edge from her tone. 'He might be good-looking and rich but his personality needs a serious makeover. He's so stiff and formal you'd think he'd been potty-trained at gunpoint.'

Rosie tilted her head again in her studying-an-exotic-creature manner. 'Maybe he'll ask you to be the brides-maid at his wedding too, I mean, since you're going to be step-siblings again.'

Audrey clenched her teeth hard enough to crack a coconut. 'Not if I can help it.'

* * *

Audrey drove out of London and within a couple of hours pulled into the country lane that led to the secluded cottage in the Cotswolds. Her mother had bought the house when she landed her first role on television. It often amazed Audrey that her mother hadn't sold it by now, but somehow the cottage remained even though several husbands and their houses had not.

It was too small to be the sort of place the press would expect to find Sibella and Harlan, so it was the first place on Audrey's list. Her mother had left a hint in the note on her doorstep, along with the invitation:

Gone to smell the daffodils with Harlan.

That could only mean Bramble Cottage. At this time of year the rambling garden was full of daffodils. Along the lane, in the fields, under the trees, along the bank of the stream—the swathes of yellow had always delighted Audrey.

Bramble Cottage was a perfect hideaway as it was on a long country lane lined with hedgerows and lots of overarching trees, creating a leafy tunnel. The lane had a rickety bridge over a trickling stream that occasionally swelled enough with rainwater to be considered a river.

When she came down to the cottage with her mother as a child, Audrey had been fascinated by the trees along the lane because they looked as if they were reaching down to hug her. Going through that shady green tunnel had been like driving into another world, a magical world where it was just her and her mother.

A safe world. A world where there were no strange men coming and going from her mother's bedroom.

No press lurking about for candid shots of Sibella's painfully shy daughter.

Audrey couldn't see any sign of activity at the cottage when she got out of her car but she knew her mother and Harlan would have covered their tracks well. On closer inspection, however, she realised the cottage looked a little neglected. She'd thought there was a caretaker who kept an eye on things. There were often months and months or even a couple of years between her mother's fleeting visits. The garden was overgrown but in a way that was part of the charm of the place. Audrey loved how the plants spilled over the garden beds, their blooms filling the air with the fresh and hopeful fragrance of spring.

Audrey left her car parked in the shade of the biggest oak tree a short distance away so as to keep her car from being seen if any paparazzi happened to do a drive-by. She did a mental high-five when she saw the marks of recent tyre tracks on the pebbled area in front of the cottage. She bent down so she could inspect the tracks a little more closely. A car had come in and gone out again, which meant her mother and Harlan hopefully weren't far away. Probably picking up supplies or something. 'Or something' being copious amounts of alcohol most likely.

She straightened and glanced up at the suddenly darkening sky. That was another thing she loved about this place—watching a spring storm from the cosy shelter of the cottage. The spare key was under the left-hand plant pot but Audrey gave the door a quick knock just in case either her mother or Harlan was still inside. When there was no answer, she unlocked the door just as the rain started to pelt down as if someone had turned on a tap.

She closed the door and looked around the cottage but it didn't look as though anyone had been there in months. Disappointment sat on her chest like an over-stuffed sofa. She'd been so certain she would find them here. Had she misread her mother's note?

She glanced at the cobwebs hanging from a lamp-shade and suppressed an icy shiver. There was a fine layer of dust over the furniture and the air inside the cottage had a musty, unaired smell. So much for the care-taker, then. But Audrey figured this would be a good test of the hideously expensive therapy she'd undergone to rid herself of her spider phobia. She pulled back the curtains to let more light in but the storm clouds had gathered to such an extent the world outside had a yellowish, greenish tinge that intensified with each flash of lightning. She turned on the sitting room light and it cast a homey glow over the deep, cushiony sofas and the wing chair positioned in front of the fireplace.

Audrey was battling with an acute sense of dismay that her mission to track down her mother and Harlan had come to a dead end and a sense of sheer unmitigated joy she had the cottage to herself during a storm. She figured she might as well stay for an hour or two to set the place in order, maybe even stay the night while she thought up a Plan B.

She reassured herself with the possibility that her

mother and Harlan would return at any minute. After all, someone had been here—she'd seen the tyre marks. All she had to do was wait until they got back and sit them down and talk them out of this ridiculous third marriage.

Audrey glanced at the fireplace. Was it cold enough to light a fire? There was kindling and wood in the basket next to the fireplace, and before she could talk herself out of it she got to work setting a fire in the grate. It would come in handy if the power was to go off, which was not uncommon during a storm.

As if by her just thinking of a power cut, the light above her head flickered and a flash of lightning rent the sky outside. A sonic boom of thunder sounded, and it made even an avid storm-lover such as she jump. The light flickered again and then went out. It left the room in a low, ghostly sort of light that reminded her of the setting of a fright flick she'd watched recently. A shiver scuttled over her flesh like a legion of little furry feet.

It's just a storm. You love storms.

For once the self-talk wasn't helping. There was something about this storm that felt different. It was more intense, more ferocious.

Between the sound of the rain lashing against the windows and the crash of thunder, she heard another sound—car tyres spinning over the pebbled driveway.

Yes!

Her hunch had been spot-on. Her mother and Harlan were returning. Audrey jumped up to peep out of the window and her heart gave a carthorse kick against her breastbone.

No. No. No.

Not Lucien Fox. Why was he here?

She hid behind part of the curtain to watch him approach the front door, her breathing as laboured as the pair of antique bellows next to the fireplace. The rain was pelting down on his dark head but he seemed oblivious. Would he see her car parked under the oak tree?

She heard Lucien's firm knock on the door. Why hadn't she thought to lock it when she came into the cottage? The door opened and then closed.

Should she come out or hide here behind the curtain, hoping he wouldn't stay long enough to find her? The *Will I or won't I?* was like a seesaw inside her head.

He came into the sitting room and Audrey's heart kept time with the tread of his feet on the creaky floorboards.

Step-creak-boom-step-creak-boom-step-creak-boom.

'Harlan?' Lucien's deep baritone never failed to make her spine tingle. 'Sibella?'

Audrey knew it was too late to step out from her hiding place. She could only hope he would leave before he discovered her. How long was he going to take? Surely he could see no one had been here for months… *Yikes.* She forgot she had been laying a fire. Her breathing rate accelerated, her pulse pounding as loud as the thunder booming outside. She'd been about to strike the match when the power had gone off and it was now lying along with the box it came from on the floor in front of the fireplace.

Would he see it?

Another floorboard creaked and Audrey held her breath. But then her nose began to twitch from the dust clinging to the curtain. There was one thing she did not have and that was a ladylike sneeze. Her sneezes registered on the Richter scale. Her sneezes could trigger an earthquake in Ecuador. Her sneezes had been known to cause savage guard dogs to yelp and small babies to scream. She could feel it building, building, building… She pressed a finger under her nose as hard as she possibly could, her whole body trembling with the effort to keep the sinus explosion from happening.

A huge lightning flash suddenly zigzagged across the sky and an ear-splitting boom of thunder followed, making Audrey momentarily forget about controlling her sneeze. She clutched the curtain in shock, wondering if she'd been struck by lightning. Would she be found as a little pile of smoking ashes behind this curtain? But clutching the curtain brought the dusty fabric even closer to her nostrils and the urge to sneeze became unbearable.

'Ah... Ah... Choo!'

It was like a bomb going off, propelling her forwards, still partially wrapped in the curtain, bringing the rail down with a clatter.

Even from under the dense and mummy-like shroud, Audrey heard Lucien's short, sharp expletive. Then his hands pulled at the curtain, finally uncovering her dishevelled form. 'What the hell?'

'Hi…' She sat up and gave him a fingertip wave.

He frowned at her. *'You?'*

'Yep, me.' Audrey scrambled to her feet with haste

not grace, wishing she'd worn jeans instead of a dress. But jeans made her thighs look fat, she thought, so a dress it was. She smoothed down the cotton fabric over her thighs and then finger-combed her tousled hair. Was he comparing her with his glamorous girlfriend? No doubt Viviana could stumble out of a musty old curtain and still look perfect. Viviana probably had a tiny ladylike sneeze too. And Viviana probably looked amazing in jeans.

'What are you doing here?' His tone had that edge of disapproval that always annoyed her.

'Looking for my mum and your dad.'

Lucien's ink-black brows developed a mocking arch. 'Behind the curtain?'

Audrey gave him a look that would have withered tumbleweed. 'Funny, ha-ha. So what brings you here?'

He bundled up the curtain as if he needed something to do with his hands, his expression as brooding as the sky outside. 'Like you, I'm looking for my father and your mother.'

'Why did you think they'd come here?'

He put the roughly folded curtain over the back of the wing chair and then picked up the curtain rail, setting it to one side. 'My father sent me a text, mentioning something about a quiet weekend in the country.'

'Did his text say anything about daffodils?'

Lucien looked at her as if she'd mentioned fairies instead of flowers. 'Daffodils?'

Audrey folded her arms across her middle. 'Didn't you notice them outside? This place is Wordsworth's heaven.'

The corner of his mouth twitched into an almost-smile. But then his mouth went back to its firm and flat humourless line. 'I think we've been led on a wild-goose chase—or a wild-daffodil chase.'

This time it was Audrey who was trying not to smile. Who knew he had a sense of humour under that stern schoolmastery thing he had going on? 'I suppose you got the invitation to their wedding?'

His expression reminded her of someone not quite over a stomach bug. 'You too?'

'Me too.' She let out a sigh. 'I can't bear to be a bridesmaid for my mother again. Her taste in brides-maid dresses is nearly as bad as her taste in men.'

If he was annoyed by her veiled slight against his fa-ther he didn't show it. 'We need to stop them from mak-ing another stupid mistake before it's too late.'

'We?'

His dark blue gaze collided with hers. Was it even pos-sible to have eyes that shade of sapphire? And why did he have to have such thick, long eyelashes when she had to resort to lashings of mascara? 'Between us we must be able to narrow down the search. Where does your mother go when she wants to get away from the spotlight?'

Audrey rolled her eyes. 'She never wants to get away from the spotlight. Not now. In the early days she did. But it looks like she hasn't been here in months, pos-sibly a year or more. Maybe even longer.'

Lucien ran a finger over the dusty surface of the nearest bookshelf, inspecting his fingertip like a foren-sics detective. He looked at her again. 'Can you think of anywhere else they might go?'

'Erm... Vegas?'

'I don't think so, not after the last time, remember?'

Audrey dearly wished she could forget. After her clumsy air kiss to Lucien—*as if that hadn't been bad enough*—her mother and his father had been ridiculously drunk at the reception of their second wedding and had got into a playful food fight. Some of the guests joined in and before long the room was trashed and three people were taken to hospital and four others arrested over a scuffle that involved a bowl of margarita punch and an ice bucket.

The gossip magazines ran with it for days and the hotel venue banned Harlan and Sibella from ever going there again. The fact that Audrey's mother had been the first to throw a profiterole meant that Lucien had always blamed Sibella and not his father. 'You're right. Not Vegas. Besides, they want us at the wedding to witness the ceremony. Not that the invitation mentioned where it was being held, just a date and venue to be advised.'

Lucien paced the floor, reminding her of a cougar in a cat carrier. 'Think. Think. Think.'

Audrey wasn't sure if he was speaking to her or to himself. The thing was, she found it difficult to think when he was around. His presence disturbed her too much. She couldn't stop herself studying his brooding features. He was one of the most attractive men she'd ever seen—possibly *the* most.

Tall and broad-shouldered and with a jaw you could land a fighter jet on. His mouth always made her think of long, sense-drugging kisses. Not that she'd had many of those, and certainly none from him, but it didn't stop her fantasising. He had thick, black, wavy hair that was neither long nor short but casually styled with the ends curling against his collar. He was clean-shaven but there was enough regrowth to make her wonder how it would feel to have that sexy stubble rub up against her softer skin.

Lucien stopped pacing and met her gaze and frowned. 'What?'

Audrey blinked. 'What?'

'I asked first.'

She licked her lips, which felt as dry as the dust on the bookshelves. 'I was just thinking. I always stare when I think.'

'What are you thinking?'

How hot you look in those jeans and that close-fitting cashmere sweater.

Audrey knew she was blushing, for she could feel her cheeks roaring enough to make lighting a fire pointless. She could have warmed the whole of England with the radiant heat coming off her face. Possibly half of Europe. 'I think the storm is getting worse.'

It was true. The lightning and thunder were much more intense and the rain had now turned into hail, landing like stones on the slate-tiled roof.

Lucien glanced out of the window and swore. 'We'll have to wait it out before we leave. It's too dangerous to drive down that lane in this weather.'

Audrey folded her arms across her middle again and raised her chin. 'I'm not leaving with you, so you can get that thought out of your head right now.'

His eyes took in her indomitable stance as if he were

staring down at a small, recalcitrant child. 'I want you with me when we finally track them down. We need to show them we are both vehemently against this marriage.'

No way was she going on a tandem search with him. 'Were you listening?' She planted her feet as if she were conducting a body language workshop for mules. 'I said I'm not leaving. I'm going to stay the night and tidy this place up.'

'With no power on?'

Audrey had forgotten about the power cut. But even if she had to rub two sticks together to make a fire she would do it rather than go anywhere with him. 'I'll be fine. The fire will be enough. I'm only staying the one night.'

He continued to look at her as if he thought a white van and a straitjacket might be useful right about now. 'What about your thing with spiders?'

How like him to remind her of her embarrassing childhood phobia. But she had no reason to be ashamed these days. She'd taken control. Ridiculously expensive control. Twenty-eight sessions with a therapist that had cost more than her car. She would have done thirty sessions but she'd run out of money. Her income as a library archivist only went so far. 'I've had therapy. I'm cool with spiders now. Spiders and me, we're like that.' She linked two of her fingers in a tight hug.

His expression looked as though he belonged as keynote speaker at a sceptics' conference. 'Really?'

'Yes. Really. I've had hypnotherapy so I don't get triggered when I see a spider. I can even say the word without breaking out in a sweat. I can look at pictures of them too. I even draw doodles of them.'

'So if you turned and saw that big spider hanging from the picture rail you wouldn't scream and throw yourself into my arms?'

Audrey tried to control the urge to turn around. She used every technique she'd been taught. She could cope with cobwebs. Sure, she could. They were pretty in a weird sort of way. Like lace...or something.

She was *not* going to have a totally embarrassing panic attack.

Not after all that therapy. She was going to smile at Incy-Wincy because that was what sensible people who weren't scared spitless of spiders did, right?

Her heart rate skyrocketed. *Breathe. Breathe. Breathe.* Beads of sweat dripped between her shoulder blades as if she were leaking oil. *Don't panic. Don't panic. Don't panic.* Her breathing stop-started as though a tormenting hand were gripping, then releasing her throat. *Grip. Release. Grip. Release. Grip. Release.*

What if the spider moved? What if this very second it was climbing down from the picture rail and was about to land on her head? Or scuttle down the back of her dress? Audrey shivered and took a step closer to Lucien, figuring it was a step further away from the spider even if it brought her closer to her arch-enemy Number One. 'Y-you're joking, right?'

'Why don't you turn around and see?'

Audrey didn't want to turn around. Didn't want to see the spider. She was quite happy looking at Lucien instead. Maybe her therapist should include 'Looking at

Lucien' in her treatment plan. Diversionary therapy…
or something.

This close she could smell his aftershave—a lemony and lime combo with an understory of something
fresh and woodsy. It flirted with her senses, drugging
them into a stupor like a bee exposed to exotic pollen.
She could see the way his stubble was dotted around
his mouth in little dark pinpricks. Her fingers itched to
glide across the sexy rasp of his male flesh. She drew
in a calming breath.

*You've got this. You've spent a veritable fortune to
get this.*

She slowly turned around, and saw a spider dangling
inches from her face.

A big one.

A ginormous one.

A genetically engineered one.

A throwback from the dinosaur age.

She gave a high-pitched yelp and turned into the
rock-hard wall of Lucien's chest, wrapping her arms
around his waist and burying her face in the cashmere
of his sweater. She danced up and down on her toes to
shake off the sensation of sticky spider feet climbing
up her legs. 'Get rid of it!'

Lucien's hands settled on her upper arms, his fingers almost overlapping. 'It won't hurt you. It's probably more frightened of you.'

She huddled closer, squeezing her eyes shut, shuddering all over. 'I don't care if it's frightened of me. Tell
it to get some therapy.'

She felt the rumble of his laughter against her cheek

and glanced up to see a smile stretching his mouth. 'Oh. My. God,' she said as if witnessing a life-changing phenomenon. 'You smiled. You actually smiled.'

His smile became lopsided, making his eyes gleam in a way she had never witnessed before. Then his gaze went to her mouth as if pulled there by a force he had no control over. She could feel the weight of his eyes on her mouth. She was as close to him as she had been to any man. Closer. Closer than she had been to him at the last wedding reception. Her entire body tingled as if tuning in to a new radar signal. Her flesh contracting, all her nerves on high alert. She could feel the gentle pressure from each of his fingers against her arms, warm and sensual.

His fingers tensed for a moment, but then he dragged his gaze away from her mouth and unwrapped her arms from his waist as if she had scorched him. 'I'll take care of the spider. Wait in the kitchen.'

Audrey sucked in her lower lip. 'You're not going to kill it…are you?'

'That was the general idea,' he said. 'What else do you want me to do? Take it home with me and hand-feed it flies?'

She stole a glance at the spider and fought back a shudder. 'It's probably got babies. It seems cruel to kill it.'

He shook his head as if he was having a bad dream. 'Okay. So I humanely remove the spider.' He picked up an old greetings card off the bookshelf and a glass tumbler from the drinks cabinet. He glanced at her. 'You sure you want to watch?'

Audrey rubbed at the creepy-crawly sensation running along her arms. 'It'll be good for me. Exposure therapy.'

'Ri-i-ight.' Lucien shrugged and approached the spider with the glass and the card.

Audrey covered her face with her hands but then peeped through the gaps in her splayed fingers. There was only so much exposure she would deal with at any one time.

Lucien slipped the card beneath the spider and then placed the glass over it. 'Voila. One captured spider. Alive.' He walked to the front door of the cottage and then, dashing through the pelting rain, placed the spider under the shelter of the garden shed a small distance away.

He came back, sidestepping puddles and keeping his head down against the driving rain. Audrey grabbed a towel from the downstairs bathroom and handed it to him. He rubbed it roughly over his hair.

She was insanely jealous of the towel. She had towel envy. Who knew such a thing existed? She wanted to run her fingers through that thick, dark, damp hair. She wanted to run her hands across his scalp and pull his head down so his mouth could cover hers. She wanted to see if his firm mouth would soften against hers or grow hard and insistent with passion.

She wanted. Wanted. Wanted the one thing she wasn't supposed to want.

Lucien scrunched up the towel in one hand and pushed back his hair with the other. 'This storm looks like it's not going to end anytime soon.'

Just like the storm of need in her body.

What was it about Lucien that made her feel so turned on? No other man triggered this crazy out-of-character reaction in her. She didn't fantasise about other men. She didn't stare at them and wonder what it would be like to kiss them. She didn't ache to feel their hands on her body. But Lucien Fox had always made her feel this way. It was the bane of her life that *he* was the only man she was attracted to. She couldn't walk past him without wanting to touch him. She couldn't be in the same room—the same country—without wanting him.

What was wrong with her?

She didn't even like him as a person. He was too formal and stiff. He rarely smiled. He thought she was silly and irresponsible like her mother. Not that her two tipsy episodes had helped in that regard, but still. She had always hated her mother's weddings ever since she'd gone to the first one as a four-year-old.

By the time Sibella married Lucien's father for the first time, Audrey was eighteen. A couple of glasses of champagne—well, it might have been three or four, but she couldn't remember—had helped her cope reasonably well with the torture of watching her mother marry yet another unsuitable man. Audrey would be the one to pick up the pieces when it all came to a messy and excruciatingly public end.

Why couldn't she get through a simple wedding reception or two or three without lusting over Lucien?

Another boom of thunder sounded so close by it made the whole cottage shudder. Audrey winced. 'Gosh. That was close.'

Lucien looked down at her. 'You're not scared of storms?'

'No. I love them. I particularly love watching them down here, coming across the fields.'

He twitched one of the curtains aside. 'Where did you park your car? I didn't see it when I drove in.'

'Under the biggest oak tree,' Audrey said. 'I didn't want it to be easy to see in case the press followed me.'

'Did you see anyone following you?'

'No, but there were recent tyre tracks on the drive-way—I thought they were Mum and Harlan's.'

'The caretaker's, perhaps?'

Audrey lifted her eyebrows. 'Does this place look like it's been taken care of recently?'

'Good point.'

Another flash of lightning split the sky, closely fol-lowed by a boom of thunder and then the unmistakable sound of a tree crashing down and limbs and branches splintering on metal.

'Which tree did you say you parked under?' Luc-ien asked.

Audrey's stomach lurched like a limousine on loose gravel. 'No. No. No. *Noooooo!*'

CHAPTER TWO

LUCIEN HAD TO stop Audrey from dashing outside to check out the state of her car by restraining her with a firm hand on her forearm. 'No. Don't go out there. It's too dangerous. There are still limbs and branches coming down.'

'But I have to see how much damage there is,' she said, wide-eyed.

'Wait until the storm passes. There could be power lines down or anything out there.'

She pulled at her lower lip with her teeth, her expression so woebegone it made something in his chest shift. He suddenly realised he was still holding her by the arm and removed his hand, surreptitiously opening and closing his fingers to stop the tingling sensation.

He usually avoided touching her.

He avoided her—period.

From the moment he'd met her at his father's first wedding to her mother he'd been keen to keep his distance. Audrey had only been eighteen and a young eighteen at that. Her crush on him had been mildly flattering but unwelcome. He'd shut her down with a stern lecture and hoped she would ignore him on the rare occasions their paths crossed.

He'd felt enormous relief when his father had divorced her mother because he hadn't cared for Sibella's influence on his father. But then three years later they'd remarried and his path intersected with Audrey's again. Then twenty-one and not looking much less like the innocent schoolgirl she'd been three years before, she'd made another advance on him at their parents' second wedding. He'd cut her down with a look and hoped she'd finally get the message…even though a small part of him had been tempted to indulge in a little flirtation with her. He had wanted to kiss her. He'd wanted to hold her luscious body against his and let nature do the rest. Sure he had. He had been damn close to doing it too. Way too close. Dangerously close.

But he'd ruthlessly shut down that part of himself because the last thing he wanted was to get involved with Audrey Merrington. Not just because of who her mother was but because Audrey was the cutesy homespun type who wanted the husband, the house, the hearth, the hound and the happy-ever-after.

He wasn't against marriage but he had in mind a certain type of marriage to a certain type of woman some time in the future. In the distant future. He would never marry for passion the way his father did. He would never marry for any other reason than convenience and companionship. And he would always be in control of his emotions.

Audrey rubbed at her arm as if she too was removing the sensation of his touch. 'I suppose you're going to give me a lecture about the stupidity of parking my car under an old tree. But the storm had barely started when I arrived.'

'It's an easy mistake to make,' Lucien said.

'Not for someone as perfect as you.' She followed up the comment with a scowl.

He was the last person who would describe himself as perfect. If he was so damn perfect then what the hell was he doing glancing at her mouth all the time? But something about Audrey's mouth had always tempted his gaze. It was soft and full and shaped in a perfect Cupid's bow.

He wondered how many men had enjoyed those soft, ripe lips. He wondered how many lovers she'd shared her body with and if that innocent Bambi-eyed thing she had going on was just a front. She wasn't traffic-stoppingly beautiful like her mother but she was pretty in a girl-next-door sort of way. Her figure was curvy rather than slim and she had an old-fashioned air about her that was in stark contrast to her mother's out-there-and-up-for-anything personality.

'Once the storm has passed I'll check the damage to your car,' Lucien said. 'But for now I think we'd better formulate a plan. When was the last time you spoke to your mother?'

'Not for a week or more.' Her tone had a wounded quality—disappointment wrapped around each word as if her relationship with her mother wasn't all that it could be. 'She left the invitation and a note at my flat. I found them when I got home from work yesterday. I got the feeling she was coming here with your dad from her note when she mentioned the daffodils. I'm not sure why she didn't text me instead. I've texted her since but I've heard nothing back and it looks like my messages haven't been read.'

Frustration snapped at his nerves, taut with tension. What if his father had already married Sibella? What if there was a repeat of the last two divorces with the salacious scandal played out in the press for weeks on end? He had to put a stop to it. He *had* to. 'They could be anywhere by now.'

'When did you last speak to your father?'

'About two months ago.'

Audrey's smooth brow wrinkled. 'You don't keep in more regular contact?'

Lucien's top lip curled before he could stop it. 'He's never quite got used to the idea of having a son.'

A look of empathy passed over her features. 'He had you when he was very young, didn't he?'

'Eighteen,' Lucien said. 'I didn't meet him until I was ten years old. My mother thought it was safer to keep me away from him given his hard-partying lifestyle.'

Not as if that had changed much over the years, which was another good reason to keep his father from remarrying Audrey's mother. They encouraged each other's bad habits. His dad would never beat the battle of the booze with Sibella by his side. The battle became a binge with a drinking buddy when Sibella was around. She had no idea of the notion of drinking in moderation. Nothing Sibella Merrington did was in moderation.

'At least you finally met him,' Audrey said, looking away.

'You haven't met yours?'

'No. Even my mum doesn't know who it is.'

Why did that not surprise him? 'Does it bother you?'

She gave a little shrug, still not meeting his gaze. 'Not particularly.'

He could tell it bothered her much more than she let on. He suddenly realised how difficult it must have been for her with only one parent and an incompetent one at that. At least he'd had his mother up until he was seventeen, when she'd died of an aneurysm. How had Audrey navigated all the potholes of childhood and adolescence without a reliable and responsible parent by her side? Sibella was still a relatively young woman, which meant she must have been not much older than Lucien's father when she'd had Audrey.

Why hadn't he asked her how it had been for her before now?

'How old was your mother when she had you?'

'Fifteen.' Her mouth became a little downturned. 'She hates me telling anyone that. I think she'd prefer it if I told everyone I was her younger sister. She won't allow me to call her Mum when anyone else is around. But I guess you've already noticed that.'

'I have, but then, I don't call my father Dad, either.'

'Because he prefers you not to?'

'Because *I* prefer not to.'

She considered him for a long moment, her chocolate-brown gaze slightly puzzled. 'If you're not close to him then why do you care if he remarries my mother or not?'

Good question. 'He's not much of a father but he's the only one I've got,' Lucien said. 'And I can't bear to see him go through another financially crippling divorce.'

Resentment shone in her gaze. 'Are you implying my mother asked for more than she deserved?'

'I'm now his accountant as well as his son,' Lucien said. 'Another divorce would ruin him. I've been propping him up financially for years. It won't just be his money he'll be losing—it will be mine.'

Her eyebrows rose as if the notion of his generosity towards his father surprised her. 'Oh… I didn't realise.' She chewed at her lip a couple of times. 'In spite of my mother's success as a soap star, she never seems to have enough money for bills. She blames her manager and he blames her.'

'Do you help her out?'

'No…not often.'

'How often?'

Her left eye twitched and then she suddenly cocked her head like a little bird. 'Listen. The storm's stopped.'

Lucien pulled back the lace curtain and checked the weather. The storm had moved further down the valley and the rain had all but ceased. 'I'll go and check out the damage. Wait here.'

'Stop ordering me about like I'm a child.' Her voice had a sharp edge that reminded him of a Sunday School teacher he'd had once. 'I'm coming with you. After all, it's my car.'

'Yeah, well, let's hope it's still a car and not a mangled piece of useless metal.'

Audrey looked at the mangled piece of useless metal that used to be her car. There was no way she would be driving anywhere in that anytime soon, if ever. Half the tree had come down on top of it and crushed it like a piece of paper. At least her insurance was up to date…or was it? Her chest seized in panic. Had she paid the bill or left it until she sorted out her mother's more pressing final notice bills?

Lucien whistled through his teeth, his gaze trained on the wreckage. 'Just as well you weren't sitting in there when that limb came down.' He glanced at her. 'Is your insurance up to date?'

Audrey disguised a swallow. 'Yes…'

His gaze narrowed. 'Your left eye is twitching again.'

She blinked. 'No, it's not.'

He came up close and brushed a fingertip below her eye. 'There. You did it again.'

'That's because you're touching me.'

His finger moved down the slope of her cheek to settle beneath her chin, elevating it so her gaze had to meet his. 'There was a time—two times—when you begged me to touch you.'

Audrey's cheeks felt hot enough to dry up all the puddles on the ground. 'I'm not begging you to touch me now.'

His eyes searched between each of hers in a back and forth motion that made her heart pick up its pace. 'Are you not?' His voice was low and deep and caused a shiver to ripple down her spine like a ribbon running away from its spool.

His eyes were so dark a blue she could barely make out the inkblot of his pupils. She could feel his body heat emanating from his fingertip beneath her chin right throughout her body as if he were transferring sexual energy from his body to hers. Pulses of lust contracted deep in her female flesh, making her aware of her body in a way she had never felt before. She moistened her mouth, not because her lips were dry but because they were tingling as if they could already feel the hot press of his mouth.

The need to feel his mouth on hers was so intense it was like an ache spreading to every cell of her body. She could feel a distant throbbing between her legs as if that part of her was waking up from a long slumber, like Sleeping Beauty.

Lucien watched the pathway of her tongue with his midnight-blue gaze and she could sense the battle going on inside him even though he had dropped his hand from her face. The tense jaw, the up and down movement of his Adam's apple, the opening and closing of his hands as if he didn't trust them to reach for her again.

Was he thinking about kissing her? Maybe she hadn't been mistaken at their parents' last wedding. Maybe he'd been tempted then but had stopped himself. It was a shock to know he wanted her. A thrilling shock. Six years ago he hadn't. Three years ago he had but he'd tried to disguise it.

Would he act on it this time?

'Were you thinking about kissing me?' The words were out of her mouth before she could think it was wise or not to say them, her voice husky as if she had been snacking on emery boards.

His gaze became shuttered, his body so still, so composed, as if the slightest movement would sabotage his self-control. 'You're mistaken.'

And you're lying. Audrey relished the feminine power she was feeling. Power she had never experienced in her entire adult life. When had anyone ever wanted to kiss her? Never, that was when.

But Lucien did.

His jaw worked as if he was giving his resolve a firm talking-to and his eyes were almost fixedly trained on hers as if he was worried if they would disobey orders and glance at her mouth again.

'I bet if I put my lips to yours right now you wouldn't be able to help yourself.' *Argh. Why did you say that?* One part of Audrey mentally cringed but another part was secretly impressed. Impressed she had the confidence to stand up to him. To challenge him. To flirt with him.

His eyes became hard as if he was steeling himself from the inside out. 'Try it. I dare you.'

A trickle of something hot and liquid spilled over in her belly. His gravelly delivered dare made the blood rush through her veins and set her heart to pounding as if she had run up a flight of stairs carrying a set of dumb-bells. Two sets. And a weight bench. Before she could stop the impulse, she lifted her hand to his face and outlined his firm mouth with her index finger, the rasp of his stubble catching against her skin like silk on tiny thorns. Even the scratchy sound of it was spine-tinglingly sexy. He held himself as still as a marble statue but she could still sense the war going on in his body as if every drop of his blood was thundering through his veins like rocket fuel. His nostrils flared like a stallion taking in the scent of a potential mate, his eyes still glittering with resolve, but there was something else lurking in the dark blue density of his gaze.

The same something she could feel thrumming deep in her core like an echo: desire.

But Audrey wasn't going to betray herself by kissing him. He had rejected her twice already. She wasn't signing up for a third. And if the gossip surrounding Lucien and Viviana was true, she was not the type of woman to kiss another woman's lover. She didn't want him to think she was so desperate for his attention she couldn't control herself. With or without champagne. She lowered her hand from his face and gave him an on-off smile. 'Lucky for you, I don't respond to dares.'

If he was relieved or disappointed he didn't show it. 'We're wasting valuable time.' He turned and strode back to the cottage and took out his phone. 'Call your mother while I call my father. They might have switched their phones back on.'

Audrey let out a sigh and followed him into the cottage. She'd tried calling her mother's phone fifty-three times already. Even under normal circumstances, her mother would only pick up if *she* wanted to talk to Audrey and even then the conversation would be Sibella-centred and not anything that could be loosely called a mutual exchange. She couldn't remember the time she had last talked to her mother. *Really* talked. Maybe when she was four years old? Her mother wasn't the type to listen to others. Sibella was used to people fawning over her and waiting with bated breath for her to talk to them about her acting career and colourful love life.

Audrey should be so lucky to have a love life…even a black and white one would do.

* * *

Lucien left a curt message on his father's answering service—one of many he'd left in the last twenty-four hours—and put away his phone. He had to get back on the road and away from the temptation of Audrey Merrington. Being anywhere near her was like being on a forty-day fast and suddenly coming across a sumptuous feast. He had damn near kissed her down by her wrecked car. Everything that was male in him ached to haul her into his arms and plunder her soft mouth with his. How easy would it have been to crush his mouth to hers? How easy would it have been to draw those sweet and sexy curves of hers even closer?

Too easy.

Scarily easy.

So easy he had to get a grip because he shouldn't be having such X-rated thoughts around Audrey. He shouldn't be looking at her mouth or her curves or any beautiful part of her. He shouldn't be thinking about making love to her just because she threw herself into his arms over that wretched spider. When she had launched herself at him like that, a rush of desire charged through him like high-voltage electricity. Just as it had at their parents' last wedding. Her curves-in-all-the-right-places body had thrown his senses into a tailspin like a hormone-driven teenager. He could still smell her sweet pea and spring lilac perfume on the front of his shirt where she'd pressed herself against him. He could still feel the softness of her breasts and the tempting cradle of her pelvis.

He could still feel the rapacious need marching through his body. Damn it.

He would have to stop wanting her. He would have to send his resolve to boot camp so it could withstand more of her cheeky *'Were you thinking about kissing me?'* comments. He wasn't just thinking about kissing her. He was dreaming of it, fantasising about it, longing for it. But he had a feeling one kiss of her delectable mouth would be like trying to eat only one French fry. Not possible.

But he could hardly leave her here at the cottage without a car. He would have to take her with him. What else could he do? When he'd first seen her at the cottage he'd decided the best plan was for them to drive in two cars so they could tag-team it until they tracked down their respective parents. He hadn't planned a cosy little one-on-one road trip with her. That would be asking for the sort of trouble he could do without.

Audrey came back into the sitting room from the kitchen and put her phone on the coffee table in front of the sofa with a defeated-sounding sigh. 'No answer. Maybe they're on a flight somewhere.'

He dragged a hand down his face so hard he wondered if his eyebrows and eyelashes would slough off. Could this nightmare get any worse? 'This seemed the most obvious place they'd come to. They used to sneak down here together a lot during their first marriage. My father raved about it—how quaint and quiet it was.'

She perched on the arm of the sofa, a small frown settling between her brows, the fingers of her right hand plucking at the fabric of her dress as if it was helping her to mull over something. 'I know, that's why I came here first. But maybe they *wanted* us to come here.'

'You mean, like giving us a false lead or something?'

She gave him an unreadable look and stopped fiddling with her dress and crossed her arms over her middle. 'Or something.'

'What "or something"?' A faint prickle crawled over his scalp. 'You mean, they wanted us both to come here? But why?'

She gave a lip shrug. 'My mother finds it amusing that you and I hate each other so much.'

Lucien frowned. 'I don't hate you.'

She lifted her neat brows like twin question marks. 'Don't you?'

'No.' He hated the way she made him feel. Hated the way his body had a wicked mind of its own when she was around. Hated how he couldn't stop thinking about kissing her and touching her and seeing if her body was as delectable as it looked under the conservative clothes she always seemed to wear.

But he wasn't a man driven by his hormones. That was his father's way of doing things. Lucien had will power and discipline and he was determined to use them. He would not be reduced to base animal desires just because a pretty, curvy woman got under his skin.

And Audrey Merrington was so far under his skin he could feel his organs shifting inside to make room.

'Good to know, since we're going to be related again,' she said with a deadpan expression.

'Not if I can help it.' Lucien was not going to rest until he'd prevented this third disastrous marriage. His father had almost drunk himself into oblivion the last time. There was no way he was going to stand by and watch that happen again. He was sick of picking up the pieces. Sick of trying to put his father back together again like a puzzle with most of the bits damaged or missing.

He picked up his keys. 'Come on. We'd best get on the road before nightfall. I'll organise someone to collect your car when we get back to London.'

She stood up from the arm of the sofa so quickly her feet thudded against the floor like punctuation marks. 'But I don't want to go with—'

'Will you damn well just do what you're told?' Lucien was having trouble controlling his panic at how much time they were wasting. His father could be halfway through his honeymoon at this rate. Not to mention his bank balance. 'You don't have a car, so therefore you come with me. Understood?'

She pursed her lips for a moment as if deciding whether or not to defy him. But then she stalked over to where she had left her overnight bag and her tote, and, picking them up, threw him a mutinous look that wouldn't have looked out of place on the deck of *The Bounty*. 'You can take me back to my flat in London. I'm not going anywhere else with you.'

'Fine.' He opened the front door of the cottage so she could walk out ahead of him. 'Go and sit in the car while I lock up.'

Audrey went to his car, sat inside and pulled the seat belt into place with a savage click. Why did he have to be so cavemanish about getting her to go with him? She could have had a hire car delivered or got a friend to collect her. Even a taxi would be worth the expense rather than suffering a couple of hours in Lucien's disturbing and far too tempting company. The last thing she wanted to do was to make a fool of herself again. She wasn't eighteen now. She wasn't twenty-one. She was twenty-five and mature enough—she hoped—to put this silly crush to bed once and for all.

Okay, so that wasn't the best choice of words.

She would nix her crush on Lucien. It was just a physical thing. It wasn't a cerebral or emotional thing. It was lust. Good old-fashioned lust and it would burn out sooner or later as long as she didn't feed it. Which meant absolutely no fantasising about his mouth. She wouldn't even look at it. She wouldn't daydream about it coming down on hers and his tongue gliding through the seam of her lips and—

Audrey pinched herself on the arm like someone flicking an elastic band around their wrist to stop themselves from smoking. This was like any other addiction and she had to stop it. She had to stop it *right* now. She would be strong. She would conquer this.

Besides, according to Rosie and her gossip magazine source, Lucien was in a committed relationship. It was weird how edgy it made her feel to think of him in a long-term relationship. Why should she care if he was practically engaged? Was he in love with Viviana Prestonward? Funny, but Audrey couldn't imagine him falling in love. He was nowhere near the playboy his father was between marriages, but neither was he a plaster saint. He dated women for a month or two and then moved on.

She sat in the passenger seat of his top model BMW as he got on with the business of locking up the cottage and putting the key under the left-hand plant pot. It seemed strange that he knew the cottage routine so well. She'd always loved the place because it was something she and her mother had shared before all the crazy celebrity stuff happened. But apparently Sibella had shared it with Harlan and now Lucien.

Audrey waited until he got behind the wheel of his car to ask, 'How many times have you been down here?'

'To the cottage?'

'You knew where to put the spare key. I figured you must have been here before or someone's told you the routine.'

He started the engine and did a neat three-point turn on the driveway. His arm was resting on the back of her seat so close to her neck and shoulders she suppressed a tiny shiver. 'I came down for a weekend once.'

'When?'

'A month or two before their second divorce.' His tone was casual but his hands on the steering wheel tightened. 'They asked me down for the weekend. They asked you too, but you had something else on. A date, your mother said.'

Audrey could remember being invited to spend the weekend with her mother and Harlan but neither of them had mentioned inviting Lucien. She'd declined the invitation, as she hadn't wanted her mother and Harlan to think she sat at home every weekend with nothing better to do than read or watch soppy movies. Which was basically what she did most weekends, but still.

Why had they invited him as well as her? They were well aware of the enmity between her and Lucien. 'Why did you accept the invitation? I can't imagine spending a weekend with them would have been high on your list of priorities.'

He drove along the country lane where leaves and small branches from the trees littered the road and along the roadside after the thrashing of the earlier wind. 'True. But I had nothing better to do that weekend and I wanted to see the cottage for myself. My father had talked about it a few times.'

'So, no hot date with a supermodel that weekend, huh?' Audrey said. 'My heart bleeds.'

He flicked a glance her way. 'How was your date that weekend? Worth the sacrifice of missing out on a weekend with your mother and my father?'

'It was great. Fun. Amazing. The best date ever.' *Stop already.*

'Are you dating the same guy now?'

Audrey laughed. Who said she couldn't act? 'No. I've had dozens since him.'

'So, no one permanent?'

She chanced a glance at him. 'What's with all the questions about my love life?'

He shrugged. 'Just wondering if you've got plans to settle down.'

'Nope. Not me.' She turned back to face the front and crossed one leg over the other and folded her arms. 'I've been to enough of my mother's weddings to last a lifetime. Two lifetimes.' She waited a beat and added with what she hoped sounded like mild interest, 'What about you?'

'What about me?'

Audrey glanced at him again. 'Do you plan to get married one day?'

He continued to look at the road in front, negotiating fallen branches and puddles and potholes. 'Maybe one day.'

'One day soon or one day later?'

Why are you asking that?

'Why the sudden interest in my private life?'

Audrey couldn't explain the strange feeling in her stomach—a dragging sensation, a weight that felt as heavy as a tombstone—at the thought of Lucien getting married one day. 'I could read about it in the gossip pages but I thought I'd ask you directly. Just in case what's in the papers isn't true.'

'What did you read?'

'I didn't read it myself but someone who did told me you're about to get engaged to Viviana Prestonward.'

He made a grunting sound. 'It's not true.'

She turned in her seat to look at him but he suddenly frowned and pushed down hard on the brakes. 'Damn it to hell.'

Audrey turned to look at the road ahead where his gaze was trained. A large tree had fallen across the wooden bridge, bringing down a portion of it and making it impassable. 'Oh, dear. That doesn't look good.'

Lucien thumped the heel of his hand on the steering wheel, then turned to look at her, frowning so heavily his eyebrows were knitted. 'Is there any other way around this stream? Another road? Another bridge?'

Audrey shook her head. 'Nope. One road in. One road out.'

He swore and let out a harsh-sounding breath. 'I don't believe this.'

'Welcome to life in the country.'

He got out of the car and strode over to the broken bridge, standing with his hands on his hips and his feet slightly apart. Audrey came over to stand next to him, conscious of the almost palpable tension in his body.

'Can it be…repaired?' Her voice came out one part hesitant, two parts hopeful. 'I mean, maybe we can call someone from the council to fix it. We could tell them it's an emergency or something.'

He turned away from the bridge with another muttered curse. 'There are far bigger emergencies than a single-lane bridge on a lane in the countryside that only a handful of people use.' He strode towards his car, kicking a fallen branch out of the way with his foot. 'We'll have to stay at the cottage until I can get a helicopter down here to take us out.'

Audrey stopped dead like she had come up against an invisible wall. But in a way she had. The invisible wall of her fear of flying. Flying in helicopters, to be precise. No way was she going in a helicopter. No flipping way. Give her a spider any day. Give her a roomful of them. She would cuddle a colony of spiders but flying in an overgrown egg-beater was not going to happen.

Lucien glanced back at her when he got to his car. 'What's wrong?'

Audrey gave a gulping swallow, her stomach churning so fast she could have made butter. 'I'm not going in a helicopter.'

'Don't worry—I'll clear out the spiders first.'

'Very funny.'

He held the passenger door open for her in a pointed manner. 'Are you coming with me or do you plan to walk back?'

Audrey walked to his car and slipped into the passenger seat, keeping her gaze averted. He closed the door and went around to his side and was soon back behind the wheel and doing one of his masterful three-point turns that, if she were driving, would have taken five or six turns. Possibly more…that was, if she didn't end up with the car in the ditch in the process. She looked at the brooding sky and suppressed a shudder. She had to think of a way back to London that didn't involve propellers.

'I should be able to get a helicopter first thing in the morning,' Lucien said. 'I'd try for one now but I'm not sure the weather is all that favourable.'

Argh! Don't remind me how dangerous it is to fly in one of those things.

'I'm surprised Britain's most successful forensic accountant doesn't have a helicopter or two of his own waiting on stand-by.'

'Yes, well, I'm too much of a bean-counter to throw money away on unnecessary luxuries. I leave that sort of thing to my father.'

CHAPTER THREE

THE SHORT TRIP back to the cottage was mostly silent, mainly because Audrey was trying to control her fear at the thought of having to leave in a helicopter in the morning. Maybe she should have got her therapist to work with her on that issue instead of the arachnophobia. But it wasn't every day she had to face a ride in a helicopter. Surely the road would be cleared in a day or two at the most? It wasn't like she'd be stuck down here for weeks or months on end.

But if the next morning's flight was a worry, there was this evening to get through first. Sharing the cottage with Lucien for one night—for one minute—was not going to help her little fantasy problem. It would be like trying to give up chocolate and spending the night in a chocolate factory.

Big mistake.

When Lucien helped her out of the car, the smell of rain-washed earth was as sweet as the perfume of the flowers in the overgrown garden. She could have got out of the car herself but she kind of liked the way he always got there first. No one had ever opened the door for her before. People always rushed to open her mother's door whenever Audrey had accompanied her to an event but she was always left to fend for herself.

She followed him back to the front door of the cottage, waiting while he got the key from under the pot, doing her best not to feast her eyes on his taut buttocks when he bent down to lift it up. He unlocked the door and swept his arm in front of his body. 'After you.'

Audrey chewed at the inside of her mouth and tried to ignore the prickling shiver moving over her skin. Had that spider had company? As far as she was concerned, there was no such thing as a single spider—they were all married with large families. What if there were dozens inside? Maybe even hundreds? Didn't heavy rain drive them indoors? What if a whole colony of them was setting up camp right now? What if they were crawling up and down the walls and over every surface? What if they were in every cupboard? Every drawer? Every corner? What if they were lurking in the shadows just waiting for her to come in? What if one dropped on her head and tiptoed its sticky legs all over her face? What if—? 'Erm…maybe you should go in first in case the spider has found its way back in.'

If he found her suggestion annoying or silly he didn't show it. 'Wait here.'

Audrey waited until he gave the all clear and stepped over the threshold, but even though it was a few hours away from sundown, the heavy cloud cover outside made the cottage seem gloomy and unwelcoming… sort of like an abandoned house, which was pretty much what it was. 'Gosh, it's getting kind of dark in here. Is the power on again yet?'

Lucien flicked one of the light switches but the light didn't come on. 'It could be hours until it comes back on. A tree has probably brought the line down somewhere.' He moved over to the fireplace where she had started preparing the fire. 'I'll get a fire going. Are there any candles about?'

Audrey went to the kitchen—where, thankfully, there were no spiders—and soon found some scented candles she'd bought her mother. It was kind of typical of her that they hadn't been used. She brought them back to the sitting room and set one on the coffee table in front of the two facing sofas and the other one on the antique sideboard. 'These should do the job.'

'Perfect.' Lucien came over with the box of matches and lit the candles and soon the fragrance of patchouli and honeysuckle wafted through the air.

Audrey couldn't stop staring at his features in the muted glow of the candlelight. His skin was olive-toned and tanned as if he had holidayed in the sun recently. The flickering shadows highlighted the planes and contours of his face: the uncompromising jaw, the strong blade of a nose, the prominent dark eyebrows and those amazing midnight-blue eyes.

But it was his mouth that always lured her gaze like a yo-yo dieter to a cake counter. His mouth was both firm and yet sensual with well-defined vermillion borders that made her wonder what a kiss from him would be like. Would those firm lips soften or harden in passion? Would they crush or cajole? Would they evoke a storm of need in her that so far she had only ever dreamed about experiencing?

'Is something wrong?' Lucien frowned.

Audrey did a rapid blink and rocked back on her heels…well, not heels exactly. She was wearing ballet flats. Although, given that Lucien was so tall, maybe she should have worn stilettos…or maybe a pair of stilts. 'Have you been on holiday recently?'

'I spent Easter in Barbados.'

She gave a little laugh with a grace note of envy. 'Of course.'

His frown deepened. 'Why "of course"?'

Audrey gave an off-hand shrug and bent down to tidy the out-of-date magazines on the coffee table. 'Did you go with Viviana Prestonward?'

'I went to see a client there. Not that it's any of your or anyone's business.'

She straightened from the coffee table and turned back to look at him. 'Just asking. There's no need to be so antsy about it.'

He turned to face the fire, stirring it so savagely with the poker the flames leapt and danced. 'I'm not a rock star like my father. I don't like my private life being splashed over every paper or online forum.' He put the poker back in its stand and turned around to look at her. 'Does it happen to you? The press interest?'

Audrey sat on the edge of the sofa and played with the fringe of the rug with her foot. 'Not much, but then, I'm way too boring. Who wants to know what a library archivist gets up to in her spare time?'

His gaze became thoughtful. 'What do you get up to?'

Audrey sat back on the sofa, and, picking up one of

the scatter cushions, cuddled it against her stomach. 'I read, I watch TV, go to the occasional movie.' She made a rueful twist of her mouth. 'See? Boring.'

'What about boyfriends? Those dozens of lovers you were telling me about earlier.'

Audrey knew if she kept going with this conversation her hot cheeks would be giving the fire in the grate some serious competition. She tossed the cushion to one side and rose from the sofa in one movement that was supposed to be agile and graceful as a supermodel's, but her foot snagged on the rug and she banged her shin on the coffee table. 'Ouch!' She clapped a hand to her leg and did a hopping dance as the pain pulsated through her shinbone. The scented candle flickered from the impact but thankfully remained upright.

Lucien came across and steadied her with his hands on her upper arms. 'Are you okay? Did it break the skin?'

'I'm fine. It's just a bump.'

He bent down in front of her and inspected her shin; his warm, dry hand so gentle on her leg she couldn't decide if it felt like a tickle or a caress—maybe it was a bit of both. The sensation of his fingers on her bare flesh stirred her senses, making her aware of each broad pad of his fingers. She suddenly became aware of the intimacy of his position in front of her. His face was level with her pelvis and her mind raced with a host of erotic images of him kissing her, touching her…*there*.

'You're going to bruise—you're starting to already.' His fingertip traced over the red mark on her shin as softly as a feather on a priceless object.

Audrey held her breath for so long she thought she might faint. Or maybe it was because no man had ever knelt down in front of her and touched her with such gentleness. Or maybe it was because she had never felt so aware of her body before—how each cell seemed to swell and throb with a need for more of his touch. Now that he'd touched her it awakened a feverish desire in her for more. What if he was to run his hands further up her legs…up her thighs? To the very heart of her femininity? What if he was to peel down her knickers and—?

Stop it right there.

There was no way she was going to act on her crush. No more clumsy attempts at flirting. No more making a gauche fool of herself. She would be sensible and mature about this. 'You can get up now.' She injected a hint of wryness into her voice. 'Unless you want to rehearse your proposal to Viviana while you're down there?'

Lucien rose from his kneeling position, his mouth so flat and hard it looked like paper-thin sheets of steel. 'I'm not proposing to anyone. You need to put some ice on that bruise. I'll get some from the kitchen.'

Lucien opened the small freezer compartment of the fridge in the kitchen and considered squeezing himself in there to cool off. Okay, so it was a little crazy to go down on bended knee in front of Audrey. Even crazier to touch her but she'd hurt herself and he'd felt compelled to do the Boy Scout thing. It was what any decent man would do…although nothing about his reaction to touching her was decent. As soon as he touched her he felt it. The little zing of electricity that he'd never felt with anyone else.

There was a simple solution: he had to stop touching her. He would keep his distance.

How hard could it be?

He took some ice cubes out of the tray and wrapped them in a tea towel and went back to the sitting room. 'Here we go.' He handed her the ice pack, taking care not to touch her fingers. See? Easy. No touching.

Audrey pressed the pack to her shin, her small white teeth nibbling at her lower lip like a mouse at wainscoting. After a moment she glanced up at him but her eyes didn't quite connect with his gaze. 'So…what do you love about her?'

Lucien looked at her blankly. 'Pardon?'

This time her gaze was direct. 'Viviana. The woman you've been dating longer than anyone else. What do you love about her?'

He knew whatever answer he gave was going to be the wrong one because he wasn't in a relationship per se with Viviana. He had got to know her after doing some accounting work for her father and they'd struck up a casual friendship. It was a charade he was helping her maintain after being cheated on and then dumped by her boyfriend. He had seen far too many relationships—most of them his father's—start in love and end in hate. If and when it came time for him to settle down, he was going for the middle ground: mutual respect, common interests, compatibility. 'I don't have that type of relationship with her.'

Audrey's eyes widened so far it looked like her eyelids were doing Pilates. 'What? But you've been dating her for weeks and weeks. Everyone assumes she's The One.'

Lucien moved across to the fire and put on another log of wood. He considered telling her he had no such plans to marry Viviana but he realised the protection of a 'relationship' could serve him well when dealing with Audrey. Or at least he hoped it would. 'For the record, I don't consider romantic love to be the most important factor in a marriage. That sort of love never lasts. You only have to look at your mother and my father to see that.'

She put the ice pack on the coffee table, a frown troubling her brow. 'Is she in love with you?'

'We get on well and—'

'You get on well?' Audrey let out a laugh that had a jarring chord of scorn. 'So that's all it takes to have a successful marriage? Silly me for thinking for all these years the couple had to actually fall in love with one another, care for each other and want the best for each other.'

'You might want to save your lecture for your mother,' Lucien said. 'How many times has she fallen in and out of love now?'

Her creamy skin became tinged with pink high on her cheekbones and her generous mouth tightened. 'We're not talking about my mother. We're talking about you. Why are you going to marry someone you're not in love with? I mean, who *does* that?'

Lucien straightened one of the trinkets on the mantelpiece. 'Look, we're clearly never going to agree on this, so why don't we change the subject?'

'I'm not finished discussing it,' Audrey said. 'Why would a beautiful-looking woman like Viviana settle for a man who doesn't love her? Oh, I get it.' She tapped the side of her head as if congratulating her brain for coming up with the answer. 'She's only with you because you're the son of a famous rock star, right?'

'Wrong.' He gave her an on-off movement of his lips that could just scrape in as a smile. 'She didn't know who my father was when we first met.' Which was a certain part—the main part—of Viviana's appeal to him as a friend. He was tired of the groupies and sycophants who only wanted to hang around him because of who his father was. He'd been weeding them out since he was a teenager, trying to decide who was genuinely interested in him or just along for the vicarious brush with celebrity.

Audrey got off the sofa and limped across to the window to check on the weather. 'Well, either way, I think you're both making a big mistake. People who get married should love each other at the very least.'

'But you're never getting married, correct?' Lucien decided it was time to direct the questions back at her to take the heat off him.

Her gaze moved to the left of his. 'No.'

'But what if you fall in love?'

Her teeth did that little lip-chewing thing again that never failed to draw his gaze. 'I can't see that happening anytime soon.'

'But what if a guy falls in love with you and wants to marry you?'

She gave a laugh that wasn't quite a laugh. 'And how

will I know it's me they're in love with or whether they want to meet my mother?'

Lucien frowned. 'Has that actually happened?'

She made a wry sideways movement of her mouth. 'Enough times to be annoying.' She moved back to the sofa and plumped up one of the scatter cushions she'd been hugging earlier. 'But then, I'm hardly in the same league as my mother in the looks department.'

Lucien wondered if her low self-esteem came from having such a glamorous mother. Sibella was absolutely stunning; even he had to admit that. It was no wonder his father kept going back to her like a drug he couldn't resist. Had it been difficult for Audrey growing up in her mother's shadow? Had she been compared to her mother and found lacking? He knew the press could be merciless in how they portrayed celebrities, but even family members often came in for a serve at times. He tried to recall any articles that involved Audrey but, since he generally shied away from reading the gossip pages, he drew a blank. 'You have no need to run yourself down.'

'At least you look like your father.'

Lucien thought about the lifestyle that had wreaked so much havoc on his father's once good-looking features. 'I'm not sure if that's meant to be a compliment or not. And, just for the record, your mother's looks don't do it for me, okay?'

Audrey's smile looked a little forced. 'Good to know.'

There was a strange little silence. Strange because Lucien couldn't stop looking at her girl-next-door features with those big brown eyes and her generous mouth and thinking about how naturally pretty she was. Understated and unadorned but still captivating. She reminded him of a painting he had glanced at once without really seeing, only to revisit it on another occasion and being stunned by its subtle beauty and hidden depths.

She had barely any make-up on and her skin had a healthy peaches and cream glow. Her dark brown hair had chestnut highlights that looked so natural he assumed they probably were. She didn't have the show-stopping beauty of her mother, and in a crowd you would miss her at first glance, but she was one of those women whose looks grew on you the more you looked at her. She had hardly changed since she was eighteen, although her figure had developed a little more. He wouldn't be worthy of his testosterone if he hadn't noticed the way her breasts filled out her clothes.

The sound of a phone ringing broke the silence and Audrey turned and fished for her mobile in her bag on the floor near the sofa. She glanced at the screen and mouthed 'It's my mother' before she answered. 'Mum? Where are you? I've called you a thousand times.'

Lucien couldn't hear the other side of the conversation but he could get the gist of it from Audrey's answers. 'What? How did you know I'm at Bramble Cottage? I… I'm with Lucien.' She turned her back to him and continued in a hushed voice. 'Nothing's going on. How could you think—? Look, will you please just tell me where *you* are?' Her hand was so tight around her phone he could see the whitening of her knuckles. 'I know you want to spend time alone with Harlan but—' She let out an unladylike curse and tossed the phone onto the sofa. She turned around and her shoulders went down on a defeated sigh. 'She wouldn't tell me a thing.'

'Nothing at all?'

She lifted her hands in a helpless gesture. 'She kept dodging the question.' Her forehead creased. 'But I've just had a thought. Remember that chateau they rented during their first marriage for your father's birthday in St Remy in Provence? She told me once it was one of her favourite places. Wasn't it one of his favourites too? What if they've gone there? It's a perfect hideaway. They used to go there quite a lot together.'

Lucien remembered the chateau more than he wanted to. He had attended the party for a short time more out of duty than any desire to celebrate his father's birthday. It was one of those parties where there was a lot of alcohol and loud music and a fair bit of debauchery. He remembered Audrey's mother doing a striptease—her birthday present to his father—and feeling embarrassed for Audrey, who'd left the room with her cheeks flaming. He wished now he'd gone in search of her and offered her some sort of comfort, but he'd been wary of being alone with her since the wedding, where she had made that tipsy pass at him. 'Did your mother give any other clue? What did she actually say?'

'She knew I was at the cottage.'

'How did she know that?'

'Phone app. She's blocked me from finding her but she can find me just by clicking on the app.' Her cheeks became a light shade of pink. 'She thought…well, never mind what she thought.'

'Was she drunk?'

Her eyes flicked away from his, her cheeks darkening. 'No, I don't think so... I got the feeling she and your dad just want to be left on their own for a bit.'

'Unusual since they both love nothing more than an audience.'

'Maybe they've both changed...' Her teeth sank into her lip, her brow still wrinkled as if she was mulling over something deeply puzzling.

Lucien had spent the last twenty-four years of his life hoping his father would change. He'd lost count of the number of times he'd been disappointed by his father's irresponsible and reckless behaviour and things didn't get much more irresponsible and reckless than remarrying Sibella Merrington. Sibella wasn't the person to help his father change. She was the one who kept him from changing. She encouraged every bad habit and, after the last time, Lucien was not going to sign up for another clean-up operation.

After the last divorce, it had taken him months to get his father back on his feet without two daily bottles of vodka on board. Numerous times he had come to his father's house and found him blackout drunk. He'd tried everything to get him into rehab but his father always refused. His doctors had warned his father his drinking had to stop or he would suffer irreparable damage to his already struggling liver. Even if Lucien had to fly to every city and village across Europe he would not stop until he found his father and put a stop to this madness. 'Yeah, well, next time you see a leopard running around without its spots, be sure to let me know.'

CHAPTER FOUR

AUDREY WENT TO the kitchen to see about some food for dinner in the pantry, where basic non-perishable items were stored. She lit another candle for the kitchen table and set to making a meal. Lucien was still in the sitting room, making the arrangements for a helicopter—*gulp*—to pick them up the following morning. She thought back over her brief conversation with her mother. She had teased her about being at the cottage with Lucien, but along with the teasing there had been a veiled warning about how far from his type she was.

As if she needed to be reminded.

Audrey had assembled a plate of crackers and a makeshift pâté of tinned tuna and sweetcorn when Lucien came into the kitchen. 'I'm sorry there isn't a gourmet meal on offer but most of the stuff in the pantry is past its use-by date. This is the best I could do.'

'It's fine. You needn't have bothered.'

'There's wine in the fridge.' Audrey nodded her head in the fridge's direction. 'It's cold even though the power's still off.'

Lucien took out a bottle of white wine and held it aloft. 'Will you join me?'

Audrey would have loved a glass of wine but she was worried she might make a fool of herself again. 'No, thanks. I'll stick to water.' She carried the meal on a platter to the scrubbed pine table and privately marvelled at how cosy it looked in spite of the meagre fare.

Lucien waited until she was seated and then he joined her at the table. He had poured himself a glass of wine but so far hadn't taken a sip. He picked up one of the crackers and took a bite and grimaced.

'Sorry, I know they're a bit stale,' Audrey said. 'I don't think my mother's been here for ages. I don't think anyone's been here, not even the caretaker.' She sighed and picked up a cracker. 'She probably forgot to pay him or something.'

Lucien took a sip of his wine and then put the glass down. 'Why does she keep the place if it's empty most of the time? Wouldn't it be better to sell it?'

Audrey thought about losing the cottage, losing the one place where she had felt close to her mother. Something tightened in her chest like a hand pressing down on her lungs. She knew it made financial sense to sell the cottage. But if it was sold that part of her life with her mother would be lost for ever and there would be no hope of reclaiming it. 'I've always talked her out of it.'

'Why?'

Audrey pushed a crumb on her plate with her fingertip. 'She bought it when she got her first role on television. We used to come down here just about every weekend. I loved the garden after living in a council flat. It was like a secret scented paradise. I'd spend hours making daisy chains with her and flower garlands for our hair.

We even used to cook stuff together. She wasn't a great cook but it was a lot of fun...' She smiled at the memory. 'Messy fun...' She stopped speaking and looked up to see him studying her with a thoughtful expression on his face and her smile fell away. 'Sorry for rambling.'

'Don't apologise.' His voice had a gravelly note to it.

Audrey looked back down at the crumb on her plate rather than meet his gaze. 'She wasn't always so...so over the top. Becoming a celebrity changed her.'

'In what way?'

She glanced at him again and saw something she had never seen in his gaze before—compassion. It made the walls and boundaries she had built around herself shiver against their foundations. 'Well...she didn't always drink so much.'

'Do you worry about her drinking?'

'All the time.' Audrey's shoulders drooped. 'I've suggested rehab but she won't go. She doesn't see that she has a problem. So far it hasn't interfered with her work on the show but how soon before it does? I keep worrying someone will smell it on her breath when she turns up for a shoot. Especially now she's back with your father. Sorry. I don't mean to blame him but—'

'It's fine.' His tight smile was more of a grimace. 'They're a bad influence on each other, which is why we have to do whatever we can to put a stop to them marrying again.'

'But what if we can't stop them? What if they get married and then go through yet another hideous break-up and divorce? What then?'

His features clouded as if he was thinking back to

the previous two divorces. Then his gaze refocused on hers. 'How did your mother handle the break-ups?'

Audrey sighed. 'Badly.'

He frowned. 'But wasn't she the one to end their relationship both times?'

'I guess it doesn't matter who ends it, a break-up is still a break-up,' Audrey said. 'She drank. A lot. She hid from the press at my flat for three weeks last time. I was worried sick about her, especially when she…' She bit off the rest of her sentence. She hadn't told anyone about her mother's overdoses. Her mother had begged her not to tell anyone in case it got leaked out somehow in the press. Why had she kept her promise?

Because inside her there was still that small child who loved being at the cottage with her mum.

'Especially when she…?' Lucien said.

Audrey pushed her chair back and fetched herself a glass of water. 'Would you like some water?' She held up a glass but was annoyed to see her hand wasn't quite steady.

Lucien's frown was so deep it looked like he was aiming for a world record. 'No water.' He rose from the table and came over to where she was standing in front of the sink. 'Talk to me, Audrey.'

She couldn't hold his gaze and looked at his mouth instead. Big mistake. It was set in its customary firm line but his evening shadow surrounded his lips in rich, dark stubble that looked so sexy she ached to touch it with her fingers. With her mouth. To taste his lips and trail her tongue over their firm contours to see if they would…

He put a fingertip to the base of her chin and brought her gaze up to meet his. 'What were you going to say?'

Audrey's chin was on fire where his finger was resting. She could feel the heat spreading to every part of her body in deep, pulsating waves. His eyes tethered hers in a lock that had an undercurrent of intimacy, which made her legs feel boneless. 'Erm... I think I will have that glass of wine, after all.' She stepped away and went back to the table, poured half a glass of wine and took a cautious sip.

Lucien came back to his chair and sat down. It was a moment or two before he spoke. 'My father drank two bottles of vodka every day after the last divorce. I thought he was going to die of alcohol poisoning for sure. I'd go to his house and find him... Thankfully he doesn't remember how many times I changed his clothes and his bed for him.'

Audrey swallowed. 'Oh, Lucien. I'm so sorry. That must have been awful for you to see your father like that. You must've been so worried about him. Have you asked him about rehab or—?'

He gave her a world-weary look. 'Like your mother, he refuses point-blank to go. He's been warned by his doctors that his liver won't cope unless he stops drinking.'

'No wonder you want to stop my mother from marrying him,' Audrey said, feeling deeply ashamed of her mother's influence on his father.

'I realise Sibella isn't pouring the liquor down his throat but he can't seem to help himself when she's with him,' Lucien said. 'It's like they're both hell-bent on self-destruction.'

'Their love for each other is toxic,' Audrey said. 'That's why I'm never going to fall in love with anyone. It's way too dangerous.'

He studied her for a moment with an inscrutable look. 'Never is a long time.'

Audrey picked up her wine and took another sip. 'So far you've managed not to fall in love. Why do you think I won't be able to do the same?'

His gaze flicked to her mouth and then back to her eyes but in that infinitesimal beat of time a different quality entered the atmosphere. A tightening. A tension. A temptation. 'Maybe you've been dating the wrong men.'

She hadn't been dating *any* men.

She was too scared she would be exploited. Too scared she wouldn't be loved for who she was instead of who she was related to. Too scared to be so intimate with someone because what if they slept with her and then cast her aside like so many of her mother's lovers had done? She didn't want to turn into an emotional wreck who turned to alcohol when her heart got broken. It was better not to get her heart broken in the first place.

Audrey took another sip of wine. Two sips. Two very big sips, which technically speaking weren't sips but gulps. 'Maybe you've been dating the wrong women. Safe women. Women you wouldn't possibly fall in love with in case you end up like your father.'

His top lip came up and his eyes glinted with his trademark cynicism. 'Right back at you, sweetheart.'

Audrey put her glass back down with a little clatter. 'Mock me all you like but I would hate to love someone that intensely. Your father is like a drug my mother can't give up. She gets herself clean but then keeps going back to him for another fix. It's crazy. It will kill her in the end.' She gave herself a mental slap for the vocal slip and added, 'I mean figuratively, not literally.'

Lucien's gaze sharpened. 'Has she ever tried to end her life?'

Audrey tried to screen her features but just recalling the memories of those times she'd found her mother with a half-empty bottle of pills was too painful to block. What if she'd taken them all? What if she hadn't found her in time? What if next time she took the whole bottle? She could feel her face twitching and her mouth trembling. 'Why would you think that?'

He continued to hold her gaze like a counsellor would a nervous patient. 'It's better to talk about it, Audrey.'

She compressed her lips, torn between wanting to offload some of the burden but worried about compromising her relationship with her mother. 'We have to stop them getting back together, okay? That's all I care about right now. We have to stop them before it's too late.'

'I couldn't agree more.'

Once they'd cleared away the lean pickings of their dinner, Audrey took one of the candles with her and went upstairs to make up the beds. She put Lucien in the room furthest from hers just to make sure he didn't think she was going to do a midnight wander into his room. When she got into her own bed and pulled the covers up, she looked at the candlelight flickering on the ceiling and thought of the times in her early childhood when she had lain in this wrought-iron bed with her mother sleeping in the room next door. She had never managed to be that happy since. Nor felt that safe. The happy memories should have been enough to settle her to sleep but somehow they weren't.

Or maybe it was because she was conscious of Lucien in the bedroom down the corridor. Would he sleep naked or in his underwear? Her mind raced with images of him lying between the sheets her hands had touched when she'd made the bed earlier. Was he a stomach sleeper or a back sleeper? Did he move a lot or stay still?

Audrey sat up and gave her pillow a reshape and settled back down. Her chest suddenly seized. Was that a spider on the ceiling? No. It was just the candlelight. She licked her dry lips. She was thirsty. The wine had made her mouth as dry as a sandbox and she would never be able to sleep unless she had a glass of water. Why hadn't she thought to bring one with her?

She threw off the covers and smoothed her satin nightgown down over her thighs. She padded out to the corridor to check if Lucien was about but his bedroom door was closed. She tiptoed downstairs as quietly as she could, wincing when she got to one of the creaky floorboards. She froze, her other foot poised in mid-air until she was sure it was safe to continue.

The kitchen was bathed in moonlight now the storm clouds had blown away. Audrey got herself a glass of water and sipped it while she looked out of the window at the moonlit garden and fields and woods beyond. Lucien was right. The cottage should be sold at some point. Her mother had outgrown it and it was sadly falling into ruin without regular visits and proper upkeep.

Wasn't that a bit like her relationship with her mother?

Audrey knew she was too old to be still hankering after her mother's affection but it had been so long since she'd felt loved by her. Sibella loved fame and her fans and had no time for anything or anyone that reminded her of her life before her celebrity star was born. It was like that person had never existed. The teenage mum with her much adored little girl was no more. In her place was Sibella Merrington, successful soap star of numerous shows that were broadcast all over the world.

And where was that once adored little girl?

No one adored Audrey now.

She couldn't be sure if the friends she had actually liked her or the fact she had a celebrity mother. There was always that seed of doubt sprouting in her mind, which made it hard for her to get close to people. She always kept something of herself back just in case the friend had the wrong motives.

She turned from the window and sighed. See? A few sips of wine earlier that evening and now she was a maudlin mess, getting overly emotional and down on herself.

Audrey took another glass of water, went to the sitting room and curled up on the sofa. If the power was back on she would have put on a soppy movie to really get herself going. And if there had been any naughty food in the house she would have eaten a block of chocolate. A family-sized block.

She rested her head against one of the scatter cushions and watched the still glowing embers of the fire in the fireplace until finally, on a sleepy sigh, she closed her eyes…

Lucien was having trouble sleeping. Nothing unusual in that, since he was often working late or in different time zones, but this time it was because he was aware of Audrey in the room down the corridor. Too aware. Skin-tingling and blood-pumping aware. He wasn't sure if it was his imagination but he could smell her perfume on his sheets. And the thought of her leaving her scent on his sheets stirred up a host of wickedly tempting images he knew he shouldn't be allowing inside his head. He could feel her presence like radar frequency in the air. His skin prickled into goosebumps and his normally well-controlled sex drive stirred and stretched like a beast in too cramped a space.

You're spending the night alone with Audrey Merrington.

Lucien shied away from the thought like a horse refusing a jump. They were in separate rooms. It was fine. Nothing was going to happen. He would make sure of that. If she came tiptoeing into his room with seduction on her mind he would be ready for her.

To *refuse* her, that was.

Not that he didn't find the prospect of a quick roll around these sheets with her tempting. He did. Way too tempting. Her luscious curves were enough to make a ninety-year-old monk rethink his celibacy vows.

But Lucien wasn't going to make a bad situation worse by complicating things with a dalliance with Audrey. Even if her mouth was the most kissable he'd seen in a long time.

Damn it. He had to stop thinking about kissing her.

He sat on the bed and sorted through a few more emails but he kept an ear out for her returning upstairs. He'd heard her go down half an hour ago. Why hadn't she come back up? He tossed his phone on the bed and wrestled with himself for a moment. Should he go down to check on her?

No. Better keep your distance.

He picked up his phone again and tapped away at the screen but he couldn't concentrate. He let out a long breath and reached for his trousers. He pulled them on and zipped them up and then shrugged on his shirt but didn't bother with the buttons.

He found her lying on the sofa in front of the smouldering fire, her body curled up like a comma and her cheek pressed into one of the scatter cushions. One of her hands was tucked near her chin and the other was dangling over the edge of the sofa. She was wearing a navy blue satin nightgown that clung to her curves like cling film. A stab of lust hit him in the groin at the shape of her thighs showing where the nightgown had ridden up. It intrigued him that she wore such sexy nightwear when during the day she covered herself with such conservative clothes. He knew he shouldn't be staring at her like a lust-struck teenager but he couldn't seem to tear his eyes away from her. The neckline of the nightgown was low, revealing a delicious glimpse of cleavage. She gave a murmur and shifted against the cushion, her dangling hand coming up to brush something invisible away from her face. Her smooth forehead creased in a frown and she swiped at her face again as if she could feel something crawling over her skin.

Maybe she could feel his gaze.

Lucien waited until she'd settled again before he carefully lifted the throw off the end of the sofa and gently laid it over her sleeping form. He figured it was safer to leave her sleeping down here than disturbing her. He stepped backwards but forgot the coffee table was in the way and the side of his leg banged against it with a thump.

Audrey's eyes flew open and she sat bolt upright. 'Oh, it's you. How long have you been here?'

'Not long,' Lucien said. 'I came downstairs for something and found you lying there. I covered you with the throw.'

She gathered it around her shoulders, using it as a wrap. It made her look like a child bundled up in a garment too big for her. Her brown eyes looked glazed with sleep and she had marks on her left cheek where the piping on the cushion had pressed against her skin. 'What time is it?'

'Four-ish, I think.'

She tugged her hair out of the back of the throw and draped it over her left shoulder. 'I hope I didn't disturb you?'

You disturb me all the time. Lucien kept his expression neutral. 'I wasn't asleep. I was working.'

She rose from the sofa still with the throw wrapped around her shoulders. 'I couldn't sleep and came down for a glass of water. I must have fallen asleep in front of the fire.' She glanced at the fireplace with a wistful look on her face. 'I think you're right though about selling this place.' Her gaze drifted back to his. 'It's a waste for it to be unoccupied for months and months on end.'

'Would you take it over?' Lucien said. 'You could use it as a holiday home, couldn't you?'

She shrugged and shifted her gaze. 'I have a pretty busy social life in town and, anyway, I couldn't afford the maintenance.'

Lucien was starting to wonder just how busy her social life was. He'd never heard her mother or his father mention anyone she was dating by name. 'You haven't thought to bring one of your numerous lovers down here for a cosy weekend?'

Her cheeks developed twin circles of pink. 'I think I'll go back up to bed.' She made to walk past him but he stopped her by placing a hand on her arm. Her eyes met his and her brows lifted ever so slightly like those of a haughty spinster in a Regency novel. 'Did you want something, Lucien?'

He let his hand fall away from her arm before he was tempted to tell her what he wanted. What he *shouldn't* be wanting. What he would damn well *stop* himself from wanting.

'No. Goodnight.'

Audrey came downstairs to the kitchen the following morning to find Lucien already packed and ready to go. 'Forget about breakfast,' he said. 'We're leaving.'

Her stomach pitched as if she were already in the helicopter. In a nosedive. 'What? Now?'

'I've managed to get a local farmer to meet us at the bridge. He's going to get us across on his tractor and then we'll pick up a hire car in the village.'

'So we're not going in the helicopter?' Relief swept through her like a rinse cycle through a load of laundry.

'No.'

'Why did you change your mind about it?'

'I don't want to draw too much attention to ourselves. The fewer people who know we've spent the night here together, the better.'

Audrey's relief collided with her anger that he disliked being seen with her in public so much. Was she so hideous he couldn't bear anyone finding out they'd 'spent the night here together'?

She bet he wouldn't be all cloak and dagger about it if it was Viviana holed up here with him. He'd be hiring the biggest helicopter on offer and parading Viviana on his arm like a trophy. He'd probably announce it on a megaphone: *Hey, look who I spent the night with— Viviana Prestonward, the most beautiful supermodel on the planet.*

It made Audrey want to puke...or to punch something. 'You know, if it pains you that much to be in my company, why then are you insisting on taking me with you? I can find my own way back to London to do my own search and you can do yours.'

'Aren't you forgetting your car is out of action and likely to be for some time?'

'I can hire one.'

A look of grim determination entered his gaze. 'No. We stick to my plan to do this together. It'll add more weight if we show a united front once we find them. I think you might be right about St Remy. My father's been there a few times over the last couple of years, so it's highly likely they've headed there.'

Audrey rubbed her lips together as if she were setting lipstick. Why was he insisting she go with him if he didn't want to draw attention to them? Wasn't taking her with him going to cause all sorts of trouble for him? 'What about Viviana?'

'What about her?'

'What's she going to think of us spending all this time together?'

A flicker of something passed over his face. 'She's not the jealous type.'

Audrey arched a brow. 'Would that be because I'm not slim and beautiful like she is?'

Lucien closed his eyes in a slow God-give-me-strength blink. 'Get your bag. The farmer will be waiting for us by now.'

Lucien drove with Audrey a short time later to the bridge, where the local farmer was waiting on the other side with his tractor. There was a hire car parked on the other side as well, presumably left by the company for them to collect. Audrey had to admire Lucien's organisational skills, but then she realised how determined he was to put a stop to his father's marriage to her mother. He wouldn't let even a broken bridge get in his way.

The farmer gave them a wave and they pulled up on the side of the lane and proceeded to cross the river a metre or so away from where the bridge had come down. The tractor climbed up the other bank with a rumbling roar and came to a stop next to where Audrey and Lucien were standing. She recognised the farmer from previous visits to the village and expressed her thanks for his helping them.

'No problem, Audrey lass,' Jim Gordon said. 'Hold on tight when you get on, now. The water's not deep but the bottom is a little uneven in places.'

Lucien handed Jim Audrey's overnight bag and her tote and then came to stand behind her to help her get on the tractor by putting his hands on her hips. His touch—even through her clothes—made her senses do cartwheels. She put her foot on the metal step and gave a spring that would have got her nowhere if it hadn't been for the gentle nudge of his hands. She wriggled to take her place on the back of the tractor and Lucien jumped up next to her and wrapped a firm arm around her waist to keep her secure. 'Okay?'

Audrey was so breathless from his closeness she could barely get her voice to do much more than squeak. 'Okay.'

Jim set the tractor on its way and soon they were across to the other side of the river. Lucien jumped down and, once he had her bags off and on the ground next to him, he held out his hands for her. She placed her hands on his shoulders and he put his hands on her waist and lifted her down as if she weighed less than a child.

For a moment they stood with his hands on her waist and hers on his shoulders. Audrey's gaze met his and it was as if someone had pressed 'pause' on time. Even the birds in the nearby shrubs seemed to have stopped twittering. The blue of his eyes was mesmerising, the touch of his hands making her aware of how close to him she was standing. His thighs were almost brushing hers. She could feel his body warmth like the glow of a radiator. His gaze lowered to her mouth for a brief moment, his hands tightening on her waist as if he was about to bring her even closer. Her heart gave an extra beat as if she'd had one too many energy drinks. She looked at his mouth and something in her belly fluttered like the pages of a book in a playful breeze. She swallowed and moistened her lips but the moment was broken by the sound of the tractor being placed in gear.

Lucien relaxed his hold and stepped back from her and turned to Jim. 'Thanks again, Jim. Really appreciate your help.'

'The hire-car people left the keys in the ignition when they dropped it off,' Jim said, nodding towards the car parked to one side. 'And I'll get the wheels moving on getting young Audrey's car towed to the workshop as you asked.'

Audrey felt like a helpless female surrounded by big, strong, capable men who were taking care of everything for her. She mentally apologised to her emancipated self and lapped it up. She followed Lucien to the hire car and he held the door open for her and helped her in.

Once he was behind the wheel, she said, 'If you drop me at the nearest train station I'll make my way back to—'

'Have you got your passport in your bag?'

'Yes, but—'

He gave her a glance that made something in her belly turn over. 'St Remy, here we come.'

CHAPTER FIVE

LUCIEN KNEW IT was probably a bad idea to take Audrey with him to the south of France but he needed her there to make sure Sibella and his father understood how vehemently they were against their marriage. It was a bad idea to be anywhere near Audrey. He had to help her on and off the tractor, but did he have to stand there staring at her mouth like a punch-drunk teenager anticipating his first kiss?

He had to get his hands off her and get a grip on himself.

But he would be lying if he said it hadn't felt good holding her close like that. Seeing the way her nutmeg-brown eyes widened and the way her tongue swept over her lips as if preparing for the descent of his mouth.

And he'd been pretty damn close to doing it too.

He'd been lost in a moment of mad lust. Feeling her breasts within inches of his chest, imagining what it would feel like to have them pressed against him skin-to-skin. Feeling her thighs so close to his, imagining them wrapped around his as he entered her velvet warmth. He had always dated super-slim women but something about her womanly figure made everything that was male in him sit up and take notice. He was ashamed of his reaction to her, especially as he was supposed to be 'involved' with Viviana.

But that was no excuse to be lusting over Audrey. He wasn't like his father, who got his head turned by sexy women even when he was involved with someone else. He was too strong-willed to let the ripe and sensuous curves of Audrey's body and her supple and generous mouth unravel his self-control like a ball of string.

Way too strong-willed.

He hoped.

Audrey considered refusing to go with Lucien to France but without a car and no spare cash to hire one she knew her search for her mother and Harlan would grind to a halt. The thought of spending the weekend at her flat with nothing better to do than watch her flatmate, Rosie, get ready to go out with her latest boyfriend was not appealing. Well, not as appealing as a weekend in St Remy. It had nothing to do with going with Lucien Fox. Nothing at all. St Remy was the attraction. She hadn't been to the south of France in ages.

But when they arrived at the airport in London, Audrey was shocked to find a small group of paparazzi waiting for them. 'Oh, no…' she said, glancing at Lucien. 'How on earth did they find us?'

His expression was so grim he could have moonlighted as a gravedigger. 'Who knows? But don't say anything. Leave it to me.'

He helped her out of the car as the press gang came

bustling over. 'Lucien? Audrey? Can we have a quick word? What do you two think about your respective parents Harlan and Sibella remarrying for the third time?'

'No comment.' Lucien's tone was as curt as a prison guard's.

'Audrey?' The journalist aimed his recording device at her instead. 'So, what's going on between you and Lucien Fox?'

'Nothing's going on,' Audrey said, feeling a blush steal over her cheeks like a measles rash.

'Is it true you spent last night alone together down at your mother's cottage in the Cotswolds?'

Audrey mentally gulped. Had someone seen them? Had Jim Gordon said something to someone? She glanced at Lucien but his expression was as closed as a bank vault. She turned back to the journalist. 'No comment.'

'What does Viviana Prestonward think of your cosy relationship with your step-sibling Audrey Merrington, Lucien?' another journalist asked with a *nudge-nudge, wink-wink, say no more* look.

Audrey was sure she heard Lucien's back molars grind together. 'At the risk of repeating myself—no comment,' he said through lips that were so tight you couldn't have squeezed a slip of paper through. He took Audrey by the arm and led her further inside the terminal to the check-in area. 'I told you not to say anything.'

'I didn't say anything—well, nothing you didn't say, that is.'

'You told them nothing's going on.' His hand on her arm tightened to steer her out of the way of an older man pushing an overloaded baggage trolley.

'That's because nothing is going on.'

'You made it sound like there was.'

Audrey pulled out of his hold and rubbed at her arm. 'I did not. What did you expect me to do? Just stand there and let them make those insinuations without defending myself? Anyway, I don't see what's your problem. No one would ever think you'd be interested in someone like me.'

His frown gave him an intimidating air. 'This is your mother's doing.'

A weight dropped in Audrey's stomach. 'You think my mother tipped off the press about us? But why would she do that?'

His mouth was set in a cynical line. 'Because she loves nothing more than a bit of pot-stirring. The more press attention on us, the less on her and my father.'

Could it be true? Had her mother done something so mischievous in order to take the spotlight off her relationship with Lucien's father? But why? Sibella knew how much Audrey disliked Lucien.

But the more she thought about it the more likely it seemed. Her mother had blocked Audrey from finding her on the phone app but her mother could still find her. Her mother could have been following her movements ever since Audrey had left her flat yesterday morning. She and Harlan were probably laughing about it over a bottle or two of wine right this very minute.

Lucien's phone rang soon after they had checked in to their flight. He glanced at the screen and grimaced and, mouthing 'Excuse me', stood a little apart from Audrey to answer. She tried not to listen…well, strictly speaking she didn't really try, but even with the background noise of the terminal it was almost impossible not to get the gist of the conversation from the brooding expression on his face. After the call ended he slipped the phone in his trouser pocket.

'Trouble in paradise?' Audrey gave him an arch look.

He shrugged as if it didn't matter one way or the other. 'Come on. It's nearly time to board.'

Audrey waited until they were seated on the plane before she brought up the topic of Viviana again. 'So, she was the jealous type after all.'

His mouth tightened as though it were being tugged on from inside. 'If you're expecting to see me fall in an emotional heap like my father then you'll be waiting a long time.'

'No. I'm not expecting that.' She clipped on her seat belt and settled back into her seat. 'My theory was right. You would only ever get involved with someone who doesn't threaten your locked-away heart.' She turned and gave him a sugar-sweet smile. 'I'm assuming you actually have one?'

He gave her the side-eye. 'I hope you're not one of those annoying passengers who make banal conversation the whole flight?'

'Nope,' Audrey said. 'I like to read or watch movies.'

'Glad to hear it.' He leaned his head back against the headrest and closed his eyes.

Audrey picked up the in-flight magazine but her gaze kept drifting to his silent form beside her. His arm was resting on the armrest, his long legs stretched out and crossed over at the ankles. They were travelling Business Class; apparently he was too much of an accountant to travel First Class. But secretly that impressed her about him. Her mother always insisted on travelling First Class, even when she couldn't always afford it. It was all about her mother's image, how the public perceived her. It seemed such a shallow existence to Audrey and she wondered what was going to happen to her mother when her celebrity star dimmed, as it inevitably would. She sighed and reached for the remote control and clicked on the movie menu. Her mother's star would dim even more quickly if Audrey didn't talk her out of remarrying Harlan Fox.

And, God forbid, it might even be snuffed out completely.

Lucien opened his eyes some time later to find Audrey sniffing in the seat beside him, her knees drawn up, her feet bare. Chocolate wrappers littered the floor and her seat, including one on his seat. She was dabbing at her streaming eyes with a bunched-up tissue—or was it a napkin from the meal tray? The credits were rolling on a movie on the screen in front of her.

'Sad movie?' he said, handing her his handkerchief.

She gave him a sheepish look, pulled out her headphones and took the handkerchief. 'I've seen it twenty-three times and I still cry buckets.'

Who watched a movie twenty-three times? 'Must be a good movie.' He leaned closer to glance at the credits and caught a whiff of her perfume as well as a stronger one of chocolate. *'Notting Hill.'*

'Have you seen it?'

'Once, years ago.'

Audrey gave a heartfelt sigh. 'It's my favourite movie.'

'What do you love about it?'

'Anna Scott, Julia Roberts's character, is one of the most famous actors in the world, but she's just a normal person underneath the fame and that's who Hugh Grant's character—William Thacker—falls in love with, only he nearly loses her because he's put off by her celebrity status. But then he finally comes to his senses when his quirky flatmate calls him a daft prick for turning her down and—' Her mouth twisted. 'Sorry. I'm probably boring you.' She pretended to zip her lips. 'That's it. No more banal conversation from me.'

'You're not boring me.' He was surprised to find it was true. He could have listened to her rave on and on about that movie for the next hour—for the next week. Her face was so animated when she talked, her eyes bright and shiny with her dark lashes all spiky from tears.

'Anyway, you've seen the movie, so...' Her eyes fell away from his and she began fiddling with the fabric of his handkerchief.

'You have chocolate next to your mouth,' Lucien said.

'Where?' She brushed at her mouth with the handkerchief. 'Gone?'

He took the handkerchief and, holding her chin with one hand, gently removed the smear of chocolate.

You're touching her again.

He ignored his conscience and dabbed at the other

side of her mouth. There wasn't any chocolate there but he couldn't resist the way her big brown eyes reacted when he touched her—they opened and closed in a slow blink like a kitten enjoying a sensuous stroke. Her pupils widened like spreading pools of ink and she gave a tiny swallow, her tongue darting out to wet her lips. Something tightly bound up in his chest loosened like the sudden slip of a knot.

He placed his thumb on her lower lip and moved it back and forth against its pillowy softness, his blood stirring, simmering, smouldering. She made a little whimpering sound—it wasn't much more than the catch of her breath, but it ignited his desire like a taper against dry tinder. He brought his head closer, closer, closer, giving her time to pull back, giving himself time to rethink this madness. His madness.

Stop. Stop. Stop.

The warnings sounded like a distant horn—slightly muffled, muted, making it easy to ignore.

He covered her mouth with his and her softness clung to his dry lips like silk on sandpaper. He pressed on her lips once—a touchdown. A test.

But he wanted more. He ached, he throbbed, he craved more.

He pressed down again on her lips and she opened her mouth on a breathless sigh, her hands slid up his chest, grasped the front of his shirt. His tongue found hers and a hot dart of need speared him. He lost his mind. His self-control. Her mouth tasted of chocolate and milk and something that was uniquely her. Her mouth was like exotic nectar. A potent potion he would die without consuming. His lips were fused to hers, his tongue dancing and flirting and mating with hers like two champion dancers who knew each other's movements as well as their own.

He slid his hands under her hair to cradle her head. A fresh wave of lust consumed him like a wall of flame, whooshing through him with incendiary heat. He wanted her with such fierce desire he could feel it thundering through his groin and tingling his spine. He groaned against her mouth, flicked his tongue in and out against hers in erotic play. He lifted to change position but Audrey pulled away with a dazed look on her face. Her mouth was plump and swollen and her chin reddened from where his stubble had grazed her.

It was a new experience for Lucien to be lost for words.

What the hell just happened?

He cleared his throat and made a show of straightening the front of his creased shirt where her hands had fisted. 'Right, well. That must not happen again.' He knew he sounded stiff and formal. Damn it, he *was* stiff. But he had to break the sensual spell she had cast over him.

Audrey touched her top lip with her fingertip, still looking a little shell-shocked. 'You didn't…enjoy it?'

He'd enjoyed it too darn much. 'Sure. But we're not doing it again. Understood?' He put on his stern schoolmaster face, not wanting to show how undone he was. Seriously undone.

She glanced at his mouth and nodded. 'Probably a good idea… I mean, you were really going for it there. I thought you might start ripping my clothes off and—'

Lucien sliced the air with his hand with such force it bumped his tray table. 'Not going to happen.' But he'd wanted to. Oh, how he'd wanted to. *Still* wanted to. 'You and me getting it on is a crazy idea.'

'Because?' Was that a note of self-doubt in her voice?

'Did you just hear what I said? I said we're *not* doing this, Audrey. No more kissing. No more touching. No more anything.'

She gave him a guileless look. 'Why are you making such a big thing about this? I'm not asking you to sleep with me. Anyway, it was just a kiss.'

Was it just a kiss? Or was it the kiss of a lifetime? A kiss from which all past and future kisses would be measured? His lips were still tingling. He could still taste her. His blood was still hammering.

He needed a cold shower.

He needed his head examined.

He needed to straitjacket and shackle his desire.

Lucien's gaze kept tracking to her mouth like a sniffer dog on a drug bust. 'Listen to me, Audrey.' He took a breath and dragged his eyes back to hers. 'We have to be sensible about this…situation. We're on a mission to stop your mother and my father from making a terrible mistake. Their third terrible mistake. It's not going to help matters if we start making our own mistakes.'

Her eyes drifted and focused on a point below his chin. 'I hear you, okay? There's no need to keep banging on about it. I get that you're not into me even though you kissed me like you were.' She gave him a little stab of a glare. 'You shouldn't send mixed signals—it can give people the wrong idea. Not that I got the wrong idea. I'm just saying you should be more careful in future.'

He sucked in a breath and released it in a quick draft. 'Let's just forget that kiss ever happened, okay?'

She sat back with a little thump against her seat and picked up the remote control. 'What kiss?' She pressed on the remote as if she were switching him off.

Lucien settled in his seat and tried to rebalance himself. Forget about the kiss. *Forget. Forget. Forget.* But every time he swallowed he tasted the sweetness of her, the temptation of her. He would never be able to eat chocolate again without thinking of her. Without remembering that kiss.

For six years he had resisted Audrey. He had been sensible and responsible about her tipsy passes.

But now he'd kissed her.

Not just kissed her but all but feasted off her mouth like it was his last meal. His body was still feeling the dragging ache of unrelieved desire. It pulled and pulsed in his groin, running down his thighs and up again as if every nerve was on fire.

But now he didn't have his 'relationship' with Viviana to hide behind, his self-control had collapsed like a house of cards in a stiff breeze. Damn it, there was that word 'stiff' again. He'd needed that relationship to keep his boundaries secure. He wasn't the sort of guy to kiss another woman when he was in a relationship with someone else, even if that relationship was only a charade.

He had standards. Principles. Morals.

But the irony was Viviana hadn't ended the charade

out of jealousy because of that mischievous tweet of Audrey's mother's but because she had fallen in love with someone on her photo shoot—a cameraman she'd known for years.

Now Lucien was inconveniently free. Inconveniently, because without the protection of a 'relationship' with someone else he was tempted to indulge in a fling with Audrey.

Seriously, dangerously tempted.

Bad idea. Dumb idea. Wicked idea. It didn't matter how many arguments he put up, his mind kept coming back to it like a tongue to a niggling tooth. They were both adults, weren't they? They were clearly attracted to each other. She didn't want marriage, nor did he.

He had always chosen his partners carefully. No strings. No promises. No commitment. He didn't choose women who made him feel out of control. He wasn't averse to a bit of passion. He was a man with all the normal desires and needs. But he'd always been selective in how that passion was expressed.

He had no such control when it came to Audrey. He knew it on a cellular level. She had the potential to undo him. To unravel the self-control he worked so hard to maintain.

But maybe if he got it on with her it would purge her from his system. Get the fantasies of her out of his head once and for all.

Audrey clicked off the remote and turned to look at him. 'You know, for someone who just broke up with the person they were thinking about marrying, you certainly moved on indecently quickly.'

She didn't know how indecent his thoughts were right now. Shockingly indecent. But he figured he might as well tell her the truth about Viviana, otherwise Audrey would never stop banging on about his attitude to love and marriage. 'We were only pretending to be dating. I was doing her a favour.'

Her eyebrows came together. 'Friends with benefits, you mean?'

'No benefits. We just hung out so her cheating ex would get annoyed she moved on so quickly.'

'Oh...' Her teeth pulled at her lip. 'That was...nice of you. But weren't you a little bit tempted to sleep with her? I mean, she's gorgeous and—'

'I'm assuming you're currently between relationships or should I be worried some guy is going to take my kneecaps out with a baseball bat?'

Her lips made a funny little movement—a quirky, wry movement. 'I haven't dated anyone for a while.'

'How long a while?'

Her eyes flicked away from his. 'You wouldn't believe me if I told you.'

'Try me.'

She looked at his mouth, then back to his eyes and he felt a strange little jolt. 'Are you thinking about that kiss?'

'No.' It was such a blatant lie he mentally braced himself for a deity's lightning strike.

'Then why do you keep staring at my mouth?'

Lucien forced his gaze back to hers. 'I'm not.'

'Yes, you are. See? You did it just then. Your eyes flicked down and then up again.'

'I was checking out the stubble rash on your chin.' He brushed his finger over the reddened patch. 'Is it sore?'

She gave a delicate shiver as if his touch had sent a current through her flesh. 'You're touching me again.' Her voice was soft and husky, making his body give an answering shiver.

Lucien dropped his hand and curled his fingers into a fist. 'While we're on the subject, why do you keep staring at my mouth?'

'Do I?'

'You do.'

Her eyes darted to his mouth. 'Maybe it's because no one's ever kissed me like that before.'

Right back at you, sweetheart.

'No one?'

'No one.'

Lucien stroked a finger across her lower lip. She closed her eyes and swayed slightly. He moved his finger under her jaw, applying gentle pressure beneath her chin to raise her gaze back to his. 'Stop that thought right now.'

Her expression was as innocent as a child's. 'What thought?'

He gave a soft grunt of laughter. 'You're thinking what I'm thinking, so don't try and deny it.'

The tip of her tongue passed over her lips and she gave the tiniest of swallows. 'How do you know what I'm thinking? You're not a mind reader.'

Desire throbbed through him, a dull pain in his groin. 'You want me.'

'So? It doesn't mean I'm going to act on it. Anyway, you said no more kissing or touching.' She batted her eyelashes. 'But maybe you only said that for *your* benefit.'

'Don't worry. I can control myself.'

One of her brows lifted and her eyes flashed with a challenge. 'So if I leaned forward and pressed my lips against yours, you wouldn't kiss me back?'

Lucien had to call on every ounce of willpower to stop himself from looking at her lush, ripe mouth. 'Want to try it and see?'

Her smile flickered, then disappeared. 'No.'

No? What did she mean, no? He wanted to prove to her—to prove to himself—that he could resist her. It had nothing to do with how disappointed he felt. He wasn't disappointed. Not one bit. Why should he care if she kissed him or not? He was trying *not* to kiss her, wasn't he?

And he would keep on trying. Harder. Much harder.

He summoned up an easy-going smile. 'Coward.'

Even after the two-hour flight to Marseille, Audrey was still reliving every moment of that kiss. They had picked up a hire car and were driving through a small village on the way to the chateau a few kilometres out of St Remy. She kept touching her lips with her fingers when Lucien wasn't looking, wondering how it could be that all this time later her lips would still feel so…so awakened. So sensitive. So alive. Every time she moistened her lips she tasted him. Every time she looked in a mirror she saw the tiny patch of beard rash on her chin and a frisson would go through her. His kiss had been passionate, thrilling, magical. Their mouths had responded to each other like the flames of two fires meeting—exploding in a maelstrom of heat she could feel even now smouldering in her core. She could feel the restless pulse of unsatisfied desire in her body—an ache that twinged with each breath she took.

Audrey looked out of the car window at the quaint village shops and houses, wishing they had time to stop and explore. The tiny village had once been surrounded by a circular wall and many of the charming medieval buildings dated back to the fourteen-hundreds.

Lucien slowed the car to allow a mother and her two children and little fluffy dog cross the narrow street before he continued. 'Did you know St Remy is the birthplace of Nostradamus, the sixteenth-century author of prophecies?'

'Yes,' Audrey said. 'And the place where Vincent Van Gogh came for treatment for his mental illness. I wish we had time to stop and have a wander around.'

'We're not here to sightsee.'

'I know, but what if Mum and Harlan aren't at the chateau?'

'I've already spoken to the owner. I called before we left London.'

Audrey glanced at him. 'What did he tell you? Did he confirm they were there?'

'No.'

'Then why are we heading there if you don't think—?'

'He was cagey, evasive, which made me suspect he's been sworn to secrecy.'

'But you're Harlan's son, so why wouldn't he tell you? You're family.'

Lucien gave a lip-shrug. 'I don't have that sort of family.'

Neither do I.

Audrey shifted her gaze from his mouth and looked at the view again. She was glad it was Lucien that had started the kiss. It gave her a sense of one-upmanship she badly needed, given their history. His attraction might be reluctant but it was there all the same. She saw it every time he looked at her—the way his gaze kept going to her mouth and the way his eyes darkened and glittered with lust. She felt it in his touch— the way his hands set fire to her skin even through her clothes.

It had surprised her to find out he hadn't been in a real relationship with Viviana. Surprised and secretly delighted. But he'd allowed everyone, including Audrey, to think he was until Viviana had called him, no doubt after seeing her mother's tweet. Did Viviana think he was now involved with Audrey? He hadn't said anything to the contrary on the phone.

But it had always seemed strange to her that Lucien would even want to get married one day in the future if he was trying to avoid love. Even arranged marriages often ended up with the partners falling in love with each other. Or was he so determined his heart would never be touched?

As determined as *she* was?

And Audrey was determined. Steely and determined. No way was she going to fall in love like her mother, losing all sense of dignity and autonomy by becoming hopelessly besotted with a man who would only leave her or disappoint her.

But that didn't mean she didn't want to experience sensuality. To feel a man's touch, to feel a man's rougher skin move against hers. To feel a man's mouth on her lips, on her breasts, his hands on her…

You could have a fling with Lucien.

She allowed the thought some traction…

He was attracted to her. *Tick*. She was attracted to him. *Tick*. They were both currently single. *Tick*.

What harm could it do? They were both consenting adults. He was the *one* person she would consider having a fling with because she knew he wasn't interested in her mother's stardom. She wouldn't have the worry about his motives. His motives would be pure and simple lust.

Just like hers.

Lucien suddenly braked and grabbed her by the arm, and for a startled moment Audrey thought he must have read her mind. 'Look. Is that your mother over there near that market stall?'

Audrey peered in the direction he was pointing. 'Which stall?' It wasn't Wednesday, the main market day, but there were still a lot of stalls full of fruit and vegetables and freshly baked bread and the gorgeous cheeses this region was famous for. Just looking at all that food made her stomach growl. But then she glimpsed a blonde head before it disappeared into the maze of the stalls. 'I'm not sure if that was Mum or not. It looked like her, but—'

'I'll quickly park and we can do a search on foot,' Lucien said. 'They might not be staying at the chateau. They might be staying here in the village. Small as it is, it's easier to blend into the crowd down here.'

CHAPTER SIX

LUCIEN PARKED IN a shady side-street and then they made their way back to the market stalls. In her attempt to keep up with his quick striding pace, Audrey almost stumbled on the cobblestones and he grabbed her hand to steady her. 'Careful. We can't have you breaking a leg.'

'I'm fine.' Audrey tried to pull her hand out of his but he held it securely. 'But wouldn't we be better to split up and search? We could cover twice the ground that way. We can text each other if we spot them.'

His fingers tightened on her hand for a moment before he released her. 'Good idea. I'll cover this side of the market area and you can do that side. I'll text or call you in ten minutes.'

Audrey started searching through the crowd but her eyes kept being drawn by the glorious food. The smell of fresh bread and croissants was nothing short of torture. She was salivating so badly she was going to cause a flash flood on the cobbled street. She saw several blonde women but none of them was her mother. Right now she didn't care a jot about finding her mother.

What she wanted was one of those chocolate croissants.

She glanced up and down the market, looking for Lucien. He was tall enough for her to see over the top of most people…ah, yes, there he was, right at the other end near a vegetable stall. She took out her purse and, recalling her schoolgirl French, bought one of the croissants. The first bite into the sweet flakiness sent a shiver of delight through her body almost the same as when Lucien had kissed her. Almost. The second bite evoked a blissful groan, but just as she was about to take her third bite she saw her mother coming out of a tiny boutique less than a metre away. Or at least a downplayed version of her mother. She was carrying a shopping bag with a paper-wrapped baguette poking out of the top as well as some fresh fruit and vegetables.

'Mumffh?' Audrey's mouthful of pastry didn't make for the best diction and she quickly swallowed and rushed over. 'Mum?'

At first she wondered if she'd made a mistake. The woman in front of her had her mother's eyes and hair colour but the hair wasn't styled and her eyes weren't made up. Her eyelashes weren't false; they weren't even coated with mascara. Her mother's normally glowing skin looked pale and drawn and there were fine lines around her mouth Audrey had never seen before. Even her mother's clothes were different. Instead of a brightly coloured *look-at-me* designer outfit, her mother was wearing faded jeans and a cotton shirt and a man's grey sweater tied around her waist. And she had trainers on her feet. No sky-high heels.

This was taking stars without make-up to a whole new level.

Sibella glanced around nervously. 'Is Lucien with you?'

'Yes.' Audrey pointed further up the market. 'Over there somewhere. He thought he saw you when we were driving past.'

Sibella grasped Audrey's hand with her free hand and tugged her under the awning of the boutique. 'Tell him you didn't see me. Tell him it was someone else who looked like me. Please?'

Audrey was shocked at the urgent tone of her mother's voice and the desperation in her gaze. 'But why?'

'Harlan and I want to be left alone without being lectured by everyone on how bad we are for each other.'

'But you are bad for each other,' Audrey said. 'You bring out the worst in each other and I can't stand by and watch it all fall apart again.'

A middle-aged woman came out of the boutique and walked past them without even glancing at Audrey's mother. Her mother was famous all over the world. Sibella couldn't walk down a deserted country lane without being recognised. What was even more surprising, her mother seemed relieved no one was looking at her and asking for an autograph or to pose for a selfie.

'Please, Audrey.' Her mother gripped Audrey's hand tighter and her eyes took on such a beseeching look it reminded Audrey of a puppy begging for a forbidden treat. 'Please just give me a few days with Harlan. He's…' Her mother choked back a tiny sob and tears shone in her eyes. 'He's not well.'

Audrey knew her mother was a good actor and could sob and cry on demand, but something about her expression told her this was no act. She was genuinely upset. 'Not well? What's wrong with him?'

Sibella's gaze did another nervous dart around the crowded market before she pulled Audrey into a quiet narrow lane. 'He only told me last night.' Her bottom lip quivered. 'He's got cancer.'

Audrey swallowed. 'What sort of cancer? Is it—?'

'A brain tumour,' Sibella said. 'I'm trying to talk him into having an operation and chemo. He refuses to have any treatment because the doctors have told him there's only a small chance of success and he might end up having a stroke or worse. But I want him to try. To give himself the best chance. To give *us* the best chance.'

Audrey was no medical specialist but even she knew of the low rate of survival for brain cancers. Surgery was fraught with danger even when there was a possibility of removing the tumour. It was a daunting prognosis for anyone to face, and for someone like Harlan, who had never been sick other than from a hangover, she could imagine it was hitting him hard. 'Oh, Mum, that's terrible… Is there anything I can do?'

'Yes.' Her mother's eyes took on a determined gleam. 'Keep Lucien away. Don't tell him you've found us.'

'But—'

'We're not staying at the chateau,' her mother said. 'I wanted to but it wasn't available, and anyway, Harlan decided we had to go somewhere different for a change. Somewhere smaller and more intimate.'

'But don't you think Lucien should know his father's so sick?'

Sibella pursed her lips. 'Harlan is going to tell him himself. But not right now. I know what Lucien is like. He'll try and talk Harlan and me out of remarrying. Harlan wants me back in his life…in what's left of his life.' She gave another choked-off sob. 'We're planning to have a private ceremony. No fanfare this time.'

Audrey thought back to the luxury vellum wedding invitation that had been delivered to her flat. 'Then why did you send that invitation if you're not going to have a big showy wedding?'

'That was before Harlan knew he was sick,' Sibella said. 'He found out last week but didn't want to tell me until we went away together. Please, promise me you won't tell Lucien you've seen me. Tell him I called you and told you we were staying somewhere else.'

'But Mum, you know what a hopeless liar I am,' Audrey said. 'Where will I say you've gone?'

'I don't care just as long as it's not here.'

'But why did you come here in the first place? Lucien knows it's one of his father's favourite haunts. Surely Harlan knew he would come here to look for you both?'

Sibella sighed and the lines around her mouth deepened. 'It was a risk he was prepared to take because he knows how much I love this village. We both love it.' She swallowed and swiped at her streaming eyes with the back of her hand. 'I guess he thought it might be the last time we will be on holiday together, so where else would he want to go but here, where we've had some of our happiest…' she gave another tight swallow '…times?'

Audrey's phone buzzed with a text and her heart

jumped. 'That's probably Lucien, looking for me.' She pulled out her phone and read the message:

Where are you?

'Please, sweetie,' Sibella said. 'Please just give Harlan and me three days.'

There was that number three again. But it was the 'sweetie' that did it. Her mother hadn't called her that since Audrey was a little kid. She didn't like the thought of lying to Lucien but what else could she do? It was Harlan's place to tell Lucien he was sick, not hers. Her mother said Harlan planned to tell Lucien himself. It would be wrong of Audrey to deliver the news he should hear from his father first-hand.

The news of Harlan's illness changed everything. What would it hurt if her mother remarried him? He might not have long to live and at least he would die happy. 'Okay, but I can't say I'm happy about—'

'I'll send you a text now and drop a hint about some other place we might be staying so at least you'll have something concrete to show Lucien.' Sibella put her shopping bag down and quickly texted a message and within a couple of seconds Audrey's phoned pinged.

She clicked on the message. 'Okay. Got it. But I still feel really uncomfortable about lying to Lucien.'

'Why? You don't even like him.'

The trouble was Audrey liked him way too much. The longer she spent with him the more she liked him. The more she wanted him with a fierce ache that radiated throughout her body. And that kiss… How would she ever be able to forget it? Would she ever stop wanting it to be repeated? She frowned at her mother. 'That reminds me. What were you thinking, making everyone think he and I were having some sort of...thing?'

Her mother had the grace to look a little ashamed. 'I know it was bit naughty of me but Harlan thought Lucien was going to ask that broomstick model to marry him. He'd dated her longer than anyone else, but Harlan knew Lucien wasn't in love with her. Apparently he doesn't believe in falling in love. He must think it's a weakness of his father's that he's fallen in love with me so many times.' She rolled her eyes in a *can-you-believe-it?* manner.

'Why did you send me to the cottage with that false lead?'

'I've had an agent look at it. I want to sell it. I thought it might be the last time you got to go there. I seem to remember you liked it quite a lot.'

Audrey's phone pinged again with another message from Lucien. 'Look, I'd better meet back up with Lucien or he'll suspect something.' She typed a message back that she was at a public restroom. She put her phone away and looked at her mother again. 'Three days, okay?'

Sibella wrapped her arms around Audrey and gave her a big squishy hug, just like she'd used to do when Audrey was a little girl. 'Thank you, sweetie. This means so much to me.' She eased back with tears shining in her eyes. 'We want to keep Harlan's illness out of the press for as long as we can. And I really want to talk him into having the operation and chemo. But in the meantime, I'm cooking him healthy food and keeping him away from alcohol.'

Audrey glanced at the fresh produce poking out of her mother's shopping bag. Could there be a bottle of wine or cognac hidden in there somewhere? 'Are you—?'

'No,' Sibella said. 'I'm not drinking. I've decided to give it up for a while, at least until Harlan gets better...' Her bottom lip quivered again and she added, 'If he gets better.'

Audrey waited until her mother disappeared out of sight from the other end of the lane before she turned back to re-enter the market area. She saw Lucien almost immediately and her heart came to a juddering halt. The acting gene had escaped her but she hoped she could still give a credible performance.

'Where the hell have you been all this time?' Lucien asked, frowning. 'I was starting to get worried.' His gaze narrowed when he looked down at her mouth. 'Is that chocolate?'

Audrey brushed at her face and her hand came away with a smear of chocolate plus a couple of croissant crumbs. Why hadn't her mother said something? 'Erm... I had a croissant.' She could feel her cheeks blazing hot enough to cook a dozen croissants.

'Was it good?' His expression was unreadable but she got the feeling he was smiling on the inside.

'Heaven.'

'Did you catch sight of your mother?'

Here we go...

Audrey rummaged in her bag for her phone. 'No, but I just got a text. They're not here. They're in Spain.'

His brows snapped together. 'Spain?'

'Yep. See?' She held her phone up so he could read the message:

Having a wonderful time in Barcelona.

Lucien looked back at her. 'My father hates Spain, in particular Barcelona.'

Audrey's stomach lurched. 'He…he does?'

'He had a bad experience with a tour director there early in his career and hasn't been back since. He swore the only way anyone could get him to go back to Barcelona would be in a coffin.'

Audrey smothered a gulp. 'Maybe he's changed his mind. People do.'

Lucien gave a snort. 'Not my father. Not about Spain. No, this is another false lead of your mother's.' He glanced around the market, shielding his eyes with one of his hands. 'I know this is going to sound strange but I can almost sense they're here.'

Audrey's heart was beating so fast she thought she might faint. *Now, there's a thought.* Maybe she could feign a faint. She put a hand to her brow and staged a slight swoon. 'Gosh, it's hot, isn't it? I think I've had too much sun. Do you think we could go back to the car now?'

Lucien took her by the arm and looped it through one of his. 'Are you okay?' He brushed a finger across her cheek. 'You do look a little flushed. There's a café over here. Let's get you something to drink. You're probably dehydrated.'

Audrey sat with him in the café a short time later, her mind whirling on how she was going to get him out of St Remy without him suspecting something. She'd promised her mother and there was no way she was going to break that promise. Three days. That was all she needed to keep him away. Why hadn't she thought to ask where her mother and Harlan were staying? Maybe they were staying in one of those cute medieval houses. They might even be able to see her and Lucien right this minute. She sipped at her mineral water and covertly watched him as he surveyed the street outside the café.

His gaze suddenly swung back to her. 'How are you feeling?'

'Erm…better, I think.' She drained her drink and smiled. 'Time to go?'

He rose from the table and helped her out of her chair. 'Do you feel up to a little walk around if we stick to the shady side of the street?'

Audrey was torn between wanting to explore the village and needing to keep him out of it. 'Why don't we drive out to the chateau? Isn't that where we're supposed to be heading?' At least she knew her mother and Harlan weren't there and she figured once Lucien accepted that he might then agree to fly back to London.

'They're not staying there.'

Audrey was starting to wonder if he was channelling Nostradamus or something. 'How do you know? I mean, apart from my mother's text, that is.'

'I spoke to one of the stallholders,' he said. 'The chateau is undergoing extensive maintenance and repairs. It's not being rented out at present.'

'Then why was the owner so cagey on the phone the other day?'

Lucien shrugged. 'Who knows? Maybe he thought I was a building inspector.'

Lucien led Audrey outside and made sure she was out of direct sunlight as they walked through the village. It was one of his father's favourite places and he had come here for a month to recuperate after the last divorce. He couldn't imagine his father would ever change his mind about Barcelona. In spite of her mother's text message, he couldn't rid himself of the sense his father was here. He would stick around with Audrey in St Remy for the rest of the weekend.

They wandered in and out of some of the shops so Audrey could keep cool, and Lucien couldn't help noticing how taken she was with everything—the medieval architecture, the flowers hanging in baskets or spilling out of tubs, the street cafés and, of course, the food. For someone who claimed to be feeling unwell it certainly hadn't tainted her appetite. He found it rather cute she was such a foodie, sneaking off to eat a chocolate croissant when he wasn't looking. He couldn't remember the last time he'd dated a woman who wasn't on some sort of diet.

But Audrey clearly loved food, which made him wonder if she was just as passionate about other appetites. He had tasted that fiery passion in her kiss. Felt it thrumming in her lips as they clung to his. Was she thinking about that kiss now? Every time he looked at her, her gaze would dart away and she would bite her lip and her brow would furrow.

Was she finding it as hard as he was *not* to think about that kiss?

'We'd better find a place to stay,' Lucien said once they'd come out of a handcrafts boutique.

Audrey's eyes flew to his as if he'd said he'd booked them a room in purgatory. 'Stay? You mean here? Here in St Remy?'

'Of course here,' Lucien said. 'I want to hang around for the rest of the weekend in case—'

'The rest of the weekend?' Her eyes were as big as Christmas baubles. 'But…but why? I mean, I—I need to get back to London. I can't flit around Provence all weekend now we know Mum and Harlan aren't here.'

'It's all right. I'll book us into separate rooms. Your virtue is safe.'

'Of course it is.' Her voice contained a note of something he couldn't identify. Was it cynicism or hurt or both? 'You'd never lower your standards to sleep with someone like me.'

'We really need to do something about that self-esteem of yours, don't we?' Lucien stepped closer to brush a flyaway strand of her hair away from her face. 'Do you really think I'm not attracted to you?' It was a dangerous admission on his part but he was unable to stop himself. He did want her. He wanted her badly. He kept trying to remember the reasons he'd put up against sleeping with her, but now none of them seemed strong enough. Maybe they had never been strong enough and all this time he'd been deluding himself he could withstand the temptation.

But now nothing was strong enough to counter the red-hot desire that moved through his body in fizzing currents and eddies. He had fought his desire for her. Fought with it, wrestled with it, battled with it and yet it had been beyond him, because deep down he knew she was the one woman to unravel his control in a way no one else could.

Her tongue came out and left a glistening sheen over her lips. 'You want to sleep with me? Really? But I thought you said—'

He ran his fingertip over her bottom lip. 'Forget what I said. We're both consenting adults.'

What the heck are you doing?

But right then, Lucien wasn't listening to the faintly ringing warning bell of his conscience. He was going on instinct—primal instinct—and reading the signals from her that told him she wanted him just as much as he wanted her.

Her lip quivered against his finger and her hands came to rest on his chest. 'But you said if we got involved it would only encourage our parents.'

'I'm not proposing marriage,' Lucien said. 'Just a short-term fling to explore this chemistry.'

She glanced at his mouth and swallowed. 'You feel it too?'

He picked up her hand and brought it to his mouth, holding her gaze with his. 'All the time.'

Audrey walked with Lucien into the luxury villa he'd booked for the weekend with her body tingling in anticipation. He wanted her. He was offering her a short-term fling. They were going to spend the weekend together as lovers.

But her mind kept throwing up flags of panic. They were still in St Remy, when she'd promised her mother she would keep him away from the village. What if he ran into his father and her mother? What if her mother thought she'd betrayed them? It was like trying to choose between two favourite desserts. Impossible.

She would have to have both.

She could have the weekend with Lucien but she would keep him off the streets of the village by indulging in heaps of bed-wrecking sex. Not that she knew much about bed-wrecking sex or anything.

But *he* didn't need to know that.

The more she thought about it, the more it seemed the perfect plan. She would have to give her mother the heads-up to avoid any chance encounters. But, since her mother and Harlan wanted time alone and with his health being so poorly, she couldn't imagine they would be out too much anyway…she hoped.

Lucien led her inside the gorgeous villa and Audrey gasped and turned in a full circle, taking it all in. The décor was simple but elegant and perfectly complemented the medieval origins of the villa. Crystal chandeliers with polished brass fittings and soft furnishings in muted tones of white and dove-grey. Persian rugs softened the tiled floors and the furniture was stylish and sophisticated with typical French flair.

She darted over to the windows to look at the view of the maze of the streets outside and the neighbouring ivy-clad villas. Flowers spilled from hanging baskets defined pectoral muscles, the flat dark nipples, the light dusting of ink-black hair that felt rough and springy and sexy under her fingertips. She brought her mouth to the strong column of his throat, her tongue licking over the bulge of his Adam's apple, his stubble grazing her tongue like sandpaper. The citrus-based scent of his aftershave tantalised her senses as if she were inhaling a psychedelic drug. The hint of male perspiration on his skin was just as intoxicating, making her long to taste him—every inch of him—as she had fantasised about doing for so long.

Lucien reached behind her and unclipped her bra and it fell to the floor. Audrey fought the urge to cover herself and stood and allowed him to feast his eyes on her. He gently cradled her breasts, touching them respectfully, reverently, worshipfully. She had never felt such powerful sensations in her body. No one had ever touched her that way before and the thrill of it snatched her breath away. He bent his head and swept his tongue over each curve—first the right breast, then the left—taking his time until her nerves shivered and danced in a frenzy. He brought his mouth to each of her nipples, sucking on them softly, taking them between his teeth in a gentle bite that made her legs almost go from under her. He circled each nipple with his tongue as if he was marking out a territory, the sexy glide making the base of her spine shiver like fizzing sherbet was trickling down her backbone.

Audrey was so turned on she could barely stand upright. She tugged at his waistband and popped the silver button on his jeans. The flat plane of his abdomen contracted under her touch and it made her emboldened to go lower. His masculine hair tickled her fingers and he sucked in a harsh-sounding breath, his hands gripping her by the waist. He released his breath in a steady stream as if trying to garner some self-control. He undid the button and zip at the back of her skirt and it, too, fell with a whisper of fabric to the floor, leaving her in nothing but her knickers.

'Do you have any idea how much I want you?' He spoke the words against her lips, dazzling her senses all over again.

Audrey licked the seam of his mouth with her tongue, a part of her shocked at her wanton behaviour but another part relishing in the feminine power she felt to be desired so fiercely by him. The potency of his erection pressed against her belly, so near to where her body ached and pulsed with need. 'I can feel it.' She licked his lower lip this time—a slow stroke that made him groan and crush his mouth to hers.

His hands went to her hips, peeling down her knickers, and he walked her backwards to the nearest wall, pinning her hands either side of her head as he feasted off her mouth. His commanding hold of her called out to something primal in her. When he lifted his mouth for air she bit down on his shoulder playfully, tugging at his flesh and then sweeping her tongue over the bite mark.

Lucien gave a low grunt of approval and eased back to step out of his jeans and source a condom from his wallet. His movements were rushed, almost feverish, echoing the storm of urgency she could feel barrelling through her body.

She wanted him *now*.

He slipped the condom in place and Audrey drank in the sight of him, marvelling that it was her who had made him feel so aroused. She stroked him with her hand, going on instinct…well, not quite on instinct alone because she'd read plenty of the sealed sections in women's magazines. But reading about it was nothing compared with doing it in the flesh. Even through the fine membrane of the condom, he felt amazing—like velvet-wrapped steel. He quivered under her touch and made another sound deep at the back of his throat and gently pushed her back against the wall.

He ran one of his hands from her breast to her belly and then below. She sucked in a breath when he came to her folds, sensations spiralling through her when he inserted one finger. 'Oh, God…that feels so good…' She gripped him by the shoulders. 'Make love to me. Please do it. Do it now.'

Lucien hitched one of her legs over his hip and entered her with a deep thrust that made her head bump against the wall. 'Ouch.'

He stopped and looked at her in concern. 'Am I rushing you? You were so wet, I thought—'

Audrey tried to relax her pelvis but the thick presence of him felt strange…as if she was too small for him or something. It wasn't painful now he had stopped but she knew if he moved again it might tug at her tender flesh, which made it even harder for her to relax. 'You didn't rush me at all. It's just you're so…so big…' Could she sound any more clichéd?

Lucien stroked her hair back off her face in a touch

so gentle it felt like the brush of a feather, his dark blue gaze intense and penetrating. 'Are you sure you want to do this?'

'Of course I'm sure.' Audrey could feel a blush stealing over her cheeks. 'I'm just a little out of practice, that's all.'

He brushed his thumb over her lower lip. 'I'll take things a little more slowly. And maybe a bed instead of up against the wall would be better.' He began to withdraw and she couldn't disguise her wince in time. He frowned again. 'I'm hurting you?'

Audrey bit down on her lip. 'Not much…'

Something flickered over his face as if he was shuffling through his thoughts and not liking what his brain produced. 'When was the last time you had sex?'

Audrey swallowed. 'Erm…not…not recently.'

'When?' His gaze was so direct she felt like a suspect in front of a very determined detective.

'Does it matter?' She tried for a casual tone but didn't quite pull it off. Yep, that acting gene certainly hadn't come her way.

Something that looked like horror passed through his gaze and his throat moved up and down over a convulsive swallow. 'Oh, my God…' He moved away from her and she had never felt so naked and exposed in her entire life.

Or so terrifyingly vulnerable.

'You're a…a *virgin*?' He said it like it was an affliction from which there was no known cure.

Audrey made a paltry attempt to cover her breasts.

He brought up her chin with his finger and meshed his gaze with hers. 'I'm not talking puppy and kitten and kid cute. I'm talking I want to carry you to the nearest bed and make love to you cute.'

She looked into his eyes and something unfurled in her belly. 'Do you mean that?'

Indecision flitted over his features as if he was weighing up the pros and cons. 'Of course I do. But I'm concerned that you might want something different out of a relationship with me. Something permanent. I wouldn't want you to get the wrong idea.'

'But I don't want anything permanent,' Audrey said. 'The last thing I want is to get married. My mother's multiple marriages has turned me off the whole notion of in sickness and in health and till death....erm...and all that.' She stumbled over the phrase 'death do us part', thinking of her mother looking after Harlan as he faced a possibly terminal illness. She'd always thought her mother's 'love' of Harlan was an obsessional type of love, a selfish sort of obsession that was all about Sibella and not much about Harlan. But after witnessing her mother's distress over the prospect of losing him, not through divorce but through death, Audrey realised her mother's love had matured into something to be admired, to be emulated.

To aspire to and want for herself.

Lucien brushed his thumb over her lower lip, his eyes still searching hers. 'Are you sure?'

She wasn't but she wasn't going to admit it. She stretched up on tiptoe and linked her arms around his neck. 'I don't want a wedding ring from you, Lucien. But I do want you to make love to me.'

His hands cupped her bottom and drew her closer to his hard heat. 'A couple of days ago I had a long list of reasons why I thought making love to you would be a really bad idea.'

'And now?'

His eyes glinted and his mouth came down to just above hers. 'Can't think of a single one of them.' And then his mouth covered hers.

CHAPTER SEVEN

AUDREY SIGHED AS his mouth came down and covered hers in a kiss that communicated not just lust and longing but also something else…something she couldn't quite describe. There was passion in his kiss but also gentleness—a slow exploration of her mouth that made her senses sing like they were in a choral symphony. His hands cradled her face, angling it so he could deepen the kiss with strokes and glides of his tongue that made her insides quake and quiver and quicken with need. She made breathless sounds of approval and her fingers delved into the thickness of his hair, wanting him so badly it was like a firestorm rampaging through her flesh. Her breasts prickled and tingled where they were crushed against his chest, her thighs heavy with desire as they rubbed against his.

Lucien dragged his mouth off hers and began to scoop her up in his arms. Audrey tried to stop him. 'No. Wait. I'm too heavy. You'll do yourself an injury.'

'Don't be silly.' He lifted her effortlessly as if she were a feather bolster instead of an adult woman who had a sweet tooth. A whole set of sweet teeth.

He carried her to the master bedroom of the villa, and, lowering her to the floor, he slid her down the length of his body, sending shockwaves of delight through her.

He brushed back her hair from her face and stood with her in the circle of his arms, his pelvis tight and aroused against hers. 'Still sure about this?'

Audrey stroked his jaw from just below his ear to the base of his chin. 'I don't think I've wanted anything more than this.'

He peeled his shirt away from her shoulders and gently cradled her breasts, his thumbs rolling over her tight nipples like a slow-moving metronome. His touch was achingly light, so light the sensations were like exquisite torture. But then his mouth came down and he laved each nipple with his tongue. She'd had no idea her breasts were that sensitive. No idea they would trigger other sensations deeper in her body as the network of her nerves transmitted pulses of pleasure from one place to another. He continued his assault on her senses by taking her nipple into his mouth and gently sucking on it. The warm moisture of his mouth and the slight graze of his stubble against her flesh made her whimper with wanton need. There was a smouldering fire between her legs and a hollow ache spreading across her thighs and belly.

Lucien laid her down on the bed and stepped back, and for a stomach-dropping moment Audrey wondered if he was going to call a stop to their lovemaking. 'What's wrong?' she said, instinctively drawing her knees up and covering her breasts.

He leaned down and placed his hands either side of her head and pressed a hot kiss to her mouth. 'Wait for me. I need to get another condom.'

Relief coursed through her. 'Oh… I thought you might have changed your mind.'

He gently stroked her cheek with the tip of his finger. 'If I was a better man then maybe I would.'

'You are a good man, Lucien.' Audrey's voice came out husky. 'I wouldn't allow you to make love to me if you weren't.'

He gave her one more kiss and left the room to get the condom. She couldn't keep her eyes off his aroused male form as he came back in and her body gave a tremor of anticipation. He joined her on the bed and sent his hand down the side of her body in a slow stroke that made every nerve pirouette. He kissed his way down from her breasts to her stomach, dipping his tongue into the shallow cave of her belly button before going lower.

Audrey tensed and clutched his arms. 'I'm not sure I—'

'Relax, sweetheart,' he said. 'This is the best way for me to give you pleasure without hurting you.'

'But don't you want to—?'

He placed a hand just above her pubic bone. 'I want to pleasure you and I want you to be comfortable. That's my priority right now.' He paused for a moment and added, 'As long as you're okay with me touching you like this?'

Audrey couldn't imagine ever wanting anyone else to touch her so intimately. Her body was feverishly excited about his touch, so excited she could feel the intense moisture gathering. 'I'm okay with it.'

'I'll make it good for you but you have to tell me if anything I do isn't working for you,' he said. 'Promise?'

'Promise.'

He stroked his fingers down over the seam of her body, his touch so gentle it was almost a tickle. He parted her folds and stroked her again, his touch featherlight, allowing her time to get used to it. She quivered under the caress, shocked at how wonderful it felt to be touched by someone other than herself. He continued exploring her, moving his fingers at varying speeds, and the pleasure grew—tight pleasure, straining pleasure, pleasure that needed just a little more of a push.

He brought his mouth down to her and stroked her with his tongue, the action so shockingly intimate, so thrillingly pleasurable she drew in a staggered breath and whimpered. He continued caressing her, building the pace and the pressure until she lifted off into a dazzling world where thoughts were blocked out and only physical ecstasy remained. Waves and pulses of pleasure rippled and flowed through her lower body, spiralling out from the tightly budded heart of her. She gasped and cried and clutched at the bedcovers to anchor herself but the orgasm wasn't finished with her. Lucien wasn't finished with her. He kept caressing her, leading her into another release that was stronger and even more powerful than the first.

He waited until she settled with a huge sigh and he smiled and glided his hand up and down the flank of her thigh. 'I hope that was as good as it sounded?'

'Better.' Audrey touched his face in a state of wonderment. 'I can't believe that just happened. I've never felt anything like that before when I've...' Her cheeks grew hot and she lowered her gaze.

He pushed up her chin with his finger. 'Hey. Why are you embarrassed about touching yourself? It's perfectly natural and sensible because it helps you learn how your body works.'

'I know, but there's still a double standard when it comes to sex,' Audrey said. 'It's still hard for women to own and celebrate their sexual desire. To not feel guilty about wanting to give and receive pleasure.'

Lucien circled her left nipple with a lazy finger. 'Tell me what you want now.'

She cupped his face in her hands. 'I want you to make love to me. I want you inside me.'

A frown flickered across his brow. 'What if I hurt you again?'

'I'm sure it won't hurt now that I'm more relaxed,' Audrey said. 'I want to feel you. I want to give you pleasure as well as receive it.'

He kissed her on the mouth—a deep, lingering kiss that made her desire for him move through her body in a rush of heat. His tongue played with hers, calling it into a dance that was thrillingly erotic. He left her mouth to work his way down her body, pressing tingling kisses to her breasts, her ribcage, her hips and stomach and back again to her mouth.

He applied the condom he'd collected earlier and gently parted her, pausing at her entrance, uncertainty shadowing his eyes. 'Are you sure you're ready for this?'

Audrey grabbed at his shoulders. 'You've made me so ready for you.'

Doubt flickered over his features but then he smiled and lowered his mouth back to hers in a mind-drugging kiss. After a moment, he slowly began to enter her, pausing every step of the way until he was sure she was accommodating him without pain. It was uncomfortable at first, not painfully so but just a tightness that eased the more he progressed. Her body wrapped around him and, while it wasn't as intense as him touching her with his fingers, the sensation eased that hollow, achy feeling. And then when he slowly began to move the sensations increased in intensity and she felt a growing urge, a growing restlessness within her flesh for more contact, more direct friction.

She moved underneath him, searching for the point of contact that would get her over the edge, soft, breathless sounds coming from her throat. Just when she thought she could stand it no longer, he brought his hand down between their bodies and stroked her until she broke free into an orgasm that lifted every hair on her scalp and sent her spinning into a vortex of feeling unlike anything she had felt before.

He waited until the last ripples passed through her before he took his own pleasure. She held him as he thrust and thrust and then he tensed and spilled in a series of pumps that made her own skin lift in a pepper of goosebumps as waves of vicarious pleasure pulsed through her body.

Audrey lay in a blissful stupor, the sensations slowly petering out inside her like the quietening of ocean waves after a storm had blown past. Never had she thought her body capable of such mind-blowing pleasure. It felt reborn, awakened, stimulated into life and she knew nothing would ever be or feel the same.

Lucien raised himself up on one elbow and played with a tendril of her hair. 'No regrets?'

'Not one.' Audrey outlined his mouth with her fingertip. 'It was amazing. You were amazing and so gentle.'

'You're the one who was amazing.' He brushed her lips with his. 'And if you weren't so new to this, I'd suggest a replay but I don't want to make you sore.'

She was touched by his concern for her but another part of her was disappointed she couldn't experience another round of his earth-shattering lovemaking right now when her body was already stirring for more of his touch. He gave her one last kiss and rolled away to sit on the edge of the bed to dispose of the condom. She stroked a hand down his back and then traced around each of his vertebrae in slow-moving circles. 'Do you think that's why my mother and your father keep going back to each other? Because of sex?'

He turned his head to look at her and gave a shrug. 'Maybe. But a marriage needs to be based on more than good sex to last the distance.' He got off the bed and held out a hand to her with a glinting look. 'Didn't you mention something about a shower earlier?'

Audrey took his hand and he helped her to her feet and she gave him a coy smile. 'I had no idea you were so into water conservation.'

He smiled and drew her closer. 'Right now I'm into you.'

* * *

Even as Lucien led Audrey into the shower his conscience kept pinging at him. He'd thought they were
indulging in a bit of itch-relieving sex, only to find out
she was a virgin. To say he was shocked was an under-
statement, especially finding out the way he had. He
wanted to be angry with her for not telling him but deep
down he understood why she hadn't. He wouldn't have
made love to her if she'd told him up front. He had never
slept with a virgin before. One or two of his lovers had
only had sex a couple of times before but no one had
ever shared their first time with him. He wasn't sure
how it made him feel. How was it supposed to make
him feel? Wasn't it a little outdated to hold a woman's
virginity up as some sort of male prize to claim? But
something about the experience touched him in a way
no one had done before. Her confidence that he would
take care of her needs made him feel as if she had given
him a precious gift.

Not just her virginity but also her trust.

He turned on the water and waited until it was the
right temperature before leading her under the spray.
He was already hard from being so close to her luscious
body. How had he refrained from making love to her
before now? Her shyness about her body made him determined to show her how much her curves delighted
him. They more than delighted him—they ignited him.
Firing up his lust until he was almost mad with it. He
always prided himself on his self-control. He wasn't a
man driven by his sexual appetite. He dealt with his
primal needs in such a way as never to exploit or hurt a

partner and if there wasn't a partner available he wasn't averse to relieving himself, or distracting himself with work. But with Audrey standing in the shower with him he could feel the throb and pound of his blood swelling him as he drank in the shape of her breasts and the womanly curve of her hips.

He brought his mouth down to hers and kissed her as the shower sprayed over their faces, adding another level of sensuality. Her hands came up around his neck, her breasts and nipples poking sexily at his chest. He slid his hands down her back to cup her bottom, holding her against the throbbing ache of his flesh. Her hips moved against him in a circular motion that threatened his hold on his self-control. He knew he should be out on the streets of the village searching for his father and Sibella, but here he was in the shower with Audrey and all he wanted was to sink into her tight, wet warmth and experience again the head-spinning rush of release.

But there was her likely tenderness to consider and there was no way he was going to put his needs ahead of hers. This wasn't like any other relationship he'd had, which was faintly disturbing…but in a nice way. This wasn't a simple hook-up or casual short-term relationship. By allowing him to share her first time, Audrey had stepped outside the boundaries he normally set on his relationships.

He was in completely new territory and for the first time in his life, he wasn't sure how to handle it. Audrey wasn't a woman he probably would never see again. Even if his father and her mother went through another marriage and yet another divorce, it still left a connection between Lucien and Audrey—a connection not so easily eradicated.

'Lucien?' Audrey pulled him out of his reverie by trailing a wet hand down his abdomen and he drew in a breath when her fingers wrapped around his erection. 'I want to pleasure you the way you did—'

'You don't have to feel obliged,' Lucien said. 'I want this to be about you, not me.'

Weird how altruistic he was becoming.

'But I want to.' She slithered down in front of him and took matters into her own hands, so to speak. 'Tell me if I'm doing it wrong.'

Lucien couldn't speak. Couldn't think. All he could do was feel the tentative sweep and glide of her tongue over the head of his erection, and then the way her mouth opened over him and drew on him softly at first, and then with greater suction. Again and again she drew on him, her mouth wet from the shower and her own warm saliva, and his self-control didn't stand a chance. He staggered under the force of his orgasm, the pulses of pleasure taking him to a place he had never been before with a partner. Was it the absence of a condom? Was it the more-than-just-a-hook-up nature of their relationship?

Or was it something else?

Something he didn't want to examine too closely. He didn't do close relationships. He didn't believe true love existed except between the title and credit roll of a Hollywood movie. Sure, some relationships survived the distance but most didn't. The only way he could see himself marrying one day would be to make sure his emotions were not fully engaged.

Audrey came back up to link her arms around his neck, her eyes shining with newfound confidence. 'How did I do for a beginner?'

Lucien wondered how could she not feel confident. He could still sense the aftershocks running down the backs of his legs. He cupped her face in his hands and pressed a kiss to her mouth. 'You were perfect.'

Her smile became crooked. 'No one's ever called me that before…'

He stroked his thumb over her cheek. 'Then maybe it's about time someone did.' And he brought his mouth back down to hers.

Audrey couldn't remember a time when she'd enjoyed a shower more. Pleasuring Lucien had felt so…so right somehow. She had never thought she would want to do something so intimate with a partner, especially if she was pressured into it. But he hadn't pressured her. He hadn't expressed any sense of entitlement. He had allowed her the choice and she had made it and relished in it.

But now the shower was over and they were dressed and Lucien was talking about going out to dinner. Even though Audrey was hungry she knew their meal out would not be simply about food or even companionship, let alone romance.

It would be about tracking down Harlan and her mother.

That was Lucien's mission, not a romantic dinner for two to celebrate their recent lovemaking.

'Why don't we order Room Service?' Audrey said.

Lucien straightened the cuffs of his shirt. 'What would be the point of that? You know how much my father and your mother love to eat out.' He frowned in concentration. 'What was the name of that restaurant they used to like? They used to go there every night because they enjoyed the food so much.'

There was no way Audrey was going to tell him, even though she remembered it well. Her mother had raved about the food and the service and the chef who had asked for their autographs and numerous photos with her and Harlan. 'I don't know... I'm hopeless at remembering French names.'

He picked up the hotel room key card and slipped it in his pocket. 'Come on. We'll have a wander around and see if we can find it. I'm sure it wasn't far from here.'

Audrey needed to text her mother to make sure she and Harlan weren't out. It wasn't likely, given Harlan was unwell, but what if they had decided to go out? Her mother was a disaster chef not a master chef. 'Erm... can you give me a second? I just want to fix my hair.'

'Your hair looks great.'

'And... I need the bathroom.' She gave him a winning smile. 'I'll be five seconds.'

Audrey dashed into the bathroom and quickly typed a text to her mother. She waited thirty seconds for her to read the text but the message icon showed the text had been delivered but not read. She turned on one of the taps and with the cover of the running water called Sibella, but the message said the phone was either switched off or not in a mobile phone reception area.

Damn. Double damn.

How was she supposed to warn her mother if she didn't turn on her phone?

There was a knock at the bathroom door. 'Are you okay in there?' Lucien said.

Audrey jumped off the closed toilet seat where she'd been sitting and pressed the flush button. She washed her hands because they were clammy with panic at the thought of her and Lucien running into her mother and Harlan. 'I'm coming.'

She opened the door with a bright smile in place. 'Sorry.'

Lucien's gaze searched hers. 'What's wrong?'

'Nothing's wrong.'

He glided a finger down her cheek where she could feel a fire burning. 'Are you sure you're not sore?'

Audrey knew if she said she was there would be no more lovemaking tonight. He was too considerate a man to put his needs ahead of hers. But how else could she stop him from taking her out to dinner? 'No, I'm not sore at all... I'm just not really very hungry.' Just then her stomach gave the biggest growl, which sounded like a gurgling drain.

His gaze narrowed slightly. 'Okay. But if you don't mind, I'll go out for a bit and have a look around for an hour or so. If you feel hungry later then just order something to the room.'

Panic was a giant claw tearing at Audrey's stomach, even worse than the pain of her hunger. She couldn't let him go out without her. She couldn't risk it. 'Erm...

I've changed my mind. I am a bit hungry…and the fresh air will be nice.'

He held out his hand and she slipped hers into it. 'Good. For a moment there you had me worried.'

'Why? Because I turned down a meal?'

He studied her for a long moment, a small frown pulling at his brow. 'Are you being completely honest with me, Audrey?'

Audrey tried to disguise a swallow but it felt as if she were swallowing a feather pillow. 'Honest about what?'

His eyes were like searchlights and every pulsing second they held hers she felt her heart trip and flip. 'You seem a little agitated.'

'No, I'm not.' She answered too quickly for it to be convincing.

He took both of her hands in his, holding them loosely but securely. 'What's troubling you, sweetheart? Is it being seen out in public with me now that we've made love? Is that it? You feel embarrassed?'

It was just the lifeline she needed. 'What are we going to tell people about us? I mean, I know my mother already led the press to believe something is going on between us, but now that something is going on…well, what *is* going on? How will we describe it? A fling sounds a bit… I don't know…a bit tacky…'

Lucien's mouth firmed as if coming to a decision in his mind. 'We'll tell everyone we're dating exclusively.'

Audrey mentally breathed a sigh of relief. She didn't want to be grouped with all the other women Lucien had had flings with in the past. She didn't want to be just another name, just another face, just another body to show up in the press on his arm.

She wanted to be special.

She wanted to be special because he made her feel special. His touch made her feel she was the only woman he wanted to make love to. She couldn't imagine making love with anyone else now she had made love with him. He knew her body better than she knew it herself. He had drawn from it responses she hadn't thought she was capable of experiencing. Her body was in love with him even if her mind refused to go there.

Was it pathetic of her to hope his body was a little bit in love with hers too?

The air was cool outside but not as cold as if the mistral wind St Remy was famous for were blowing. Lucien's arm was around Audrey's waist as they walked out of the hotel and, while one part of her was thrilled at being in his company, the other part was dreading the prospect of running into his father and her mother. She had checked her phone for any texts back from her mother but her text still appeared unread. She tried to relax because she could feel Lucien's contemplative gaze on her from time to time.

There were several restaurants along the street their hotel was on and Audrey knew the one he was thinking of—the one her mother and Harlan frequented—was only a couple of streets away. She stopped in front of a quaint restaurant that had a sandwich board on the footpath with a menu of specials written on it. 'This one looks good.' She pointed to the sign. 'Even with my shocking schoolgirl French I can see it has my favourite dessert.'

'There are more restaurants further along this street. Don't you want to check them out first before we make a decision?'

'But I'm now starving and it will take ages to check out all the other restaurants.'

Lucien shook his head as if dealing with a small child whom he couldn't resist indulging. 'All right. Here it is.'

He led her inside and with perfect French he asked for a table for two. The waiter asked if they would prefer a table near the window or in a more private corner.

'Window,' Lucien said.

'What if I wanted to sit in the private corner?' Audrey said once they were seated with wine and mineral water and two bread rolls fresh from the oven in front of them. Well, one bread roll was left because she had already eaten hers.

His gaze met hers. 'You're not convinced Sibella and my father are in the village, are you?'

Audrey was glad the lighting in the restaurant was low because it would at least hide the way her cheeks were glowing. 'They could be anywhere by now.'

'Have you heard anything since that last text?'

She had to think for a minute which text he meant. 'No. Nothing.' She waited a beat before adding, 'What makes you so convinced they're here?'

He picked up the single glass of red wine he'd ordered and took a measured sip. He put the glass back down with a sigh. 'My father came here for a month after their last break-up. After I got him back on his feet, that is. I think it was what saved him, actually—a month just pottering about the village being a normal person instead of a rock star. He came back looking refreshed and tanned and the healthiest I'd seen him in ages.'

Audrey pushed a crumb around her side plate with her finger. 'My mother really struggled after that last divorce too.' She stopped pushing the crumb and glanced at him. 'I mean, *really* struggled.'

Concern entered his gaze. 'What do you mean?'

She let out her breath on a long exhalation. Why shouldn't she tell Lucien what she had gone through with her mother? He'd told her about the dramas he'd been through with his father. 'She took a couple of overdoses when she was hiding out at my place. Not enough to require hospitalisation but enough to terrify the heck out of me.'

His expression communicated compassion as well as concern. 'What a shock it must have been for you to find her like that. But why didn't you insist on her going to hospital?'

'I begged her to let me call an ambulance or even to drive her there myself, but she got all hysterical and weepy about her fans finding out so I relented,' Audrey said. 'I managed to get her to agree to let me call her doctor, who checked her out at home. He said she had only taken enough to be a bit sleepy and wobbly on her feet.'

His frown was so heavy it closed the distance between his eyes. 'That was a big risk to take. What if she had taken more than she'd said?'

'I know it was risky, but her doctor assessed the situation. And then I stayed home from work for the next few days until I was sure she was safe.'

'You said she took a couple of overdoses,' he said. 'When did she take the other one?'

'Actually, she took three in total,' Audrey said. 'One a week for three weeks.'

'And you or the doctor still didn't insist on her going into hospital?'

Audrey didn't care for the note of criticism in his voice. 'Look, I did my best, okay? Her doctor thought she would be worse off in hospital with fans trying to get in to see her. He thought it best for her to have some quiet supervision at home out of the spotlight. I didn't want to break her trust, which I might add I've just done by telling you. She's the only mother I've got—the only parent—and I didn't want to damage our relationship by acting against her wishes. The overdoses were a cry for help so I gave that help and I continued to give it until she didn't need it any more.'

'I'm sorry, I didn't mean to criticise—'

'Did I criticise you for not getting your father into rehab? No. I realise how hard it is with a difficult parent to get them to do what you think is best for them. But have you ever considered that maybe what we think is best for them isn't always best for them?'

He looked at her for a moment with a quizzical look on his face. 'What are you saying?'

Audrey wished she'd kept her mouth shut. 'I don't know… I guess if we can't stop them remarrying then maybe we should just accept it. Who knows? If we stop criticising from the sidelines, this time their relationship might actually work.'

'You can't be serious?'

She forced herself to meet his incredulous gaze. 'Have you ever said anything nice about my mother to your father? Something positive instead of negative?'

Lucien frowned as if mentally sorting through his compliments folder in his head. 'Not that I can recall.'

'Exactly my point, because I can't think of a positive thing I've said about your father to my mother, either,' Audrey said. 'They're not bad people, Lucien. They just make bad choices. And the more we fight their being together then the more they'll want to prove us wrong.'

His forehead was creased in lines like isobars on a weather map. 'So you're saying we call off the hunt? Just let them get on with it and hope for the best? I can't do it. I'm sorry but I'm not going to let your mother destroy him a third time.'

'But what if she doesn't destroy him?' Audrey said. 'What if she's the best thing for him right now?'

Lucien's expression went from frowning to suspicious. 'What's brought about this change of heart? You can't stand my father any more than I can stand your mother.'

'That's not true,' Audrey said. 'I can think of heaps of positive things to say about your father.'

'Go on.'

She chewed at her lip. 'Well…he's a fabulous musician for one thing.'

'And?'

'And he's good-looking, or at least he was when he was younger.'

'And?'

Audrey sighed. 'Okay, so it's a little hard to think of stuff, but I haven't spent a lot of time with him. And I certainly haven't made an effort to get to know him. I've always felt a little bit intimidated by him, to be perfectly honest.'

'By his fame, you mean?'

'That and because I always feel as if he's comparing me to my mother.' She gave another sigh. 'The first time I met him he asked if I was adopted.'

Lucien reached for her hand across the table. 'I'm sorry he hurt your feelings. He can be a bit of a jerk at times. Most of the time, actually.' His fingers stroked hers. 'I've lost count of the number of times I've felt hurt or let down by him.'

'Why do you keep trying to have a relationship with him if you don't even like him?'

He gave a soft laugh. 'Yeah, well, that's the thing, isn't it? I don't like him much as a person but I love him because he's my father. Doesn't make sense, does it?'

Audrey squeezed his fingers. 'It makes perfect sense. My mother drives me nuts but I still love her and would do anything for her. I guess because before all the fame stuff happened she was a pretty good mum. Much better than her own mum because her mother kicked her out of home when she got pregnant with me.'

'Are they still estranged?'

'Permanently because now my grandmother is dead,' Audrey said. 'She was killed in a car crash before my mother could repair the relationship. I think it's one of the reasons she drinks so much when she goes through a break-up or a disappointment of some kind. It triggers all those feelings of rejection. It's also why she draws unnecessary attention to herself in order to be noticed.'

She couldn't believe how much she had told him about her mother. About her feelings about her mother. There were so few people she could talk to. Really talk to. She was always conscious of 'tainting her mother's brand' or afraid she wouldn't be believed. But now it felt as if a weight had come off her shoulders, as if she were shrugging off a heavy overcoat.

Lucien had a thoughtful expression on his face. 'That's sad. I guess I didn't consider the circumstances that had contributed to your mother's personality. I took an instant dislike to her because she seemed to bring out my father's reckless and irresponsible streak. But then, he probably brings out hers.'

Audrey gave a wry smile. 'I heard once that people who fall in love at first sight are actually falling in love with each other's emotional wounds. Their relationship doesn't usually last unless they address and heal those wounds.'

He gave a *that-makes-sense* lip-shrug. 'Interesting.'

'What's yours?'

He frowned. 'What's my what?'

'Your wound.'

His half-smile didn't reach his eyes. 'Whoa, this is starting to get heavy. Let's see… I guess I'm a little wary of investing too much of myself in a relationship because I've been let down so many times.'

'By your father?'

'Not just my father,' Lucien said, with a flicker of

pain in his gaze. 'My mother died when I was in my final year of school. Of course, it wasn't her fault or anything. She had a brain aneurysm, so it wasn't as if she could give me any warning. One day she was alive, the next she wasn't.'

'I'm so sorry,' Audrey said, thinking of the secret she was keeping about his father's health and how it might hurt him to be excluded from it. 'What did you do? Did you go and live with your father after that?'

He made a sound that was part laugh, part snort. 'No. He gave me a heap of money instead to set myself up in a flat so I could finish my year at school. He didn't even come to her funeral. He was doing a show in Europe that he didn't want to cancel. After I finished school, I went to university and lived on campus.'

Audrey hadn't realised he'd had to be so self-sufficient...but then, hadn't she too had to fend for herself more times than she could count? 'It's funny how people on the outside see us as lucky to have famous parents but they don't realise it comes with a cost. A cost no amount of money can fix.'

'So what's your wound?' Lucien asked.

Audrey wished now she hadn't started this heart-to-heart. It made her feel exposed and needy when she'd spent years trying to give him the opposite impression. 'I guess it's what we talked about the other day. I have trouble believing people want to be with me because of me or because of who my mother is.'

His eyes held her with a tender beat of understanding that made something tight in her chest soften. 'So how will you heal it? Your wound, I mean.'

Audrey couldn't hold his gaze and looked at her mineral water instead, pretending to be fascinated by the tiny stems of bubbles in the glass. 'I guess one day I might be lucky enough to meet someone who loves me for me.'

There was a strange silence…like the collectively held breath of an audience before a crucial scene in a play.

Lucien was the first to break it but his voice sounded distinctly husky. 'I'm sure you will, Audrey.'

But it won't be you…

CHAPTER EIGHT

LUCIEN DIDN'T ALLOW his thoughts to run to what sort of man would fall in love with Audrey. Not because he didn't want her to find happiness but because he didn't want to examine too closely the strange sense of discomfort he felt at the thought of her with someone else.

Someone other than him.

Which was quite frankly ridiculous of him because he wasn't in the market for a long-term relationship. None that involved emotions like love. Never had been, never would be. Too many complications when things turned sour, as they nearly always did. He was still cleaning up the financial messes from every time his father had fallen in 'love'.

He liked his life the way it was. Dating didn't have to be complicated when you were clear about your terms. And he was always clear. Although, he had to admit, this thing he had going with Audrey was a little blurry around the edges. He couldn't just have a weekend fling and set her free. Not after sharing her first time. She was still finding her way sexually and it would be cruel to cut it short. Cruel to her and cruel to him because he had never had such intimate sex before. Sex that was intensely physical but with an added element of emotional depth he hadn't expected.

She hadn't just shared her body with him. They had both shared confidences they hadn't shared with anyone else. He'd told her more than he'd told anyone about his father—even stuff about his mother. They had talked as intimately as they had made love. No holds barred, no screens or barriers up.

No secrets.

He was surprised by her change of heart over her mother's marriage to his father. What had brought that about? Or was she tired of traipsing around the country looking for people who didn't want to be found? He was a little tired of it himself but he was sure his father was here. He couldn't explain it. He wasn't normally one for relying on gut feelings. He was a numbers and data man. But ever since he'd driven with Audrey into St Remy he'd sensed his father's presence and he wasn't going to leave until he knew one way or the other.

Lucien watched Audrey eat her chocolate *religieuse*, somehow without getting any traces of chocolate on her mouth, which was a pity because he could think of nothing better than kissing it off. And not just kissing her mouth, but every inch of her body. He was getting hard just thinking about it. Uncomfortably hard. *I-want-you-now* hard.

She suddenly looked up from her dessert and caught him watching her. She picked up her napkin and dabbed it around her mouth, her expression a little sheepish. 'I think you can see now why I don't have my mother's figure.'

He smiled. 'I like your figure just the way it is. In fact, I'm having wicked fantasies about your figure right now.'

Her cheeks gave a delicate blush and her toffee-brown eyes twinkled like fairy lights. 'Didn't you want to go for a walk after dinner?'

It was scary how easily she could distract him from his mission, and if it hadn't been for her inexperience, he would have taken her straight back to the hotel and made love to her again and again and again.

But it wasn't just about pacing her. He had to pace himself. He was acting like a lovestruck teenager, all raging hormones and out-of-control feelings. Feelings he wouldn't allow any purchase because he wasn't going to be a fool like his father and fall in and out of love and leave a trail of despair and destruction behind. 'Walk first, bed later,' he said, softening his words with another smile.

A flicker of disappointment flashed over her features. 'Do we have to walk now? We've been on the go all day and—'

He took her hand and brought it up to his mouth, kissing her bent fingers. 'Just a short walk, okay? That's what we're here for, remember?'

Her eyes skittered away from his. 'How could I forget? It's not like you really want to be here with me. I'm a convenient bonus bit of entertainment while you get on with your mission of breaking up your father's relationship with my mother.'

Lucien frowned at her tone and brought her gaze back to his with a finger beneath her chin. 'That was your mission too, up until today. And I'm here with you because I want to be here with you.'

Because right now I can't imagine being with anyone else.

Audrey gave him one of her cute pouts that made him want to kiss her so badly he had to glue his butt to his chair. 'Do you mean that?' Her voice came out whispery soft.

He stroked her cheek with his thumb. 'It kind of scares me how much I mean it.' It scared him even more to have admitted it out loud.

Her eyes went all shimmery as if she was close to tears but she blinked rapidly a couple of times and gave him a tight smile. 'Sorry. I know this is just a fling and I promise I won't get all clingy and start dragging my feet past jewellery shops or anything, but I just want for once in my life to be special to someone, even if it's for a short time.'

Lucien brought her hand back up to his mouth, holding her bent knuckles against his lips. 'You are special, sweetheart.' So special he was having trouble recalling his reasons for keeping his relationship with her sensibly short. 'You're amazingly special.'

'I think you're pretty special too.' She gave him a wry smile and, pulling away from him, added, 'Not special enough for me to fall in love with but special all the same.'

He didn't want her to fall in love with him, so why did her throwaway comment sting like a dart? In the past, things always got a little messy when any of his lovers had said those three little words, and these days he carefully extricated himself from the relationship well before it could happen.

But now he felt a strange sense of emptiness…a hole inside him that opened up like a painful fissure at the thought of Audrey saying those words to another man. He had never said them to anyone apart from his mother and even then he hadn't said them enough times. It was one of his biggest regrets that he hadn't told his mother how much he loved and appreciated her for all the sacrifices she had made for him. He couldn't even remember the last time he'd told her, which was even more distressing.

Audrey did her lip-chewing thing. 'I'm sorry. Have I offended you?'

Lucien quickly rearranged his frowning features into an easy-going smile. 'Why would I be offended?'

'I don't know…you were frowning so heavily, I thought I must have upset you.'

'I was thinking about my mother, actually,' Lucien said. 'I can't remember the last time I told her I loved her before she died. It's niggled at me for years.'

'I'm sure she knew it without your having to say it,' Audrey said. 'You probably showed it in heaps of ways.'

He gave her a crooked smile. 'Maybe.'

There was a little silence.

'Have you told your father you love him?' Audrey asked.

'No.' He had never felt comfortable enough within his relationship with his father to say it. He had only realised he cared about his father in the last few years, especially seeing him go through the last break-up with Sibella. It had made Lucien realise how much he cared about him when he thought he was going to lose him.

And yet he hadn't told him he loved him.

Was it anger that held him back? Anger at the reckless way his father had always lived his life? Anger at the way he had left Lucien's mother to struggle on her own as a single mum with no support? Anger that even now, when his father should be acting responsibly and sensibly, he was doing the opposite?

Audrey winced as if she found the thought of him not saying it to his father painful. 'Maybe you should…you know, before it's too late…or something…'

He let out a long sigh. 'Yeah, maybe I should.' He drummed his fingers on the table for a moment, then pushed back his chair to stand. 'Come on, little lady. Time for some fresh air before bed.'

'Can I use the bathroom first?'

'Sure. I'll settle the bill and wait for you at the front.'

Audrey dashed into the bathroom and checked her phone. The message still hadn't been read by her mother, which meant Sibella had her phone switched off. Normally her mother never switched her phone off in case her agent wanted to call her. It used to drive Audrey crazy whenever she spent time with her because her mother would always be checking her phone instead of listening to her. Why hadn't she thought to ask exactly where her mother and Harlan were staying?

She went back out to where Lucien was waiting for her at the front of the restaurant and when he smiled her heart gave a little kick. They had talked like a real couple over dinner, sharing hurts and disappointments about their lives that she—and she suspected he—had never shared with anyone else.

But they weren't a real couple. Not in the sense that this relationship—this fling—could go any significant distance. Which would have been perfectly fine even a couple of days ago because back then she hadn't seen herself wanting any relationship to go the distance, especially the distance towards marriage and happy-ever-after.

But after running into her mother and seeing the heartfelt love and distress on her face at the thought of permanently losing the love of her life Audrey had undergone a change—a change that both surprised and terrified her. She had promised not to fall in love with Lucien. She had told him it wasn't going to happen.

But hadn't it already happened?

Hadn't she already opened her heart to him both literally and figuratively? By sharing her body with him, by allowing him to be her first lover, it had made it darn near impossible not to fall in love with him. He'd been so gentle and considerate. He insisted on putting her needs ahead of his. He made her feel special. Damn it, he even told her she *was* special. He'd sounded pretty damn convincing.

Was it too much of a pipe dream to hope he might love her?

Lucien led her outside with her arm looped through one of his. The night had cooled down considerably but there were still plenty of people out and about. Audrey hoped none of them would be Harlan or her mother, but who knew what they might want to do, since this might be Harlan's last few months or even weeks of life? They might risk the threat of exposure by the press to enjoy a romantic dinner out, or a leisurely walk through the quaint village at night, when it was less easy to be recognised.

Within a block they came to the restaurant Harlan and Audrey's mother had frequented in the past. 'That's it,' Lucien said. 'It's had a name change but that's the building.' He looked through the window for any sign of his father and Sibella while Audrey's heart began a bumpy ride to her throat.

After a moment, he sighed and turned away from the window. 'No sign of them in there.'

'That's because they're in Barcelona.' Audrey hated lying to him. She felt tainted, soiled by the secret her mother had begged her to keep.

For the first time she saw a tiny flicker of doubt pass across his features. 'Maybe, maybe not.' He gave her arm a gentle pat. 'It's getting late anyway.'

They walked back to their hotel in silence. Audrey felt torn at the way she was keeping her knowledge about his father's illness from him, especially when he'd told her how gutted he'd felt when his mother died. What if something happened and he never got to say those words to his father? She opened her mouth a couple of times on the way back to the hotel but then closed it again. She had made a promise to her mother. And it was Harlan's place to deliver the news to Lucien, not hers. Not only that, but she also knew how determined Lucien was to end Harlan and Sibella's relationship. She had been just as determined a matter of days ago. What would a couple more days do? Her mother had asked— *begged*—for three days to be left alone with Harlan. One of those days was almost over. Two more to go.

'You're very quiet,' Lucien said when they got back to their room.

Audrey forced a smile to her lips. 'Just tired, I guess.'

He gathered her close, brushing her hair back from her face with a touch so gentle it made her heart contract. His eyes searched hers for a pulsing moment before they went to her mouth. 'I told myself I wasn't going to kiss you when we got back here tonight.'

A tiny ping of hurt bruised her chest. 'Why not?'

'Because I can't seem to stop at a kiss any more.' His fingertip moved over her lips like the slow sweep of a sable brush. 'You have done some serious damage to my self-control.'

Audrey leaned closer, her hips pressing against his and her arms going around his waist. 'Yeah, well, mine's not in such good shape, either.'

'That's why I didn't kiss you at the wedding three years ago.'

Audrey blinked. 'You were going to kiss me? Really?'

'Yes. But I knew if I did I might not be able to stop.' He smiled and bent down to brush her mouth with his. 'There. I'll ration myself. One kiss.'

She lifted herself up on tiptoe and pressed a soft kiss to his mouth. 'That's one apiece. Dare you to go two apiece.'

His hands moved so they were cupping her bottom and he drew her closer so she could feel the ridge of his arousal. 'Mmm…not sure that's wise.'

'Go on,' Audrey said. 'You're not going to back down from a dare, are you?'

His eyes glinted. 'You're playing with a fire that is already burning out of control.'

She moved against him and shuddered with the same longing she could feel in his body. 'I don't want you to be in control. I want you to make love to me.'

Regret tightened his expression. 'It's too soon. You need time to—'

'I need you, Lucien,' Audrey said, holding his face in her hands. 'I need you now.'

He lowered his mouth to hers in a long, sensual kiss that made every cell in her body ache for his possession. His tongue entered her mouth in a sexy glide that mimicked the intimate entry of his body, tangling with hers in an erotic combat that made her inner core clench with need. He groaned against her mouth and his hands on her bottom gripped her even tighter against the swollen heat of his erection. 'I want you so damn much it hurts,' he said.

'I want you too,' Audrey said, planting kisses on his mouth one after the other. 'Want, want, want you.'

He led her to the bedroom, stopping every couple of steps to place another kiss on her lips. Once they were in the bedroom, Audrey kicked off her shoes and slipped out of her clothes, her gaze feasting on him as he did the same. They came back together naked, skin-on-skin, and she sighed with delight. 'If anyone had told me a couple of days ago I'd be stripping off my clothes in front of you without flinching in embarrassment I would have said they were certifiably crazy.'

Lucien gave her a teasing smile. 'Does that mean you're not going to blush any more?'

'Urgh. I hate how I blush.'

He stroked a lazy finger down the slope of her cheek. 'I think it's cute. I only have to look at you a certain way and off you go. There. You're doing it now.'

Audrey grimaced. 'That's because you're looking at me like you're going to eat me.'

His eyes glittered and he guided her towards the bed, drawing her down beside him. 'That's exactly what I'm going to do.'

Audrey shivered when his hand came down on her belly, her legs trembling at the thought of the pleasure and raw intimacy to come. He parted her first with his fingers as gently as if she were a precious hothouse orchid that needed careful handling. Then he brought his mouth to her, using his tongue to trace her, sending her senses haywire like a sudden power surge. Electric sensations flickered through her pelvis and down her thighs in little pulses and currents. He continued the sensual torture until she was tipped over the edge of a precipice, falling, falling, falling into an abyss of sublime pleasure that ricocheted through her body, making even the arches of her feet contract. 'Oh. My. God…'

Lucien moved back up her body, planting kisses on her flesh along the way: her hips, her belly, her ribcage and then her breasts, finally making it to her mouth. Tasting her essence on his mouth was so intensely erotic and it made another barrier around her heart come down like paint peeling off a wall. 'You're so sexy when you come,' he said.

Sexy. Now, that was a word she had never used to describe herself. But she felt it when she was with Lucien. She felt sexy and beautiful and…and special. She smiled and traced his mouth with her finger. 'Sexy, huh?'

He captured her finger and sucked on it deeply, releasing it to say, 'Extremely sexy.'

Audrey slipped her hand down to caress him. 'I think you're pretty sexy too.'

He drew in a deep, shuddery breath as her hand moved up and down his shaft. 'You can keep touching me like that if you like.'

'What? And not have you inside me where I want you?'

He placed a gentle hand on her belly once more, his gaze full of concern. 'The last thing I want to do is hurt you again.'

Audrey brought his head down so his mouth was within a breath of hers. 'You worry too much. You won't hurt me.'

For a moment she thought he was going to pull away but then he gave her a lopsided smile. 'See how dangerous you are? You're making me shift all my boundaries.'

Not quite all of them.

It would be foolish to hope he would unlock his heart for her, but who said she wasn't foolish? She'd been foolish from the first moment she'd met him. But that schoolgirl crush had morphed into something far more dangerous. Dangerous because she was never going to be happy with a simple, no-strings fling. How could she have thought she would be? She wasn't built that way. She was more like her mother than she realised. She wanted marriage. She needed the security of a formal commitment.

She needed to be loved, not just lusted over.

Lucien kissed the side of her neck, his evening stubble tickling her skin and making her forget all about her reservations over their current relationship. This was what they had now—this mad lust for each other that made everything else fade into the background.

His mouth came back to hers in a deep kiss that rocked her senses like an earthquake in a glass factory. She shivered as his tongue played with hers, calling it into a seductive dance that made her toes curl with pleasure. He moved down her body, kissing and caressing her breasts, teasing the nipples into hard peaks.

He left her momentarily to reach for a condom, coming back to position himself above her, his legs in a sexy tangle with hers. 'Tell me if I'm going too fast for you.'

'You're not going fast enough,' Audrey said, lifting her hips to receive him, sighing with sheer delight when he entered her with a smooth, slick but gentle thrust. She could feel her body wrap around him, triggering pleasurable sensations in her intimate muscles.

He moved within her body, slowly at first, making sure she was comfortable until increasing his pace. If she hadn't been in love with him before, his lovemaking would have surely tipped her over. She could feel his restraint, the way he was gauging every gasp and whimper of hers, treating her with the utmost care and respect while tantalising her senses into a frenzy of delight. He stroked her intimately to give her that extra bit of friction she needed to finally fly. The orgasm swept her up in a whirlpool that made her thoughts fade to the background until she was only aware of the ripples and waves of ecstasy that were consuming her entire body. His release came soon after hers and she felt it shudder through him. He pressed against her, totally spent, his breathing heavy and uneven against her neck.

Audrey stroked his back and shoulders, content to hold him close in the blissful aftermath. But her thoughts kept drifting to the future...the future he wasn't promising to share with her. Who else would she love other than him? Who else would she want to make love with and lie like this with her body still tingling from his touch? She couldn't imagine a future without him and yet there was no future with him. Not unless he changed his mind. Not unless he fell in love with her as deeply as she had fallen in love with him.

Lucien lifted his head and gave a long, deep sigh, not quite meeting her gaze. 'I guess this was always going to feel a little different with you.' He picked up a strand of her hair and tucked it behind her ear. His eyes meshed with hers for a beat before he looked back at her mouth. 'A nice different, of course.'

'Because we already had a relationship of sorts?' Audrey screwed up her mouth and added, 'Well, hardly a relationship. An acquaintance maybe?'

He gave a wry smile and found another stray hair to tuck away. 'I guess I hadn't realised how much in common we had with our parents, acting like out-of-control teenagers all the time. Plus, I've been fighting this attraction for longer than I care to admit.'

'You're good at hiding what you're feeling. I thought you hated me.'

His crooked smile returned. 'Hate is a strong word. I guess what I hated was the way you made me feel.'

'What did I make you feel?' The question was begging to be asked, so she asked it, even though she was worried she might be disappointed with his answer. But before he could answer there was the sound of her phone ringing from inside her bag in the other room.

'Do you want to get that?' he said.

'Whoever it is can leave a message.'

He frowned. 'What if it's your mother?'

Audrey sighed. 'You're right.' He moved aside so she could get off the bed but before she could get to the bedroom door the phone had stopped. She slipped on a bathrobe, tied the ends loosely and padded out to where her bag was. She took the phone out and saw the missed call was from her mother. She was about to press 'redial' when it started to ring again. There was no way of hiding the call from Lucien because he had followed her out of the bedroom and was standing near by. She took a breath and answered the phone. 'Hello?'

Her mother was a television star but right then her voice sounded as if it were theatre-trained. It projected out of the phone as if she were trying to reach the back row of a five-thousand-seat auditorium. 'Oh, thank God you answered. Harlan's collapsed. He had a seizure and I can't bring him round. Help me. Please help me. I don't know what to do!'

Audrey glanced at Lucien's shocked face and before she could answer he took the phone from her. 'Sibella, it's me, Lucien. Have you called an ambulance?' His brow was so tightly furrowed it looked as if it would split the bones of his skull. 'Where are you?'

Audrey swallowed a triple knot of panic. Panic for Harlan. Panic for her mother. Panic for Lucien. She listened as her mother said they were in St Remy in a farmhouse a short drive away.

'Okay, listen to me,' Lucien's voice was calm and authoritative. 'Give me the address. I'll call an ambulance. You stay with him and check his breathing and pulse. Do you know how to do CPR? Good. Try and stay calm and we'll be there as quickly as we can.'

He ended the call and used Audrey's phone to call an ambulance. She listened to him give the information in that enviably calm voice and wondered how he was ever going to forgive her if his father didn't regain consciousness.

'Get dressed,' he said as soon as he ended the call with the emergency services.

Audrey got dressed and later wondered how she'd managed to do it without putting something on back to front or inside out. Her heart was beating in her throat like a pigeon stuck in a pipe and her palms were sweaty and her legs trembling so much she could barely get them to transport her to Lucien's car.

He drove like a rally driver, only managing to remain within the designated speed limits because he wasn't the sort of man to put others' lives at risk. 'Damn it. I knew they were here,' he said, his hands gripping the steering wheel so tightly she could see the whitened bulge of his knuckles.

Should she tell him she'd known it too? She was ashamed for thinking he might not have to find out. Her mother hadn't said anything to betray her part in the secrecy. There hadn't been time with all the panic that was going on. Maybe nothing would be said. Maybe her part in the cover-up wouldn't be exposed. 'Lucien…' She moistened her bone-dry lips and tried to get her voice to cooperate past that scratchy whisper of sound.

'I *knew* she would do this to him.' He banged one of his hands on the steering wheel with such force she thought it would snap off the steering column. 'I knew she would kill him in the end. They've probably been drinking for days and God knows what else.'

She wanted to express her hurt at his misjudgement of her mother but knew it would be pointless. She sat in a miserable silence, not even able to access the words of comfort she knew she should be giving him at such a harrowing time.

He flicked her a quick glance. 'Sorry. I know she's your mother but if I find out she's played any role in making him unwell…' He didn't finish the sentence but his jaw locked so tightly she could see a muscle working overtime.

'It's okay…'

The ambulance had already arrived by the time they found the farmhouse. Lucien rushed inside with Audrey just as they were loading his still unconscious father onto the stretcher. He went to his father's side and grasped one of his limp hands. 'Dad?'

It nearly tore Audrey's heart out of her chest to hear him say that word. She had never heard him refer to his father as anything but 'Harlan' or 'my father'.

Audrey's mother stood wringing her hands and sobbing uncontrollably. Audrey went to her and gathered her close, trying her best to comfort her but knowing it would never be enough. 'Try not to panic, Mum. They'll take good care of him. The sooner he's in hospital the better.'

Sibella pulled out of Audrey's hold. 'I need to go in the ambulance with him.'

'No,' Lucien said, stepping in the way.

Sibella straightened like a flagpole defying a hurricane. 'You can't stop me, Lucien. You're not his next of kin. I am. I'm his wife. We got married yesterday.'

CHAPTER NINE

AUDREY HAD NEVER seen anyone look more furious than Lucien at that point. But somehow he managed to control himself enough to step aside to let her mother get into the back of the ambulance. His eyes flashed like lightning when he took Audrey's hand to lead her back to his car, the grip of his hand around hers painfully tight. 'No doubt they've been celebrating ever since they tied the knot. He's probably got alcohol poisoning or something. Excessive alcohol can cause swelling on the brain. It can set off seizures.'

She closed her eyes for a brief moment, wishing she could open them again and find this was all a bad dream. 'Lucien…there's something I—'

'You know what really gets to me?' he said before she could complete her sentence. 'The way she crowed about their marriage. What was that about next of kin? I'm his only child. *I'm* his next of kin. She's just another one of the wives he's loved and who's left him.'

Audrey drew in a breath that clawed at her throat like a fishhook. 'She *is* his legal next of kin, Lucien. That's the whole point of marrying someone you love—so they can be with you at all the important stages of your life. He wanted to marry her and he did. You shouldn't be questioning it. You have to accept it. They love each other and want to spend any time that's remaining with each other.'

She felt his glance like the thrust of a dagger. The silence building in tension, stretching, stretching, stretching like an elastic band pulled too tight.

'You knew they were here.' He thumped the steering wheel again, his breath leaving his mouth in a rush. 'You knew they were here, didn't you?'

Audrey couldn't look at him and looked instead at her hands in her lap. 'I've been trying to tell you—'

'When did you find out?' His voice was so hard she was surprised it didn't shatter the window on her side of the car.

'Today.'

'Today?' She could almost hear the cogs of his brain ticking over. 'Before or after we had sex?'

Audrey put a hand to her forehead. 'Don't do this, Lucien. Please. Isn't everyone upset enough without—?'

'You've taken prostitution to a whole new level.' The words were as savage as lethal arrows. 'You saw your mother at the market, didn't you? You saw her and then lied to me. You lied to me and then offered yourself like some sort of boudoir distraction to stop me from continuing the search.'

She swallowed without speaking, unable to look at him, unable to witness the caustic loathing and hatred she could hear in his words.

'Answer me, damn it!'

Audrey flinched and fought back tears. 'I made a promise—'

'A promise?' Scorn dripped from his tone like corrosive acid.

'I ran into my mother at the market and she begged me not to tell you that your father was unwell with a brain tumour,' Audrey said. 'She wanted to talk him into having surgery. He was refusing all treatment and she was trying to talk him round. She loves him, Lucien, and he loves her. They want to be together with whatever time is remaining. They were both worried you would try and talk them out of being together. I agreed to keep their location a secret because…because I wish someone loved me like that.'

Her words dropped into a cavernous silence.

'Let me get this straight…you've known since earlier today that my father was critically unwell and you didn't see it as a priority to inform me of that fact?'

How could she explain her motivations when he put it like that? How could she tell Lucien his father hadn't wanted him to know about his illness until after he was married to her mother? It seemed too cruel to dump that on him now when he was already so upset. 'I made a promise to my—'

'I don't care what promise you made to your mother,' he said. 'This is about my father, not your mother. I had the right to know he was unwell.'

'I know… I'm sorry. I should have told you but I didn't want to hurt her. She trusted me and I wanted to honour that trust.'

'And what about the trust that had developed between us?' His eyes bored into hers, as determined as a drill through steel. 'Didn't that count for something?'

'We're having a fling, Lucien. It's not the same as a committed or formal relationship.'

He pulled into the hospital entrance with a squeal of brakes. He parked the car before he spoke, his hand still gripping the steering wheel with white-knuckled force. He didn't turn to look at her but stared fixedly straight ahead. 'Would you have entered into a fling with me if you hadn't run into your mother today?' His voice was so cold it made her skin shiver.

'Yes. Yes, I would.'

His glance was so pointed she felt as if she'd been jabbed with a pin. 'Sorry but I don't believe you. You offered yourself to me because you knew it would be enough of a distraction to stop me trawling the streets of the village.'

She took a breath and continued. 'That's not true. I wanted to make love with you. I settled for a fling but I think we could have more than that, Lucien. I think you know that too. We're good together—you said it yourself. You said how different it was between us than your other—'

'Oh, you thought this was going to *go* somewhere?' The derision in his tone was as savage as a switchblade. 'So you lied to me about that too. You told me you never wanted to get married. But all the time you've been hanging out for the fairy tale. Well, guess what? It's over. I'm ending it right here, right now. I should have trusted my instincts and left you well alone.'

Audrey had been preparing herself for this moment

but now that it had come it was even more devastating than she'd thought. He was upset, of course he was, and he had every right to be. She would be too if the situation was reversed. He needed time to come to terms with the shock of his father's illness. Maybe he would change his mind once he talked to his father...her stomach swooped...*if* he ever got the chance to talk to his father. 'Can we talk about this later, when you've had time to—?'

'Did you hear me?' His voice contained an edge of steel that made every hair on her head shiver at the roots. 'I said it's over.'

Audrey couldn't look at him and quietly gathered her bag from the floor. 'I'm just going to see my mother and then I'll get a cab back to the hotel to collect my things. I'll stay with her until the...the crisis is over with your father.'

'Fine.'

Fine? Was that all he could say after what they'd shared? Nothing was fine about this. Audrey's heart felt like it was jammed between two solid, splinter-ridden planks, every breath she took increasing the pressure. Her eyes stung with tears but she refused to cry in front of him. She couldn't bear the humiliation of him witnessing her heartbreak.

She followed him into the hospital but he barely gave her a glance. He went straight to the desk to ask where his father had been taken and Audrey peeled away to find her mother.

She was in the waiting room outside the emergency room and Audrey went straight to her and enveloped her in a hug. 'Oh, Mum, I'm so sorry. Is there any news?'

Sibella lifted her tear-stained face off Audrey's shoulder, her bottom lip trembling. 'They're going to do a CAT scan to see what's going on. They think he's having some sort of intracranial bleed from the tumour. They're going to fly him to Paris for surgery because they don't have the facilities here. I can't bear the thought of losing him. Not now that I've finally got him back.'

'I know, it's so sad,' Audrey said, blinking back her own tears. 'But you've been with him for the last few days and made him as happy as you could. Hold on to that.'

'We had such a lovely wedding ceremony,' Sibella said, taking the tissue Audrey handed her and mopping at her eyes. 'So intimate and private at the farmhouse in the garden. I'm sorry I didn't invite you and Lucien but Harlan wanted it to be just us this time. No fanfare. No fuss. Just us.'

'I think you did the right thing,' Audrey said. 'I'm glad you two got married again. I couldn't be happier for you. Well, I could if Harlan wasn't so unwell.'

Her mother looked at her with reddened eyes. 'You really mean that, don't you?'

Audrey smiled. 'Perhaps you and Harlan do belong together. You're lucky to have experienced such passionate love not once but three times. I hope and pray he gets through this so you can prove all the doubters wrong.'

'Speaking of doubters,' Sibella said, glancing past

Audrey for any sign of Lucien, 'I hope I haven't made things difficult between you and Lucien.'

Audrey wasn't going to burden her mother with her own heartbreak at this point, if ever. Sibella had enough emotion to deal with without Audrey dumping more on her. 'No, it's fine. He's upset about his father, of course. It's been a terrible shock for him.'

Her mother's gaze searched hers. 'You're not in love with him or anything, are you?'

'In love?' Audrey made an attempt at a laugh but it sounded more like a choke. 'We had a bit of a fling but we've called time on it. It was never going to work. I'm not his type and he's not mine.'

Sibella chewed at her lower lip for a moment, her brow creased in a tiny frown. 'It's not always about being the right type of person, sweetie. It's about the right type of love you feel for each other. It took me three times to find that love with Harlan but now I've found it I'm going to hold on to it no matter what.'

'Lucien doesn't love me, Mum,' Audrey said in a quiet voice. 'I don't think he's capable of loving anyone like that.'

'Mrs Fox?' A doctor with an English accent came towards them and stopped in front of Sibella. 'The air patient transfer has been arranged so we're taking your husband soon. He's not conscious but if you'd like to spend a couple of minutes with him before the flight to Paris that would be okay.'

'Oh, thank you,' Sibella said and followed the doctor away to where Harlan was being held.

Audrey sighed and went back to the waiting room to

wait for her mother to return, wondering if it would have been wiser to leave now before there was any chance of running into Lucien. Had he had a chance to spend time with his father?

Lucien walked out of the hospital after speaking to his father's doctor and stood for a moment trying to get his emotions under control. His father had cancer. A brain tumour. It was operable but the risks of permanent damage were huge. His fun-loving, irresponsible and reckless father might turn into a comatose body on a ventilator. He couldn't understand why his father hadn't told him he was ill. He handled all his father's financial affairs, fixed up every mess and monitored every detail of his father's life and yet his father had shut him out of this health crisis. What sort of father did that to his only son? Didn't his father realise how much he cared about him?

But it was Audrey's role in the cover-up that was eating at him the most. She had only slept with him to distract him from finding out where his father and Sibella were. He'd thought…he'd thought… Damn it. He wasn't going to think about it now. He wasn't going to think their relationship was different from anything he'd experienced before because it wasn't different. It was just a fling that had turned sour. But it had only turned sour because she'd deceived him. Openly lied to his face, making him believe…

No. No. No. Don't go there.

He had to stop thinking she might have been The One. The one person—the only person—he could see himself building a future with that involved trust and openness and, yes, even love. But it was all a bald-faced lie. Their relationship had sprung up out of her desperation to keep him from the truth about his father's and her mother's whereabouts.

Had she been working against him from the start?

He mentally backtracked through the last couple of days, wondering how he could have been so stupid to be hoodwinked by lust. That was all it was, of course. Lust. He refused to consider it as anything else. He'd lusted after her and she'd seen it as an opportunity to manipulate him. Now his father was dying and his next of kin was that attention-seeking, wine-swilling witch Sibella, who gloated over his father's unconscious body about her brand-new status as his wife.

For the third freaking time.

Lucien dragged in a lungful of cool night air, trying to loosen the tight feeling in his chest. It might be hours before his father came out of surgery in Paris. It might be hours, days even, before there was news, either good or bad. He didn't want to see Audrey. He never wanted to see her again. Seeing her would remind him of every cunning and clever lie she'd told him and how he'd foolishly fallen for it.

Fallen for her.

No. Damn it. No. He'd fallen in lust. He wasn't going to name it as anything else. What was the point in admitting she had done what no other woman had done? What he had allowed no other woman to do. He had lost his head over her. Lost everything he had worked so hard to maintain. Her betrayal had stung him, more than stung him, but it was the fact she had got into his heart that hurt the most. He should never have allowed it to happen. He should have taken greater care. He should have resisted her.

Lust, not love. Lust, not love. Lust, not love. If he had to say it like a mantra until he believed it then that was what he would damn well do.

Lust was all it was and now it was over.

CHAPTER TEN

AUDREY HADN'T BOTHERED collecting her things from the hotel and had flown with her mother to Paris as soon as she could organise a flight. By the time they arrived at the large and busy Paris hospital, Harlan was still on a ventilator but the bleed had been controlled and a large section of the tumour had been removed. The neuro-surgeon had expressed cautious optimism that Harlan would regain consciousness in a few days when the swelling had receded.

Audrey had been terrified of running into Lucien when she and her mother came to the hospital, but, given the size of the place, somehow she had managed to miss him and hadn't seen him since the night they'd followed the ambulance to the smaller hospital in St Remy.

The time spent supporting her mother was just the distraction she needed to take her mind off her own heartache. But in spite of the warm and loving chats with her mother, the visits to the hospital and the day-to-day duties she assigned herself at the small Airbnb they were staying in, Audrey still had plenty of time to feel the stinging pain of Lucien's rejection. How different would this time be if he'd allowed her to support him as well as her mother?

How different would it be if he loved her as she loved him?

Audrey wanted what her mother had with Harlan this third time around. The right type of love. A mature and lasting love. A love that wanted the best for the other partner—a love that gave sacrificially instead of selfishly taking.

But Lucien had locked his heart away and built an impenetrable fortress around it. It pained her to think he thought so badly of her after all they'd shared. But he had refused to listen to her explanation and had cut her coldly and clinically and cruelly from his life.

On day five Harlan woke when his doctors removed him from the ventilator. The first person he asked for was Sibella and Audrey sat outside ICU while her mother was taken in to see him. She couldn't help thinking how special it must be to be the first person a desperately ill patient asked for when they woke from a coma. Would she ever be that special person to someone? Would anyone love her the way Harlan loved her mother? Or would she always be lonely like this? Sitting alone in the waiting room of life.

When her mother came out a short time later she was crying but with happy tears. 'Oh, sweetie, he's awake and even managed to make a joke. He's still not out of danger but the doctors think he might be well enough for chemo in a week or two, if we can convince him to go through it.'

Audrey hugged her mother so tightly she worried she might snap a rib. 'I'm so glad he's made it this far. So very glad.'

Sibella pulled back from the hug but still held on to Audrey's arms. 'He's asking for Lucien. Do you think you could call him? I'm not sure he'll take a call from me.'

Or from me.

Audrey took out her phone and pulled up his number. Even seeing his name there on her screen made her heart clench and her stomach sink. She pressed 'dial' and held the phone to her ear but it went straight to his message service. She tried to think of something to say but her mouth wouldn't cooperate. In the end she hung up the phone and sighed and faced her mother. 'No answer.'

'I suppose the hospital will call him,' Sibella said and scraped a hand through her blonde tresses. 'I could do with a drink.' She grinned cheekily at Audrey's frown. 'Coffee, okay? Harlan and I are booked in to do couple's rehab. I reckon we'll have more chance of kicking the habit better together than doing it alone.'

Audrey smiled and linked her arm through her mother's. 'Coffee sounds great.'

Lucien sat by his father's bedside in ICU later that day when he'd flown back in from London. He'd had some work to see to for a client awaiting his report for court so he hadn't had any choice but to fly back to London and sort it out. His father had been sleeping on and off but had woken a couple of times to speak to him. It was strange having that time with his father. Alone time, if you could call it that when you were surrounded by machines and monitors and multiple medical staff milling about as they attended to their duties.

Whenever he'd spent time with his father in the past there were always managers or publicists or other band members about. When he'd met his father for the first time when he was ten years old there'd been twenty other people in the room.

But now it felt as if it was just the two of them. A father and his son just…hanging out.

Harlan opened his eyes again and gave Lucien a lopsided smile. 'I thought you'd have something better to do than hang around here.'

'Nowhere I'd rather be right now.'

Harlan's eyes watered. 'I haven't been a good father to you, Lucien. Thing is… I didn't know how to be a dad. Mine was a mean, sadistic bastard who beat my mother up and sold our belongings to feed his gambling habit. Beat me up too. Heaps of times.' His fingers gripped the sheet under his hand as if he was remembering each and every blow of his father's fists. 'It made me worried I might do the same…you know…if I got too close to you.'

Lucien had never heard his father mention his own father. He'd had no idea his dad's childhood had been so grim. Was that why his dad drank and partied to cover up his pain at how he'd been treated? He took his dad's hand, suddenly realising it was the first time he had ever touched him in such an affectionate way. 'You're a better father than I am a son. I've been too critical of you, too judgemental. I haven't taken the time to see the man behind the fame.'

Harlan squeezed Lucien's hand. 'I know you don't care for Sibella but I love her and want to spend whatever time I have left with her. We've been bad for each other in the past but we've made some changes. Good changes. Tough changes. I hope one day you get to feel the same sort of love for someone. Don't settle for anything less. Promise me that.'

Lucien was finding it hard to find his voice. He had already found that sort of love. What he felt for Audrey was so much more than lust. If it had been simply lust then why was he still feeling so empty? Why was he feeling like his heart had been severed from his chest? He'd been pushing his feelings from his mind. Shoving them back like a shirt in his wardrobe he couldn't bring himself to look at for the memories it triggered. He hadn't been able to stop thinking about her. Torn between dreading running into her at the hospital and yet feeling bitterly, achingly disappointed when he didn't. Tempted to call her so much he'd turned off his phone. He'd pushed her away because he'd believed she had disappointed him, betrayed him. Lied to him.

But who was the bigger liar?

He was. He'd been lying to himself for years. Six years. It had started when Audrey flirted with him at his dad's first wedding to her mother. And he'd continued lying to himself when Audrey approached him the second time, smiling up at him with those big brown eyes of hers.

And what had he done? Each time he'd pushed her

away. Cruelly rejected her. She'd given herself to him. He was her first and only lover. Didn't that mean something?

His gut clenched, his heart gave a spasm and regret tasted like bile in his mouth.

It meant he'd made a terrible mistake.

Lucien brought himself back to his conversation with his father with an effort. 'Why didn't you tell me you were ill? I could have organised the best medical—'

'I made Sibella promise not to tell you,' Harlan said. 'I wanted her to know first, and then, when we got the wedding out of the way, we were going to tell you and Audrey. I didn't want either of you to try and talk us out of it. You know what you two are like. Fricking fun police, the pair of you.'

Lucien swallowed again. 'So when did Audrey find out you were ill?'

'When she ran into Sibella the other day,' Harlan said. 'She made Audrey promise not to tell you because that's what I wanted. I insisted on telling you in person but only when I was ready to. She was only acting on my wishes, Lucien. Please don't be too offended I didn't tell you first. But you have to understand Sibella's my go-to person now. The person I want to tell everything to, the good stuff and the bad stuff. It doesn't mean I don't love you. I do in my own inept and clumsy way.'

Lucien put his other hand on top of his father's and somehow managed a smile. 'I love you, too… Dad.'

Harlan blinked away tears but he was still wearing his bad-boy rock star smile. 'If you tell anyone I've been bawling like a teething baby I'll have to kill you, okay?'

* * *

Lucien walked out of ICU a short time later in a daze. What had he done? He'd destroyed his only chance at happiness with Audrey. He'd ruthlessly, cruelly cut her from his life. He hadn't given her time to explain anything. If only he'd listened. If only he'd realised his feelings for her weren't a bad thing. She was the best thing that had ever happened to him. Just like Sibella was for his father. The love Sibella and his father shared had matured into something that could withstand illness, even death.

It was exactly the sort of love he felt for Audrey. He had fought so hard not to fall for her. He had fought so hard not to lose control. But she had been too much for his willpower. She had always been too much for his willpower, which was why he'd held her aloft for so long.

His chest cramped as if someone had kicked him square in the heart. What if he'd lost her? Was it too late to tell her? Was it too late to hope she might forgive him? Sweat prickled his back and shoulders. A sick feeling churned in his stomach. He couldn't lose her. Not now. Not now he'd finally realised he'd been waiting for this sort of love for most of his adult life.

He couldn't lose her.

Oh, God. If he lost her...

Audrey left her mother chatting to some fans in the hospital cafeteria. The press had been around when they'd first arrived at the hospital but she had managed to avoid them. Sibella had issued a press release about

Harlan's condition and asked for privacy and, thankfully, that was mostly what they'd had. Now that Harlan was a little better, Audrey knew it would soon be time for her to go back to London. She knew she should have already made arrangements well before now but hadn't been able to let go of a gossamer thread of hope Lucien might seek her out and tell her he'd changed his mind.

She was walking along the wide corridor when she saw him walking towards her. She considered darting into one of the storage rooms out of sight, but his stride length increased and so did his speed. Before she could make up her mind which door to choose he was within arm's reach. 'Audrey?' The way he said her name made her heart skip. Was that a note of…of desperation in his voice?

She kept her face blank and turned with her spine so rigid and straight it looked as if she'd just graduated as star pupil from deportment school. 'Yes?'

His expression was hard to read but she thought she could see a flicker of worry in his eyes. 'I need to talk to you.'

'I think you've said all that needs to be—'

He held her by the upper arms, his voice gruff and with that same note of desperation she'd heard before. 'Please, sweetheart. Just hear me out. I know I don't deserve it after the way I cut you from my life the other day. I was wrong to blame you for not telling me about my father's illness. You were acting on his wishes and I would've done exactly the same if the tables were turned.'

Audrey wasn't ready to forgive him. Why should

she when he'd treated her so cruelly? He could apologise all he liked but it wasn't an apology she wanted from him. She wanted his love and that was unlikely to be why he was standing in front of her now. He was too proud a man to grovel. He was probably clearing his conscience after his cosy little chat with his father. 'Oh, so now you're apologising because he's told you he was the one who insisted you not be told? How terribly gallant of you, Lucien.'

He gave a slow blink as if her words pained him like a vicious stab but he still maintained his hold on her arms. 'I'd already realised I loved you before my father told me he'd insisted I not be told.' His hands slid down her arms to grasp her hands, holding them gently. 'I love you, Audrey. I think I've been in love with you ever since you hit on me at our parents' first wedding.'

Audrey couldn't find her voice. She opened and closed her mouth and blinked a couple of times to make sure she wasn't imagining this conversation. 'You...you love me? Really and truly love me?'

He smiled a wide smile that made his dark blue eyes shine. 'Really and truly and desperately love you. I've been such a fool for denying it all this time. I don't know why I did. It's so obvious you're the only one for me. You're the other half of my heart. I feel so empty without you. Will you marry me, sweetheart?'

Audrey beamed up at him and threw her arms around his neck. 'You're the only person I want to marry. I love you. I don't want anyone else but you. I think that's why I never dated all these years because I've been secretly waiting for you.'

'The wait is over, my darling,' Lucien said, holding her close. 'We belong together. I can't imagine how miserable my life would be without you in it.'

'I was so sad when you ended our fling—'

'Don't call it that ever again.' He grimaced as if in pain. 'It was never a fling. It was never just about lust, even though I kept telling myself it was. It was always about love. How could I have been so deluded as to convince myself otherwise?'

'I did it too,' Audrey said, holding on to him to keep herself from falling over out of sheer relief and joy. 'I pretended I hated you. I couldn't even hear your name mentioned without wanting to grind my teeth to powder. But I was always a bit in love with you.'

He grimaced again. 'I can't bear to think we might have missed out on being together. I've been such an idiot. Forgive me? Please?'

'Of course I forgive you. I love you.'

He brushed her hair back from her face. 'I want to build a life together. Do you want children? God, I can't believe I'm even asking that in a hospital corridor.'

'Do you want them?'

'I asked first.'

Audrey gazed into his twinkling eyes. 'I only want them if they're yours.'

He smiled and brought his mouth down to hers. 'I'll see what I can do.'

EPILOGUE

Ten months later...

LUCIEN SAT NEXT to Audrey at the dining table at Bramble Cottage. She reached for his hand under the table and, smiling at him, gave it a squeeze. His heart gave a leap just as it always did when her beautiful brown eyes looked at him like that. He smiled back and winked at her and, yes, she still blushed.

'Hey, you two, the honeymoon should be well and truly over by now,' Harlan said, from the other side of the table. His hair hadn't grown back yet from the gruelling chemo but his cranial scar was fading and his specialists were happy with his progress so far. So far. No promises were being made about a complete recovery but Lucien was determined that, no matter what awaited them in the weeks and months ahead, his father's happiness would be a top priority.

And no one made his dad happier than Sibella.

'Like you can talk,' Lucien said, smiling at the way his father's arm was around Sibella's shoulders and how she was beaming at Harlan with such love in her eyes it made him feel ashamed of how he had misjudged her in the past. His father and Sibella weren't perfect, but he had come to a place where he accepted them as they were and didn't expect them to change to suit him.

'Mum, Dad, we have something to tell you,' Audrey said, looking like she was about to burst with the secret she'd been keeping for the last couple of weeks until they hit the twelve-week mark in their pregnancy.

It just about made Lucien's heart explode with emotion every time she called his father 'Dad'. It spoke of the deep affection she had for his father, and her care and concern and nursing abilities over the last few months had made Lucien, and of course his father, love her all the more.

And now Lucien was to become a father. In the not so distant future a little person would look up at him and call him Dad.

'Will you tell them or will I?' Audrey said, smiling at him.

He took her hand and brought it up to his mouth. 'Let's do it together.'

And so they did.

* * * * *

TAMING HER TYCOON

YAHRAH ST. JOHN

To my friends and colleagues Mary Dillard,
Alana Guinard and Mica Reinhardt for providing
an ear when I needed a sounding board.

Chapter 1

"I want Brooks and Johnson," Lucius Knight told his lawyer and best friend, Adam Powell, as the two sparred in the boxing ring of their favorite gym on a Wednesday afternoon. It was one of Lucius's favorite pastimes when he needed to blow off some steam, and today was one of those days.

"I know. I've been acquiring the shares like you asked, but why?" Adam inquired as he squared off against his six-foot-two friend.

Lucius put his gloves down and looked him in the eye. "Does it matter? I want it."

"Yeah, it does," Adam said. "I've never seen you so focused on a company before. Why is it so important to you?"

Lucius couldn't tell Adam the real reason he was interested in Brooks and Johnson, an organic retail company, was its cofounder Naomi Brooks. Known for his playboy lifestyle, Lucius hadn't been able to settle for anyone or anything, let alone a woman. But Naomi Brooks was different. He liked her story. She was a no-nonsense type of woman, a real do-gooder who not only believed in what she was selling—organic products that ranged from shampoos and conditioners to body lotion—but had also become successful in her own right. Who would have thought that the nerdy sophomore with the boyish figure and acne problems who followed him around during his senior year in high school would someday turn her basement business into a national success story?

Lucius understood that kind of determination.

Because he'd done the same thing. A reformed bad boy turned businessman, Lucius had experienced a chaotic relationship with his mother and had chosen to live with his grandmother in the Rose Park neighborhood of Long Beach.

Adjusting to the neighborhood and being a loner hadn't been easy for Lucius. He'd rebelled and gotten into trouble often in school. Eventually, he'd met Adam, and a friendship that would last decades had been formed. Lucius had gone on to obtain an MBA before investing in his first business venture, an up-and-coming technology firm. The gamble paid off, and he'd made his first million before he was thirty. And thanks to his shrewd sense for recognizing opportunities, he'd formed Knight International and was now a wealthy tycoon with holdings across multiple industries.

"Hey, hey." Adam waved a gloved hand in front of Lucius, jolting him from looking back down memory lane.

"You do that again and you'll get knocked out," Lucius joked, effectively ending their conversation about Brooks and Johnson.

"I doubt that." Adam gave him a jab in the side. "Who do you think taught you how to fight?"

Lucius answered with a blow of his own to Adam's middle. "You did. But as in the stories of old, sometimes the student becomes the teacher."

Adam laughed heartily. "We'll see about that."

The two men continued to spar for another hour before they finally took a break. The gym along Santa Fe Avenue was starting to fill up with locals, which signaled it was time for Lucius to roll. Even though he still liked coming to the old neighborhood because it reminded him of days gone past, Lucius also knew the hundred he'd paid to the kid outside to watch his Bentley to ensure no one would scratch it wouldn't last too much longer.

"How about a beer?" Adam said as they jumped down from the ring and walked toward the benches where their gym bags were.

Lucius smiled as he reached for a towel to wipe the perspiration from his forehead. "After a shower, you're on."

"Kelsey, whatever you're cooking up smells wonderful," Naomi Brooks said from her bar stool as she watched her business partner and best friend, Kelsey Johnson, stir a fragrant concoction on the stove of her four-bedroom home in Belmont Shore that afternoon.

Kelsey shrugged her shoulders, tossing her blond curls. "It just kind of came to me. I've been stirring this pot for an hour trying to get the consistency just right."

"In your condition—" Naomi eyed Kelsey's growing belly "—you don't need the extra exertion. Plus, we have a development team that handles new creations for us."

Kelsey turned from the stove to face Naomi. "I'm only six months pregnant, not completely fragile. And I kind of miss the days when it was just the two of us toiling away on our new business."

Naomi nodded. She remembered those days, too. How could she forget? She and Kelsey had had the bright idea of starting an organic-products business eight years ago due to the sensitive skin and allergies they had in common. Naomi had suffered terribly in high school with bad acne. It had just been a notion, but soon they were in the kitchen testing out their ideas. Their parents had thought they were crazy. They'd just received their four-year liberal arts degrees and now their daughters wanted to start a new business with no experience?

They'd shown them.

Naomi and Kelsey had researched the hell out of the organic industry and slowly started building their brand. They initially sold candles, shower gels and bubble baths from Kelsey's apartment. Word of mouth about their little business began to spread in the local community, especially when they began attending farmer's markets. Soon, they were expanding to include shampoos and conditioners. And once their business hit a stride, they could no longer make their products out of Kelsey's apartment. There had been some serious discussion about the next steps for their growing business. They'd also decided that selling online rather than going retail was the best way to promote and market their products.

It worked.

Their online presence had quadrupled their sales, causing the need for an office and a manufacturer who could distribute their growing product line. Once they'd topped several hundred million in revenue, they'd moved forward with an IPO and gone public, putting 49 percent of their shares on the open market but retaining 51 percent. It was important that they maintained majority interest in *their* company.

Naomi glanced at Kelsey. It was hard to believe just how far they'd come. "It was just the two of us for a long time," she finally commented wistfully. But times had changed. Especially when Kelsey had two miscarriages and had a difficult pregnancy with her first child, Bella. Since then,

Kelsey had opted to work from home, only coming into the office when needed.

"I know." Kelsey stirred the concoction in the pot. "But having this second baby is making me reevaluate things and think about what's more important."

Naomi frowned. She didn't like where this conversation was going. "What do you mean?"

Kelsey sighed heavily. "I'm thinking about whether I want to stay in the business."

Naomi jumped off her bar stool and walked over to Kelsey at the stove. "Why? I don't understand? Where is this coming from? Is Owen putting pressure on you to quit?"

Kelsey stepped away. "He would rather I focus on our growing family and he has encouraged me to sell. He thinks the stress of pregnancy and working full-time has taken a toll on my body. And he's right, to a degree, but I'm torn. Brooks and Johnson means a lot to me, but…" Her voice trailed off.

"But what?"

"I don't know. It's just not the same anymore like when we first started out. Some of the joy has gone out of it."

"Because we're successful?" Naomi inquired. "It's what we've always wanted, what we worked so hard for." She turned away and walked over to the sink and grabbed both sides with her hands. "Or at least I thought so."

Several seconds later, she felt Kelsey's hands on her shoulders. "Don't be mad, okay? I'm just being honest and telling you how I feel. Just like I did when I first met you and saw you needed a little help in the beauty department."

Naomi chuckled and turned around to stare at Kelsey. At five foot four, Kelsey's petite figure was still recognizable even though she was expecting, due to a regime of vegan food, yoga and Pilates. "Don't sugarcoat it now. I believe you called me a hot mess."

Both women laughed.

"Well, you were," Kelsey responded with a grin. "You had acne and you wore your hair in a ponytail, and the clothes…" She snorted. "You were straight out of the '90s. You wore those baggy jeans and plaid shirts. It was no wonder you couldn't get a date."

Naomi rolled her eyes.

"Now look at you." Kelsey eyed Naomi's figure up and down. "Your skin is clear and bright from using the proper facial products. And you finally listened to me telling you relaxers were killing your good hair, so it looks healthy now."

Naomi fingered the soft spiral curls that reached her shoulders and complemented her long face. She'd fought Kelsey in the beginning about going natural, but the look suited her. Though it had taken some practice and a good stylist to learn how to work her natural curls into coil and twist styles, she'd mastered it. "Yeah well, I'll give you that one."

"And?" Kelsey countered. "Look at your clothes? We finally found your style—bohemian chic."

Naomi was wearing a bat-wing sweater with distressed jeans, fringed boots and clunky jewelry adorning her ears, neck and wrists. She was finally learning to show off her killer size-four figure. "I can't thank you enough," Naomi replied, "for taking in such a socially inept, fashionless woman as myself, but that still doesn't change the fact that you're ready to bail on our business after all we've endured."

Kelsey stirred the mixture on the stove one more time before turning off the burner. She was quiet for several long moments before responding. "You know I love you,

Naomi, but my priorities have changed. I have to put my family first. But listen, I'll give this some more thought before making any decisions."

Naomi gave her a bear hug. "Thank you. That's all I could ask. But while you're figuring things out I'll be doing the same. Perhaps I can buy your shares."

"Naomi, that would be a steep sum and a lot of responsibility. Can you afford it and are you really ready to take on all the responsibility?"

"I don't know, but I have to find out," Naomi replied. Because although Kelsey posed some good questions to give Naomi pause, she had to *do* something. Otherwise, the future of Brooks and Johnson, a company they both started, was in jeopardy.

After showering at the gym, Lucius and Adam headed to a local gentlemen's club they liked to frequent. The service was top-notch and the scantily clad women that delivered them their drinks more than made up for the overpriced menu.

"Ah." Lucius sipped on his scotch neat and leaned back in the lounge chair to face Adam. "I needed this after that workout."

"Yeah." Adam nodded. "Seems like you had some steam to let off today. What gives?"

Lucius shrugged. "It's nothing." He wasn't altogether keen on talking about the real reason for his bad mood.

His mother, Jocelyn Turner.

"Bull," Adam stated. "I know when you have something on your mind."

Lucius frowned at Adam. He could always read Lucius even though outsiders never could. Lucius strove to always have a poker face in his business dealings. Most people never knew what was going on in his mind, and he liked it that way. It kept people off-kilter and gave him the element of surprise, which he needed when deciding whether to take over or dismantle a company.

But Adam knew him too well.

"It's Jocelyn," he replied. "She's coming to town." His grandmother Ruby had told him his jet-setting socialite mother would be stopping in for one of her semiannual trips.

"Oh." Adam nodded his head thoughtfully. "That explains it. How long is she staying?"

"Don't know. Don't care."

Why should he? Jocelyn Turner had never cared about him. He'd had countless nannies before she'd finally sent him to a junior boarding school at the age of nine, and he'd acted out accordingly, so she'd handed him over to his grandmother. And bless her heart, his grandma done right by him. She'd brought Lucius to live with her in Long Beach and tried to instill good values in him, but Lucius had always known he was an afterthought.

His mother didn't want him, and his father? Hell, he didn't even know who he was, and Jocelyn refused to tell him no matter how many times he asked or pleaded. Lucius had begun to suspect that his father was a married man. So what did that make his mother?

At a young age, he'd learned to harden his heart and toughen up. It was a lesson that had served him well in life and in business. Of course, it also happened to get him in a lot of trouble as a teenager. His grandmother had been called constantly because he was getting in fights or being suspended from school. Lucius had gotten something of a reputation in high school as a bad boy because he rebelled against authority. Meeting Adam had changed his life and shown him he wasn't as alone as he'd felt in the world.

"I don't think that's true," Adam interrupted Lucius's

musings. "It's because you care. Every time your mother visits, you get riled up."

Lucius took a long drink of his scotch. "That's not true."

"Do you remember the last time she was here? You were so out of sorts that it nearly cost us that Corinth deal because you insulted the man right when he'd agreed to not fight you on the takeover."

"Yeah, well, he deserved it," Lucius commented, even though he knew Adam was right. His hotheadedness was one of his flaws. "Speaking of takeovers, let's talk about Brooks and Johnson."

"Ah, are you ready to tell me why you're so interested in the company?"

"Have you seen the numbers they've been bringing in?" Lucius commented. "They've grown steadily over the last three years, and their revenue is impressive and can double now that they've been public for a few months. And I've learned that one of the principals might be open to selling. So we should strike while the iron is hot."

"Kelsey Johnson or Naomi Brooks?" Adam inquired. "Why would either of them sell?"

Lucius rubbed his chin. "Didn't the dossier on Kelsey Johnson say she's pregnant with child number two? She could be thinking of downsizing and focusing on her family. That could be our in."

Adam leaned back in his chair. "I would think business is the last thing on her mind."

"We need to convince her that now is the right time to sell."

"And what about Brooks?"

"Let me handle her," Lucius said. He was eager to reconnect with his high school classmate and see how the once nerdy kid he remembered had turned the tables and become a successful entrepreneur. He'd also seen a picture of her recently, and she'd blossomed into a fine-looking woman. A woman he wouldn't mind getting to know better.

"You should be aware that Lucius Knight has been silently buying up Brooks and Johnson's stock since the IPO," Bill Andrews, Naomi's vice president, told her the next morning after they went over some company business.

Naomi was leaving for Anaheim later that afternoon because she wanted to get a jump on traffic leaving Long Beach. She would check in to the hotel, pick up her registration packet and get settled before the trade show and conference started tomorrow. But first, she'd come into the office to take care of a few items. She hadn't expected Bill to tell her that corporate raider Lucius Knight, her former high school crush, was interested in her company.

"Since when?" Naomi asked, staring up from her Mac-Book.

"A couple of months ago," Bill responded. "At first I dismissed it, but then Knight International recently picked up another 5 percent, making his total stake in the company 30 percent."

Naomi closed her MacBook. "That's not good."

"No, it isn't," Bill said. "Every time Lucius Knight sets his sights on a company, he either dismantles them or they wind up as part of his portfolio."

"But why would he be interested in us?" Naomi asked. "We're a far cry from his other holdings." She too had done her research on the man. Ever since college, she'd kept her eye on her former crush—Knight International had a mix of industries in its portfolio, but they were mainly centered on technology.

Bill shrugged. "He could be looking to diversify. And given the success of Brooks and Johnson, he could get in on the ground floor. I received a call from his attorney Adam Powell—he'd like a meeting with you."

"A meeting?" Naomi hated that her voice hitched and the question came out more like a squeak.

"How would you like to handle it?"

"Ignore it," Naomi responded. "I'm not interested in talking to Lucius about my company or anything else."

Bill stared at her.

"What?" she snapped. She knew Lucius was a large shareholder, but she didn't care. "Why are you looking at me like that?"

"Because I haven't seen you this passionate before unless perhaps we're talking about a new product or launch."

"Well…well, I just don't like the thought of Knight thinking he can railroad me or my company. I'm no one's pushover."

"Never thought you were, Naomi," Bill replied. "What you and Kelsey were able to accomplish is phenomenal."

Naomi's burst of anger fizzled, and she smiled back at Bill. "I'm sorry if I was a little abrupt," she said. "I just get angry at the thought of someone trying to take something I worked so hard to build."

"We won't let that happen, Naomi. But he's a major shareholder now."

"I'm aware, Bill." She began packing her computer and some work files into her leather briefcase. When she was done, she snapped it shut and reached for her purse inside a drawer. "However, I trust that you'll keep the hounds at bay at least while I'm at the conference. When I get back, we'll address this." She started toward the door.

"Absolutely, boss."

"I'll see you when I get back." Seconds later she was headed toward the elevator lobby.

She stabbed at the down button as she waited for the elevator.

Lucius Knight wanted her company? Her baby? Hell, no. There was no way she was going to let the man—no matter how good-looking—weasel his way in and take over everything she'd built. She would show him and every other local who'd discounted her in high school and thought she was less than just how strong she'd truly become.

Chapter 2

"Grandma." Lucius softened his tone when he heard his grandmother's voice on the other end of his iPhone. "It's so good to hear from you."

"I hope that remains the case when you hear what I have to say," she replied.

"I could never be angry with you, Grandma." He loved the older woman with all his heart. She'd been the only mother he'd ever known and the only person who loved him unconditionally, except maybe Adam. "What's going on?"

"I spoke with your mother today."

"And?"

"Don't act dense, Lucius. It doesn't suit you," she responded. "She said you haven't returned her calls."

"I know."

"Well, when do you intend to?"

Lucius snorted. He hated the reproachful tone in her voice. He counted from one to three to remind himself to remain respectful. Grandma Ruby deserved it. She hadn't had to take him in when he was a young boy. She'd raised all her children. Three, to be exact—his mother, Jocelyn, his aunt, Deborah, and his uncle, Troy. But she had taken him in. And she'd been in his corner ever since.

He finally responded. "Soon."

"I wish you two would try to get along," his grandmother said. "It takes so much energy to hold on to all the bad blood."

"Have you told her this?" Lucius asked. "The only thing I've ever asked of that woman is tell me who my father is. And to this day, even though I'm thirty-four, nearly thirty-five years old, she refuses to tell me."

"Perhaps some things are best left unsaid."

Lucius was silent. He'd always wondered if his grandmother knew the truth, but she'd point-blank told him that if she did, she would tell him.

When he continued to remain silent, his grandmother said, "I have to go. I'm heading to the grocery store, but do go and see your mother, Lucius. You might regret one day that you never resolved things between you. Promise me you will."

He was being guilt-tripped and he didn't like it. "All right, Grandma. For you, I'll make the effort. Satisfied?"

"Immensely. Love you, Lucius."

"Love you, too, Grandma." Lucius ended the call and sat back against the plush cushions of the limousine. He knew she meant well, but her meddling in his and Jocelyn's relationship wouldn't help the situation. He would never see eye to eye with his mother until she was honest with him about who he was.

Until then, they'd always be at an impasse.

Naomi was excited as she checked in to the Anaheim Hilton. A valet immediately greeted her when she disembarked from her car and took care of her baggage while she checked in to the hotel.

She glanced around and took in the modern decor done in beiges and dark wood. It was classic yet modern. It would serve as a good backdrop for the natural products expo where she hoped to get Brooks and Johnson even more into the public consciousness. She wanted people to start using their products, which were now inclusive of not only personal care products, but home cleaning products and a new baby line as well.

The baby line was Kelsey's brainchild. It was still in its early stages but included baby washes and baby powders. They would soon expand to include diapers, rash cream and wipes. Naomi was just as passionate about having organic products for her goddaughter, Bella, and her soon-to-arrive godson, Caden.

With Lucius Knight circling like a vulture, Naomi just hoped that she could convince Kelsey not to sell her shares so they retained majority interest in the company they'd built.

"Good afternoon, Ms. Brooks," the front desk attendant greeted her. "Great to have you back with us again."

Naomi smiled. "Thank you. I'm glad to be back."

"I can't tell you enough how much I love the Brooks and Johnson body wash and lotion line. It's done wonders for my skin." The attendant caressed her cheek.

Naomi beamed with pride. This was exactly what she liked to hear when meeting customers. "Glad to hear it!"

"We've put you in one of our signature suites, complete with a queen-size bed." She handed Naomi two room key cards. "I sincerely hope you enjoy your stay, and if there's anything else you need, please don't hesitate to let me know."

"Thank you, and I will." Naomi accepted the envelope and headed for the elevator bank.

* * *

Just as Naomi entered the elevator, Lucius's limousine pulled up to the Hilton's entrance. Just as he'd promised his grandma Ruby, he'd called Jocelyn. Thankfully she hadn't answered, so he'd left a message, giving him a reprieve from an unpleasant conversation.

The chauffeur opened the door of the limo, and Lucius stepped out, buttoning up his suit jacket as he entered the building. He was used to five-star establishments but knew that he needed to get in front of Naomi Brooks. He'd heard that she would be attending the expo, and the only way he could do that was to be as approachable as possible. Thus, he would stay in the same hotel with all the other attendees and exhibitors.

Content to handle business himself, he made short order of checking in. After obtaining his card, he headed for the elevator.

Some might consider his tactics a bit sneaky, but he needed to figure out Naomi Brooks. What were her strengths, her weaknesses? A smart businessman knew his opponent, because only then could he use the knowledge to his advantage. He was determined to add Brooks and Johnson to his portfolio. Having a company of that caliber under his wing would only lend itself to making Knight International more credible. He didn't just want to be known as a corporate raider. He also wanted to be known as a man who stood for something, and this acquisition would give him credibility.

Disembarking from the elevator, Lucius headed to his two-bedroom suite. He glanced down the hall, wondering where Naomi was staying. It was just a matter of time before they met.

Naomi dressed simply yet professionally for the trade show and conference the next day. She'd knotted her wild curls into a bun off her face to show off her neck and cheekbones. Then she teamed a crisp three-quarter sleeved white shirt with a taupe pencil skirt and a thick brown belt with matching heeled sandals. She finished the look with a gold bangle set and long gold necklace. She glanced at herself in the mirror. The outfit was suitable for the office and could transition for an evening afterward.

She grabbed her briefcase and hobo purse and excitedly hurried toward the door. Fifteen minutes later, she'd already checked in with Brooks and Johnson's event coordinator to make sure their booth was being set up and would be ready when the trade show opened later that afternoon. Assured that everything was under control, Naomi decided she could attend some of the workshops. Perhaps they might give her some inspiration?

She found one to her liking and headed to the right convention room. They were just starting, and there were many empty seats in the back of the room, so Naomi slid into one of them.

She was listening rapturously to the professor when she felt the seat beside her suddenly become occupied.

The scent of cedar washed over her nose as a strong thigh brushed against hers. Naomi's breath hitched in her throat as she tried to focus on the lecture and not on the man sitting beside her. Whoever this stranger was, he smelled delicious, and Naomi couldn't resist licking her lips.

"Good topic?" the deeply masculine voice asked from beside her.

Naomi didn't turn around. She didn't want to. For just a little bit longer she wanted to stay enveloped in his scent and let her imagination roam as she wondered who the owner of the rich masculine voice and sensual cologne was.

"Yes, it's very timely," she commented.

"Undoubtedly."

Naomi frowned. The masculine voice beside her sounded familiar. Like she'd heard it dozens of times before, like when he'd told some bullies in high school to leave her alone. Except now the voice had matured and was stronger, more confident. Naomi turned and stared directly into the dark brown eyes of Lucius Knight.

Does she recognize me? Lucius wondered. *Or does she just know of me? Is she aware I'm after her company?*

Naomi didn't speak for several seconds; she just eyed him warily before turning back to face the front of the room. He could feel her tense beside him almost immediately. He'd hoped their first meeting would be smoother. He prided himself on his ability to charm the socks off almost anyone, including most women, but it seemed Naomi wasn't interested.

Instead of replying to his earlier comment, she continued to focus on the lecture until the hour was complete. When it was over, Naomi rose and so did Lucius. "So where are you headed?"

She glanced over her shoulder at him. "To gather info and maybe learn something like everyone else." And without another word, she left his side and walked up the aisle to speak with the professor. Lucius had no choice but to take action.

He purposely walked toward the duo. "Professor Duvall, great talk," Lucius said.

"Coming from you, Mr. Knight," the professor said, "that's quite a compliment."

Naomi said nothing from his side. Lucius could see she was fuming, because he hadn't taken the hint to take a hike. "Lucius Knight." He turned to her and offered his hand.

She would have to shake it if she didn't want to appear

unprofessional. When she did, Lucius was surprised by the reaction he felt when their hands touched. There was a spark, but she also didn't offer her name. Instead, she snatched back her hand.

"I'm eager to hear more, professor. Perhaps we can have coffee sometime later?" Lucius reached inside his suit jacket and produced his business card. "Call me." He nodded to the professor and strode purposely toward the door. He'd accomplished what he'd intended. Naomi knew he wouldn't be ignored.

Lucius stepped away to take an emergency call from Adam about another acquisition and missed the next few lectures and a chance to catch up with Naomi.

After he'd put out the fire and grabbed some lunch, he was ready for the trade show that opened at 3:00 p.m. He showed his badge and was allowed entry into the show. He was perusing many of the exhibit booths that ranged from agriculture and beauty to fitness products when a certain curly-haired updo caught his attention.

Naomi.

Lucius made a beeline in her direction.

She was bent down, smelling some cocoa beans, when he approached.

"Smell something you like?"

You, Naomi thought when Lucius's familiar scent drifted toward her. He probably tasted just as sweet as one of the organic milk chocolates in front of her. Why did she have to run into him now? She wasn't ready and hadn't had enough time to put on all her armor. Nor was she in any way prepared for the depth of the attraction she'd felt at the merest touch of his hand earlier.

It had startled her. That now, nearly sixteen years later,

Lucius Knight would still have an effect on her. She was no young ingenue anymore.

"Did you hear me?"

Naomi blinked several times, bringing Lucius back into focus. "Excuse me?"

"I asked if you smelled something you like." He inclined his head to the cache of cocoa beans she was holding.

"Oh, yes, it has some interesting notes that might work well for one of my product lines."

"You own your own business?"

Naomi rolled her eyes. Really? Were they really going to play this game? Well, if he wanted to act like he didn't know who she was, she would do the same. "Yes, I do. I own a line of organic personal and home care products, among other things."

"So this expo is right up your alley."

"Yes, and you? Why are you here?" Naomi realized her question was blunt, but it was to the point.

Lucius smiled but answered. "I own a variety of businesses and am interested in expanding my reach. The rise of organic products and healthy living has really caused me to evaluate what I want to venture into next."

"Sounds reasonable." Naomi handed the beans back to the exhibitor and began moving to the next table.

Much to her chagrin, Lucius followed. "How long have you been in business?"

"Eight years."

"Impressive. Not many start-up businesses make it past the first year."

Naomi shrugged. "We had a lot of support from the community. And you? How did you get your start?"

Lucius stared at her sideways. He seemed surprised by the question but answered her anyway. "I had a knack for determining companies worth investing in."

"How vague," Naomi replied.

An amused smile crossed his face as he looked down at her. And Naomi swallowed, shifting uncomfortably in her sandals.

A strange invisible pull was between them, and Naomi didn't like it. Nor did she like the way Lucius stared at her like he wanted to gobble her up with a spoon or something. What was happening between them? It didn't make any sense. She hadn't seen him since she was fifteen years old, when he'd graduated from high school. She shouldn't be feeling this way. Not again. And not now. Not when Lucius wanted to take away something very precious to her.

"I have to go." She walked to another table several feet away.

"Why?" Lucius asked to her retreating back. "I thought we were finally getting somewhere."

"Oh, yeah? Where was that?"

"If we're both lucky, to a bedroom."

His arrogant and shameless words caused Naomi to turn on her heel to face him. "What did you just say?"

Lucius's smile was devastatingly handsome and also a bit devilish as he walked toward her. "You heard me. But if you want to act like you didn't feel what I felt when we touched earlier or just now, I'll bite and play the game."

"Of all the nerve." Naomi refused to even give what he said credence—even though he was right. If the simplest of touches could cause that kind of reaction, it was obvious there was something underlying, but Naomi wouldn't be acknowledging it. Instead, she turned and walked away.

"Naomi, Naomi." She heard her name being called and could see Alexis, her intern, waving her over to the Brooks and Johnson table. When she'd hired the interns, she'd told them that they were all on a first-name basis and could call her Naomi.

"No need to yell, Alexis," Naomi said when she arrived. Her salespeople were already occupied with other customers, so Naomi headed straight for her. "What can I do for you?"

"Well, this gentleman wants to know how they might go about carrying our products at his stores," Alexis replied with a smile.

Naomi smiled and hid her purse under the table. Now *this man* she could handle and knew what to do with. She immediately started explaining Brooks and Johnson's mission statement and how they would be a great addition to his business. It didn't take long for the man to hand her his card and tell her he'd be in touch to talk terms.

"That went wonderfully," Naomi said five minutes later to Alexis, who was standing avidly by, soaking it all in.

"How'd you do that?" the young woman asked. They'd hired her to help with the trade show and she was still green.

"Experience," Naomi replied. "Don't worry, the more you're exposed to these types of environments, the more you'll learn."

Applause sounded from behind Naomi. She didn't need to know who was praising her. Lucius. The man refused to go away. He was like a puppy nipping at her heels.

"I couldn't have said it better myself, Naomi Brooks," Lucius responded. He held out his hand. "Pleasure to officially meet you."

Chapter 3

Naomi thought about leaving Lucius hanging, but since she was in front of her intern, who looked to her as a mentor, Naomi had no choice but to accept the handshake. Lucius's hand clasped her small one, and a ripple of excitement went up her spine at touching him again. He studied her face, waiting for a reaction.

Damn him!

She quickly released his hand and turned to her intern. "Alexis, I'd like you to meet—"

"Lucius Knight?" the girl finished. "*Black Enterprise* businessman of the year."

"One and the same." Lucius smiled broadly, and Naomi couldn't fail to notice he had straight, pearly-white teeth. His charm hit the poor intern like a ton of bricks, and she blushed from ear to ear, her cheeks turning red.

"Oh, my God!" Alexis's hand flew to her mouth. "It's a pleasure to meet you."

"You as well," Lucius said and turned back to stare at Naomi. His eyes pierced hers, and Naomi felt her heart hammer foolishly in her chest. She hated that she was having such a reaction to his obvious interest in her. If this had been sixteen years ago when she'd loved his rebel-without-a-cause image, she would have welcomed it, but not today.

"You could learn a lot from this woman," she caught Lucius saying. "Naomi and her partner started this company from nothing and have grown into a multi billion-dollar enterprise, or so I've heard, while I've just gambled on the right companies."

"Clearly your gambles paid off," Naomi responded.

Lucius laughed heartily. And Naomi had to admit she liked the sound of it. "They usually do."

"Arrogant," Naomi muttered underneath her breath.

"What was that?" Lucius asked.

"Oh, nothing," Naomi said. "Alexis, I'm going to get back to the trade show. The salespeople are available—" she motioned to her sales team, who'd finished with their customers "—as am I if you need me again, all right?"

"Sure thing, Naomi." Alexis smiled.

Naomi retrieved her purse and started toward the other table, but stopped. "Are you coming?" she asked Lucius. Since it was obvious she wasn't going to shake him, she might as well try to use his interest to find out more about what he had in store for Brooks and Johnson.

His face creased into a sudden smile. "Love to."

Lucius was happy that Naomi softened toward him as the afternoon progressed. If she'd kept the hardened stance from earlier this morning, he would have his work cut out for him. But this more laid-back Naomi was more his speed. And if he played his cards right, their relationship would be more than just business.

When he'd seen her sitting there in the workshop, he couldn't believe his luck. It was an opening for him to get to know Naomi and how she'd changed from awkward teenager to brilliant businesswoman. He hadn't found out everything he wanted to know about Brooks and Johnson that afternoon, but he enjoyed her company. Perhaps it was because he found Naomi extremely attractive.

A luscious mane of spiral curls was piled atop her head, allowing him full view of her delicate neck and shoulders. Or was it the way she carried herself now? She was more confident and assured in that pencil skirt that hugged all the right places. The white shirt, though professional, gave him just a hint of cleavage that he was dying to find out what secrets were underneath.

Lucius didn't know this version of Naomi Brooks. He remembered a gangly teenager who was so socially awkward the students in their high school made fun of her. He'd protected her once when a gang of bullies razzed her. Adam probably thought he didn't remember, but he had. She'd looked so small and innocent back then, unable to take care of herself.

But this new Naomi Brooks was a force to be reckoned with. Lucius had a feeling that a takeover of her company wouldn't be as easy as he'd thought. Naomi wasn't just going to lie down and roll over. She was going to fight him, but Lucius was more than ready for the challenge.

"How about a cocktail?" Lucius asked when they'd both seen enough of the east wing of the trade show and everyone was starting to pack up for the end of the day.

"I don't think so."

"C'mon," Lucius said. "What are you going to do? Go back to you room and order room service?"

Naomi chuckled, and Lucius suspected that was exactly what she was going to do. "Only if I get to take off this outfit and put on something more comfortable."

Visions of Naomi naked sprang to Lucius's mind, but he blinked them back. "Deal. How about I meet you downstairs in the lounge in fifteen minutes?"

"You're on."

* * *

Ten minutes later, Naomi paced her hotel room after she'd changed into jeans and a tank top and let down her hair. It was her usual attire after a long day, but the reason why wasn't. Why had she agreed to a drink with Lucius? The man couldn't be trusted. He'd already acted like he didn't know who she was when she knew darn well he'd done his research on her. Did he remember they'd gone to high school together? Did he remember when she'd followed him like a lovesick puppy dog after he'd saved her from some bullies?

Of course he didn't. He was Lucius Knight, international playboy and heart stealer. Why would he remember a gangly, pimple-faced teenage girl?

It was no wonder her heart had palpitated around him, because that was Lucius's appeal. He reeled women in then tossed them aside when he was done. She'd read the tabloids, seen him with gaggles of beautiful women, models and actresses alike. Naomi wouldn't become one of those women.

But those dark eyes. They seemed to look into her soul. And those lips…they were full and kissable.

Stop. Stop. Stop.

She had to remind herself that she was in control. Of her own destiny and her company's fate. She would and could resist Lucius, even if he turned on his full charm, which she was sure he would do tonight. But she would be on her guard.

Lucius rose from his lounge chair when he saw Naomi enter the room. Damn, the woman was fine as hell! She made ripped jeans and a tank look like she was wearing the slinkiest dress ever. As she walked toward him, Lucius was aware of how the jeans rode low and snug around her hips. How the tank clung to her breasts, tapering down to her narrow waist. Lord almighty, he was in trouble.

"Naomi." He pulled out her chair.

"Lucius." She sat down and he joined her in the opposite chair.

"What can I get you to drink?" He motioned the nearby waiter over.

"I'll have a pomegranate martini."

He rattled off her order to the waiter and turned back to face her. "I like you in casual attire. It suits you."

"More than my business attire?"

Lucius shook his head. "Not more than, just that you appear more yourself."

"And how would you know that?" she countered.

He dodged her question. "Am I wrong?"

She laughed and leaned back in her chair. "No, I prefer jeans to suits and skirts, but it's a necessary evil at times."

"Agreed. So tell me, Naomi, how does someone as young and vibrant as you decide to take on starting her own business?"

Naomi shrugged. "It might have been a notion to some, but Kelsey and I—that's my business partner," she added, even though he already knew this information, "didn't want a nine-to-five job. We wanted to be in charge of our own destiny."

"I can understand that," Lucius responded. "I wanted the same thing. To be my own man."

"From the looks of it you succeeded," Naomi replied.

"Wow. That sounds like an insult coming from you."

Naomi shook her head. "Not an insult, just the truth. You've done quite well for yourself, Lucius Knight. Not only are you in the business magazines as a self-made millionaire, but you're also in every gossip rag, thanks to your dalliances with beautiful women. Unlike most rich men, you're not spoiled, but you definitely have their confidence and arrogance."

"And I take it those are traits you don't admire?"

"Quite the contrary. I admire confidence and believing in oneself."

"But not my arrogance?"

Her brow rose. "Wasn't it you who pretty much *ordered* me to meet you down here for a cocktail?"

"I didn't order you. You were welcome to decline the invitation."

"I doubt you would have taken no for an answer."

He threw back his head and let out a peal of laughter. She was right. He wouldn't have taken no for answer, not when he suspected that Naomi found him equally as attractive as he found her. "All right, Naomi. I suppose you're right. Would it also surprise you to know that I knew who you were before we met?"

"Not at all. My vice president informed me of Knight International's interest in *my* company."

The waiter returned with their order and placed the drinks in front of them.

He noted her emphasis on the word *my*. Naomi knew of his desire to control Brooks and Johnson, which made her a formidable adversary. "So you've prejudged me? You should know my interest is not only professional, but personal."

Naomi chuckled, reached for her drink and took a few calming sips before answering. "C'mon, the only reason you're trying to charm me is so you can find out more information on Brooks and Johnson."

"That's not the only reason." Lucius sat upright and leaned closer to her. His eyes caught and held hers over the circle of light from the votive candle on the table between them. His dark eyes bored into hers and spoke with-

out words of his desire for her. She dropped her eyes under
his intense scrutiny.

Naomi might be confident in business, but just then
he'd seen a flash of the old Naomi. The sensitive, innocent Naomi who'd once admired him. Now, however, he
didn't want her admiration—he wanted her to *want him.*

Naomi couldn't hold Lucius's gaze and lowered her
lashes. His eyes had darkened dangerously with what
Naomi felt was akin to lust. His face was hard and lean,
just like his body. A body that was emphasized by the
wine-colored polo shirt that revealed his bulging biceps
and black jeans that showed off his trim waist and long
legs.

Naomi felt an unwelcome surge of excitement. Her
body felt heavy and warm due to his unrelenting gaze.
She reached for her drink, and Lucius caught her hand.
Naomi's pulse pounded at the smoldering flame in his eyes.

"Why don't we stop playing games? Let's quit acting
like there isn't a mutual attraction sizzling between us."

"There is no attraction," Naomi threw back at him caus-
tically.

"Don't deny it. The chemistry has been there from the
moment we reconnected."

"Only a rich, arrogant millionaire intent on getting his
greedy hands all over my company would say that." She
rose from the chair she was seated in. "Neither I nor my
company is for sale, Lucius."

She stalked out of the lounge with as much dignity as
she could muster given that he was partly right. There was
something there between them. She had to be on her guard
with Lucius at all times. She couldn't—wouldn't—fall prey
to his charms like most of the women he encountered.

She was in the elevator and the doors had nearly shut

when Lucius caught up to her and worked them open with his large hands before stepping inside.

They were alone in the elevator.

Lucius glanced at the elevator buttons. "We're on the same floor, fate is bringing us together."

Then he walked purposely toward her, and Naomi automatically shrank back a couple of steps. But when she did, her back hit the wall—not a good position to be with a dangerously sexy man like Lucius. His hands splayed on either side of her face, caging her in.

"You do want me," Lucius countered, "even if you won't admit it." He reached for a strand of her hair and twirled it around his index finger. "How about we put your resolve to the test, hmm?"

Naomi caught the challenging gleam in his eye right before his lips descended on hers. Naomi thought the kiss would be hard, but it was soft, as were his lips. She'd always wondered what they'd taste like, and now she knew. He sipped at her lips until she gasped and a low moan escaped her lungs. Lucius used it to his advantage, demanding full entry between her lips at the same time his hands slipped from the wall to cup her bottom so he could press her to him.

Naomi felt his hard, flat stomach and his broad chest as he held her firmly to him. She also felt the swell of his erection that sprang to life against her stomach. His hands ran up and down her body, and Naomi trembled.

Lucius lifted his head long enough to stroke her hair back from where some had fallen around her face, his eyes searching hers for a sign to stop. Finding none, he lowered his mouth once more to engage hers. He kissed her top lip, wetting and nibbling it with his tongue before going to her bottom lip. He sucked on it voraciously, and Naomi felt her nipples become taut and expectant. Of what?

Of Lucius's mouth on them?

The elevator doors suddenly opened, and Naomi sprang from his embrace as if they were two randy teenagers caught making out underneath the bleachers. The bell-man smiled at them both and pressed the button for the next floor.

Clearly, he knew what they'd been up to.

Did she?

What had possessed her to kiss Lucius back? Naomi knew what Lucius wanted, and she had no intention of succumbing. And as soon as the bellman was gone, she would tell him so.

She didn't have to. Once he'd disembarked two floors up, Lucius turned to her. "That was bad timing. I should have waited until we were in my room."

"Your room?" Naomi asked. Her shoulders squared. "I'm not going anywhere with you."

Lucius's hand rubbed his neatly cropped head. "Really? Are you going to act like you didn't enjoy that kiss just now? Like if that bellman hadn't interrupted us, you wouldn't have been mine for the taking?"

"Of all the…" Naomi stabbed at the elevator button. She couldn't wait for her floor to arrive.

Lucius leaned back against the wood paneling inside the elevator, regarding her quizzically. He watched the rise and fall of her chest, and his gaze immediately dropped from her eyes to her breasts. Was he assessing their size? Did he prefer huge breasts to her B-cup ones?

His eyes returned back to her face, and she felt flushed. He couldn't know what she was thinking, could he?

"All right, Naomi. I'm going to let you go tonight."

"*Let* me go?"

He smiled at the challenging tone in her voice. "That's right. Because, trust me, if I tried, I could seduce you into my bed tonight, but I won't. I want you to come there willingly."

"There is no way in hell that's happening."

The elevator chimed and doors opened, indicating it was their floor. She stepped out and turned around long enough to hear Lucius say, "We'll see. We'll see."

Chapter 4

Naomi was in a foul mood the next morning for the final day of the conference. She hadn't slept well, having tossed and turned due to the melodramatic threat Lucius made the previous evening. He'd made it clear that the inevitability of them becoming lovers was a foregone conclusion.

Was he right?

Naomi didn't want him to be.

Or did she?

He was right in that they had chemistry in spades, but how could there not be when he stared at her like he was dying of thirst in the desert and she was his oasis? It was enough to put any red-blooded woman on alert.

Once she'd returned to her hotel room, her mind had gone haywire. The memory of Lucius kissing her, his tongue delving deep inside her mouth, the way her nipples had turned rock hard along with the telltale sign of wetness between her legs, tormented her. It had been shocking how turned on she was by one kiss from Lucius. Naomi's face flamed at the realization she'd wanted him—or at least her body did.

Was this a sign that her former crush on Lucius had

never gone away and instead had just been buried deep in the recesses of her mind until his kiss brought it forward?

Why did this have to happen now? When she might possibly have to fight to keep her company? If Kelsey did indeed want to dissolve their partnership and sell her shares, it would leave Naomi vulnerable to an attack from Knight International. And not just on the business front. Lucius was coming for her *personally.*

She'd seen the determined look in his eye last night as the elevators doors shut. A look that told Naomi he meant to have her.

Would she be strong enough to fight him off when her own traitorous body found him irresistible?

Lucius woke up the next morning feeling surprisingly refreshed given there was no valet or butler to assist him for the day. He was on his own. And perhaps that was just as well. He suspected that to get through to Naomi he would have to be himself.

There were no airs to Miss Brooks. Instead, she was a woman who appreciated the simple, basic things in life. So he was sure it came as a shock to her that she too could be led astray by the desires of the flesh. She'd probably been bedding nice guys who had no idea how to bring out the vivacious woman he'd seen last night.

But she was there. He'd seen it in her eyes and body language.

And he was just the man to bring out the sensual side of her nature. Once he got her alone, he would seduce her. Last night, when his hands had roamed over her body, he'd had just a sample of what it would be like to touch that beautiful body of hers, and he craved more.

An added bonus was that while he was rattling Naomi's cage, Adam would be working on Kelsey. The soon-to-be second-time mother might be his way to get enough shares of Brooks and Johnson for a takeover.

But first things first—he had a certain woman to woo.

Downstairs in the convention center, Lucius discovered that finding Naomi wasn't all that easy. If he didn't know any better, he'd think she was avoiding him. After reading the itinerary for the second day of the expo, he attended a lecture he'd thought would surely interest her, but when he'd arrived he'd found the lady wasn't in attendance. Nor was she in the second lecture later that morning.

Lucius was quickly becoming annoyed that he'd yet to spot her—until he arrived at the trade show. Naomi was standing in front of her display talking to several customers. And she was doing a heck of a job. She'd convinced him, and he was only standing a few feet away.

She looked feminine in a sleeveless pink wraparound top and gray slacks and pink peep-toe pumps. Glittering silver earrings adorned her ears and only emphasized her beautiful face, on which she wore very little makeup other than a touch of blush, mascara and pink lipstick.

When she was done and had handed her business card to one of the customers, he applauded her.

She turned, and when she saw him, her smile faded. "Lucius."

"Good morning," he responded, not allowing her lack-luster response to faze him. "I missed you this morning."

"Duty calls."

He raised an eyebrow.

"One of my salespeople came down with a bad case of food poisoning and is currently in their room praying to the porcelain god, so I'm here in their stead."

"So it wasn't my charming personality that kept you away?"

"You wish." Naomi bent down and retrieved several

cellophane-wrapped Brooks and Johnson products from underneath her display table.

"I was actually hoping I could steal you away and talk about how Brooks and Johnson might benefit from being part of Knight International."

"Changing tactics, I see," Naomi stated. She began stacking the promotional items on the table. "I have executives that handle that kind of stuff for me. Besides I'm needed here."

"Don't hide behind your work," Lucius responded, glancing around him. "The trade show is going to slow down for lunch anyway, and you have to eat."

Naomi let out a long, beleaguered sigh. "Fine. If it'll get you off my back." She turned and whispered something to her staff.

Lunch at a nearby bistro was not only delicious, but the conversation was less charged than their previous encounters. The change of flow seemed to please Naomi immensely, and she became more at ease during the course of the meal. They talked about politics. The Lakers. Even some charity work she'd started doing. Until eventually the conversation turned to business and the purpose for the lunch.

Lucius explained the reach of Knight International and how having a distribution arm like his would allow Brooks and Johnson to not only be a national phenomenon but an international success. "We could sell B and J products in stores abroad."

"That's all fine and good, Lucius," Naomi responded, "but I'm happy with where the company is right now."

"C'mon, don't tell me you don't have big dreams."

"I do, but I also want to be approachable. I can't do that overseas. I do want a family someday."

Lucius frowned. *Family.* There was a dirty word in

his vocabulary, and one he wasn't altogether fond of. If it wasn't for his grandma Ruby, he wouldn't have any to speak of.

Naomi caught his frown, because she asked, "Are you not close with your family?"

His sat upright in his chair, his shoulders stiff. "No, I'm not."

She must have detected his body language and the note of finality in his tone, which said he didn't wish to continue on the subject, because she dropped it. "I have to get back." Naomi used the napkin in her lap to wipe her mouth.

"So that's it?" Lucius asked. "You're not going to give my proposal any more thought?"

Naomi's eyes narrowed. "I did. I gave you the benefit of lunch and you didn't convince me that the company *I* started, *I* nurtured since infancy, belongs with someone who doesn't even believe in the word *family*. Good day, Lucius."

Lucius stared at Naomi's retreating figure as she went through the revolving doors of the bistro. How had their lunch gone so horribly wrong? He'd been certain he could convince her that Knight International was the next logical step in the evolution of Brooks and Johnson. But not only had he failed at that, he'd also struck a nerve with Naomi when he'd cut down her attempt to open up about his family.

Had he killed any hope that Naomi Brooks would ever give him the time of day again?

"You won't believe who was at the conference," Naomi told Kelsey the next day when she made it back to Long Beach and phoned her friend from her three-bedroom craftsman-style bungalow in Belmont Heights' historic district.

"Who?" Kelsey asked from the other end of the line.

"Lucius Knight," Naomi replied, placing the teakettle on the stove.

"Lucius. Now there's a blast from the past," Kelsey responded. "You haven't spoken of him since college, when you told me about the monumental crush you had on him."

"Yeah, well, that ship has sailed," Naomi responded, turning on the burner. "He's not the bad boy of every teenage girl's fantasy anymore. Instead, he's a pompous, arrogant, conceited jerk."

"Wow!" Kelsey laughed. "I've never heard you speak that way about someone. He must have really gotten your goat."

"He did."

"What happened? Do tell—married women such as myself have to entertain ourselves with sexy single girl stories."

"Wh-what? There's no sex in this story."

"Naomi, chill. I was just kidding. What's gotten into you?" Kelsey inquired. "Did seeing Lucius again really upset you that much?"

Naomi sighed. "Yes—I mean, no."

"Which is it?"

"He was just so smug and confident, saying that I'm attracted to him and that we would eventually sleep together."

Kelsey perked up. "Oh, really? And why would he think that? Did you give him fodder to think he'd have the time of day?"

"No…"

"Hmm…it sounds like you're not being one hundred with me, Naomi. Give up the goods. What happened between you two?"

"All right, all right. We kissed," Naomi answered in a

rush as she leaned back against the counter to wait for the teakettle to boil. "Are you happy now?"

"I would be if you were happy about it. Was he a terribly bad kisser? You know, the ones that slobber all over you, or their tongue is like a lizard darting in and out of your mouth. I used to hate that when I dated. If a man didn't know how to kiss, he got the boot."

Naomi chuckled. "I wish that was the case, but Lucius is far from being a bad kisser. In fact, he's the best kisser I've ever had."

"Is that a fact?"

"It is. And that's also why I have to stay away from him."

"Why? What's wrong with having a little fun? If his reputation is anything to go by, Lucius knows how to treat—or should I say please—a woman. Perhaps Lucius, with his exceptional expertise, is exactly what you need to light your fire."

"Kelsey."

"I'm just being honest. When was your last date? Or relationship?"

"Lucius Knight isn't interested in a relationship with me. He's interested in sleeping with me and buying my company, and not necessarily in that order."

"That's true."

Naomi stood upright. "Why are you agreeing? Did something happen while I was away?"

"His attorney Adam Powell came to see me."

"And why would he do that?" Once the kettle began to whistle, Naomi turned off the burner and poured the boiling water in a teacup.

"To offer me an outrageous sum of money to sell my shares."

"And what did you tell him?"

"No, of course. I would never do that to you, Naomi, and not to our friendship. I promised you I would take time to think through my decision, and I'm doing just that. No amount of money thrown at me would change that."

Naomi released the long sigh she'd been holding in. "Thank you, Kels. I guess I just got a little nervous, is all."

"What I want to know is how would they even know to come to me out of the two of us?"

Naomi rubbed her chin and thought about Kelsey's questions. "Clearly, they were looking for the weak link, and they think you're it, given you're married with a child and another on the way. It's apparent that Lucius doesn't play fair and is looking for my Achilles' heel."

It was just another thing that Naomi was finding she didn't like about the man other than his proclivity against family. Or was it marriage and children? Or all of the above?

Lucius was angry. He'd called and left repeated messages on both Naomi's cell phone and at her office, and yet she continued to ignore him. He'd thought at the very least he and Naomi had formed a pseudofriendship during the couple of days they'd spent in Anaheim.

On their last day together, he'd tried to show her that if they worked as a team, Brooks and Johnson's transition into the Knight International brand would be seamless, but Naomi wanted none of it. Or maybe her ire went deeper? Was she upset because he'd come on so strong about their obvious attraction? Was this her way of telling him to take a hike? If so, she was wrong on that score.

Lucius never gave up on something he wanted. He wanted Naomi. *And* her company.

Since returning from Anaheim nearly a week ago, he'd dived back into work full force, trying to erase the memory of the curly-haired beauty from his mind, but he couldn't. He would daydream about what it had been like to kiss her in that elevator, and his dreams went farther into what would have happened if that door had *never* opened.

He imagined taking Naomi against the wall. He'd have stripped her of any clothes, spread her legs and licked her until she begged him to make love to her. Only then would he have pushed down his jeans and plunged deep inside her wet heat. He knew she'd been wet for him. The way she'd squirmed in his arms had told him exactly what he'd needed to know. Naomi was as hot for him as he was for her.

He just had to get the woman to admit it.

She was as stubborn as a mule, and this last week had proved so. But he wasn't going to take this lying down. He was going to make Naomi acknowledge that not only was Brooks and Johnson a good fit for his brand, but more importantly, Naomi was a good fit for him.

Chapter 5

Naomi called it quits. It had been a long day. A late one, actually—she'd stayed well past 6:00 p.m. But it had been worth it. Today's think tank meeting had yielded some great ideas for the product line.

She waved at the security guard manning the entrance to the building as she made her way outside. One of the perks of having her own company was she got a prime parking space right outside the building rather than having to use the parking garage in the rear.

Naomi pushed open the glass door and breathed in the cool night air. She quickly buttoned up her peacoat and glanced up at the sky. Fall was here, and it felt good.

Or at least so she thought, until her gaze lowered and she saw Lucius standing outside a limousine several feet away.

"Join me for dinner?"

"I don't think that's a good idea, Lucius." Naomi started toward her Audi A5 coupe that was parked several feet away, but Lucius rose from where he'd been leaning and blocked her path.

"Please."

Naomi was sure Lucius never used that word often. He was used to issuing commands and people followed them, but he wasn't doing that now. Her head told her to keep walking, but instead, she walked toward the limousine. Lucius reached across and opened the door, and Naomi climbed inside. She scooted onto the plush leather passenger cushions. The limo was well furnished, but then again, this was how the rich and famous lived, right?

Lucius slid in beside her, and when he did, Naomi swallowed tightly and her pulse skittered alarmingly at being so close to Lucius. "And where are we going?"

"You'll see," Lucius said. "Just sit back and relax." He pressed on the intercom button and said to the driver, "You know the destination."

Lucius didn't like that Naomi was uneasy around him. Her guard was up and he wanted to get through to her, get her to see that he had a solid plan for Brooks and Johnson. An added benefit would be her becoming putty in his hands when he seduced her.

He did not, however, like the look of fear in her eyes, and so he engaged her in conversation. "You can stop fearing for your safety, Naomi. I won't harm you."

He watched her shoulders visibly sag. "I wanted to speak with you, but you didn't really give me much choice since you've ignored my calls.

"Perhaps there was nothing you had to say that I would be interested in."

"Ah." His index finger circled her face. "There's the feisty Naomi I know and like."

"Flattery will get you nowhere."

"No?" Lucius said. "Let's see if that holds true at the end of the night."

"You think you'll make it that long?"

"Until you've listened again to my pitch. After that—" he shrugged "—I'm going to guess that you won't want to."

Naomi folded her arms across her chest. "You don't know that."

"I know that you're curious as to why I contacted you and why I waited for you tonight."

"You waited for me?" Naomi's brow furrowed.

Lucius didn't speak, he just let Naomi marinate on that thought while he reached for the bottle of champagne that was chilling in the bucket beside him. "An aperitif?"

"I suppose. I'm not much of a drinker. So why is it I only seem to drink around you?"

"Perhaps it's a way for you to release your inhibitions."

That comment brought a frown from Naomi, and she turned to silently stare out the window while Lucius uncorked and poured each of them a glass of champagne. "Here." He held out the flute to her. She accepted but didn't look at him.

"Naomi, this night will turn out far better if you perhaps acknowledge that you don't dislike me as much as you protest."

Her head spun around, and she glared at him underneath mascara-coated lashes. He noticed that she had more makeup on than he'd seen her wear on prior occasions. She was more put together, in a black and tweed dress that reached her knees and black pumps. Lucius didn't like this stuffy Naomi. He much preferred the natural, more organic Naomi, who was more comfortable in jeans and a tank top.

She finally spoke. "I—I don't dislike you."

"What then?"

"As I said before, you're arrogant, but I also find you untrustworthy and unscrupulous."

"Unscrupulous? That's a strong word."

"Did you or did you not send your attorney to speak

with my partner, Kelsey, while I was in Anaheim so you could double-team us?"

Lucius sipped his champagne. So she knew about that? No wonder she'd ignored his calls.

"Are you going to deny it?" she asked when he didn't answer.

"No, that would be dishonest," he responded curtly.

"Which proves my point." Naomi took another gulp of champagne. "I can't trust you."

He turned to face her. "Do you want to?"

"Wh-what?"

"You heard the question. Why does my behavior bother you so, Naomi?" His steady gaze bored into her in silent expectation.

"I don't care one way or the other."

"Who's lying now?" he asked quietly.

She stared wordlessly at him, and Lucius knew it was time to tell her the truth. "C'mon, Naomi, did you really think I'm that callous that I don't remember the awkward fifteen-year-old girl that used to follow me around in high school?"

Naomi's entire face flushed, and he could see he'd hit the nail on the head. She had remembered him. She gulped down the remainder of her champagne.

"So you know who I am." She set her empty flute in the cup holder. "What of it?"

"So I know that you used to harbor a schoolgirl crush on me way back when. And I know that I thought you could be cute if you'd just take off those stupid glasses, get some better facial products, do something with your hair and stop trying to hide your figure. It seems I was right on all fronts."

Naomi sucked in a sharp breath. He could see he'd embarrassed her, but he wasn't above using sentimentality to get his way. He leaned back slightly so he could assess her frankly. "Your skin is clear, which I'm sure is due to Brooks and Johnson products. You wear contacts now, and your hair, well—" he reached out to finger several tendrils "—natural looks good on you. And as for the figure..." His gaze lazily roved over her entire body. "I like everything I see."

"I'm so glad you approve," Naomi replied flippantly.

"Don't be upset." Lucius scooted closer to Naomi, and this time she didn't move away from him. "It was a compliment." He stroked the soft skin of her cheek. "You've turned into a beautiful woman. A woman I am very much attracted to."

His gaze immediately went to her lips. Lips he wanted to kiss. Had been craving to kiss since the elevator in Anaheim. He glanced upward to her neck and could see her pulse quickening. Gone was the embarrassment of a moment ago, and in its place he could feel the electricity he'd felt since they'd met.

He bent his head and claimed her lips. He kissed her nice and slow so she didn't push him away. He needed her to acquiesce. At first she remained still, but as his mouth covered hers hungrily, Naomi gave up the pretense she didn't want him and her arms snaked around his neck.

Lucius groaned as he broke the barrier of her lips and teeth and she allowed his tongue to surge inside her mouth. He left no part of her mouth untouched. He tasted every nook and crevice of its honeyed interior, but what was most surprising was how he felt while doing it. Instead of making her burn for him, he was burning for her. His hands threaded through her hair as he devoured her mouth. He had an aching need to forget all semblance of romance and just bury himself deep inside her right now in the back of this limo.

Fate was on her side, because the limo came to an abrupt stop, causing him to slowly ease away from Naomi. When he glanced in her direction, Naomi's hair was tousled and her lips looked swollen, because he'd thoroughly made love to them.

Naomi used her fingers to comb her hair back into place. She didn't say a word when the driver came around and opened her door. She just disembarked and waited for him on the sidewalk.

Lucius exited right behind her and reached for her hand, but Naomi ignored it and walked inside without him.

Naomi stared at Lucius after they'd been seated by the hostess and placed their order with a very supercilious waiter. In the limo, he'd told her that he was very aware of her when they were in high school. "Why did you say it? To get me off track from the real reason you're so desperate to contact me?"

"Say what?"

"That you found me cute back in high school. You said it to disarm me, so I'd let down my guard. Very sneaky, Lucius."

"I meant it."

Naomi snorted. There was no way a man or boy as good-looking as Lucius had found an awkward outcast like her remotely attractive.

"You don't believe me?" Lucius watched her across the rim of his glass. "Of course you don't, because I'm ruthless and can't be trusted. Is everything so black-and-white to you, Naomi? Or don't you see in shades of color?"

"I see you very clearly, Lucius. And I won't be played."

"Yes, I'm relentless when I want something, but one doesn't negate the other. It doesn't mean that I don't find you desirable and want you in my bed."

"There!" She pointed her index finger at him again. "You're doing it again. Trying to seduce me."

"I don't have to try." Lucius leaned back in his chair. "I think that was pretty obvious from the way you responded in the limo."

Naomi didn't answer and reached for her water glass. All of a sudden, she felt very thirsty. Perhaps it was Lucius's hungry gaze that was making her parched. She drank liberally, giving herself time to gather her thoughts.

"You have a way with women, Lucius. Everyone knows it. And I know it. It's not surprising that you could garner a reaction from me. I imagine you're quite skilled in that department."

"I am," Lucius said. "Skilled in the bedroom and out of it. And that's why you and your partner shouldn't toss aside the deal my team has presented. It's more than fair."

"We're not interested."

The waiter returned at that moment with the expensive bottle of wine Lucius ordered. He poured Naomi a taste, and once she'd sipped and nodded in agreement, he filled her glass and Lucius's.

Once he'd gone, Lucius wasted no time getting back to the topic at hand. "Am I the reason you're not giving this offer credence? Are you doing this just to spite me?"

"Spite you?" Naomi's head fell back with laughter. "You give yourself a lot of credit, Lucius. There are other wolves just like you waiting to pounce in the wings." She wasn't about to tell him that her partnership with Kelsey was on rocky ground because motherhood and family had become central to Kelsey. And that *she* might be interested in his offer. "But I'll tell them the exact same thing I'm telling you—I'm never giving up controlling interest in my company."

He watched her warily, as if he was assessing her answer. Naomi sensed that he wanted to say more, but he didn't.

The waiter returned with their entrées of succulent shrimp risotto and spiced duck. They both indulged in the delicious dishes in contemplative silence before Lucius took the conversation down a different path.

"It's clear, Naomi, we've reached an impasse on all talk of business for tonight, but that doesn't mean the evening has to be a bust. So can we toast to having an enjoyable evening?"

Naomi thought about it a moment. She didn't know how she was going to do that. The wariness she felt for Lucius was armor for her to deflect the attraction she felt. Without it, she was forced to admit to herself that she enjoyed his company. Having removed his jacket, he looked gorgeous in the white button-down shirt that was open at the collar and black slacks. His hair was trimmed so that the wave in it was noticeable. His deeply set dark eyes stared directly across the table at her, waiting for her answer.

"Yes." She held up her flute reluctantly. "I suppose I can do that."

An irrepressible grin slid over his incredibly full lips.

Naomi swallowed. It was going to be a long night.

Lucius was happy with how the evening progressed between him and Naomi. They'd adjourned from the restaurant to sit beside each other—Lucius on one side of a padded wicker love seat and Naomi far away on the other—on the terrace outside and enjoy the crisp fall evening with an after-dinner drink. The terrace was dimly lit by thin strings of light and strategically placed candles.

Lucius regarded her silently.

Sure, his interest in her company had been met with

outright hostility, but once they'd agreed to put their differences on the shelf, he found Naomi a breath of fresh air.

There was no pretense with her. What you saw was what you got. She wasn't like other women, who, once they found out who he was or how much he was worth, were eager to fawn all over him or want him to buy them things. Naomi Brooks was nothing like them. In fact, she couldn't care less about things. She cared about people.

It was evident in the way she passionately spoke about her family. Throughout the course of the night, he'd learned her parents were still together after thirty-five years of marriage and she had a brother and a sister whom she loved dearly. Then there was her volunteerism—Naomi was involved in several charitable organizations that supported helping children and fighting breast cancer.

Lucius wasn't sure he'd ever met anyone quite like Naomi. She was more selfless than anyone he'd ever known.

"What?" Naomi was staring back at him.

He blinked several times. "I'm sorry, say again?"

"Am I boring you?" she inquired. "I know I'm not like some of the actresses and models you've dated, who I'm sure indulge in more titillating conversation."

Lucius laughed broadly. "Boring? Ha. That's the last adjective I would use to describe you, Naomi. I was just musing on the difference between you and my usual companions."

Naomi eyed him suspiciously. "Am I really all that different?"

"You've certainly changed from the nerdy tomboy in baggy jeans and plaid shirts," Lucius countered.

"And you?" She eyed him in return. "You're just as dangerous as you were as a teenager, which is why I must be cautious of you, Lucius Knight, despite how charming you're being." She glanced down at her watch. "We should call it a night. I have a busy day in the morning." She rose from the love seat.

Lucius hated for the night to end. He wanted to spend more time with her, but he would have to bide his time. "Of course." He stood. "Shall we?" He offered her his arm.

At first, he thought she wouldn't take it, but she must have realized she was out of danger at least for tonight, so she accepted his proffered arm as they walked to the elevators.

Several minutes later, they were back in his limousine and driving to her office so she could pick up her car. She was quiet on the way back, deep in thought. He wanted to know what was on her mind and why she had a concerned wrinkle on her forehead, but he doubted she would reveal her troubles to him. Why? Because she didn't trust him.

Lucius didn't know why it bothered him, but it did. He wanted her to trust him.

They made it back to the Brooks and Johnson building too quickly, in his opinion. Before Naomi could reach for the door, he used the intercom button to tell the driver he would need a minute.

Naomi turned to him in confusion.

"I really enjoyed our evening together," Lucius stated.

She looked relieved, as if she thought he was going to pounce on her. "So did I." She reached for the handle, but Lucius grasped her hand. "Lucius, don't…"

"Naomi…" He used his index finger to turn her head to face him. He glanced down at her mouth. Her lips were slightly parted, and he watched when her tongue darted out to lick them nervously. That was his undoing.

He reached for her and dipped his head to taste her mouth. Once, then twice before he began to devour her.

* * *

All the air in Naomi's lungs left her at Lucius's electric kiss. Every cell in her came alive, and her heart hammered loudly in her chest. Damn it! She'd tried to get out of the limo as quickly as she could without being rude, but he'd done it again. He was kissing her with no mercy until she had no choice but to return his kiss.

He raked his tongue across her top and bottom lips until she parted them for his tongue. His arms vised around her body, pulling her close enough and positioning her underneath him. That's when he began kissing her deeply and so passionately, Naomi's head spun.

He made her feel alive, desired. No other man had ever made her feel like this. And she hadn't known that she could. He tore his mouth from hers long enough so his tongue could glide a wet path along the base of her throat and upward to her neck. And when his teeth made their way to her ear and he began tonguing it, Naomi moaned gently from underneath him as a wild rush of emotions began to rip through her system.

Good God! What the man was doing to her was making her wet between her thighs.

"Naomi..." Lucius groaned her name as his teeth and tongue left her ear to snake their way down. He pushed her peacoat aside so he could mold her breasts through the tweed fabric of her dress.

Naomi could feel them turn into pebbles beneath his skilled touch. She wanted to feel not just his hands but his mouth *on her*. She didn't resist when his hands roamed over her hip, thigh and leg. She didn't stop him when she felt the hem of her dress being lifted. She could only feel.

When Lucius's fingers reached the thin, lacy fabric of her bikini panties and pushed them aside to cover her warm cleft, Naomi shuddered. He touched her intimately, and Naomi let out a long hiss.

"Look at me." Naomi heard Lucius through the haze of emotions whirling through her.

She glanced up at him as his finger slid inside her. The glittering shine of hunger in his eyes was unmistakable as he stroked her in and out, over and over again until Naomi was a quivering mass of nerve endings.

"Come for me, Naomi." His fingers slowed their movements as they played with her swollen clit, time after torturous time, going deeper.

"I—I…" Naomi couldn't think. Lucius had her on the verge of coming. It was a mixture of ecstasy and agony rolled into one. She was panting for more, and when Lucius placed a second finger inside her and played her like a violin, Naomi broke, splintering into a thousand pieces.

She closed her eyes and waited for her breathing to return to normal. She couldn't look at him now. She was too embarrassed that he had just made her lose all control in the back of a limo. She was sure he was used to doing this kind of thing all the time with all sorts of women, but she wasn't one of them. And she wouldn't be used for his satisfaction. She had to put a stop to it.

Lucius was nibbling on Naomi's delicious neck when he felt her resistance. He stopped immediately and pulled them both upward. "What is it?" He searched her face for a sign of what had changed between them.

That's when he saw the tears in her eyes. "Naomi, I'm sorry…"

"Don't." She held up her hand. "I was an equal participant."

"Then what's wrong?" He was confused. Naomi had

enjoyed that kiss as much as he had. He'd felt it. She'd felt it. And she'd had an orgasm. Was that what scared her?

"I can't do this with you, Lucius. I should have never allowed this evening to continue after that first kiss," she said as she began rearranging her mussed clothing. He'd very much enjoyed finally having the opportunity to touch her body and feel her respond to him.

"Clearly I'm not immune to you," Naomi continued. "So I'm going to have to keep my distance." She reached for the handle. "And I suggest you do the same."

Before Lucius could react, she'd jumped out of the limousine. "Naomi!" He rushed toward the door, but she was racing to her car and was inside before he made it out of the vehicle.

Lucius watched as she started her car and sped away.

Slowly he slid back into the limo. Why was she running from him? He'd rather thought they were off to a good start. He'd hoped to convince her to spend the night with him, but that wasn't going to happen tonight—or any other night in the foreseeable future, if Naomi had anything to say about.

She'd been right when she said she wasn't immune to him, and Lucius intended to use it to his advantage. He wanted Naomi more than he'd wanted a woman in a long time. He would just have to wear down her defenses until she saw they could make beautiful music together.

Chapter 6

Images of Lucius kissing her in the back of the limo while his fingers were deep inside her flooded Naomi's mind as she drove to her parents' for dinner on Sunday. She was grateful for some semblance of normalcy after the crazy week she'd endured.

Seeing Lucius again after all these years, spending time with him and then finally that last passion-crazed night in which she'd made out with him in the limo not once, but twice, was troubling. She'd tried unsuccessfully to get him out of her mind, but he kept coming back like a boomerang. The way he'd kissed her, the way he tasted, the way he'd made her come with *his fingers*!

That night when she'd gotten home, she'd been mortified that she'd allowed their encounter to unravel. A kiss she could blow off, but she'd allowed him to take liberties with her body. To touch her. Make her orgasm. And what made matters worse was that now her body craved more. Her traitorous body wanted to feel him buried deep inside her, wanted to feel that gut-clenching, overwhelming sensation she'd felt when he'd made her come.

Naomi blinked several times as she pulled into her

parents' driveway next to her brother's minivan and her sister's scooter. It was bad, really bad. She was developing feelings for Lucius Knight again when she should be on her guard. The man didn't just want her. He wanted her company, too.

Turning off the engine, Naomi reached for the apple pie she'd made earlier that afternoon and exited the vehicle. She used her key and entered her parents' house moments later.

"Thanks, sweetie." Her mother, Ava Brooks, a petite woman with Naomi's same naturally riotous curls, greeted her in the hall with a kiss and relieved her of the pie. "You know you didn't have to make anything."

Naomi shrugged as she removed her jacket and hung it up on the coatrack in the foyer. "I know, but I wanted to. Where's everybody?"

"You know your dad and brother are in front of the tube watching football. Audrey's in the kitchen."

Naomi waved at her sister-in-law, Audrey, and rushed toward her father sitting in his recliner in the adjoining family room. "Dad." She gave him a squeeze around the neck.

"How's my baby girl?" Benjamin Brooks asked, glancing up at her with eyes as dark as midnight. With her caramel coloring and small frame, Naomi favored her mother, while her father had chocolate skin and a football player's build and was six feet tall.

"Just fine, Daddy." Naomi smiled as she came over to give her brother, Timothy, a hug.

"What's up, sis?" Timothy said, barely taking his eyes off the screen, not wanting to miss a play.

"Where's Gemma?" Naomi glanced around for her sister. As the youngest in the family at twenty-four, Gemma was the baby, but she was also the troublemaker and resident screwup. Naomi suspected by the time her parents got to Gemma they'd lightened up their parenting style dramatically. If Timothy or Naomi had done half the things Gemma did, they would have gotten in trouble or been kicked out of the house.

"Outside, I think," her father said. "Wanna beer?" He motioned to the cooler he kept by his side on game day.

"Sure." Her father opened the cooler and handed her a can. "Thanks." She popped the top and left them to find her sister.

She slid the door next to the family room open and found Gemma on the patio whispering on the phone. "Hey, Gemma," Naomi said from the doorway.

Startled, Gemma glanced up. "Oh, hey. How long you been here?"

"Not long. What's going on?"

Gemma placed her hand over the receiver. "Wrapping up a call. Can we talk later?"

"See you inside." Naomi wondered what she was up to but went inside anyway. She couldn't clean up any more of Gemma's problems. Her sister couldn't keep a steady job, but it was time Gemma stood on her own two feet.

She returned to the kitchen, where her mother and Audrey were making dinner. "Need any help?" Naomi asked, sitting on a bar stool at the breakfast bar.

"No, we have it under control," her mother replied. "So why don't you tell us what's new with you, such as the wealthy businessman who's interested in acquiring Brooks and Johnson? I ran into Kelsey's mom and she mentioned it."

Naomi rolled her eyes. She wanted to strangle Kelsey's mom. The last thing she wanted to do today was discuss Lucius Knight, but it looked like fate was not on her side.

"Yeah, actually I went to high school with him back in the day."

Her mother stopped stirring whatever she was cooking in the pot to glance at her. "Really? Were you friends?"

We definitely were not friends, Naomi thought. "No, I didn't really know him."

"And now he wants your company?"

Naomi nodded. "I'm not selling."

"Kelsey's mom told me that she might be," her mother replied.

Naomi took a swig of beer. "With the new baby, she's considering it, but I told her to let me know before she makes a final decision so I can buy her out."

"Can you afford to do that?" her brother asked. Timothy leaned against the breakfast bar behind her and reached across into the popcorn bowl sitting on the bar. He tossed a few kernels in his mouth. "You would need to come up with a lot of capital, and that's after you'd finally cleared all your debt with the IPO. It wouldn't be advisable."

Naomi knew this was right up her accountant brother's alley. "I don't know," she answered honestly. It was the first time she was admitting she might have a hard time raising that kind of money.

"Perhaps you need to give the offer some thought as well," her mother chimed in. "I mean, what you've done is amazing, but are you really ready to take B and J to the next level?"

"Thanks a lot, Mom." Naomi took another swig of beer.

"I'm sure your mom didn't mean anything by it." Her father came to her mother's rescue as he joined everyone in the kitchen. "*We* both believe in you, Naomi—always have. We wouldn't have given you the start-up money if we didn't."

Her parents and Kelsey's had loaned them the money

for the initial investment in Brooks and Johnson until they could pay them back. Naomi would always be grateful for their help, but this was something she would have to figure out on her own.

"I wish you guys would help me out like you helped Naomi," Gemma said, closing the sliding door to the pool.

"Of course, it's always about you, Gemma," Timothy said, glancing in her direction. "We were talking about Naomi."

Gemma made a face at him, and they all laughed.

"Dinner is ready," her mother stated. "Now, how about you guys help me and Audrey bring everything to the dining room?"

Ten minutes later, the entire Brooks family was seated at the dining room table. Benjamin said grace before they dug into the roast and sides Ava and Audrey had prepared.

"Looks good, Ma," Timothy commented.

Ava smiled. "Thank you, baby."

"So." Timothy turned to Naomi, who was seated on one side while his wife sat opposite him with Gemma. "Who is the businessman that's interested in B and J?"

Naomi had hoped the conversation was over. No such luck. "Lucius Knight."

"Knight, did you say? Isn't he that guy you used to fawn over in high school?" Timothy inquired.

Naomi blushed. "I did not fawn."

Gemma chuckled from across the table. "Liar. Look at how she's blushing." She pointed in Naomi's direction.

Naomi shifted uncomfortably in her seat as everyone at the table stared at her. "Fine. I may have had a crush on him, but for Christ's sake, I'm a grown woman now."

"Have you seen Lucius lately?" Gemma asked. "He was recently featured in *Black Enterprise* magazine as a rising star in the business world because of his shrewdness in takeovers. *And* he's simply gorgeous."

Naomi cast her eyes upward. Trust her sister to keep track of these things. "I hadn't noticed."

"So you've seen him?" Gemma picked up on what she hadn't said.

"Yes, I met him at the conference in Anaheim." Naomi figured that tidbit would be enough to appease her family.

"And was he as sexy as all the photos?" Gemma inquired.

"Gemma!" her father cautioned her sternly.

"C'mon, Dad. He's a known womanizer. I'm just asking if he's made a play for Naomi."

"This topic of conversation is extremely inappropriate," their mother scolded Gemma.

Gemma shrugged.

"If Gemma's right," Timothy said from her side, "then it might be wise to start reviewing your finances to be sure you can raise the capital if Kelsey wants to sell. A man like Lucius might not have any scruples about driving a wedge between longtime friends and business partners."

Naomi turned to stare at her brother. He had a point. She'd never thought about just how far Lucius might go to get what he wanted.

"If you want, I can help you look over your books and your finances to see what we can come up with."

"I would love that, Tim."

"Consider it done."

"Then let's move on to a new topic," her father said as he gave her a wink. She was thankful that he'd sensed her unease and she could get off the family hot seat, because Naomi suspected that she was far from out of the fire. In fact, she suspected that now that Lucius smelled victory, he would keep coming on strong.

* * *

Lucius would have loved to focus on business, Naomi or anything else other than deal with his mother, but he'd promised Grandma Ruby. His mother had already been back for a week and hadn't taken kindly to the fact that he hadn't spoken to her on the phone or come for a visit.

What did she expect, for Christ's sake?

She'd been MIA for most of his life. And just because she wanted to play the mommy role now did not mean he was about to roll over.

When Lucius arrived early that evening to Jocelyn Turner's penthouse, which she kept for her visits to Long Beach, she was happy to see him.

"Lucius, my darling." Rather than a hug, his mother kissed him on both cheeks and ushered him inside. "I'm so glad you finally decided to visit me."

Lucius heard the derisive note in her voice as he headed for the formal living room. He didn't intend on staying long. Time with his mother always got under his skin, and he wanted to keep it to a minimum. "I have a busy schedule, Jocelyn. Perhaps if you would schedule these visits I could put you on my calendar." He walked over to the wet bar on the far side of the room. He took the top off the decanter of scotch and poured himself a drink.

"I'm your mother, Lucius. I shouldn't have to be put on your calendar." She followed him in the room with her arms folded across her chest.

Lucius glanced backward at her. She was dressed in a silk lounge set that clearly was designer and quite costly. Her shoulder-length hair was in a loose chignon, and several expensive baubles adorned her neck, ears and fingers. Whoever she was seeing was quite wealthy and kept her in jewels. And had for years.

As for her face, his mother was a stunningly beautiful

woman. He'd inherited her smooth café au lait–colored skin and dark brown eyes. A flaw could not be seen on her impeccable complexion, and her figure was just as impressive. Even at fifty-four, Jocelyn Turner was still a head turner.

Lucius sipped his scotch before responding to her last comment. "You haven't earned the right to make unannounced visits. I owe you nothing."

"I'm still your mother, Lucius."

"Only when you seem to remember it and aren't traipsing the globe and hanging as an adornment on some rich man's arm."

"Lucius!" His mother covered her mouth with her hands and rushed out of the room and onto the terrace several feet away.

As soon as he said aloud the words he'd been thinking, he regretted them. Why did Jocelyn bring out the worst in him? Ever since he was a little kid, he'd been angered by her refusal to tell him who his father was. And because of it, he'd hardened his heart toward her. So much so that whenever they were within a few feet of each other, his claws came out.

Putting down his drink on the table, Lucius joined her on the terrace. He placed his hands on her shoulders, and they sagged at his nearness. "I'm sorry. I shouldn't have said that."

She patted his hands and turned around to face him. Her eyelashes were wet with tears. "Why do you despise me so? Haven't I given you everything?"

Lucius swallowed. He hated to see the hurt in her eyes, but he also wouldn't act as if she hadn't kept the truth from him his entire life. She was no mother of the year. "You haven't given me the one thing I want most, Mother."

He didn't use the title often, but in this instance he was trying to make amends as best he could.

"You know I can't do that."

And just as quickly the sentiment passed and Lucius stepped away from her. "You mean you *won't*."

"It's not the same."

"Like hell it isn't," Lucius stated. "How long will you continue to keep me in the dark? My whole life? What if I have a family of my own someday? Don't I have the right to know who I came from? My genetic makeup?" His investigation into his paternity had included researching men in his mother's past. He'd even researched men with the last name Knight, but had come up empty.

"Family?" She spun around to face him. "Have you gone and gotten one of the social climbers you associate with pregnant?"

"Of course you would think that," Lucius responded with an eye roll, "but I wouldn't want to end up like you. I suppose that's why you wish you'd never had me."

He turned to look out over the city. The sun would be setting soon.

He felt Jocelyn's hand on his arm, tugging him around to face her. "I've never regretted having you, Lucius. I love you. But I do worry about the women you choose to spend time with. Some of them would love to trap a man of your considerable wealth into a loveless marriage, and it would cost you a fortune to get rid of them. I would never want that for you."

Lucius regarded her quizzically. "Is that why my father never left his wife for you? Because he chose his money over love?" His mother turned away and didn't answer him. It seemed she'd been talking from personal experience. "I'm right, aren't I?"

"You don't understand, Lucius."

His fingers curved around her arm. "I don't because you've never helped me to understand. You've always kept the truth from me. What can it matter now? I'm a grown man. I don't need or want anything from my father. I just want to know who I am."

She stared at him with fresh tears in her ears. "I'm sorry, Lucius."

Lucius frowned and clenched his teeth. Yet again, as soon as he got too close, she shut him out. "So am I, because I can't continue to do this."

"What do you mean?"

"I won't be coming to visit you again."

"You can't mean that."

"I do mean it. I'm tired of playing this merry-go-round with you, Jocelyn. Either you tell me the truth of my parentage or you can consider yourself childless."

"You're giving me an ultimatum?"

"Damn right. So what's it going to be?" He folded his arms.

She shook her head as if she couldn't believe it was happening. "Please don't do this, Lucius." She rushed off the terrace and back into the living room, where she began pacing the floor.

"Do what?"

She stopped pacing momentarily to say, "Make me choose."

"I would think the choice is pretty clear. You can choose to have a relationship with me, *your son*. Or you can choose to continue to be *his* side piece. Always living in the shadows. Never his top priority. Never coming first."

She turned away to face the mantel that held several pictures of Lucius at various stages of his life. Stages she'd missed. There was one of him in his Boy Scout uniform with his grandma Ruby, another when he played football during the seventh grade and another with him in his cap and gown standing next to her and Ruby. Jocelyn had managed to make his high school graduation.

"Lucius, I know you can't understand this, but I vowed I would never reveal your father's identity, and I've honored it all these years. It hasn't been easy, I promise you that. Each and every time you've asked me, begged me—" her broke voice "—pleaded with me, I've wanted to tell you, but it was my choice to have you, not his and I have never regretted giving birth to you. My biggest regret is that I haven't been the best mother and can't give you the one thing you want most."

Lucius was stunned, and tears bit at his eyes, but he refused to let her see she'd finally broken him. He didn't know why, but he'd always held out the hope that one day she would tell him the truth. One day, she would put *him* first, but now he realized how foolish he'd been. She would never do that. He would always be last on her list of her priorities.

Lucius would never understand it. He walked toward the wet bar and chugged the scotch remaining in the glass. "Then consider this the last time we'll meet." He placed the glass back on the bar and strode toward the door.

She reached him at the door and tugged his arm. "Lucius, please forgive me. I'm so sorry."

He shrugged her away. "I'm finished with you. And this time for good."

Chapter 7

Lucius could use another stiff drink. It was usually how he felt after an encounter with his mother, but instead he chose a long walk on the beach to clear his mind. The sun in shades of red, orange and yellow was already setting in a half-moon shape on the horizon. Plus, it was an unseasonally mild evening, and he could use the fresh air. He discarded his jacket in the car and removed his shoes and socks, rolled up his trousers and headed to the ocean.

Why did he always wish for the impossible? Jocelyn was never going to tell him who his father was. She was always going to act like she was the put-upon, long-suffering mother and he was the ungrateful son. He shouldn't play into the role, but Jocelyn had a way of bringing out the worst in him.

Ever since he could remember, he'd been angry with her for a life denied to him. It had hurt the most when he was younger, when other little boys would talk about their fathers, or Father's Day would come around and his would be MIA. He would long for a tall, strong man to come and scoop him up in his arms and take him away from it all, but that day never came. And with each passing year, Lucius became angrier with Jocelyn for keeping the secret.

Lucius was kicking pebbles with his bare feet when he saw a figure in the distance.

Could it be?

It couldn't be.

As the shapely figure in denim capris and an oversize sweater continued to walk toward him, Lucius realized he was right. It was Naomi.

Naomi stared in disbelief at the tall, imposing man striding toward her with a purposeful walk. Of all the odds, on all the days, why did Lucius Knight have to end up on her beach now? She'd come for a little space and peace of mind after the Brooks family dinner had ended with her on the hot seat.

Her family had been extremely curious about Lucius, his intentions and her former feelings for the man. Though lately, those feelings weren't all that former. Since his return to her life, Naomi hadn't been able to get the man off her mind. He had a way of stirring up emotions and passions in her that she thought had been buried.

She continued walking and only stopped when they were a few feet from each other. Lucius was wearing a frown.

"What are you doing out here?" he inquired. "It'll be getting dark soon and you shouldn't be walking on a beach alone at night. It isn't safe."

Naomi laughed and began walking backward. "Actually, I'm probably a lot safer than when I'm with you."

"What's that supposed to mean?"

Naomi shrugged and turned around to go back toward her car.

"Wait up!" Lucius ran after her. He fell into step beside

her. Instead of commenting on her statement, they walked together in silence. Eventually he asked again. "What are you doing out here *alone*?"

She hazarded a glance at him. "Same as you, I suspect. Needed some solitary time."

"Rough night?"

Naomi shook her brown curls. "No, I was with my family."

"Sounds like a rough night."

"Oh, that's right, because you don't believe in family," Naomi replied, stopping in the sand to turn and stare at him. "Well, it isn't like that for me, Lucius. I love my family. They were just a bit more opinionated than I would have cared for tonight. And it gave me food for thought, is all." She started walking again, and Lucius followed by her side.

"Hmm…" he murmured. "Care to share?"

"Not really. And why are you out here alone on the beach? I would think you could find any number of obliging females to make a *From Here to Eternity* movie scene come to life."

He turned to stare blankly at her and paused midstride. "Excuse me?"

Naomi laughed and stopped abruptly. "You're not much on old black-and-white movies, huh?"

Lucius chuckled. "No, I'm not. What's it about?"

"It's an oldie but goodie. It's about three soldiers and stars Hollywood legends like Burt Lancaster, Montgomery Clift and Sinatra. All the action takes place in Hawaii before the attack on Pearl Harbor. Deborah Kerr is the love interest and has an affair with Burt Lancaster's character. They share a steamy moment on the beach in the sand and surf."

"And would *you* like one of those Hollywood moments?" Lucius teased as he smiled down at her.

She hated that even now Lucius looked just as sexy to her as he had all those years ago in high school. Except now he seemed more relaxed and less dangerous than he had in all their other encounters.

Naomi grinned broadly. "Wouldn't you like to know."

She turned on her heel and began walking again.

"Why can't you keep still?"

"Like you, I came for a walk, and we keep stopping."

"Would you prefer to be alone?"

Naomi glanced at him but didn't stop walking. "No, I don't mind the company."

"Good, because I'm not leaving you out here where anyone could harm you."

"How gallant of you."

"Don't be smart—" he wagged a finger at her "—or I'll throw you in the surf and give you your *From Here to Eternity* moment. I'll just bet that would quiet that mouth of yours."

Naomi's eyes grew large. He wouldn't dare. Would he? She stared in his deeply set dark brown eyes. And the answer was emphatic—yes, he would.

Lucius loved teasing Naomi and watching her get all riled up. There was a bright-eyed innocence to her that he found refreshing. He hadn't found it in the beautiful models and actresses he'd dated. He couldn't go beneath the surface with them, but with Naomi he could. Hell, even wanted to.

"What's on your mind, slick?" Naomi asked.

"Slick?"

"Yeah," Naomi laughed. "Kind of suits you."

"Yeah, well, it sounds like you don't think I'm genuine," Lucius responded, and for some reason the thought bothered him. He wanted Naomi to know that he had feelings, real emotions. He wasn't made of stone. An evening with his mother had shown him that.

Naomi turned to stare at him questioningly. "I'm sorry. I didn't mean to offend you."

"You didn't." He bent down, snatched up a rock and threw it into the surf.

"Hmm…kind of sounds like I did, and I'm sorry. What brings you out on an evening stroll, Lucius?"

He shrugged. He didn't want to talk about himself or his reunion with his mother and their nerve-racking fight. He was tired of the same ole song.

"You can talk to me. Maybe I can help."

Lucius glanced back at her. "There's nothing you can do to help," he responded, "except help me forget."

"And how would I do that?"

Her question was all innocence, but the idea of how she could make him forget was not lost on him. He could think of a number of wicked things he'd love to do to her right now on the beach. How he would enjoy nothing better than to strip her naked and take her in the surf, plunging deep inside her as the waves crashed around them.

"Hmm… I see your mind is in the gutter," Naomi said. "And here I was thinking we were finally getting someplace."

He frowned. "We are. And if you must know, I was upset after seeing my mother."

"Why would that upset you?"

"It's a long story, but suffice to say she and I don't see eye to eye. Never have, and that's never gonna change."

Naomi reached out and touched his bare arm. A spark of electricity jolted straight through him, and he turned to her. Her eyes lowered, and he was sure she'd felt it, but he didn't act on it. Instead, he continued. "I wish I had a family like yours, Naomi. You're close and actually enjoy spending time with each other."

"Yes. We do. I don't know what I'd do without them. They're my support system."

"You're lucky. Not all of us get to have that."

"Wait a second, what about your grandmother? I thought I read somewhere that she's been a big part of your life."

Lucius smiled when he turned to Naomi. So she'd been reading up about him. It gave him hope that Naomi was more interested than she let on. "Yes, she is, but it's not the same as having a mother and father who love you. Siblings. God—" he shook his head "—I remember being a little kid and wishing I had a brother or sister. Someone I could talk to or lean on, but there was no one except Grandma Ruby. And don't get me wrong, she did her best and I'm glad I had her, but there's always been something missing, you know?"

Naomi nodded in understanding.

Lucius was surprised at how much he'd shared with her. He usually kept his feelings and thoughts closer to the vest, but with Naomi, he could open up. Be himself.

"I'm sorry, Lucius. It must have been awfully lonely for you."

"It was, but I made do. And eventually I made friends with Adam."

"Your attorney. The one who contacted Kelsey?"

Lucius nodded, chuckling softly. "Adam is my man. There is no one I trust more than him."

"And what about your father?" Naomi inquired. "The article never mentioned him."

Lucius stood up straight. "I don't have one."

"What do you mean? Everyone has a father."

"I don't."

"Then you've missed out," Naomi said, "but you don't have to anymore. You should come with me to Sunday dinner. You could meet my parents and siblings. See what it's like to be part of a real family."

Why the hell had she just invited him to her parents' for dinner? The words were already out of her mouth and Lucius was staring back at her dumbfounded before she could take them back. The invitation was pure impulse, but her reaction to hearing his story wasn't. She felt for the little kid who'd grown up essentially an orphan without either of his parents. Naomi wanted to show him that there was more to life than the hand he'd been dealt.

Of course, the way he was looking at her was giving her serious reservations about the hastiness of her invitation.

Eventually, however, Lucius spoke. "Come to your parents' with *you*?"

Naomi nodded. All of sudden her throat felt parched, and she felt like she was dying of thirst. She always had this reaction around Lucius, especially when he looked at her. Except this time, there was something different than the lust she usually saw—there was something akin to gratitude.

"Thank you, I think I might like that."

"You would?"

A grin spread across his gorgeous, sinful lips. "Yeah, does that surprise you?"

"Actually, yes. Lucius Knight at a family dinner."

He shrugged. "Well, it's as you've said. I've never been a family man."

"Well, perhaps it's time you tried it on for size."

And Lucius was willing to do just that, especially if Naomi was included in the package. The more time he spent with her, the more he knew that she was something special. She was single-handedly starting to renew his faith in human kindness and compassion. Something he'd long since forgotten.

"Well, we've made it to my car," Naomi said several seconds later when they arrived in the nearly deserted parking lot. Lucius rolled down his trousers and put on his shoes. Naomi did the same, pushing down her capris and donning the flats she'd been carrying.

She unlocked her car door with her keyless entry. "Thanks a—"

Naomi never got another syllable out, because Lucius covered the ground between them in a split second and scooped the lower half of her against him and then crashed his mouth down on hers. He'd wanted to kiss her from the moment he'd seen her on the beach, but he'd reined in his desire for her.

But now, before she left, he wanted to taste her. Tilting her head for better access, he plundered her mouth like he'd never done with any other woman. He wanted this to be better than any kiss she'd ever had from another man.

He tantalized and tasted her with gentle strokes of his lips. His tongue glided across hers, exciting them both until she moved her hands to his shoulders. She slid her arms around his neck and held his head to hers. And when he seductively, expertly, slid his tongue between her lips, she responded with provocative probes of her own. The way she was responding to him was wildly exhilarating.

He pressed farther into her, backing her up against the car so she could feel the hard evidence of his arousal. Naomi moaned, ramping up the fierce passion surging through him. Lucius meshed their mouths together, driving for more pleasure.

His heart was pounding loudly in his chest. He was so

damn hot for her. He didn't care that he was damn near sexing her on the street. He just wanted more. He clutched her bottom, grinding her even closer, and that's when he felt her nipples rake against his chest. If he didn't stop himself, she would goad him into losing control. What was she doing to him? She was like a drug that he just had to have a hit of.

It took effort, but Lucius pulled back, breaking their kiss. When he did, they both sucked in air, but he didn't let her go. He liked having Naomi against him. He stared down into her eyes—they were wild and dilated. "I want you, Naomi, but it can't be here. It can't be now."

They were in plain view of anyone walking by, and he was sure they'd already given the odd passerby quite a show.

Slowly, he shifted, loosening his grasp, and opened the driver's side door. He tucked Naomi inside. "But we will be together soon," he whispered. "You can count on it."

"He said, you'll be together soon and that you could count on it?" Kelsey asked as Naomi laid out her mat at her Lamaze class several days later at Long Beach Memorial, where Kelsey would be having her baby.

Naomi had agreed to be a fill-in for Kelsey's husband, Owen, who'd had to leave unexpectedly on a business trip. Naomi had to admit that she was thrilled for some time with her best friend. With their busy schedules and Kelsey working from home, sometimes it was hard to link up.

"Yes," Naomi answered.

"And when was this again?"

"A few days ago," Naomi said, offering Kelsey her hand so she could help her onto the mat, "when we ran into each other on the beach."

"Are you sure that was just a coincidence?" Kelsey inquired, accepting her hand. "I mean, he did follow you to Anaheim for the conference."

"That isn't what happened."

Kelsey's brow rose. "No? First we get an offer from Knight International and then suddenly you run into him at a natural products expo?"

"I suppose you're right, but the beach was different. He was visibly upset and genuinely shocked to see me. He'd just had a run-in with his mother that I gathered didn't go well."

"A man at odds with his family? That isn't good," Kelsey replied.

"It's not like that," Naomi defended Lucius. "His mother has been MIA since he was born and from the little bit I've gathered, he doesn't have a father. You should feel compassion for him."

"I don't need to. You're doing enough of that for the both of us, Naomi. You always did have a soft heart. And I fear that Lucius is playing right into it."

"I disagree. And even if I did, it doesn't matter now, because I invited him to my parents' for dinner."

"You did what?"

The Lamaze instructor clapped her hands. "Class, is everyone ready to begin?"

"I invited him to dinner," Naomi whispered in Kelsey's ear as the class began. "To let him see a real family in action."

An hour later, as Naomi rolled up the mat, Kelsey picked the conversation back up.

"This is a bad idea, Naomi," Kelsey said once she was on her feet, "letting this man into your life. You know little to nothing about him and suddenly he's meeting your parents?"

"Kelsey, I'm not introducing him as my man or anything. Why are you getting so bent out of shape?"

"When was the last time you introduced your parents to the man in your life?"

Naomi rolled her eyes upward. When was the last time? She couldn't remember.

"That's right. Do the math, Naomi. You've never invited a man to meet your family, now suddenly you've invited Lucius Knight? I don't think you're being completely honest with yourself or me. I think you feel more for this man than you're letting on. And I'm just afraid for you, darling. You wear your heart on your sleeve, and Lucius is just the kind of rotten scoundrel to stomp all over it."

Was Kelsey right? Her feelings for Lucius had grown exponentially since seeing him again a couple of weeks ago. And the attraction between with them hadn't cooled. In fact, it had gotten stronger, more potent and more palpable. Sitting at work, all she had to do was think of Lucius or his kisses and her blood pressure would skyrocket. Was she going down a rabbit hole? *Would* Lucius stomp all over her heart?

"So what's going on with your quest to obtain Brooks and Johnson?" Adam asked Lucius when they met up for drinks the next day at a gentleman's club. Lucius had been busy working on another takeover project and hadn't had time to catch up with Adam, though he'd left several messages. "You haven't mentioned it in days. I thought you wanted the company."

"I do." Lucius loosened his tie. After wearing a suit for a long day at the office, he was ready to relax. His jacket was already slung over the back of his chair. "But as you know, Naomi isn't interested in selling."

"But there's always her partner, Kelsey."

"And how has that been coming?"

"Slowly," Adam replied. "I've spoken with her once and since then she's given me the cold shoulder. Said she was too busy to get back to me."

Lucius leaned back in his chair and regarded his friend. "I suspect Naomi is the reason for Kelsey's lack of interest. I'm sure she's pitching to her that selling would not be in the best interest of their company."

Adam reached for his glass of bourbon. "But our offer is more than generous. Kelsey would be a fool to turn it down."

"You haven't met Naomi. I've never met a more stubborn woman in my entire life. She's infuriating and opinionated and tenacious…" He stopped speaking when he noticed that Adam was staring at him strangely. "What?"

Adam shrugged. "Sounds like you're pretty hung up on the woman all of a sudden."

Lucius laughed and attempted to make light of the situation. "No, what I want to do is put her over my knee and spank her." An image of Naomi lying over his thigh with her bottom facing him sprang into his mind. He'd love nothing better than to give that delicious little bottom of hers a spank before he…

"Lucius!"

He blinked. "What?"

Adam shook his head while an amused grin spread across his lips. "You've got it bad, dude."

"For Naomi?" Lucius sipped his scotch neat. "You couldn't be more wrong. What I do have is a little bit of sexual frustration, and once it's released, I'll be right as rain."

"Sure," Adam responded. "If you think that's all it is."

Of course that's all it is, Lucius thought. Despite his sexual attraction toward Naomi, he didn't want or need any romantic complications. Naomi was the type of woman that a man got serious about and married. Lucius was not the marrying kind. And never would be. He needed to focus on his two objectives. One was getting his hands on Brooks and Johnson. The second was getting Naomi in his bed, and the dinner with her family was his ticket in.

Chapter 8

Naomi was nervous as she waited for Lucius to come pick her up at her home in Belmont Heights. Why hadn't she asked him to meet her at her parents' instead of picking her up? Now he not only would know where she lived—though he probably already had a file on her—but this was starting to look a lot like a date. She hadn't had one of those in God knew how long. Brooks and Johnson's rapid growth had caused Naomi to put her love life on the shelf.

She'd focused on building her brand rather than making any lasting connections with men. And it had cost her. At thirty-two, she'd only had one or two serious relationships, and dating had been nonexistent the last couple of years. She'd envied Kelsey. Her friend had always made time for romance and subsequently had met and fallen in love with her husband, Owen, five years ago. Now Naomi was all alone and forced to face the dating scene solo. And since she'd always been awkward around men, the thought of going out clubbing or online dating hadn't appealed to her. Which would explain why she was so nervous. She was about to spend the evening with Lucius Knight. He was not only her high school crush and the first boy she'd ever wanted, but he also happened to be one of the sexiest men alive, in her opinion.

She knew she shouldn't, but Naomi couldn't help herself and dressed with Lucius in mind. She wanted him to see her as desirable. She'd taken care by spiral rodding her natural curls so they now hung in ringlets to her shoulders. And she'd dressed in a fuchsia maxi skirt with a button-down denim shirt and extra-wide belt that showed off her curves. Naomi fully expected Lucius to be shocked when he saw her.

She was right.

Lucius stared at Naomi when she opened the door to her home. He hadn't known exactly what the appropriate attire for an evening with her family would be and hoped that his casual approach of dark jeans, plaid shirt and cable-knit V-neck sweater was the right look. He'd been right, because she was wearing a high-waisted maxi skirt that showed off her amazing slender waist and hugged her hips. He liked that the denim shirt was open just enough to allow her gold necklace to dangle between her breasts and show him a slight swell of cleavage.

Lucius swallowed. How was he supposed to keep his hands to himself when she dressed like that?

"I'm ready," Naomi stated with her hobo bag over her shoulder and a light jacket in her hand. Before he could take a step inside her home, she closed the door behind her.

He smiled. If that was how she wanted to play it, that was fine, but Lucius knew that before the night was over, he would be coming inside, and not just in her home.

"Great, let's go." He gently placed his hand at the small of her back and led her to his Bentley parked outside on the curb, but not before whispering in her ear, "By the way, you look gorgeous."

She glanced up at him. "Thank you."

After helping her inside, he came around to the driver's side and hopped in. "You lead the way," he said as he started the engine.

They chatted easily on the twenty-minute ride to her parents' home. Naomi told him about their history. "You'll love them. They've been married for thirty-five years and are as still in love as they were when they first met."

"That's pretty amazing considering the divorce rate," Lucius responded.

"I know, right?" Naomi gave him a sideways glance. "Trust me, I know how lucky I am to have my parents together after all these years."

"And you have a brother, Tim, and sister, Gemma, right?"

She smiled when she looked at him again. "You remembered."

"I do listen," Lucius said, "it's a must in business."

"And is that what tonight is?" Naomi asked, a frown quickly spreading across her mouth. "Because I didn't ask you here on business. I asked you as a friend."

"Duly noted," Lucius replied. "And I am here as your *friend*." He emphasized the word even though he didn't want to be her friend. He wanted to be her lover. "I've put business on the shelf tonight."

"Glad to hear it."

They parked in front of her father's Mercedes-Benz several minutes later and exited the vehicle. Lucius grabbed the rare bottle of wine he'd obtained from the gourmet store for dinner along with a bouquet of calla lilies for Naomi's mother.

"You didn't have to do that," Naomi said when he met her at the front door just as she was opening it.

"I know, but my grandma Ruby did raise me with some manners," he answered with a smile.

"Naomi!" A beautiful petite woman with a caramel complexion and dressed in a wraparound print dress met them in foyer. She had Naomi's exact same riotous curls.

"Mom!"

Lucius watched Naomi bend down to lean into her mother's embrace and felt his heart constrict. He and Jocelyn never hugged. They barely touched.

"And you must be Lucius," her mother said, and before he could answer she enveloped him in a warm, motherly hug. Surprise must have been evident on his face, because he noticed Naomi mouth *it's okay*, so he hugged her back.

"Thank you for having me, ma'am," Lucius responded when they parted. "I brought you some flowers and wine." He presented her with the bouquet and bottle of rare wine.

Mrs. Brooks beamed with pleasure. "You shouldn't have, but thank you. They're lovely. Come on inside." She slid her arm through his and led him into the home. "So you can meet the rest of the family."

Five minutes later, Lucius had been introduced to the entire Brooks family. Her father, Benjamin, was a big bear of a man with a grip to match. Her brother, Tim, who although not as muscular as his father was just as tall as Lucius, eyed him suspiciously. Tim's wife, Audrey, was a quiet, unassuming woman who suited him to perfection. And they had a precocious four-year-old daughter, Grace, who wanted to be the center of attention. Then there was Naomi's sister, Gemma. She was sassy and just as fiery as Naomi, if not more. She wasted no time firing questions at him. He liked them all immediately.

"So, Lucius," Gemma asked when they all sat in the living room, "do you remember going to high school with my sister?"

Lucius sat beside Naomi on the love seat while her father sat in a recliner, her mother stood passing around appetizers and refreshments before dinner, while her brother and his wife sat opposite them on the sofa.

He felt Naomi tense at her sister's question, but he patted her knee lightly. "Actually, I do," he said with a smile. "I remember Naomi was a bit shy."

"Shy?" Gemma laughed out loud. "She was more like a nerd!"

"Gemma!" Her mother wagged her finger at her. "That's not nice."

"Sorry, Mom." Gemma acted like she was remorseful, but Lucius highly doubted it. As the youngest, he suspected Gemma was used to being coddled instead of being given the discipline she so desperately needed. The Brooks family wasn't perfect, but that's what made them real. "But you know it's true," she continued. "Back then, all Naomi did was have her head in a book."

"Unlike you?" Naomi responded. "Who was always into cheerleading and boys."

"Hey, don't hate me because I was popular," Gemma replied with a smirk.

"And were you popular, too?" Her brother directed a question to Lucius.

"Not at all." Lucius slid his arm along the back of the love seat behind Naomi. It was a casual move, but told Tim man-to-man that his interest in his sister was of a romantic nature. He saw Naomi's eyes widen, but she didn't say anything.

"Afraid not," he finally answered. "Like Naomi, I was more of an outcast."

"A bad boy, if the papers tell it correctly," Timothy responded.

Lucius shrugged. "Bad boy, outcast. Does it really matter now?"

"Not at all," Mr. Brooks stated from his recliner, "only matters what a man makes of himself when the dust settles. And from the looks of it, you haven't done too bad for yourself, Lucius."

"No, sir. I've done quite well."

"Dinner is ready," Mrs. Brooks said when she reentered the room. Lucius hadn't even seen her leave. He'd been so engrossed in the family dynamics. Was this what it was like being part of a family? If so, he could get used to this.

Naomi smiled as she watched Lucius interact with her family. He was a natural and fit right in. He was charming to her mother. Forthright to her father. And accommodating to Tim, who pulled no punches in his direct questioning of Lucius.

Her brother had drilled Lucius, wanting to know how he'd gotten his start, when he created Knight International and more. Naomi was just glad that Tim had heeded her earlier call when she'd begged him not to bring business or Lucius's interest in Brooks and Johnson into the conversation. Her father also wasn't stopping. He made sure to question Lucius about his background. That's when she felt Lucius's mood change.

"So tell us about your family?" her father asked. "Your mother and father, what do they do?"

"Dad," Naomi interjected. "You remember I told you that Lucius was raised by his grandmother." She glanced to her side and saw the firm set of Lucius's jaw.

"Oh, of course, I'm sorry, son," her father replied. "I didn't mean anything by it."

"No offense taken," Lucius responded. "My background

is no secret. My father wasn't around, and my mother chose not to raise me. Lucky for me, my grandma stepped in."

Naomi noticed he plastered a fake smile on, but she knew otherwise. This topic of conversation made Lucius uneasy.

"Do you even know your father?" Gemma asked from the other end of the table.

Naomi choked on the water she'd been sipping and her brother had to pat her on the back. She shot Gemma a cold look as she wiped her mouth and watched Lucius warily. His eyes were impenetrable and she couldn't fathom what was going on in his mind.

"No, I do not." He was to the point and it was stated with such finality that even Gemma busied herself with refilling her wineglass.

"Well, how about some dessert?" her mother asked.

Bless her heart. Naomi couldn't have been more thankful for the distraction and change of the conversation. The set of Lucius's mouth was grim, and the smile that had been on his face throughout the course of the evening had faded. In its place was a sullen and withdrawn man. A man who reminded her of the teenage boy she'd once fallen for.

Dessert continued with Naomi and her mother doing their best to revive the conversation. Lucius made polite chitchat and was never rude in any way, but Naomi could tell that the earlier conversation had rattled him.

After the meal, she and Lucius said their goodbyes as her family walked them to the door. Her father shook Lucius's hand while her mother once again enveloped him in a hug. As he bent down to accept it, Naomi could see Lucius warm up slightly at the contact.

"Thank you both for having me over," Lucius said once they'd parted. "I truly appreciate the hospitality."

"You're welcome any time, son," her father said, placing

his arm around her mother. Then he turned to Naomi. "So feel free to bring this young man around again."

Naomi smiled. Then she stood on her tiptoes to give her father a kiss on the cheek. "Thanks, Daddy."

Lucius opened the front door and once again placed his hand on the small of her back and led her outside.

Naomi shivered slightly. The air had turned crisp. Lucius wrapped his arm around her as he walked her to the car. Once inside, she glanced up and saw her parents peeking at them through the curtains. She smiled and shook her head as Lucius hopped inside.

They were quiet on the drive back to Belmont Heights. She knew he didn't like talking about himself and family was a sore spot for him, but she wished she knew more and why he was closed up about that side of himself. Transparency was not his strong suit. Whereas she wore her heart on her sleeve.

When they made it to her house and he turned off the engine, Naomi turned to him. "Did you have fun tonight?"

Lucius slid around to face her in his seat. "I did. You have a really great family."

Naomi stared at him questioningly. "Are you sure about that?"

His brow furrowed. "Why would you ask that?"

"Because... I think you were having a good time until my sister asked you about your father. After that, well, let's just say you were a cold fish."

He grinned. "A cold fish?"

"Yes, and don't go grinning like that," Naomi said, pointing her finger at him, "and trying to be all charming now. Where was this guy an hour ago? I want to know where he went and why."

"If you let me inside, perhaps I'll tell you why," he countered. His steady gaze bored into her.

There was a maddening arrogance to him that drove Naomi crazy. She hated that when he looked at her she was powerless to resist him. If she let him in, Naomi knew what it meant, and it caused her heart to jolt and her pulse to pound. There was no denying that alone in her house with no distractions, no interruptions, she would give in to her attraction to Lucius. She'd been trying to fight it for weeks. What would happen if she unlocked her heart, her soul, her body to this man? Should she chance it? She'd always wanted this man, wanted to know what it would be like to be with him. What was wrong with allowing herself this one night of pleasure with her heart's desire?

She knew her answer and spoke quickly before she changed her mind. "Come inside."

Lucius felt triumphant when he walked through the doors of Naomi's home. It had been no easy feat getting Naomi to let go, but she finally had. However, there was a catch. He would have to open up and bare part of his soul to her in exchange.

He rarely spoke of his feelings about his family or lack thereof to anyone. What he'd told her before was more than he'd told any of his former companions—and yet she still wanted more and he would give it to her. What did that mean? Was she becoming more to him than just a means to an end?

He looked up from the sofa where he'd made himself comfortable while Naomi busied herself in the kitchen with refreshments. Did she need liquid courage to be with him? Or was it for him so he would feel more comfortable talking about his past?

He liked Naomi's house. It was warm and inviting, like the woman herself. He liked the outside with the covered front porch, travertine stone walkways, landscaped planters and mature palm trees. The inside was just as appealing as the exterior, with hardwood and ceramic tile floors in the front of the house. The living room had a built-in wet bar and etched French doors that led to a large balcony, which he was sure had gorgeous sunset views.

He turned around when he heard footsteps. Naomi returned with a tray holding a bottle of cabernet sauvignon, two wineglasses and an opener. She set the tray down on the unusual cocktail table that was made of treated wood and sat on the sofa.

"Would you mind uncorking?" She handed him the wine opener.

"Not at all." He uncorked the bottle and poured them both glasses. He handed her one and held up his glass. "To new beginnings."

"Is that what this is?" Naomi asked. Her eyes were unreadable.

"I hope so." He placed his glass on the table and turned to face her. "You asked me in, so it's a start."

She leaned back against the sofa cushions. "I did. So why don't we start with why you got so standoffish after my sister's inquiry."

So they were jumping right into the deep end? No preamble. He sighed. "All right, I suppose I was a little guarded."

"Yes, why is that, Lucius?" She sipped her wine. "The other day you mentioned your relationship with your mother isn't good."

There was no judgment in her eyes, just questions. So he answered honestly. "Because it's a sore subject for me. Family, that is. I don't like talking about my lack of one."

"Because you don't know your father?" Naomi pressed, "Lots of kids today are growing up without their father around."

Lucius chuckled. "So are you telling me to get over myself?

"Not at all, I'm just saying that fatherless black children are no longer the exception, but the rule. While I'm the exception, having both my parents together."

"Your family is truly exceptional," Lucius stated. "I really enjoyed them tonight."

"Thank you, but don't try to deflect the conversation. You're not getting off that easy."

He smirked. "I didn't think I would. The thing is, Naomi, I'm angry. I'm angry because I've been denied the right to know my father."

Naomi blinked with bafflement. "I don't understand."

"When I say I don't know my father, I'm not saying I don't have a relationship with him," Lucius replied. "I mean I don't know *who* he is. My mother refuses to tell me."

"Has she told you why?"

He shook his head. "Not in so many words, but I suspect that he's married."

"That's awful."

"And no matter how much I beg and plead, it falls on deaf ears. She won't give up his identity. Last week, when you found me on the beach, I'd just come from seeing her. You see, she comes for a visit every now and then to ease her conscience that she isn't a terrible person and mother. And every time I ask her who my father is, she denies me."

He could see tears well in Naomi's eyes and knew she felt sorry for him. Lucius hated pity, but since he was going into the deep end of the ocean, he might as well go all in. "All my life, I've looked in the crowd, wondering if that man or that man—" he pointed in the air "—could be my father. You have no idea how demoralizing it is. I know I'm someone's bastard, but whose?"

Naomi quickly rose, set her wineglass on the cocktail table and scooted closer to him. "Don't say that, Lucius." She grabbed his chin in one hand. "You're nobody's bastard."

When she let him go, he continued, "I know that here—" he pointed to his head "—but not here." He pointed to his chest. "Why shouldn't I feel this way?" He could feel tears biting the backs of his eyes, but he never cried. "So if I'm guarded or have walls up when it comes to this subject, that's why. And tonight, seeing your family and how much you guys love each other and show affection, it—it touched me." His voice broke as he placed his hand over his heart.

Naomi reached for him then, pulling him into her arms. She squeezed him hard, letting him know that it was all right to feel the emotions he was feeling. Lucius didn't realize just how much he'd needed to say the words and let out emotions he'd carried inside for years, to share his burden with someone else. What was it about Naomi that caused him to be so open? Was it that he'd finally found someone with depth, something he'd avoided his entire life?

Lucius didn't know why. All he knew was that her hug felt good, and he held on tighter, breathing in her feminine scent. He buried his head in her neck and inhaled deeply. She smelled so good, so sweet. He liked having her against him, feeling her nipples against his chest. If someone asked him later when her embrace turned from comfort to something else, he couldn't tell them, but it did. He pulled away from Naomi and his eyes raked her boldly seconds before they reached for each other and began kissing passionately.

Chapter 9

Naomi had to have this man. She'd imagined this moment in her teenage fantasies but never thought it would actually come true, but even her dreams were not as perfect as this moment. She swayed in his arms and they fell backward onto the couch. She knew how wrong this could turn out for her. What if he was just interested in her business and not her? The way he kissed her told her he felt *something* for her, even if it was just lust. A wild tingling formed in her breasts and her nipples had turned to bullets.

When he pulled away and rose from the couch, Naomi thought he might be having second thoughts, but instead, he scooped her up in his arms and started down the hall. "Bedroom?"

"Door on the left," Naomi murmured as Lucius's lips swept over hers again.

When she glanced up, she was in her room and Lucius was laying her down on her king-size bed. She'd always loved how large and sumptuous it was, and now she would have someone to share it with.

She watched Lucius toe off his shoes and shed his cable-knit sweater and plaid shirt until he was standing in front of her in dark jeans slung low on his hips. Naomi drank him in. He was sexy as hell and had a physique to go with it. His chest was broad and hairless, letting her know he kept up with his manscaping. His pectorals and abs were equally impressive. She couldn't wait to see what the rest of him looked like.

Lucius was so male that it stirred every female sensation within her. She could feel her toes curl in anticipation of what was to come. With openmouthed awe, she watched him unzip and remove his jeans until he was in nothing but his boxer briefs. His erection was straining against the fabric, and her mouth watered.

He stepped forward and joined her on the bed, his weight lowering the mattress. "Did you like what you saw?"

Naomi smiled. "I loved every minute of the striptease."

"Good," Lucius murmured huskily. "Because it's your turn."

Naomi's heart fluttered in her chest. She knew she had a nice body, but she wasn't used to being on display. She tried to sit up, but Lucius lightly pushed backward.

"Oh, no." He wagged his finger. "I intend to unwrap this gift, one delicious moment at a time, but first..."

She could think of nothing else because Lucius's mouth covered hers and demanded a response. His tongue dived inside her mouth, swirling around hers in a delicious duel that Naomi wanted to lose. Feeling his warm skin against hers made her suck on his tongue voraciously, devouring him as his hands roamed up and down her body. His muscles were so hard and it fascinated her, she couldn't wait to explore him with her fingers, but Lucius was in control.

There wasn't an inch of her he didn't touch. His hands outlined the swell of her breasts, her hips and the curve of her bottom. He pulled her closer into his manhood, and

Naomi moaned. She wanted him desperately, more than she'd ever wanted another man. As if sensing her urgency, he unbuckled her wide belt and tossed it aside. Then his hands were at the waist of her maxi skirt, sliding it down her hips ever so slowly. He stopped kissing her long enough to ease the skirt off and let it fall to the floor.

He looked down at her, his hard, muscular forearms on either side of her. "I can't wait to see more of you." He reached for the buttons of her denim shirt, and Naomi felt cool air as Lucius opened the shirt to his openly admiring gaze. His fingers played with the latch of her front-closure bra until the snap unlocked and her breasts spilled out.

Lucius's eyes darkened. "You're beautiful," he said. "I have to taste you." He lowered his head and feasted on her brown globes and chocolate nipples. He took one nipple in his mouth and rolled his tongue across the sensitive tip. Naomi squirmed underneath him. Heat whooshed at the apex of her thighs as if driven by some primal instinct of being with this man.

She cupped the back of his head as he continued nibbling gently. She didn't want him to stop. And she needn't have worried, because he kept his attention on the task at hand, which was sampling her other breast. Lucius seemed intent on exploring every inch of her body with leisurely strokes of his tongue. All she had to do was lie back and enjoy it.

Naomi Brooks was a feast for any man, Lucius thought. Soft curves, ample breasts, long legs and a flat stomach. She was every man's fantasy, and he couldn't wait to take her, but he would do so slowly, reverently, because he'd waited long enough to have this woman. Taking a woman to bed usually came easily for him, but Naomi was different. She'd made him work for the privilege of being with her, and he respected her for it, which made him want her all the more.

Lucius lifted his head and looked into her passion-glazed brown eyes. Naomi was expressive and showed him she enjoyed everything he was doing.

"I-is something wrong?" she asked softly.

"Not at all. I'm just enjoying the view." Lucius's hand roamed from her breasts down her rib cage to her stomach and lower to her panties. He hooked his hand around the band and slid them down her thighs until she was completely naked. She wasn't embarrassed—not when he stared at her with open admiration. Lucius allowed himself to stroke her hips, then her thighs, until he came to the heat of her. He rested his hand there for a moment and felt Naomi tremble beneath his touch. How much more would she when his tongue and fingers were buried inside her?

He had to find out.

His thumb caressed her softly, playing with the soft folds of her womanhood. He licked his lips when he found she was wet for him. He lowered his head to lick and suck on her breast whilst he slid one long finger inside her. She was hot and tight. Damn.

"Oh!" she cried out.

His body thickened, tightening in painful response, but he had to wait. He wanted her ready for him. He tormented her with his hand as his mouth swept a trail of hot kisses down her abdomen to arrow in on the dark springy curls at the entrance to the intimate part of her. He could smell her womanly scent. It was heady for any man, and he was no different. He dipped his tongue into the soft folds of her sex, intent on driving Naomi to a fever pitch. He exulted in tasting all of her sweet wetness. He grasped her bottom so he could stroke her over and over with his tongue.

Naomi's moans were letting him know that tension was

building up inside her. She clutched at his shoulders and tried to tug his body over hers, but he didn't oblige, not yet. He wanted to send her over the edge and only then would he join her on the ride. His tongue darted farther inside her until he reached to the hilt, and Naomi screamed.

"Lucius!" Her hips bucked and her back arched off the bed.

He licked all her slick juices as her orgasm hit her full force. When he lifted his head, he saw the glaze in her eyes and smiled. He slid off the bed long enough to find the condom packets he'd thrown in his pocket. He'd been sure that tonight was the night he'd make Naomi his, and he'd been right.

As he rejoined her on the bed after protecting them, she whispered, "I need you inside me."

"I'm happy to oblige," Lucius said, using his weight to push her legs apart. He'd been aching for her and now he would find out just how good she felt. Lucius surged into her slick passage. The fusion of their two bodies together caused a torrent of sensations to explode through him. He wasn't prepared for it, and being with her would cause him to lose every vestige of control.

Naomi reached for Lucius, circling her arms around his neck, and he dropped his head so he could ravish her with his mouth. She'd just had a soul-shattering climax that had ripped through her body, but there was more waiting. She wanted all of Lucius and locked her legs around him, taking him deeper to the very edge of her. She clamped around him and moaned at the intense satisfaction of having Lucius buried inside her. Her hands slid up and down his back clamoring for the sensations that were electrifying her each time Lucius thrust into her.

Both were eager and impatient to go over the edge to

complete and utter satiation. They moved together in unison, rocking their hips. A storm was brewing and they rode it, hurtling over and over at a breakneck speed as if their very lives hung in the balance of this one moment. Lucius quickened his pace, and Naomi could feel her body tighten, her inner muscles flex. And when he thrust inside her one last time, they both reached the peak and shattered violently, sending them both flying over the precipice.

Naomi's arms dropped from his shoulders and flopped onto the mattress. She was amazed. Sex had never been this good. She'd never known it could be this way, but Lucius had brought out something in her she hadn't known existed. No matter what happened between them, she would always be grateful for that. She was a sexual woman and now she knew it.

"Look who's grinning like a Cheshire cat," Lucius commented as he propped on one elbow and looked down at her. He wondered what she was thinking, feeling. It appeared she was happily satisfied with tonight's outcome and that she didn't regret her decision to be with him.

Her mouth quirked. "I'm not the only one. You seem pretty smug yourself."

He grinned. "Mmm…that was very good." Their lovemaking had been a fantastic journey—her response to him and how it made him feel had been a cataclysmic moment. They'd both free-fallen on a sweet cloud of ecstasy. And now they were in a relaxed embrace, with his other arm holding her against him.

He usually wasn't the cuddling type, but he was tonight. Maybe it was the sweet scent of her skin or her wispy damp curls that he twirled between his fingers or the rise and fall of her breasts. Whatever it was, he liked it and he didn't want to leave. Plus, he hadn't nearly had his fill of

Naomi. He'd been driven by a need to take Naomi, to possess her. And he had. He couldn't explain the animal instinct that had taken over him, but the chemistry between them went deep. He wouldn't be satisfied until he'd fully explored it and Naomi.

The next morning, Naomi was exhausted, but satiated because she'd been woken up twice by Lucius during the night to slow, erotic caresses, which instantly stimulated her all over. The first time together had been epic because they'd been frenzied, wanting to rip each other's clothes off and come together. In the wee hours of the morning, he'd lingered, touching every curve, making Naomi exultant in her womanliness. Then they'd both begun an exploration of each other's bodies.

She now knew every intimate detail of his muscled frame. Had even aroused him when she'd taken his shaft between her palms and heard his sharp intake of breath. She'd experimented, stroking him with light touches, then with flicks of her tongue over steel until she'd taken him into her mouth. He'd moaned her name, clutching the back of her head to help her take him even deeper. She'd loved giving him head and how it had made her feel skilled that she could arouse a man like Lucius.

He was an expert lover, and each time was more marvelous than the last. Naomi hadn't been prepared for how incredibly exciting it was to be free of her inhibitions sexually. With Lucius, she'd discovered a world of endless possibilities and heightened pleasures she hadn't known existed.

When she finally rolled over to look at him, he was still asleep. His brilliant dark eyes were closed, but his face was just as strong and handsome as ever. Naomi sighed all over again at how absolutely gorgeous this man was. He had the right amount of muscles to his well-proportioned body and loads of sex appeal. She didn't have any regrets over the amazing night she'd spent with him.

Careful not to wake him, she slid out of bed.

Lucius stretched his arms leisurely as he awoke. He hadn't expected Naomi to be all liquid heat and trembling passion in his arms, but she had been. She'd been bold and daring with him, he suspected more than she'd ever been with her previous lovers.

He'd delayed his own satisfaction several times during the night to ensure that she was completely satisfied.

"Coffee?"

Lucius blinked into focus and saw Naomi dressed in a robe and standing beside her bed—holding out an unstylish mug that looked like she'd made it. Obviously it was for him, so he sat up, pushing the pillows against the headboard, and accepted the proffered mug. "Thank you." He took a sip of the coffee. "You're up early."

"Couldn't sleep."

"That means I didn't do my job and tire you out," he said with a gleam of amusement. "Perhaps I need to try again." He placed his mug on the nightstand beside him, and before Naomi could say no, pulled her back onto the bed and into his lap.

"Lucius…" Her shock at his manhandling caused her mouth to gape open, and his tongue immediately slid inside. He kissed her slowly, confidently until he felt her sweet sigh of surrender.

He pulled at the belt that held her robe closed until it loosened and he could feast his eyes on her breasts. He reached for them, the fullness just enough for his palm, as if they were made for him and only him. Her nipples grew into buds at his touch. He liked that he had that effect on her.

He bent his head and suckled languorously on each nipple, circling the engorged tips with his tongue until they were stiff and wet. He glanced up at her and saw that her eyes were shut tight, so he licked his way down her body. He couldn't wait to come to her sex and once again make Naomi his.

"Inside me," Naomi pleaded when she felt Lucius tongue swirling into her navel. She appreciated all the foreplay. Lucius was a master at it, but she wanted him inside her.

"Shh," he soothed, reaching up to press his palm against the lower part of her stomach. "Relax, I promise to give you everything you want and more."

Didn't he know how impossible it was to be still when he was doing all kinds of wicked things to her? His tongue had found its way to her exposed sex and was now circling her core, and then she felt his fingers.

"Lucius," Naomi moaned in pleasure. He was playing her like an instrument, and it was like her body knew every melody. It was responding to him, and the sensations were exhilarating, just like being on a roller coaster ride. Her belly tightened, and her thighs quivered.

He slid away from her body until her back was flat against the mattress. Then he flipped her onto her stomach. She heard the rustle of the foil unwrapping, and then his large palm splayed across her stomach, bringing her bottom into direct contact with his thick erection. Lucius's body curved around hers as he kissed and nibbled on her neck. It was incredibly erotic and even more so when his fingers found their way inside her and began stroking her again.

Naomi sucked in a deep breath. Mercy. The man had a way with his hands.

Lucius scooped her up to place her on her knees, his hands grasped her hips and he surged into her. Holding her firmly, he began to rock back and forth, slowly at first, withdrawing slightly so as to not hurt her, brushing her curls aside so he could kiss the back of her neck. Then he would thrust in again until he was buried deep.

She could hear his heavy breathing as he pounded into her, feel his thrusts coming faster and faster. Naomi clutched at her duvet as sensation after sensation assaulted her. Pressure was building up inside her, tighter and tighter, threatening to break. She clenched her inner walls to hold him snug inside her, but it didn't work. The dam burst, and her entire body spasmed as wave after wave of pleasure engulfed her.

Lucius roared behind her and lifted her off the bed, clutching her body to him as his orgasm struck. Then they both fell forward, glued to each other in a mass of limbs. Eventually, he rolled off her and onto his back, but Naomi was spent and could only lie there with her hot face pressed against the cool pillow.

A delicious feeling of peace came over her. She was finding every aspect of this scenario and each orgasm he gave her extremely satisfying. How in the world would she ever get tired of making love to this man? But she would have to, because Lucius Knight was a no-commitment kind of guy.

Chapter 10

Naomi couldn't think, much less concentrate on anything but the torrent of sensations still assailing her body after spending yet another night with Lucius. She hadn't intended on becoming intimate with Lucius when she'd invited him to dinner at her parents' nearly two weeks ago. She'd wanted to show him what a normal family looked like. She'd had no idea how Gemma bringing up Lucius's parentage would send their relationship down a different course.

She hadn't known what to expect after spending the night with Lucius, didn't have much in the way of experience with casual relationships. She most certainly wasn't prepared that she'd see him every evening afterward, but she had. And it had been sheer and utter bliss ever since.

Lucius called her every day at work or texted her just to say hi. Or he would ask her to dinner, taking her to fine dining establishments that, although she could now afford them, she had never frequented. One Friday after work, he'd called her and told her to put on her sexiest outfit because he was taking her out dancing. She'd done as he'd asked and was happy to discover that Lucius was just as good at dancing as he was at every other task he put his mind to. His moves were smooth and assured on the dance floor, and he handled her with ease.

Naomi recalled a particularly sensual moment when he'd slid his leg between hers and gyrated his hips against hers. She blushed at the memory of the heated sensations that had flooded her body and the way he'd made love to her later that night until she begged him to ease the ache between her thighs.

Other times, they spent the night at her home, cooking dinner or ordering in and vegging out on her sofa. She was exposing him to life like a regular joe and he was onboard. To her astonishment, they enjoyed the same compelling television shows, like *The Walking Dead* and *Game of Thrones*, and laughed at badly made reality television shows.

"Are you sure you don't want to go out?" Naomi asked one evening after a week of domestication.

Lucius shook his head. "I'm enjoying this. It's a sense of normalcy I've never had before."

The last two weeks with Lucius had been nothing short of pure perfection, especially because he was an amazing lover who knew how to please her. At times fast and furious and other times soft and tender, Lucius knew how to draw out every delicious moment of their time together.

The man had put some kind of spell on her. But hadn't she always somehow known that it would be that way with him? That only *he* could unlock her sexuality unlike any other man?

Instead of going to lunch, Lucius chose to run on the treadmill at his office gym. He was hoping he would figure out what was going on with him. He'd been with Naomi nearly every night the last two weeks since the first night they'd made love except the one night when he'd had to work late. He'd thought he would be able to move on once he'd sampled Naomi's sweetness, but instead he found himself wondering what she was up to and if she was having a good day. More than that, he *wanted* to spend time with her, no matter if they were dining out, dancing or just spending time at home.

He'd never been this comfortable with a woman, so much so that he'd actually done household chores. He'd been positively baffled when she'd asked him to help her change the linen one morning.

"Lucius, do you even know how to make a bed?" she'd asked.

He'd stared at her, a vision in his white dress shirt that barely reached her thighs.

"Why should I have to?" he'd inquired. "I have a maid service."

"Didn't your grandma ever teach you?" she'd asked, stuffing a large down pillow into a pillowcase.

He'd smiled broadly. "Grandma spoiled me. I didn't have much in the way of chores except maybe taking out the trash and mowing the lawn."

"Lucky you." She bent over to tuck the fitted sheet under the mattress. "But you need to learn."

His eyes had traveled to where the shirt she wore was steadily rising up the back of her thighs. He'd abandoned all thought of making the bed and instead walked toward her and spun her around. The shirt had flown upward to her chin, revealing her bare breasts to his hungry gaze.

"Lucius—" Naomi pushed her shirt down "—what are you doing?"

"Having my way with you," he'd said and lowered his lips to hers. She'd responded to him as she always did— with complete abandon, giving her mouth over so his greedy tongue could invade it. His hands had traveled to the shirt, unbuttoning it until her breasts were free, then he'd left her mouth so he could lave one chocolate bud with the tip of his tongue. He wanted to tease her. Play with her.

Anticipation was half the fun and would only increase their appetite. And it had that night. He'd satisfied a hunger until they'd both lain spent and sweaty on the damp linen.

Lucius groaned and began running faster.

He was losing his mind over this woman. Just this morning, they'd left for work together, showing true domesticity like a normal couple. He'd never spent this much time with another woman, but Naomi tempted him to be a different man when he was with her. The weeks he'd just spent with her were pleasure filled and he couldn't believe he actually wanted more of it.

He had to be in some sort of alternate reality or universe because this wasn't him. He didn't do relationships or commitments of any kind. Women were usually invited into his circle for a limited run, but Naomi was quickly becoming a standing engagement. And one he couldn't wait to revisit every night. What did it mean?

Lucius was bewildered. Even more so, because time was winding down. Kelsey Johnson would be having her baby in a couple of months. What would that mean for him and Naomi?

Later that afternoon, Naomi put her growing feelings for Lucius aside for the meeting she had with a bank she hoped would lend her the money to buy out Kelsey's half of their shares. She'd dressed appropriately for the occasion in a business suit and pumps but was nervous as she sat across from the bank executive.

She was less so when she heard his news.

"I'm sorry, Ms. Brooks, but I'll have to turn down your

request for a loan of this size," the bank executive told her as they sat across from each other.

Naomi had been hoping against hope that given the large amount of business Brooks and Johnson was doing at their bank, they would consider loaning her the necessary funds.

"Are you absolutely certain?"

"You don't have much collateral other than your own shares in Brooks and Johnson to leverage," the balding man replied.

"But the company has gone public and I'm quite wealthy," Naomi responded. "I'll have more than enough funds to pay you back."

"True," he stated, "since the IPO, Brooks and Johnson is financially sound and flush with cash, but that could all change in a heartbeat with a down market. It's a huge risk for us. And what about you, Ms. Brooks? If you're unable to pay back the loan, you could potentially lose all your shares in the company you built. Is it really worth it?"

Naomi pondered that very question on her drive back into the office. The bank executive had a point. Was she ready to risk all her shares if B and J's success lulled or they had a bad year? She didn't know; she couldn't predict the future. But what did she do now?

As if he sensed she was thinking of him, her smartphone rang and the display indicated it was Lucius.

Naomi's heart began to flutter. Even knowing they were at odds in business, they were still very much connected physically. Her body had literally ached for his all day.

"Lucius."

"Hey, beautiful," Lucius said on the other end. "How was your day?"

Naomi thought back to her conversation with the

banker. "Not as productive as I'd hoped. No, let me correct that—it was downright disappointing."

"Is there anything I can do?"

She chuckled to herself. *Stop going after my company?* "No."

"Are you sure about that?" he asked huskily. "I have my ways."

"Then perhaps you should come over and show me."

Lucius stared down at the phone in his hand and a large grin spread across his lips. Had Naomi just propositioned him? Yes! And he was more than ready to oblige her. He'd been unable to get Naomi off his mind all day. When he should have been focusing on figures for his next acquisition, his mind wandered to how her hair looked spread out over her pillow. Or the way her eyes dilated when she came.

He licked his lips. He was getting hard just thinking about it. "When should I be over?"

"By seven p.m. And bring dinner."

"I'll see you then," Lucius said. They wouldn't need dessert, because Naomi was a dessert he intended to sample all night long.

Once he'd ended the call, he tried to return to work, but his mind was shot. He could only think of Naomi. She was consuming his thoughts. He'd been useless most of the day. He would much rather have stayed in bed with her all day until he quenched the hunger he had for this woman.

He couldn't understand the hold she had on him, but she did, and if he wasn't careful, he might lose his head. And for Lucius Knight, that simply would never do. He always knew exactly where he was going in his previous relationships and what he wanted, but not with Naomi. With her, he wanted more, always more. And lucky for them both, tonight would be no different.

Lucius arrived to Naomi's an hour later with two large paper bags with dinner. And from the looks of it, she'd had time to shower and change because she was dressed in a silk lounge set. He was aware of how the fabric clung to her hips and the low V-cut of the top showed him she wasn't wearing a bra. Her nipples were easily visible underneath.

Naomi pulled him inside. "Come in. I'm famished."

Once in the brightly lit hallway, Lucius's eyes once again zoomed to her breasts. "I hope you don't answer the door like that for everyone," he murmured huskily.

"Only for you." She took the bags from him and began walking down the hall.

Lucius had no choice but to follow her and enjoy the view of her silk pajama bottoms. The outline of her firm behind was clear and he knew she couldn't be wearing anything other than a thong. His mouth watered at the thought that his sweet Naomi was pretty much naked underneath the ensemble except for that tiny piece of fabric. He was going to have difficulty not jumping her bones before dinner.

He joined her in the kitchen and watched her from the doorway as she seamlessly pulled out wineglasses, plates and flatware and laid out the spread of pasta and salad he'd brought for them.

"I hope you don't mind, I brought a little bit of everything."

She glanced up with a smile. "It looks great and I'm starved. Care to open the wine?"

After he'd taken care of the cork, he poured them each a glass and they took it, along with their plates heaped with pasta and salad, to Naomi's adjoining dining room. They filled each other in on their days since the last time they'd seen each other nearly twelve hours ago.

It had seemed like an eternity to Lucius. He'd wanted to call her all day but hadn't wanted to appear too eager, so he'd waited until later afternoon. Had she been thinking the same?

"Care to share your disappointment from earlier?" he inquired.

Naomi shook her head. She couldn't tell him that her last hope of saving her company had fallen through. She didn't want to ruin the evening with talk of business. *What difference would it make anyway? Would it change the result?* She'd run out of options, and Lucius had the advantage.

"All right," Lucius said slowly, "if you're sure."

"I'm sure." She dug her fork and spoon into the pasta.

She was thankful when he turned the topic to an art show he'd been invited to. They began discussing art, both classic and modern. Naomi found Lucius to be well versed in not only art, but literature, too, especially when he quoted a poem to her.

"Do you always quote love sonnets to your women?"

His brows furrowed. Lucius couldn't remember ever having done it with anyone else. "No, I don't recall that I have, but you're not one of *my women*."

"Aren't I?" Naomi said with a chuckle, reaching for her wineglass.

Lucius placed his hand over hers, halting her action. "No, you're not. I don't see you that way."

"But—"

He silenced her protests with his index finger. "No *buts*." He reached for her hand and pulled her to her feet. He wasn't ready to share with Naomi exactly what his feelings were, but he could show her. "Come."

He walked her to her bedroom. His eyes were dark with intense desire that only Naomi could quench. When they made it to her bed, the depth of his attraction for her took over. They undressed quickly and Lucius went to work. He kissed every part of her, lingering in certain areas like her navel, the backs of her knees, the undersides of her thighs and finally her womanly nub that was achingly sensitive.

He touched her intimately with his tongue and gripped her hips, lifting them off the bed to bring them closer to his mouth. He pushed her over the edge of control with sweeping thrusts of his tongue at her core. Moans erupted from Naomi's throat. He loved the effect his mouth, tongue and eventually his hands had on Naomi. He wanted to pull everything from her, any resistance she had to him, and make her see that *she* was special, different from the others.

When she gripped his shoulders and held on as if her life depended on it, his tongue dived deeper, penetrating her until she splintered, screaming out his name.

"Lucius!"

He didn't stop; he continued his frenzied quest, using his tongue until she begged him to take her. "Lucius, please."

Only then did he reach for one of the condoms they kept by her bedside table and sheathe himself. Then he was back in place, straddling her hips to enter her in one smooth thrust. Her reaction was instant, and her greedy body milked him. He had no choice but to move, quicker, faster and harder.

Naomi kissed him, winding her legs around his calves, taking him deeper and gripping his buttocks as he rode her. He shuddered inside her as she moved to his rhythm.

When a maelstrom of sensations hit him, Lucius gasped aloud as a tidal wave of pure pleasure surrounded him. He let out a long shout and finally let go. Naomi joined him as her inner muscles clenched tight around him at her own release. The power of his orgasm was so strong it caught Lucius unaware, because the feeling was so foreign, so alien that he wasn't sure he understood its meaning. All he knew was that Naomi was the cause.

Chapter 11

Naomi was scared. Last night, she'd lost herself in Lucius. The feelings, the sensations he evoked when he kissed her, touched her, was buried deep inside her. When she closed her eyes and allowed herself to go there, she could still *feel* him inside her.

Naomi shuddered at the depth of her growing feelings for this man. She didn't want to name it, but she suspected she was falling in love with the tycoon.

"Ms. Brooks, Ms. Johnson is here to see you," her assistant, Sophie, said from the intercom, interrupting Naomi's thoughts.

"Send her in."

Naomi was rising to her feet when Kelsey opened the door.

"Hey, stranger. I didn't expect to see you here," Naomi said, strolling toward her best friend. "What brings you by?"

"I do work here," Kelsey said, waddling farther into the room. In the last couple of weeks her partner had blossomed. Her belly protruded in the maternity jeans and tunic she wore, and her cheeks were round and ruddy.

Naomi smiled. "Of course you do. You've just been cutting back on your hours, as you should," she added, "so I'm just surprised, that's all, and you didn't bring Bella."

"Darryl said he was having trouble replicating the sample I sent him, and I couldn't bring Bella—you know she'd be into *everything*," Kelsey responded.

"The one you cooked up in your kitchen a few weeks ago?"

"One and the same, so I thought I'd come in and lend a helping hand," Kelsey stated, rubbing her belly.

Naomi frowned. "Are you sure that's a good idea? I mean, you are in your last trimester."

"And everything is going fine," Kelsey stated. "I still have two more months to go. You and Owen need to stop worrying. I mean, I know I had a difficult pregnancy with Bella, but I've been feeling great this time around. The morning sickness was nothing like with Bella."

Naomi remembered that all too well. Kelsey had been intent on working for as long as she could until her due date, but her first pregnancy had been riddled with problems, the worst being her hyperemesis gravidarum. She'd had such a severe form of morning sickness, with constant vomiting, crippling weakness and dehydration, that she had taken a leave of absence.

"I'm glad to hear that, Kels," Naomi responded, "but you should still take it easy."

"And I will. While my mother is watching Bella, I'm going to get a couple of hours in downstairs in the lab. I just want to be sure he gets it right. I slaved on the stove a long time to get just the right scent."

Naomi released a long sigh. "Only if you're sure." She was hesitant to allow Kelsey to work at the office instead of her home, this late in her pregnancy. Her gut told her it wasn't the best decision.

"Yes, I'm sure," Kelsey tried to reassure her.

"Well, get on down to the lab before your mom starts calling you that Bella has gotten into her makeup bag again and we'll talk later." There was so much they needed to discuss, primarily her burgeoning relationship with Lucius, if she could call it that. And more.

Kelsey gave her a suspicious look. "All right. I'll stop in before I leave."

Once her door closed, Naomi trotted to her large executive chair and plopped down. Kelsey had known something was wrong and uncharacteristically decided to let the matter drop. And thank God she had. Naomi wasn't looking forward to telling Kelsey the other reason for her distress—she was no closer to raising the money to buy her out than she'd been a month ago when she'd returned from Anaheim. In that short time, her financial team had arranged for meetings with three separate banks and all of them had turned her down. Not a one of them was willing to take a risk on her.

It reminded Naomi of when she and Kelsey were first starting out and no one would loan them the money. The only difference was back then, it had been her and Kelsey against the world, but now she was alone—and she had run out of options.

"Naomi was turned down for yet another loan yesterday," Adam said when he walked into Lucius's office later that afternoon wearing the latest in designer men's suits. The look of pure glee and satisfaction in his eyes as he rubbed his hands together made Lucius feel slightly ill. And why was that? Adam was only doing what *he'd* asked. He was trying to get Lucius Brooks and Johnson.

"Is that right?" Lucius inquired as he put down his pen. "And how many does that make now?"

"Three since she first started inquiring," Adam stated as he sat in one of the two leather chairs opposite Lucius, unbuttoning his suit jacket.

Lucius nodded. Naomi failing to find the necessary funds to buy out Kelsey should have excited him, but instead he felt apprehensive. Brooks and Johnson meant everything to Naomi, and if she lost it, it would kill her.

Since when had he started to care about her feelings? Since he'd begun sleeping with her, Lucius thought to himself. Ever since they'd become lovers, Lucius was beginning to feel different about his quest to obtain Brooks and Johnson.

"What's wrong?" Adam inquired. "I thought this was what you wanted—Naomi on the run. Well, she is now. And with Kelsey's baby due in a couple of months, her back is against the wall."

"Nothing's wrong," Lucius responded, rising from his chair. "I'm just not sure that taking over Brooks and Johnson is what I want anymore."

"Since when?" Adam folded his arms across his chest. "You've been singularly focused on acquiring this company's stock for months, and *now* you're not interested? That's not the reason at all."

"Oh, no? And what's the reason?"

"Naomi. You have the hots for the woman, and it's making you soft. I don't know if you've acted on your attraction, but maybe if you did, you'd get back to having that killer instinct you've always had."

Lucius remained silent, because Adam had hit the nail on the head. An image of Naomi popped inside his mind and he could feel his member get thick. If just thinking about her caused this kind of reaction, then he was hot for her—more than that, he craved her.

"Wait a sec." Adam sat forward in the chair with his

feet planted firmly on the ground. "You've already acted on your lust for the woman, haven't you?"

"A gentleman never kisses and tells."

Adam snorted. "You don't have to tell. I know you, Lucius. And you've hit that." He stared Lucius directly in the eye. "And if I'm on the money, more than once."

Lucius swallowed hard. He hated the way Adam was talking about Naomi, like she was one of the women he usually spent time with who wanted his money, power and fame. Naomi was nothing like them. She was beautiful and sexy, yes, but she was genuine with a kind heart.

"I don't want to talk about this anymore."

"Why, because I dare to call you out on your bull?" Adam inquired. "Fine, have it your way." He rose from the chair, rebuttoning his suit jacket, and started toward the door. "The only reason I've been hell-bent on getting you Brooks and Johnson was because that's what you said you wanted. Why don't you let me know when you're ready to get back down to business, all right?"

Lucius snorted when Adam closed the door behind him. If anyone else had dared to speak to him like that, they'd have been fired on the spot, but Adam was his closest friend and the only person other than his grandma Ruby that he would allow to talk to him any kind of way.

Speaking of his grandmother, he hadn't seen her in weeks. It was time he paid her a visit. And maybe talking to her would help him put his priorities back in order and figure out why he was losing his edge where Naomi was concerned. There was no place in his life for more than a casual fling. Or at least that's what he told himself, but the harder he clung to the thought and denied what he wanted, the more his body betrayed him, as it had done just now with Adam.

Yes, he would go to talk to his grandmother and get some perspective.

* * *

"Naomi, come quick." Darryl's voice came through the intercom.

"Darryl, what is it? What's wrong?" Naomi asked when she picked up the receiver.

"It's Kelsey. She's bent over in pain. I think something is wrong," the chemist said from the other end of the line.

He never got to finish his sentence because Naomi had already dropped the phone and was racing toward the laboratory. Naomi didn't even bother with the elevator; instead she took the stairs two at a time from the fourth floor to the first. She ran down the hall to the lab, where she found Kelsey seated on a chair, hyperventilating.

"Kelsey." Naomi rushed to her side and fell to her knees. "What is it?"

Tears were streaked down Kelsey's cheeks, and her face was flushed pink. "It's the baby, Naomi. Something's wrong."

Naomi took Kelsey's hand in hers and gave it a gentle squeeze. It was cold and clammy. "It's going to be fine, okay? Did you call an ambulance?" She looked up at the chemist.

"Yes, of course. As soon as she started having contractions," he answered.

"Contractions?" Naomi's eyes grew large as she looked into Kelsey's baby blues. "Kels—are you sure?"

Kelsey shook her head. "Yes, no, I don't know. But it's just so painful." Just then another pain must have stabbed Kelsey in the abdomen, because she cried out, doubling over in pain. "Oh, my God, this can't be happening now. It's too soon, Naomi. It's too soon."

Naomi was worried. Why hadn't she gone with her instincts and sent Kelsey home when she'd arrived? And now look at her. "Breathe, baby girl. Breathe." Naomi mimicked the breathing techniques they'd practiced during Lamaze class. "C'mon, breathe with me. One. Two."

Her calmness was enough to begin to quiet Kelsey's hysteria until the ambulance arrived a few minutes later. As they placed her in the back, Kelsey held Naomi's hand tightly. "Please don't leave me."

"Of course not, sweetie," Naomi stated. "I'm with you." She joined Kelsey in the back of the ambulance as they shut the double doors. She squeezed Kelsey's hand. "I'm here for you. Right here with you."

Lucius arrived at his grandmother Ruby's house later that afternoon and found her sitting outside on her large wraparound porch, crocheting in her rocker. He'd tried unsuccessfully to move her to a nicer home in a better neighborhood, but she'd been stubborn and told him this was her home and she wasn't going anywhere.

"Lucius?" his grandmother called out to him after he'd parked and approached the house.

"Yes, it's me, Grandma." He climbed the steps of the porch and came to her side.

Ruby Turner wasn't an average grandmother and didn't sit at home waiting to get older. She walked several miles a day and had an active social life, attending church and her women's group functions. Lucius supposed that's why she'd been able to maintain her figure. At eighty-two, she was still as slender and spry as when he'd come to live with her when he was nine years old and had gotten kicked out of one too many boarding schools. She dressed in the latest fashions, thanks to the generous stipend he placed in her bank account each month. There was no way his grandma would live off Social Security benefits alone. With her smooth café au lait complexion, Ruby didn't look a day over sixty.

"You're looking beautiful as always," Lucius said just before he kissed her on the cheek.

"Oh, you charmer you." She waved her hand at him. "Come sit with me and have some sweet tea."

His grandmother's answer for everything was a jug of her famous sweet tea. He supposed it came from her having been raised in Georgia before moving out west because his grandfather worked in the shipping business.

"Sweet tea sounds great, Grandma." Lucius joined her in the adjacent rocker next to hers. He watched her pour the tea into a mason jar. "Thanks." He accepted the jar and took a sip. "Just as good as I remember."

"I'm a Georgia peach," his grandmother responded with a smile. "Of course I know how to make sweet tea. But enough about me. What brings you by in the middle of a workday?"

Lucius gave her a sideways glance. "Can't I just come by to visit my grandma?"

She threw her head back and laughed. "C'mon, Lucius. I raised you. Don't you think I know when there's something on your mind?"

He shrugged. "I suppose."

"Then out with it. I don't have all day."

Lucius laughed to himself. Of course, she didn't, his grandma stayed busy. "There's this woman."

"Of course," she murmured, "it had to be a woman."

He glared at her, but then his grandmother gave him the evil eye and he quickly corrected his look before she backhanded him. "The thing is, I've been seeing this woman. Naomi's her name."

"And?"

"And she has me twisted, Grandma," Lucius stated, leaning back in his chair. "The only reason I sought her out was because I wanted her company, but when I met her—I don't know. Something just kind of clicked. And we kind of fit together, ya know?"

"And that scares you," his grandmother finished, judging the situation rightly. "Your feelings for this woman?"

He nodded. "How did you know?"

"You've always held your emotions in check, Lucius. You have since the moment you came to live with me. Nothing and no one could get to you. You wouldn't let them. You've built walls so high and so thick, but I always knew it was just a matter of time before someone would break through the barriers you have erected around your heart."

"I don't know about all that," Lucius said. "All I'm saying is that I'm conflicted. I wanted her company and…"

"And now you might want the lady instead?"

"I dunno. Maybe. It's too soon to tell. All I know is she's causing me to feel all these emotions that I've never wanted. And I don't know what to do about them."

His grandmother eyed him suspiciously, as if she didn't believe a word that was coming out of his mouth.

"Why are you looking at me like that?"

"What are you so afraid of, Lucius?" his grandmother asked. "Of loving someone? Of being loved?"

"I love you," he returned.

"That's not the same and you know it," she said softly. "Is it because of your mama? Did she damage you that much that you can't allow yourself to be happy and to love this woman?"

Lucius's cell phone vibrated in his jacket pocket and he reached for it. It was Adam. "Yes?"

"I don't know if you're interested in this news, but I reached out to Owen Johnson to talk about the selling his wife's shares and he informed me that Kelsey was taken by ambulance to Long Beach Memorial Hospital. If ever there was a time to strike while the iron is hot, it's now. If the stress of work—"

Lucius didn't allow Adam to finish his sentence and ended the call. He rose from the rocker and started for the steps. "I'm sorry, Grandma. I have to go. It's an emergency and can't be helped."

"Wait!" She jumped from her recliner as fast as she could and rushed toward him. She grabbed both sides of his face in her small palms. "Lucius, if you're starting to fall for this woman, don't run away from it. Embrace it. You'll never know just how much joy love can bring into your life if you're not willing to allow it in."

He nodded and then bounded down the porch steps to his Bentley. He had to get to the hospital. To Naomi. She would need him.

Chapter 12

"This is all your fault," Kelsey's husband, Owen, yelled at Naomi as soon as he saw her in the hospital corridor.

Naomi was so taken aback, she could only stand there in shocked disbelief. She'd just left Kelsey's side and was stepping outside to handle some Brooks and Johnson business when Owen attacked.

"You're the reason Kelsey's in there." He pointed to the hospital room behind him.

"Listen, Owen, I know you're upset."

"Upset?" His voice rose. "I'm furious. Kelsey had no business being at the office. You and I both know that the doctor told her to take it easy with this pregnancy after her two miscarriages and difficult pregnancy with Bella, but you just couldn't let it rest, could you?" He circled around her, letting all of his anger and rage out on her.

Naomi was strong enough to take it, because she knew she'd done nothing wrong. She hadn't asked Kelsey to come to the office. In fact, she'd advised her to leave, but Kelsey had a mind of her own and was going to do what she wanted to. But Naomi wasn't about to tell Owen that—not when he was enraged.

"You had to get her all riled up when you reminisced about the past and how you both started the business. But things have changed, Naomi. It isn't just you and Kelsey against the world anymore. Kelsey is a wife. She has a family and husband and people who need her. I know that might be hard for you to understand since you've always been alone, but—"

Owen never got to finish his sentence, because Lucius stepped in between them.

"Now wait just a darn minute," Lucius said, facing the red-faced man who'd been bullying Naomi when he arrived on the maternity floor. He'd expected they'd be pulling together in a time of crisis, but instead the man was unleashing his hurt on Naomi. It wasn't fair. But she was just standing there, taking it. It made him respect her even more, because she refused to kick a man when he was down. "This isn't Naomi's fault."

"Isn't it? She's the reason my wife was in the lab because she was afraid to let go and allow Kelsey to sell her shares."

"Naomi is not responsible for Kelsey's condition. Now what you need to do is calm down and then go in there—" he pointed to the door "—and be with your wife."

Owen huffed but didn't speak another ill word to Naomi as he entered his wife's room.

Lucius pulled Naomi aside and touched her arm. "Are you okay?" He searched her eyes for a sign that Owen had upset her.

"Y-yes, I'm fine." She stared back at him. "But you, what are you doing here? How did you know?"

Lucius wasn't about to tell Naomi that Adam was speaking with the Johnsons on his behalf. "I called your office and asked for you. Sophie told me you were in the hospital."

Naomi nodded, accepting his answer. "Well, thank you for that." She glanced at the door Owen had just disappeared behind.

"Why in heaven's name were you allowing him to speak to you that way? If I hadn't gotten here when I did, he would have decimated you."

"I—I don't know…" Tears immediately formed in her eyes, and he could see her blinking them back, trying to keep them at bay, so he slid his arms around her shoulders and brought her closer to him.

"It's all right, baby," he crooned softly in her ear as he rubbed her back. "It's okay. I've got you."

Later, once she'd calmed down, Naomi sat with Lucius in the waiting room. He'd gone to the cafeteria earlier to get her some dinner, which now sat uneaten in the disposable container it came in. Naomi didn't have an appetite—not after everything that had happened.

Kelsey being rushed to the hospital and Owen unloading his anger at her. Thank God for Lucius. If he hadn't gotten there when he did, who knew what other hurtful words would have spewed from Owen's mouth. But she would never tell Kelsey what went down. Her friend was battling to keep her baby in her womb.

Naomi had never been so frightened in her entire life. Despite what Owen thought, she would never want anything to happen to the baby and Kelsey. So what, Naomi couldn't hang on to her company? Naomi wasn't that superficial. She valued her friendship, her sisterhood with Kelsey more than any company. She hoped Kelsey knew that and resolved to tell her just as soon as she could.

"It's okay," Lucius said, breaking into her thoughts. She felt his firm grip on her trembling hands.

Naomi turned to him. "Thank you for being here."

"You don't have to keep thanking me."

"Well, I'm sure this is not how you wanted to spend your evening."

"Don't presume to know what my plans were," Lucius said sharply. "I *want* to be here."

Naomi was surprised by the stern tone in his voice. He *meant* what he said, and she believed him. Did that make her a fool? Was he playing her so he could get closer to her and to Kelsey? "I won't presume," she finally responded, "and I'm sorry. It's been a long, emotionally taxing day."

"You don't have to apologize, either," Lucius said softly. "Your best friend and partner suffered a scare, but I'm positive that everything is going to be okay."

Naomi glanced down the corridor. "If I didn't know any better, I'd purposely think Owen is not updating me on Kelsey to spite me."

"I wouldn't put it past him."

"Excuse me for a moment." Naomi rose and stepped away from the waiting area. She used her smartphone to call Kelsey's mother, who was at home with Bella.

Several minutes later, she returned to the waiting area and Lucius looked up from his iPhone. "Everything okay?"

"Oh, yes." Naomi slid next to him in the low-backed chair. "Kelsey's mom told me she's doing good and the contractions have stopped."

"That's wonderful news."

Lucius didn't get a chance to continue, because Naomi saw Owen walking toward them. She inhaled sharply and steeled herself for another attack.

When he reached her, Owen said stiffly, "Against my better judgment, Kelsey has asked to see you."

Naomi jumped up and rushed out of the chair. She was nearly down the hall when she remembered Lucius and he mouthed, *go.*

Upstairs in the maternity ward, Naomi was so excited to see Kelsey, she immediately started crying tears of joy when she entered the room.

"Please don't cry," Kelsey exclaimed as Naomi rushed toward the bed to gingerly sit before pulling her friend into a hug. "I'm okay." She returned her hug.

Naomi pulled away and looked into Kelsey's blue eyes. "Are you sure? You gave us such a fright."

Kelsey nodded. "Gave you a fright? Lord, I thought Owen's head was going to explode. But I'm fine. The medication appears to be working, because the contractions have stopped."

"I'm so relieved." Naomi scooted backward onto the edge of the bed. "Owen wasn't too happy with me."

"Was he terribly dreadful?"

Naomi waved her hand dismissively. She would never say a word to Kelsey about how abominably he'd behaved. She had enough to deal with. "Nothing I couldn't handle."

Kelsey sighed. "He was just scared, Naomi, as am I. And—" She paused as if trying to find the right words, but Naomi already knew what she was going to say.

"And that's why you're going to sell your remaining shares?" Naomi finished.

Tears welled in Kelsey's eyes, and she nodded her head. "I'm so sorry, Naomi. I wanted to give you more time to raise the capital. But I can't turn down what Knight International is offering me. It is well above market value and this would secure *my* future, *my children's* futures. Please don't be upset with me."

Naomi reached for Kelsey's hand across the thin hospital blanket. "Don't worry about me, Kelsey. I'll be fine. You have to take care of you and this baby." She touched her rounded belly. "That's all that matters."

"But if I sell, Lucius will have majority interest in the company." Kelsey sniffed, wiping away her tears with the back of her hand.

Naomi patted Kelsey's thigh. "You let me worry about that."

She wouldn't belie her fears about what Lucius's take-over of her company might mean. Would she be out as CEO? Would he want to make sweeping changes? Would her staff lose their jobs? Somehow, someway, Naomi would figure it out with the man she now realized she'd fallen hopelessly in love with. She had to. Otherwise she would end up shattered because she'd let the playboy tycoon into her heart.

Chapter 13

"I heard from Kelsey Johnson," Adam told Lucius as they played basketball at the fitness center inside Knight International's offices a couple of days later. Encouraging a healthy lifestyle was important to Lucius, which was why he'd installed a state-of-the-art gym in the headquarters, complete with exercise and weight equipment, racquetball, and group fitness classes. He supported his employees' goals for living long, healthy and productive lives.

"Oh, yeah?" Lucius tried to act nonchalant as he dribbled the ball toward the basket.

Adam blocked him, so Lucius did a fake to the right before spinning around left to shoot the ball. The basketball slid easily inside. Nothing but net.

Adam ran over to rebound the ball and caught it before Lucius could get there. "She's ready to sell," he continued, "I think that hospital incident scared her and her husband. We already own 30 percent of Brooks and Johnson—with Kelsey's shares, we're poised to own 55 percent of Brooks and Johnson. You just have to tell me if you're ready to pull the trigger, but the company is yours for the taking."

Lucius took advantage of Adam's chattiness to steal the

ball from him and fast-break down the court to the other side. He rushed the net and did a quick layup.

"Son of a—" Adam yelled when he finally made it down the court, slightly out of breath.

"You snooze, you lose," Lucius laughed.

"Ha-ha," Adam responded. "You still haven't answered my question. I think your play was a way to deflect my attention away from the matter at hand."

Lucius stopped dribbling and snatched the ball up. "And what's that?"

"Your inability to make a decision where this company is concerned because of your latent feelings for its owner."

"I don't have feelings for Naomi." As soon as the words were out of his mouth, Lucius knew they were a lie. He'd been struggling for weeks with his feelings for the woman, and then the other night his protective side had come out. His instinct to protect someone close to him was usually reserved for his grandmother. Needless to say, he was confused by his actions. He'd been ready to beat Owen to a bloody pulp for hurting Naomi.

"Lie to me all you want," Adam responded, "but stop lying to yourself, man. You need to figure out how you feel about Naomi and if you want the relationship to lead somewhere."

Lucius frowned. "Lead where?"

Adam shrugged. "I don't know. To what normal people want. Marriage. Babies. A house. All that. Because, trust me, that's the type of woman Naomi is. She's not the usual woman you've dated and discarded, Lucius. She's the kind of woman you marry."

Lucius thought about Adam's words long after their basketball session ended at the gym and he was drinking a glass of scotch on the balcony of his penthouse.

Adam was right. He was torn. Torn between being the

ruthless corporate raider he'd always been and the man he was with Naomi. When he was with her, he was different, felt different. He needed more time. He had to take Adam and his grandmother's advice and figure out exactly where he stood with Naomi.

A thought sprang into his head, and he had the answer. Now he just hoped that Naomi would go along with it. If not, he would have to use persuasive measures to convince her.

Naomi felt sick to her stomach after meeting with Tim to review her finances. It was done. There was no way she would have enough capital to buy out Kelsey. She would have to leverage all the profit she'd made, wipe out nearly all her savings and mortgage her house to buy Kelsey out. If Brooks and Johnson's stock suffered or the company had any setbacks, she would feel the brunt of it as major stockholder. Was being in charge that important to her that she would risk her entire nest egg and her home?

Naomi was grappling with the question when her cell phone rang. She glanced down and saw it was Lucius.

Why did he have to call now when she was a wreck?

If she ignored the call, he would just call her personal line at the office.

She quickly reached for her phone and swiped to answer. "Hello, Lucius."

"Naomi. How are you? How's Kelsey?"

Naomi released a long sigh. So this call was about Kelsey and her shares, not about her. "I'm fine, and Kelsey's been released from the hospital and is at home resting comfortably."

"That's wonderful," Lucius responded.

"Yes, I'm relieved. Though Owen may not believe it, I only want the best for Kelsey."

"That guy is a real jerk. Although I'd like to use another word to describe him."

Naomi laughed. "I echo that sentiment. So, what's the purpose for your call?"

"Do I have to have one?" Lucius replied.

"No, I just—" Naomi sighed. Figuring out her finances was her problem; Lucius had always been honest with his intentions and his desire to buy B and J. She just wasn't sure how to handle losing controlling interest in her company to the man she was in love with. "It's just been a long day. What's up?"

"I wanted to invite you up to my cabin at Big Bear. I thought perhaps we could enjoy some skiing or perhaps a dip in the hot tub as we look at the stars. What do you say?"

Joy raced through Naomi. Lucius wanted to spend uninterrupted time with her? What did it all mean? There was only way to find out. "Yes, I would love to," she responded.

"Great!" She heard the smile in Lucius's voice at her acceptance. "If you can get off a bit early, we could leave tomorrow morning before traffic gets bad and have more of the weekend."

"Sure. I'm the boss, so I can take the day off."

When they ended the call several minutes later, Naomi was brimming with excitement. Deep down, she wanted more from Lucius, but she was too afraid to allow herself to go there. But now, they would spend the entire weekend together. Perhaps after that Naomi would know once and for all how Lucius truly felt about her and whether he wanted her, the company or both.

As Lucius drove to Naomi's house the next morning, he didn't feel an ounce of nerves. Of one thing he was certain—he enjoyed Naomi. He couldn't wait to get her underneath him and would waste no time doing so. He'd been battling his desire for her and his ambition with ensuring Knight International was a force to be reckoned with.

He was hoping the weekend would give him clarity. Show him what it was he truly wanted from Naomi. Was she just a very sexy outlet for his overzealous libido? Or was there more, as his grandmother and Adam had said? Regardless, he couldn't wait to have his way with her. And they would have the entire weekend with no interruptions, at least not on his end. He'd told Adam in no uncertain terms that he was MIA for the weekend and to call him at his own risk. It had better be something just short of a tsunami for him to disturb him. He had plans for Naomi Brooks.

When he arrived at Naomi's, she was already packed and looking hot. She was wearing a cream-colored sweater with a scarf around her neck and skinny jeans that showed off her slim but curved in all the right places figure.

"Hey, babe." He reached for Naomi, circling his arm around her waist so he could bring her closer for a kiss. She didn't pull away and instead grabbed both sides of his face and kissed him full and deep on the mouth, returning his ardor.

They pulled away several moments later. "Hi." She smiled up at him.

That's when Lucius knew it was going to be one helluva weekend.

The drive to Big Bear went smoothly since they'd gotten a jump start on traffic on 91 east and Interstate 10. During the scenic drive into the San Bernardino National Forest and passing the snowcapped mountains, Naomi regaled Lucius with tales of her family road trips, songs, mishaps and generally how much fun they'd had. It made Lucius a bit envious to hear her family stories when he had none to share of his own. He and Grandma Ruby had never vacationed. And the only time he'd traveled was the odd trip to visit his mother in whatever new villa or penthouse she was staying at abroad, none of which had ever amused Lucius. After a time, Jocelyn had stopped sending for him.

Eventually, they made it to the cabin he'd rented for the weekend.

"You call this a cabin?" Naomi asked, looking up at the house as he unloaded their bags from the trunk.

Lucius had to admit the travel agent had outdone herself. The grand driveway entrance led to an impressive log and stone chalet on top of a hill that overlooked Big Bear Lake. And this was just the outside. He couldn't wait to see what the inside looked like.

"This is more like a château. And this place is beautiful and it smells of wood smoke," Naomi commented, wiggling her nose.

"That's because I ensured they started the wood-burning fireplace for us, so we could get cozy and out of this cold."

Naomi shivered. "It is pretty chilly. The weatherman said the high here was only going to be thirty degrees today."

"That means we'll have to find other ways to keep warm." Lucius gave her a conspiratorial wink. "C'mon, let's get inside."

When he opened the door of the chalet and dropped their bags, they both stared at the sheer size and beauty of this cabin. There were windows everywhere, and large glass doors gave them a spectacular view of the town.

"This is breathtaking." Naomi walked on the rich wood-planked floor of the main living area toward the windows and deck that overlooked the mountains. She paused on the way, stepping over the bearskin rug to finger the elaborate stone wall that held a large flat-screen TV and fire-place below it.

Lucius followed and came behind her to circle his arms around her waist. "I'm glad you like." He glanced behind him at the rug and couldn't wait to make good use of it.

Naomi spun around in his arms. "I *love* it!" She circled her arms around his neck, and he leaned forward to brush his lips across hers.

They continued touring the lower level of the home, ooh and aahing over each new discovery.

The main living area had big comfy camel sofas, hand-made wooden tables and a poker table, but the best was yet to come. They found an in-home movie theater with reclining seats and a game room, which had a pool table and built-in stone bar. Lucius doubted though they would be using the movie room, as he intended to keep Naomi on her back much of their visit. He had a lot to work through. Only then could he could make sense of these feelings he was having.

There was a state-of-the-art kitchen with stainless steel appliances, rich oak cabinetry, granite countertops and even a cappuccino machine. The kitchen led to a deck on the main level, which included a large Jacuzzi. Lucius planned to make good use of it. The upstairs was just as spectacular as the downstairs. The master bedroom had the same matching stone wall with fireplace and television and its own deck with a panoramic view. The bathroom was a modern marble masterpiece, complete with sunken Jacuzzi tub, walk-in rainfall shower and dual vanities.

"What would you like to do now?" Naomi asked once they were back in the master suite.

Lucius grinned wolfishly.

"Besides that," she said with a smile. "That's later."

"Promise?"

A wide grin spread across her lips. "Oh, absolutely. You *will* get lucky tonight."

And Lucius couldn't wait.

Naomi was having the time of her life. She didn't know it was possible to feel this relaxed, yet excited all at the same time. After she and Lucius had toured the house, she'd thought they'd need to go out for provisions. But when she'd looked in the double-sided refrigerator and pantry, she found Lucius had ensured they were fully stocked, including liquor. It was like he'd prepared for the zombie apocalypse.

He'd humored her and they'd gone into town to walk around Big Bear Village to find someplace for dinner. She knew what was on his mind. He'd been ready to take her to bed the instant they arrived. She'd seen the hungry look in his eye when they'd stood in the master bedroom and she'd asked what he wanted to do next. She'd wanted the same thing, but she'd never been to Big Bear and wanted to see some of the town before they indulged in extracurricular activities.

Lucius held her hand as they walked down Main Street side by side, popping into the odd shop or just window-shopping. Or in Lucius's case, actually buying something. Naomi was shocked when he pulled her inside a jewelry store and bought her a diamond pendant necklace.

They ended the evening at Madlon's, a local family-owned French restaurant. They both ordered something different so they could try each other's food. Naomi's duck dish was simply divine, but she equally liked Lucius's veal dish with mustard sauce. They chatted and talked while enjoying dessert and an after-dinner drink.

She indulged and plopped a sweet and sticky treat into her mouth and was looking for a napkin to wipe her fingers, when Lucius reached for her hand and took each sticky finger into his own mouth and suckled on them.

Her reaction was swift. Naomi thought she'd implode with desire and drew in a deep breath at the sheer delight of having Lucius's mouth around her fingers.

Times like these amazed Naomi. Lucius wasn't the same man the media made him out to be—this ruthless tycoon with no conscience. She found him to be not only caring, funny and gregarious, but downright romantic. She liked this side of him and wished more people could see it.

"Why are you looking at me like that?" Lucius asked, peering at her strangely. "Is there something in my teeth?" He showed off his pearly whites.

Naomi chuckled. "Nothing so indelicate. I was just thinking that there are many sides to you. Sides you don't share with the world."

He stared solemnly at her and then reached for his wine-glass, taking a sip. "Only with you, it seems."

Naomi didn't know what to make of that. "Does that scare you?"

How intuitive of her, Lucius thought as he stared across at Naomi in the candlelight. That she could pick up on his anxiety where she was concerned. But he'd never been one to show weakness, and he wouldn't now. Not when he hadn't even figured it out himself.

"Of course not," he replied. "It's more surprising than anything. You bring out the best in me, Naomi Brooks."

He loved the wide grin that spread across her beautifully shaped mouth. A mouth he couldn't wait to devour. His gaze rested on her pouty bottom lip and he wanted to suck it. Lucius felt his groin begin to ache. "Are you ready to get out of here?" he murmured huskily.

She nodded.

Perhaps she sensed that she'd awakened the animal in him that couldn't be kept at bay any longer.

He quickly dispensed with the bill and they headed to the car. With minimal traffic, they were back at the chalet within minutes.

As soon as the door closed, he covered the ground between them. He crushed Naomi to him, plundering her lips as he'd wanted to do at the restaurant. She matched his hunger and they eagerly undressed in the hall, yanking off their scarves, coats and boots. Once free, Naomi surprised him by jumping into his arms and locking her legs around his waist.

Lucius held her tightly in his arms and carried her upstairs to the master bedroom. Once there, he tossed the duvet cover back and sat Naomi atop. Naomi yanked him by his shirt, pulling him hard against her. When his lips grazed hers, he felt the points of her breasts against his chest, igniting a fire inside him. He licked her lips, seeking entry, and she gave in to him, openly giving herself so he could deepen the kiss. Did she feel the same feverish passion that was rising within him?

He got his answer at her eager surrender of her mouth to him. Excitement seeped through him like wildfire, reaffirming everyone's opinion that he was starting to fall for this beautifully seductive woman. He was consumed by her responsiveness to his kiss and it made their connection more powerful, more real. He'd never been so aroused just from a kiss!

Naomi wanted Lucius more than she'd wanted any other man. She was burning up with the need to have this man inside her.

When he finally tore his mouth from hers, her heart was pumping wildly in her chest. And when his hands went to the hem of her sweater, all she could do was lift her arms so he could rid her of the garment. She wanted to be naked against him. She reached behind her and unclasped her bra, releasing her breasts.

His eyes widened, but that didn't stop him from yanking his sweater over his head in one fell swoop until they were both naked from the waist up.

Naomi reached for his belt buckle, unlatching it and his zipper. Lucius rose from the bed and pulled his pants and briefs free until he stood as naked as the day he was born, and with one hell of an erection. Naomi motioned him over with her index finger. He did as instructed and she unzipped her jeans. Then she fell backward on the bed so Lucius could tug then down her hips and legs and toss them aside.

She wasn't embarrassed wearing only her bikini panties, because the passion glazing Lucius's eyes told her that he wanted to *see her*. She raised her hips and he slid his thumbs along the waistband to slide the delicate fabric over her hips until she was naked.

She scooted farther onto the bed and Lucius crawled up on top of her. The breath whooshed out of her as he lowered his mouth back down over hers while one of his hands spread her legs apart. She welcomed his touch; she was already wet and ready for him and writhed against his searching fingers.

When he lifted his head and saw her dilated eyes, she conveyed without words just how much she wanted him. He leaned over to the nightstand and produced a condom from the box he'd brought and set in plain sight. After he'd sheathed himself, he returned to her. Using his knees to spread her thighs apart, he surged inside her.

They came together in a rush of lust, heat and passion. Their desire-drenched bodies made shadows in the firelight as they ascended the highest peak. Naomi clasped her legs around Lucius's buttocks as they both reached infinity at just the same time and began to free-fall back toward earth.

Chapter 14

Naomi marveled at Lucius's stamina. They'd gone throughout the night and his libido hadn't waned. He'd been able to take them to new heights, and she'd felt waves and waves of sensual pleasure. The morning came slowly, and Naomi awoke first, which allowed her time to watch Lucius as he slept. His body was nestled next to her, one arm resting possessively over her bottom.

Her skin smelled like his musky scent, a heady combination. And a losing battle. She'd fallen in love with Lucius. She knew it was a fool's mistake when he was only using her until his passion for her cooled, but that didn't help with the predicament she'd put herself in. This man she loved had the power to destroy her life's work.

Brooks and Johnson was all she had. And yes, she did have her family to support her, but B and J was her baby. Without it, where would she be?

But where would she be without Lucius?

Just then, he began to stir beside her, pulling her toward him. "Good morning," he said, wiping the sleep from his eyes.

"Good morning."

"Did you sleep okay?"

"I slept like a log after you wore me out."

Lucius smiled sheepishly. "Oh, don't act like you didn't like it."

"Did I?" Naomi responded cheekily.

"How about I remind you." He leaned over her and sought her lips with his own.

While he deepened the kiss, Lucius felt Naomi's hands sliding down his body to find the swell of his penis. Then she shocked him by reaching for the box of condoms on the nightstand and pulling out a packet. He loved that she took it upon herself to protect them. Before he knew it, she'd swiftly moved to straddle him.

He was both surprised and delighted by her boldness. His hands immediately went to her hips to help ease her onto his throbbing erection. He watched her eyes close as she slowly took him inside her body inch by delicious inch. Then she began to torment him with the rise and fall of her body atop his. At times she would come down slowly onto his manhood, other times fast and deep, holding him until he had no choice but to start pumping underneath her. With her hands on his chest, she stopped him.

He understood without her having to speak. That's how attuned they were to each other. This was *her* ride. She was in control.

It was as if a deep ache in Naomi's stomach had to be quenched. She began to ride him faster and faster. When she reached the precipice, she cried out and tremors shook her entire body, causing her to fall on top of him.

Lucius took advantage and flipped her onto her back, rolling her beneath him. This time he was the one in control and thrust inside her in one fell swoop. He took his time making love to her. Cupping her breasts in his hand, he took one sensitive bud into his mouth and suckled while the lower half of his body slowly moved of its own accord. Naomi clutched at muscles in his back with her hands as he climbed them toward infinity.

When he felt convulsions tighten her body and her inner muscles clutched around him, it caused Lucius's own tidal wave of an orgasm to come crashing down. Only then did Lucius give in and surrender himself to its power.

Later that morning after cooking breakfast, Naomi and Lucius set out for a fun day in the snow. Naomi wasn't too keen on skiing, so instead Lucius arranged for them to go snowmobiling and tubing after they'd dressed in several layers due to the bitter cold.

After a scenic chairlift ride to the top, the two of them went down by bobsled on the alpine slide. They each navigated their own sled down a quarter-mile-long cement track. Naomi got a thrill from every twist and turn. And so did Lucius, because he whooped and hollered from his bobsled.

Although it was freezing outside, Naomi couldn't recall having so much with another person. Seeing this light-hearted, fun-loving side to Lucius was more than she could have ever dreamed, and she liked—no, she loved it. Loved him. Armed with the knowledge of her feelings for this incredible man, Naomi did her best to hide how she felt about him. She didn't want Lucius to feel like he had to share them. Her feelings were her own. He'd never offered her anything more than what they'd experienced, and she would just have to be happy with that and live in the moment.

But there was a part of her, in the deep recesses of her mind, that yearned for more. Wished that Lucius shared her feelings. She knew that he enjoyed being with her.

Why else would he have invited her for the weekend? But it was just physical for him. She craved the intimacy that came from true love between a man and a woman. Would she ever find a man that loved her as much as she loved him? Or was Lucius that man and he didn't know it yet?

To warm up, they ended the evening much as they had spent the day, having fun at the Big Bear Lake Brewing Company, where they sampled the restaurant's best craft and microbrews while munching on an assortment of appetizers.

Naomi was stuffing a fry topped with their famous homemade beer-cheese sauce, grilled onions and bacon crumbles in her mouth when she saw Lucius smiling at her. "What's so funny?" she asked with a mouthful of decadent French fry.

"You. You are really something."

Naomi used her napkin to wipe her mouth. "In a good way, I hope?"

Lucius grinned. "Definitely a good way. I doubt I would ever get one of my usual dates to dine on—" he motioned to the monster honey-chipotle wings and beer-cheese fries on the table "—to ever let me take them to someplace so casual. But you, you don't mind at all."

Naomi chuckled. "Well, I don't eat like this *all* the time," she emphasized, "but I don't mind having a beer and wings. I'm not that uppity. Perhaps you've been dating the wrong sort of woman."

Lucius stared at Naomi. She was right. He had been dating beautiful, vain and materialistic snobs who wouldn't be caught dead in a place like this. Let alone accompany him bobsledding and get their ski outfits dirty. Naomi was different. She was down-to-earth and looked darn fine in the outfit he'd purchased for her of a ski jacket with a lambskin collar, turtleneck and snug leggings that hugged her behind just how he wanted it.

He'd enjoyed spending the day with her. It had been nothing short of magical. There was a twinkle in her eye as she'd wholeheartedly gone for whatever activity he suggested. He could be real with Naomi. And she was the only woman he'd opened up to about his past, his lack of a father and his yearning to be part of a family.

She'd gone a step farther by inviting him to her parents' home so he could see what it was like. Lucius had to admit that he wouldn't mind being part of a large family. Maybe then he'd finally feel like he belonged somewhere, to someone. *Someone like Naomi*, an inner voice suggested.

Lucius wasn't ready to admit to that. What he did want to do was go back to their chalet and get Naomi in a skimpy bathing suit so he could indulge in the hot tub on deck. "What do you say we head out?"

"Absolutely." Naomi pushed away the plate of fries. "Otherwise, I'll eat all of these."

He took care of the bill, generously tipping the great waitress, and they headed back to the chalet. "I was thinking we could try out the hot tub," Lucius commented giving Naomi a sideways glance. "What do you say?"

"Sure. I'm game."

Twenty minutes later, Lucius was sitting in his swim shorts waiting anxiously for Naomi. He couldn't wait to see her in her bathing suit.

Naomi exited the master bathroom wearing a feminine ruffled two-piece leopard-print halter bikini and wearing high heels. For some reason, Lucius had expected her to wear a one-piece, so he was pleasantly surprised by her confidence in her figure as she walked toward him. He felt his manhood jump to attention.

"You like?" She spun around to give him a better view

of the itsy-bitsy bottom that showed him more cheek than an average bathing suit.

Lucius's mouth watered. "I love it!"

She beamed with pride, and he could see a blush spread across her breasts. Breasts he couldn't wait to suck in the immediate future.

"Let's go."

They donned thick terry-cloth robes and embarked downstairs to the kitchen, but not before Lucius slid a foil packet into his pocket. He stopped long enough at the countertop to grab the champagne and flutes he'd left out before opening the screen door.

The air was crisp and cold. Steam was already coming up from the bubbling hot tub.

"Ooh, it's so cold out here." Naomi shivered a bit and her breath steamed.

"You won't be cold for long," he said as she eased off her robe. He helped her up the steps and watched her slide in the water. He swiftly tossed aside his robe and climbed in behind her.

The water was warm and bubbling around them. Naomi sat across from him while Lucius took care of popping open the bubbly. He poured them each a glass and handed one to her.

"Thank you."

"To the best day ever," Lucius said, holding up his glass.

A large grin spread across Naomi's face. "To the best day ever."

Naomi was overjoyed as she sipped her champagne and looked at him through her lashes. She couldn't believe Lucius had enjoyed the day as much as she had. It gave her hope. Even though she knew she should be careful and not get carried away by the statement, she did.

It also didn't help that Lucius was looking at her like she was the cherry on an ice cream sundae. The lust in his eyes mirrored the desire that was churning within her. Every time she was around this man, there was an undeniable attraction she couldn't contain.

Lucius set his flute aside on the built-in cup holder. "Come here," he ordered.

Naomi happily obliged and placed her flute on the cup holder nearest her. Then she walked slowly toward Lucius through the swirling bubbles. His legs were open and she walked between them. He grabbed her around the waist and pulled her tight against him seconds before his mouth claimed hers in a searing kiss.

The kiss took her breath away. Naomi wasn't sure if that was his intention, because she fell into his lap at the sheer force of hunger in his kiss. She felt his teeth at her bosom untying the knot that kept her breasts from him, and the skimpy material floated away. Then she felt the cool air against her nipples and then Lucius's hot hands caressing one mound as his wet tongue closed around one nipple. He licked it until it turned into an engorged bud, and Naomi moaned uncontrollably, her head falling back. Then he turned to the other and laved it with his tongue.

When he pulled away, Naomi wanted to cry out for him not to stop, but it was only long enough for him to free her of the matching bottom. He tossed them onto the deck along with his shorts. He reached for his robe, and much to Naomi's surprise, he pulled out a condom and sheathed his bulging erection. He'd thought of everything for this moonlit encounter.

Thank goodness the house was secluded and no one could see them outside in the nude and making love in the hot tub. Not that Naomi cared. She wanted Lucius, right here and right now. When he sat back down and motioned her over, she straddled him and her stomach tightened in anticipation of what she knew was to come. She eased down slowly until he filled her to the hilt, and a low gasp escaped her lips. She thought she was going to ride him, but instead he flipped positions and had her on the back on the steps of the hot tub. He began moving inside her, slowly, gently. Back and forth. Back and forth. She moved with him, squeezing him tightly with her inner muscles until he began to thrust more vigorously.

"Yes, Lucius. Yes, like that!" she cried.

She saw his jaw clench as he tried to resist the sensations. He grabbed hold of her hips and held her in place, slowing down the pace, so he could once again thrust slowly inside her.

The intensity was building, and Naomi couldn't hold on any longer. She was making so much noise, moaning and groaning, someone had to hear them, and when Lucius kissed her deeply, the kiss sent her entire body into a spasm, contracting around his.

Her response triggered Lucius to shudder violently and throw his head back, eyes shut, and he came with a loud shout. "Naomi!"

When their orgasms subsided, Lucius withdrew and sat beside her on the step.

"What are you doing to me, woman." Lucius had lost control and shown no finesse a moment ago. All he could think about was a driving need to lose himself in her. And he'd tried, but Naomi had given as good as she got and matched him in every way.

"Am I supposed to answer that?" she inquired. "Because I could ask you the same thing. This is completely out of character for me."

Lucius turned to stare at her boldly. "So I bring out this side of you?"

Naomi regarded him warily. "Don't get cocky, Lucius Knight. You know you're a good lover. I'm sure I'm not the first woman to tell you so."

She wasn't, Lucius thought, but she was the first to make him glad he was. And that he was the man who could bring out the sexy temptress in Naomi. "Come, we should go inside before we catch a cold."

They returned to the master bedroom and slid under the warm covers. He pulled her sideways into a spoon position so he could wrap his arm tightly around her. Naomi released a happy-sounding sigh, and soon her breathing slowed, telling Lucius she'd fallen sound asleep after great sex.

Sleep eluded Lucius, however. It wasn't just sex between them anymore. Every time he was with Naomi, he *made love* to her. She was unlike any of his usual women, and that scared him. His uncharacteristic behavior and response to her made Lucius see that commitment would be the only solution for a woman like Naomi. Was he ready for that? He came and went as he pleased. He didn't have to answer to anyone. He'd always enjoyed his bachelor lifestyle and hadn't been looking for a change.

Until Naomi.

Naomi had him reevaluating everything he held dear. He was in uncharted territory and had no idea where to go. Those were his last thoughts as he eventually drifted off to sleep.

Brrring. Brrring.

"Lucius." He could feel Naomi pushing his shoulder. "That's your phone."

"Hmm...?" He was luxuriating in lying close to Naomi.

His hand was on her breast and he could register her heart-beat, which had gradually returned to normal after their lovemaking session in the hot tub caused them to retire to the bedroom. He'd wanted to sleep in, have a leisurely morning sexing her like crazy again before they had to get back on the road to Long Beach.

The shrill of the phone continued until Lucius had no choice but to throw the covers back and jump out of bed. Annoyed, he snatched up the phone and without looking at caller ID said, "This had better be good."

"Lucius, I need you."

"Who's this?" Lucius recognized the voice, it was his mother, Jocelyn.

"What do you want? And how did you get this number?" Not many people knew his personal cell phone number other than his grandmother, Adam and Naomi. He'd only ever given Jocelyn his work cell phone, which he'd purposely not brought with him to the cabin. And since their last meeting had been less than pleasant, Lucius hadn't expected to hear from her.

"Something terrible has happened. You'll see. It's all over the news. And I need your help. I called Adam and he told me where you were and gave me your number. He didn't want to, but this is urgent."

"Don't be overly dramatic, Jocelyn."

"This is life and death, and you need to come quick, Lucius. I'm at…" She began rattling details into the phone.

"Wait! Wait!" Lucius searched for a pen, saw one on the desk and rushed over to take down the particulars. "Okay, go ahead."

Seconds later, after she'd given him the information, the phone went dead.

Lucius stared down at the phone in shock. Jocelyn had never asked him for anything, much less his help. And it would have to be serious for Adam to break his confidence and give Jocelyn his personal phone number. Then he frowned.

Uncaring of his nakedness, he walked over to the nightstand to grab the remote. He clicked on the television, whirling the room with light as he turned to the local news. That's when he saw it.

"Socialite Jocelyn Turner was found in bed with married shipping magnate Arthur Knight, who has been rushed to a Los Angeles hospital from what appears to be a massive heart attack."

"Lucius." Naomi was behind him. He glanced down and saw she'd wrapped a sheet around her torso. "What is it? Who is that?"

He turned to Naomi. "I suspect that man is my father."

Naomi was hurt. After watching the news report, she'd wanted to accompany Lucius to the hospital. It was his mother, after all, and she was in one helluva mess, having been caught in bed with a married man. Arthur Knight had a wife and a son. The fact that he'd been having an affair with Lucius's mother would be big local news. And if Lucius's suspicions about Arthur were true, he would need her.

But Lucius didn't want her to go with him. Instead, after they'd showered and dressed, they'd packed in a hurry and fled Big Bear to get back home to Long Beach. And instead of taking Naomi with him, he'd given her a quick kiss on the forehead and dropped her off at home with a terse "I'll call you," which he'd thrown over his shoulder as he'd raced back to his car.

She knew she shouldn't be upset. He was dealing with a lot. On the drive home, he'd called Adam and ordered him to contact their public relations department. Adam must have fussed about it being a Sunday, because Lucius had stated quite clearly he couldn't care less. It still didn't mean that she didn't want to be there to support him. Who would be in his corner?

Tears sprang to her eyes as her love came pouring out with no place to go.

"How bad is it?" Lucius asked Adam when he met him in the hospital garage. He'd driven to the hospital on autopilot. His mind spinning with the knowledge that after all these years, he'd finally found him. His father. Lucius had finally decided to park rather than come through the front entrance, where a throng of reporters had already congregated.

"Pretty bad. Every major news outlet is all over this story," Adam said as he walked into the hospital with Lucius. He was dressed in jeans and a pullover sweater, same as Lucius. Adam grasped his shoulder. "Perhaps you and I should talk before—"

Lucius shrugged off his hand and interrupted him. "No, I have to go now. Where is she?"

"In the waiting room."

"Take me to her."

They marched down the hall toward the waiting area, where Lucius found his mother curled up in a ball in the corner sobbing into a handkerchief. She wasn't in her usual fashionable attire. Instead, she was wearing jeans, a tank and cardigan that she must have thrown on before the ambulance arrived.

"Mother?"

She looked up when she saw him and jumped out of her chair to rush into his arms. "Oh, Lucius. It was so horrible." She sniffed into his shoulder. "And the press.

They're such monsters. Saying all kinds of terrible things. And calling me names."

Lucius patted her on the head. Unsure of how to handle this Jocelyn. "I'm here now. And I'll take care of everything."

She glanced up at him with tearstained cheeks, "Can you help me see him?" Hope evident in her voice.

He took hold of her by the shoulders. "That's not a good idea. You do realize how serious this is? The repercussions of how salacious this story is. You were caught with a married man in bed, they'll think he died during sex."

She jerked away from him. "I don't care about the darn repercussions. I care about Arthur. I want to see him. Matter of fact, I'm going now." She pushed past him.

Lucius glared at Adam before following her quickly down the hall. "Jocelyn, this is not a good idea. Besides, we *need* to talk. I have some questions that *need* answers."

"I don't care about what people think," she replied over her shoulder. "I have to know how he's doing. We can talk later."

When they rounded the corner, they saw a group of people huddled at the end of the hall. The instant they saw his mother, Lucius knew she'd made a critical mistake.

A tall, elegantly dressed woman with a smooth mocha complexion rushed toward his mother.

"You hussy!" she cried. "How dare you show your face here!"

His mother stepped backward, recoiling from the harsh words and Lucius watched the whole scene play out as if he was an observer instead of a participant. "And look who you brought with you? Arthur's bastard son!"

Chapter 15

Lucius nearly choked when he heard aloud what he'd begun to suspect as he drove back from Big Bear. His mother had been caught in bed with *married* shipping magnate Arthur Knight. *His* last name was Knight. How had his investigators missed their affair? During their research, they'd found no connection between Jocelyn Turner and Arthur Knight. Clearly, they'd been good at covering up their deception.

But now, he finally knew his biological father's identity.

Lucius stared wide-eyed at the woman and then turned to his mother.

"Oh, don't act like you didn't know," the woman continued. "You and your harlot of a mother have been basking in Arthur's money for years."

"Mother." A tall, caramel-toned, clean-shaven brother with deep-set dark eyes and an athletic physique came forward. He was dressed in dark trousers and pale blue dress shirt. "What do you mean for years? Are you saying Dad has another son?" The shock in the man's face was clear, because it mirrored Lucius's. He, too, had no idea what had been going on between his father and Lucius's mother.

The woman turned and caressed her son's face in her delicate slender hands. "I'm so sorry, Maximus, but that's exactly what I'm saying."

"No, it can't be," Maximus responded, glaring in Lucius's direction. "It can't be. Dad wouldn't do that to you. To us."

"It's true, Max," she whispered softly, "and I'm sorry for blurting it out this way, but I couldn't hold it in any longer. Now seeing the evidence—" she motioned to Lucius "—of their affair, right in front of my face. The truth has to be told."

Maximus's face hardened and his eyes turned cold as he looked at Lucius and then at Jocelyn. "That may be true, but you don't need to do this *here* and make a scene. Let's go." He tightened his hand on her arm and began leading her back down the hall, where their remaining group stood in shocked disbelief.

Lucius caught Maximus's long glare before he turned and huddled back with the group.

"Lucius..."

He heard his mother's voice, but it was as if it were in the distance. He couldn't breathe. He had to get out of there.

He blinked several times, trying to clear the fog in his head. "Adam, can you take my mother home, please?"

The look of pity in his best friend's eyes angered Lucius.

"No problem. I'll call you later."

Lucius barely heard a word as he turned on his heel and stormed down the corridor.

"Is everything okay, baby girl?" Naomi's father asked later that evening when she arrived glum faced to their weekly Sunday dinner. She hadn't been in the mood for socializing, but knew if she didn't attend it would raise more suspicions. So instead, she'd arrived an hour early, because she'd wanted some alone time with her father before Gemma and Tim got there. They'd retired to the den while her mother finished dinner.

"Is it because that young fella, Lucius, didn't accompany you?" he inquired.

Naomi shrugged and reached for the chip bowl. She grabbed a large Ruffle and took a generous scoop of onion dip before placing it in her mouth. "Partly," she answered with her mouth full.

Her father mimicked her and she smiled. They'd always been alike. She was a daddy's girl, through and through.

"Talk to me," he said, reaching for another chip. "What's going on?"

"I take it you haven't been watching the news," Naomi replied.

Her father shook his head. "You know Sunday is football day, but eventually I'll get to it. Is there something I should know?"

"No! No one should, but instead Lucius's life is being played out in public, in front of everyone, and I'm powerless to help him."

"What's being played out?"

"The fact that Lucius's mother has been having an affair with a married man."

"Oh."

"That's right. And on top of that, Daddy, he suffered a heart attack while in bed with her and was rushed to the hospital. Lucius barely had time to get dressed before we left Big Bear."

"Big Bear?" Her father's brow rose. "A weekend away sounds awfully romantic, if you ask me."

Naomi waved her hand. "Forget about me right now, if you can, Daddy. I'm worried about Lucius. As soon as he heard about it, he—he changed right in front of me. He became so cold and distant."

"You mean he became the ruthless corporate raider you'd read about?"

She nodded. "But he's never been that way with me. Ever. If you could have seen him this weekend, Daddy. We were having so much fun, laughing, talking, going bobsledding or just enjoying a beer like a normal couple."

"So you admit that you're dating?"

"I don't know if I'd call it that."

"You have to remember that he's not like us, baby girl," her father said, rising to his feet. "He might not have the same life experiences or the coping skills to deal with life's curveballs that I hope I've taught you. I suppose the only way he can deal with all the turmoil is turn off his emotions."

"With me, too?" Naomi knew she sounded weak, but if she couldn't be honest with her father, whom could she be honest with?

"Sometimes we hurt those we love the most."

Naomi snorted. "Love? I doubt that word has ever crossed Lucius's mind when it comes to me, Daddy. I'm just—"

She never finished her sentence, because her father clutched her shoulders. "Don't you dare make light of this, young lady. I taught you better than that. I taught you not only how to love, but that you *deserve* it. And you should settle for nothing less."

Tears welled in her eyes. "I know that, Daddy, I do, but—" She spun away from him. She didn't want him to see her despair.

"You don't think he returns your love?" her father asked.

How had he guessed her feelings? Probably because she was an open book, just as Kelsey had said. She nodded.

He grabbed her chin and turned her to look at him. "I don't know if that's true, baby girl. The man you brought to dinner was head over heels for my daughter."

Naomi shook her head. "You're wrong. He only wants me for sex."

Her father didn't blush at her words. They'd always had an open and honest relationship, and she didn't mince words.

He lowered his head and was silent for several beats. "That may be so, but I also think that young man doesn't know what to do with the feelings he's developing for you. Why? Because he's never had an example. Didn't you tell me he was raised by his grandmother? That his mother has been nonexistent in his life?"

"Yes."

"So, he's never seen real and abiding love between two people until he met me and your mother. It's foreign to him, Naomi. You've got to give him time to come to terms with it. And if what I saw the night you brought him here is true, he'll find his way back to you."

"Do you really think so?"

Her father nodded.

She wanted to believe that Lucius could love her. But was her head in the clouds?

Knock. Knock. Knock.

Naomi wiped the sleep from her eyes. What time was it? She glanced at the watch on her nightstand. It read 2:00 a.m. After coming home from her parents', she'd given up on hearing from Lucius and retired to bed. They'd made it back that afternoon and he'd had plenty of time to go to the hospital, help his mother and still phone her. But he hadn't.

He was showing her exactly what he thought of her. She was good enough for a romp between the sheets on any given day or in a destination of his choosing, but when it came to matters of the heart, he was closed off to her.

That's what she thought, at least, until she padded to the front door and saw a haggard Lucius leaning against the side of her door. His eyes looked haunted, as if he'd seen a ghost. "Lucius?"

"Can I come in?"

"Of course." She grabbed his hand, pulling him inside. She led him to the sofa in her living room, but instead of sitting, he started pacing her wood floor. So she sat with her legs underneath her and waited for him to talk.

"I can't believe it." He shook his head. "I still can't believe it. Even though I heard it with my own ears."

"Believe what?"

"That *I*—" he pounded his chest "—*am Arthur Knight's son.*"

Naomi sucked in a deep breath. Of all the things she'd been expecting to hear, that bombshell wasn't one of them. "What did you say?"

"You heard me. I learned tonight—or should I say yesterday, at the hospital—that I'm Arthur's bastard son. Apparently he and my mother have been carrying on some elaborate affair for over *three*—" he held up three fingers "—*three* decades. How is that even possible? That kind of duplicity? And that she would go along with it? For God's sake, has she no shame?"

Naomi knew he meant it as a rhetorical question and didn't answer. Her heart broke for Lucius. To find out this sort of news like this—so publicly. It was a horrible thing for a mother to do to her son. She should have told him the truth long ago. If Arthur didn't make it, it might be too late.

"Wow!" Lucius finally sat down in the large chair opposite Naomi and held his head in his hands. "I—I don't know what to do with this news, Naomi. What do I do with it?" He glanced at her, and she could see tears glistening in his eyes. "My entire life I've been yearning for the truth, but not like this." He shook his head. "Not like this."

Naomi immediately sprang from the sofa. "Lucius…" She wanted to comfort him, but instead, he gripped her robe by the waist, pulling her to him. She held his head to her body. "I'm so sorry, baby," she whispered as he cried. "I'm so sorry."

She held him, and once he began to quiet, she sat in his lap holding him to her bosom. When he lifted his head, his dark brown eyes were hooded and cloudy with tears. She wiped them away with her hands. "Let me go get you some Kleenex."

She rose, but he grasped her around the waist and brought her back to his lap. "Don't leave me."

Naomi used her index finger to raise his chin. His eyes bored into hers as if they were looking into her very soul. She was startled by the intensity and cast her eyes downward, but Lucius wouldn't let her.

Instead, she felt a tug on her robe as he released it and it fell to her shoulders. Naomi wasn't wearing much, only a satin nightie that showed a fair amount of her cleavage and barely reached her thighs.

Lucius's eyes darkened, turning from hurt and anger to blazing passion. He clutched the back of her neck and brought her lips to his. His mouth was soft and tender at first, but then he steadily increased the pressure, his kiss becoming harder and greedier.

And so were his movements. Naomi felt him reaching between them to unzip his jeans just as he laid Naomi down onto the floor with only her robe to cushion her. He kicked off his shoes and pushed her nightie up and over her head. Then he was kissing and touching and caressing her all over. Causing her entire body to purr with delight.

She heard the tear of a wrapper, but she was too engrossed in the sensual licks of his tongue on her breasts or the nips of his teeth to notice. She only felt. Felt him drive into her. She'd never been taken so strongly before; she couldn't even cry out because all the air had been sucked out of her lungs.

Lucius thrust into her with rapid, deep thrusts that were so intense they consumed her mind, body and soul.

"Lucius…" There was almost a need for him to stop and let her catch her breath, but he was relentless as he awakened her body.

When he reached his climax, Lucius shouted, "Naomi!" and collapsed on top of her.

They lay breathless for minutes, still joined together. Even though she hadn't come, Naomi knew he'd needed the release. Then she felt Lucius swelling inside her. He was *still hard.*

She glanced up at him and grabbed both sides of his face as he started a new tempo. This one was slow with deliberate motions to send her into overdrive so she too could feel sensual bliss. So much so that when they both reached the peak and came spiraling back down to earth, Naomi whispered, "I love you," right before she fell asleep with Lucius in her arms.

Lucius picked Naomi up as she slept, exhausted from his exuberant lovemaking. He carried her to her bedroom and slid her beneath the cool sheets, kissing her forehead.

He shouldn't have come here tonight. It wasn't fair of him to use Naomi as a release for his pain. But instead of calling him out on it, she'd offered herself up to him as a salve. He'd made love to her with such intensity that the depth of their encounter had scared him. As a result, he'd heard words that he'd never thought he'd hear from a woman.

Naomi loved him.

He hadn't imagined it. Although she'd whispered it, he'd heard her loud and clear. Which was why he had to leave. He'd been feeling an emotion some might call love, but it was just a sentiment.

He had no place for love in his life. *Look at me*, he thought. *I'm a disaster. I've a liar for a mother and a cheat for a father. What could I possibly know about love or give to a woman as special as Naomi?*

Picking up his shoes he'd discarded earlier, he quietly tiptoed out of Naomi's house. And maybe out of her life.

Chapter 16

"Hey, man, how you doing?" Adam asked Lucius as he gave him a one-armed hug before walking inside his penthouse later that morning.

"Fine." Lucius closed the door behind him. He'd called his assistant earlier and advised her he would be taking the day off and was accepting no calls.

"I doubt that's true." Adam turned around to face him. "I was there, remember? I heard everything." He watched as Lucius strolled in and sat on the couch.

Lucius rolled his eyes. How could he forget? Hell, the entire hospital had probably learned his mother was Arthur's mistress and he was his illegitimate son. They probably would have learned a lot more if his *brother*, Max—or whatever Latin name they'd called him—hadn't stepped in.

Brother!

He had a brother that he knew absolutely nothing about.

He'd always wanted siblings. A brother or sister, he hadn't cared. He'd just wanted someone to talk to, to confide in, who would be there for him. And all along he'd always had one. But thanks to his parents' deception, he

didn't know him. And if the look Maximus Knight gave
him at the hospital was any indication, he didn't want to
know Lucius, either.

"What can I do? What do you need?"

"Ha!" Lucius laughed out loud and jumped to his feet.
"What do I need?" His voice rose. "I needed not to find
out who my father was in front of a bunch of strangers!
What I needed was for all this to come out years ago when
I had time to prepare for the fallout, not when the man has
a heart attack."

Adam released a long heavy sigh. "I know that, Lucius.
But what's done is done. There is no going back. All we
can do now is damage control."

"Why?" Lucius laughed derisively. "I couldn't care less
what the world thinks of me. They already think I'm a
spoiled playboy, a corporate raider—the title of illegitimate son won't matter much."

"What about your mother?"

Lucius eyes turned cold. "What about her?"

"With Arthur's standing in the community and the business world, the press are going to have a field day with
this, Lucius. If they haven't already. This story is juicy and
certainly salacious. Not to mention your potential stake in
Knight Shipping."

Lucius waved his hand in the air. "I don't want his
money. I never did."

He shook his head. He couldn't think about that now.
He was trying to make sense of the last twenty-four hours.

"I know you don't," Adam replied, "but if something
happens to him—"

"Don't you dare." Lucius poked Adam in the chest,
"Don't you dare. I can't hear that right now."

Adam threw his hands up in the air. "I'm sorry, all right.

As your friend, I'm just trying to help, Lucius. But I have to tell you, I don't know where to begin."

"Neither do I!" Lucius yelled. "My whole world has been turned on its axis, Adam." He ran his hand over his cropped hair.

Ding. Dong. Ding. Dong.

Lucius stormed toward the door. "I told the guard I wanted no visitors." He swung the door open and found his mother on the other side.

She was wearing all black and sporting a large brimmed hat and sunglasses. She looked more like she was going on vacation than attempting to appear incognito.

"What do you want, Jocelyn?" He held on to the door, keeping her outside in the hall.

"We need to talk."

"That time has long since passed."

She snatched off her sunglasses. "That may be so, but I have some things to say, and you might want to hear them." Being several inches shorter than he, she crouched underneath his arm and strolled inside. "Hello, Adam."

Annoyed, Lucius slammed the door and strode in behind her with his arms folded across his chest.

There was a long, uncomfortable silence as he and his mother just stared at each other.

Adam finally reacted. "Well, uh, I'm going to go—" he pointed toward the door "—to the office and do whatever I can to keep the press at bay until you're ready to make a statement."

His words caused Lucius to look up from his battle of wills with Jocelyn. "Statement?"

Adam nodded from the foyer. "You'll need to say something, Lucius. This is big news. The press will be looking for a sound bite."

"And what do you expect me to say?"

Adam shrugged. "I don't know, you'll figure it out. Ms. Turner." He inclined his head to her and seconds later he was gone, leaving Lucius and his mother alone.

"Oh, joy, what do we do now?" Lucius rubbed his hands together. "Oh, I know. How about you explain why you kept Arthur's identity a secret? Or, I don't know, why don't you tell me why on earth you would *choose* to be that man's mistress for decades? How about we start there?"

"I know you're hurt, Lucius, upset with me about the turn of events, but there's so much you don't know."

Lucius walked over to a nearby chair and sat. "Enlighten me."

"Very well." His mother removed the large hat and placed it and her sunglasses on his glass cocktail table and sat down on his black leather sofa opposite him.

Several beats went by before Lucius said, "I'm waiting."

"May I have a glass of water?" She touched her throat. "I'm feeling a bit parched."

"Ever the drama queen." Lucius rose and returned a couple of minutes later and handed a glass to her. "Let's get on with it, Jocelyn. I don't have all day, because I have to figure out how to fix the mess you've created not only of *your* life, but *mine* as well." He sat down in the seat he'd vacated.

She nodded and took a sip of water. "I met your father at a party after I'd snuck out of Mama's house when I was eighteen years old. Arthur was everything I wasn't. He was twenty-one years old and had just graduated from Stanford. He came from an upper-middle-class family and was going places. We were immediately drawn to each other and embarked on a passionate love affair that summer. Arthur talked to me about his dreams of owning his own business and being his own man outside his father's control."

"Sounds romantic." Lucius snorted, placing his right leg on his opposite thigh.

She ignored the dig and continued. "I thought Arthur was going to marry me because we were head over heels for each other, but later I learned I was wrong. He was already promised to Charlotte Griffin, a beautiful debutante whose father was going to help Arthur get his business off the ground."

"So this boils down to money. He was a greedy bastard who left you pregnant and penniless to marry another woman?"

His mother shook his head. "It wasn't like that, Lucius. I'd planned on telling him I was pregnant with you, but that's the night I found out about Charlotte. I loved him so much that I couldn't stand in the way of his happiness. So I didn't tell him I was pregnant even when your grandma threatened to disown me. And so Arthur married Charlotte and I had you."

Lucius eyes narrowed. "Sounds plausible, but that doesn't explain why you were never around. Why you left me with Grandma Ruby."

"Honestly?"

"That would be appreciated."

"I left you because I couldn't bear to look at you." She turned away from him and sniffed into her handkerchief. "Every time I looked it you, you reminded me of Arthur and the love we'd shared. It was too much. So I took the easy way out."

"That's all fine and good, and maybe it explains your indifference toward your own child. But what about the money? Where did it come from? The boarding school, fancy clothes and vacations. It had to have come from him."

His mother rose from the sofa and walked over to the

French doors of his balcony. She swung them open and sunlight flooded the room—in direct opposition to Lucius's dark mood.

He strode over to her and grasped her shoulders, "I asked you a question, Mother. And I want the truth. *Finally.* I think I deserve that much."

She nodded. "You do. And I'm here to give it to you and endure your wrath."

"My wrath?" Lucius released her. "I just want the T-R-U-T-H. Why is that so hard for you?"

"Because," she shouted. "I loved him. I loved him with all my heart and still do, but I could never *have* him. I was forced to live in the shadows and watch another woman bear his child. Watch him raise another son as his firstborn when it should have been you."

"And whose fault is that, Mother? Yours."

She stepped away from him. "Don't you think I know that? I'm to blame for all of this. I should have told him when the summer ended, but I didn't. And when we reconnected when you were five years old, I couldn't tell him then, either. How could I tell him about the child I'd denied him? Oh, my God!" She let out a long sob. "Instead, I was selfish and rekindled our affair. I allowed him to lavish me with nice things, but I didn't just take it for myself." She turned to Lucius. "I used the money for you, so you could have a better life. But the joke was on me, because you wanted no part of it."

"That's right, Mother. I hated the nannies and boarding schools you put me in because I wasn't with *you*! Don't you get it?" He pointed to his temple. "I just wanted a mother, but you couldn't be bothered."

"I know that. And I felt guilty, so I cut things off with Arthur and tried to move forward with my life. How could I be with him when I was keeping this terrible secret from him? So instead I filled my life up with men and parties as an escape from my past."

"And, well, here we are," Lucius replied. "We've come full circle, Jocelyn. And it's all out there for everyone to see."

"Don't you think I know that? It's been my secret shame."

"So I'm your shame?" Lucius pounded his chest. "Thanks a lot. Now I know how you truly feel."

"No, no." She rushed toward him. "I didn't mean you, Lucius. Never you. I've been ashamed of how I treated you, of how bad a mother I've been to you."

"But you're not ashamed of being his mistress?" Lucius asked, gritting his teeth. "Because clearly you didn't stay away from him."

"No, I didn't," she admitted. "We kept in touch over the years. I suppose we could never fully let each other go. Arthur has never been truly happy with Charlotte even though she bore him a son. And a couple of weeks ago, when I came back here to see you, Arthur asked me to dinner. He was so unhappy and I guess one thing led to another—"

"And you ended up in bed? Again?" Lucius shook his head. Never in a million years could he have dreamed up this story.

"Yes." She lifted her chin, meeting his icy gaze straight on. "It was beautiful and I won't be ashamed, because I love him, and despite all the odds, Arthur still loves me."

Lucius clapped his hand. "What a touching love story you two have. But what about me, Jocelyn? Where do *I* fit in the picture? Do you mean to tell me that he has no idea of my existence?"

Her face clouded with uneasiness, and he noticed her biting her lip as she looked away from his probing eyes. "Well?"

She shook head. "No, he doesn't know."

"That's bull," Lucius snapped. "A man like that had to have known. He had the means to keep track of you and I bet he did for years. *He knew.* And that begs the question as to why he never came forward to meet me, claim me."

"No, he couldn't have known." She shook her head fervently and her face flushed. "If he did, he would have contacted you."

"So naive," Lucius said with contempt. "You—" he pointed to his mother "—I get. I was a constant reminder of a love you could never have. It would be easier to keep me at arm's length. But him? The great Arthur Knight is a coward. He couldn't face me man-to-man and tell me he's my father."

"Don't say that." Jocelyn placed her hands over her ears. "He's a good man."

"He's a rich man that was afraid to lose his fortune if his wife and second son found out my identity. But wouldn't you know, she knew anyway. It was just as easy for her to keep me in the closet, same as him. Because then Charlotte Knight got to stay in the lifestyle she'd grown accustomed to as lady of the manor. It's all coming to me now. It was a win-win for all you while Max and I are in the dark."

"Max?"

"My brother," Lucius responded. "I saw him last night. Saw the devastation on his face to learn he had a brother he knew nothing about and the lies and deceit our parents have lived with for decades."

He strode toward the door and held it open. "Get out!"

"Lucius…"

"I heard what you had to say and now I want you to leave."

"But—"

"Go, Jocelyn. Haven't you done enough? You denied me

my birthright, the father I've longed for my entire life, refusing to tell me time and time again when I pleaded with you. And now I find out he's been right under my nose the entire time?" He laughed contemptuously. "I don't want anything to do with either of you, ever again. I'm tired of the lies. It's time I start living the truth, *my* truth."

She grasped her hat, sunglasses and purse and headed for the door. "What does that mean, Lucius?"

"I guess you're just going to have to wait and see like everyone else." And he closed the door behind her.

Chapter 17

Naomi couldn't believe it had been two days since she'd heard from Lucius. He'd sneaked out of her house like a thief in the middle of the night, stealing her heart along with him. Why, oh, why had she been so foolish as to let her feelings slip from her lips? He had to have heard her whisper she loved him. That's why he stayed away.

Lucius didn't do commitment. She'd known that from the start. He was a love 'em and leave 'em playboy. And she'd just been left.

It hurt knowing that he didn't feel the same way about her. She'd given him all of herself, and she'd thought that his coming to her after hearing such devastating news was his way of opening up to her, letting her in.

She'd been wrong.

Instead, she got silence. Her calls, texts and emails went unanswered. At first she thought he was just avoiding her, but then his assistant had finally taken pity on her and told her he hadn't been into the office in days.

The savvy media had put two and two together and realized that Lucius Knight was indeed Arthur's illegitimate son. There was much speculation in the local paper about what that would mean for Maximus Xavier Knight, heir apparent to Knight Shipping. Would he have to share his inheritance if his father died?

Arthur Knight was hanging on, but the prognosis wasn't good, probably because the man couldn't get any peace worrying about his entire life turning on its ear. Not that Naomi could feel sorry for him. He had to have known Lucius existed and had done nothing about it. Never acknowledging he was Lucius's father was a pretty heartless thing to do.

Despite how much she hurt for Lucius, life had to go on. Naomi would soon find herself out of a job if Lucius bought Kelsey's 25.5 percent. It would make him majority shareholder.

Naomi wasn't ready for that, and she most certainly wasn't ready to have to work with him every day. It would be a reminder that he didn't love her, and that she couldn't abide.

She needed to talk this out, so she called Kelsey, who was at a park near her home. Apparently, she'd been going stir-crazy in the house with Bella and had told Owen she had to take her out so she could run off some excess energy.

Naomi found Kelsey seated on a park bench watching Bella play on the slide. "Hey, Kels." She smiled when she saw her pregnant friend's very large belly.

"Wow! Have you blown up overnight." Naomi couldn't resist speaking her thoughts aloud.

Kelsey's brows pulled together. "Thanks a lot, Naomi. Don't you know you're not supposed to criticize a pregnant woman's weight? We're very sensitive."

"Oh, please, heifer," Naomi laughed, "you have much too much confidence. Plus, you're all belly anyway."

Kelsey's cheeks were a touch round, but her biceps and legs were exactly the same.

"That's because I was working out up until Caden—" she rubbed her belly "—decided to give us a scare."

"You look fantastic and you know it."

"Two months to go."

Naomi smiled. "That's right, you have to keep that bun in the oven. So no stress, all right?" She pointed her finger at her.

"I'm not stressed." Kelsey glanced at the slide her daughter was playing around. "Bella, stay where I can see you!"

The blue-eyed blonde with the gorgeous ringlets was the spitting image of her mother and quickly complied thanks to the stern tone of Kelsey's voice.

Kelsey turned to her. "I'd be a lot less anxious if Adam would return my or my husband's calls. I thought he wanted our shares."

"You've heard the news?"

"That Lucius could be Arthur Knight's son?" Kelsey inquired. "Yes, and it was pretty shocking. How's he dealing with it?"

Naomi shrugged. "Wouldn't know. I haven't seen or heard from him since the night he found out. He's MIA."

"Oh, Naomi." Kelsey reached across the short distance between them to pat her hand. "I'm sorry, honey. I told you to be careful about falling for that man."

"Too late." Tears formed in Naomi's eyes, "I already did. I'm in love with him, Kelsey, but he doesn't want me."

"You can't save him, Naomi," Kelsey said. "He's always been a loner. It's the only way he knows how to be. Perhaps he doesn't know what it's like to have love in his life."

"That—" Naomi pointed her index finger "—that I could understand if he talked to me. Then we could maybe work through it, but he's shut me out. He'd prefer to deal with this on his own."

"I'm sure it's hard to break old habits, Naomi. Here's a man who has never had a father, never known the kind of love that you and I have. He could be struggling to make sense of things. Maybe you can give him a little slack until he comes to grips with the situation."

Naomi stared back at Kelsey, stunned. "Where is all this compassion coming from? I thought you didn't like Lucius."

"I've never disliked Lucius," Kelsey replied. "I've just always been worried that you might love him more than he loves you. I worry that you're more invested, because when you love, you love deeply and with your whole heart. And—and—" her voice broke as she fought back tears "—I just want you to find someone who's worthy of that love, Naomi."

"Aw, Kelsey." Naomi leaned in for a hug, but she didn't make it very far with Kelsey's belly between them.

They both laughed. "I can't even hug you right." Kelsey chuckled. "I really have become big overnight."

"Big and beautiful," Naomi said with a genuine smile. She would try to remember Kelsey's words. Perhaps she was right. Maybe all Lucius needed was time to come to terms with his parentage in his own way. Naomi would give him all the time he needed. She just hoped that when he was ready, he would come back to her.

Dead. Arthur Knight was dead. Stunned, Lucius ended the call on his cell phone and sat back on the sofa in his living room. He'd suffered a second heart attack in the hospital and they'd been unable to revive him.

He'd only just found out he had a father three days ago.

He'd been trying to come to terms with the lot he'd been dealt in life, only to have Arthur suddenly ripped away.

It wasn't right.

It wasn't fair.

How could this have happened? Why hadn't he gone to him and tried to make some sort of peace when he had the chance? Instead, he'd wasted time and now it was too late. He was gone.

Lucius would never know the truth. Were his suspicions right? Had Arthur known about him? How had he felt about Lucius? Lucius would never have the answers he so desperately needed.

His mother was partially to blame for this travesty. She'd kept the truth from him when he could have had years getting to know the man. They might not have had a normal father-son relationship, but at least they would have had something.

Instead, all he was left with was regret. Although, he'd only known of Arthur's existence for a short time, he could have pushed past that she devil of a wife of his and made his presence known. Instead, he'd reverted back to his teenage years, sullen and withdrawn. It came easy to him, because it was his comfort zone. Heaven forbid he would ever do the unexpected.

He bet the Knights had counted on that, counted on his cowardice, and he'd proven them right.

Lucius needed to escape. Flee from the present. Run from the past and drown in his sorrows. And he knew just the place to go to make him forget.

"Tim, what are you doing here?" Naomi asked when her brother stopped by to visit her at work two days later. He was dressed in his usual office attire of trousers and a collared shirt as he approached her desk.

She'd just finished listening to a pitch on some new products they were considering. They were all great ideas, but Naomi hesitated debuting any of them while she was unsure of her place in the company. Once Lucius purchased the lion's share of Brooks and Johnson stock, he would have enough leverage to convince the board to replace her, the founding partner, if he wanted to.

Not that she knew what was going on with Lucius. She'd seen reports that Arthur Knight had died on Wednesday. She'd been heartbroken for him, knowing now he would never get a chance to get to know the man with whom he shared a bloodline. Naomi had again reached out to him, calling repeatedly, but nothing.

Lucius didn't want to be found, and he sure as hell didn't want to talk to her.

Tim frowned, and Naomi became uneasy. She'd never seen this look on his face before, a mixture of sadness with a tinge of relief. "What's going on?"

"You haven't heard?"

"Heard what? I've been in a closed-door session all morning," Naomi responded, rising from her chair and walking toward him.

"Then it's good I got here first." Tim reached for her hand. "Come sit with me."

"Why?" Naomi asked as he led her to the sofa in her sitting area. "Tim, you're scaring me."

"I'm sorry. I don't mean to do that, but I thought you might need me after you see this." He pulled a newspaper from behind his back and showed her the front page.

Naomi stared in horror at the headline: Playboy vs. Heir Apparent—Who Will Win? But that wasn't the worst offense. There, in color for the entire community to see, was Lucius, cuddled up with an unidentified half-dressed female who was darn near sitting in his lap.

Naomi turned her head away. "I don't want to see that."

Tim tossed the tabloid in the trash can nearest to him. "Better you see it now and know who you're dealing with, Naomi. During lunch, when I saw everyone reading it, I knew I had to get to you."

"Why? To show me what a fool I've been for thinking that Lucius actually cared for me?" Naomi laughed derisively.

"No." Tim reached for her and pulled her into his embrace. "Because I know how much you care for him. That night when you brought him over to meet the family, I could see how besotted you were with the man. The same way you'd been when you were fifteen. And I knew this would hurt."

"It does." Naomi nodded against the comfort of her brother's chest. She wanted to cry, but instead all she felt was anger. "It helps me see how stupid I've been to think I matter to Lucius."

"You're not stupid, Naomi." Tim took her chin between his thumb and forefinger and forced her to look up at him. "You're trusting and open. And it made you susceptible, given your former feelings for this man. He took advantage of that, and instead of appreciating the woman he had in front of him, he looked elsewhere."

Naomi blinked back tears that threatened to fall. "True, but I knew who he was, Tim. He never said he was going to change or offered me anything more than living in the moment. I was the one who was foolish to think we'd shared something special. Now I see I was wrong. Lucius has moved on."

She stood up.

"What are you going to do?" Tim asked as he rose.

"I'm going to move on, same as him." Naomi knew saying the words were easier said than done. She was putting on a brave front with Tim because she didn't want him to see how truly devastated she was. She wanted to fall apart in private.

Tim caressed her arm. "All right, kid." He pulled her into one last hug and kissed the top of her head. "Call me if you need *anything*."

Naomi breathed in heavily, holding on to her sorrow. "Will do." She glanced up at Tim and gave him a brief smile as he left her office.

Only once he'd gone did she clutch her hand to her mouth and release the sob she'd been holding inside.

"Well, well, well, I finally found you," Adam said the next afternoon when on a whim he decided to check the gentleman's club he and Lucius liked to frequent. "I've been looking for you everywhere."

Lucius didn't look up as he stared into his nearly empty scotch glass. He'd been at the club for nearly forty-eight hours drinking away his troubles. The barkeep hadn't seemed to mind, because he knew it would be one helluva bill given Lucius only drank top-shelf liquor. He'd also ensured Lucius hadn't lacked for company, and several women—including one waitress who'd been his favorite bedmate in the past—had been his companions for the entire evening.

She knew the right words to say to stroke his ego, and they'd sat in a corner booth, drinking and smoking stogies for much of the night. However, when she'd suggested a private room upstairs, Lucius had declined. As beautiful as she was, he wasn't interested. There was only one woman that lit his fire. Naomi.

Adam snapped his fingers in front of Lucius's face. "Are you listening to me?"

Lucius greeted him with an icy stare. "Perhaps I didn't want to be found. Did you ever think of that?"

"Yeah, I did," Adam replied, "because you've always been a sulker, even when we were teenagers, but I thought I'd weaned you off that habit."

His good-natured response caused Lucius to glance up, and a slight smile creased the corners of his mouth.

"See, I can still make you laugh," Adam said with a grin.

"Yeah, well, I don't have a lot to laugh about these days."

"That's bull, Lucius. I'm not going to give in to your pity party." He tried snatching the glass away, but Lucius held on to it with a death grip.

"Don't mess with my drink."

"I know you're angry, man. Hurt, even, and I'm truly sorry Arthur passed away before you ever got a chance to know him, but that's life, Lucius. Sometimes bad things happen. So what you didn't get to have a daddy? You grew up just fine without one. You had your grandma Ruby, who has loved you unconditionally from the jump. And look at what you've been able to accomplish—I bet the old man secretly admired all you were able to do without him in your life. You used your past to inspire you to greatness. Not many men can say the same. So what Arthur Knight didn't acknowledge you as his son. You're a wealthy man in your own right. It should taste all the more sweet."

Lucius didn't like hearing what Adam had to say, even though he knew there was some truth to his words. He needed time to think about his next move, to get his footing and figure out his place now that he was part of the Knight family and all that would entail. "I don't need or want your pep talk, Adam. Can't you just leave me in peace to drink?"

"I could, but we have business to attend to. If you want to position yourself to be the majority shareholder of Brooks and Johnson, you have to act now and lock in Kelsey's stock before she sells it to someone else."

"If that's what you're here to pester me about, just do it," Lucius said. He motioned to the bartender to refill his drink.

"Are you sure about this?" Adam asked leaning against the bar stool. "You don't want to talk to Naomi first?"

"Naomi?" Even saying her name caused an ache in his belly, but he couldn't deal with that part of his life right now. He was too deep in his own misery to take someone else's feelings into account.

"Yeah, the woman you've been hitting the sheets with for weeks," Adam responded. "And the very same woman who is ready to read you the riot act for this." Adam threw down a tabloid.

"What's this?" Lucius snatched up a local tabloid magazine and saw the headline, Playboy vs. Heir Apparent— Who Will Win? There was a picture of Lucius slouched in a booth with a cigar in one hand and the waitress from last night in his lap, along with another picture of Maximus Knight, looking debonair in a business suit, standing in front of the Knight Shipping compound. "What the hell?" He turned to Adam. "When did this come out?"

"This morning. It's one—though not the only—reason I wanted to reach you. The press is really going to play you against your brother over who will run Knight Shipping."

"I couldn't care less about Knight Shipping."

"You should. You could be entitled to a share of it."

"I care about Naomi. If she saw this—" he pointed to the paper on the bar "—she'll think…" He couldn't say the words aloud. She'd think he'd been with another woman after she'd been there for him. Comforted him. Made love to him. Loved him. "I have to go. Can you take care of the bill?" Lucius jumped off the bar stool and started toward the door.

Adam nodded. "Sure thing. And the shares of Brooks and Johnson?"

"I'll take care of it." Lucius waved him off as he rushed out the door and to Naomi's.

Chapter 18

When Lucius arrived home to shower and change before he went to Naomi's, the press was everywhere. He found his penthouse swarming with reporters, cameramen and television trucks. He barely made it into his garage through the throng. On his way out, he'd have to be stealthy if he didn't want them following him to his intended destination.

After a shave and an overdue long, hot shower to clear his head, Lucius dressed in trousers and a dress shirt sans tie. He hoped Naomi would believe him. Although he hadn't clearly defined his feelings for her, he didn't want her to think he was callous enough to jump from her bed into another woman's with no regard for her feelings. He wished he could offer her more than that, but he was confused. The last several days had been a whirlwind for him. He hadn't been prepared for the flood of emotions that had enveloped him upon learning his heritage only to have it so violently taken away from him.

Arthur's death had set him down a dangerous path. If Adam hadn't gotten to him, he would have gone farther into the rabbit hole. Then there was his mother. Jocelyn wasn't letting up on calling him, and she'd recruited his grandmother. He didn't want his grandma upset and planned on going to see her after he'd cleared the air with Naomi.

Lucius arranged with the apartment complex for one of the bellmen to take his place in the vehicle he'd arrived in, while Lucius would take a different car. His plan worked out perfectly. When he pulled out of his garage in his Porsche, the press had disappeared, having followed the bellman in his Bentley. He was free and clear.

As he drove, Lucius reflected on what he was going to say Naomi. If she'd seen the tabloids, he would apologize and tell her that the press got it all wrong. He hoped that it would alleviate any qualms she might have, but deep down Lucius wondered exactly what Naomi's reaction would be when he showed up to her door unannounced.

Naomi swung open the door and was surprised to find Lucius on her doorstep, given he'd systematically ignored her for the last five days, since he'd sneaked out of her bed. She didn't speak to him; instead she closed the door in his face and walked away.

"Naomi, wait!" Lucius caught the door before it shut and entered her bungalow.

She turned around and gave him a hostile glare. "Did I ask you in?"

"No," he began, but she interrupted him.

"Then perhaps you should leave," Naomi replied. "Because there's nothing for you here. That is, unless you want to hit it one more time for the road before you go back to being the playboy."

"I suppose I deserve that for how I left you the other night," Lucius responded. "But I'd like to talk to you." He reached for her arm.

"Don't touch me!" Naomi snatched her arm away. "Don't you dare touch me!"

Lucius held up his hands in the air. "All right, all right. I won't touch you, but we have some unfinished business."

"Ha." Naomi snorted and padded over to her couch. She sat down with her legs folded underneath her. She didn't bother looking to see if he was following, because she knew he was. He'd come to say his peace, and although she wouldn't believe a word that came out of his mouth, she'd listen.

Lucius joined her in the living room, but rather than sit beside her, he wisely chose the adjacent chair. He leaned down and faced her with his arms resting on his thighs. He let out a long sigh as if pondering his words. She noticed him glance at her coffee table to see the tabloid and the picture of him with the other woman across the front page. She'd retrieved it from the trash in her office as a reminder to never be stupid again where Lucius Knight was concerned.

"Well?"

His dark eyes glanced up and focused on hers, and Naomi felt the familiar tug whenever she was around him. She was angry that he could still make her feel lust for him when she knew he wasn't interested in anything other than sex from her.

"You saw the tabloid?"

She didn't answer, she just glared at him. She'd think that much was obvious.

"And I suppose you think that I've been using you this entire time and couldn't wait to get back to my former lifestyle?" Lucius surmised.

Still she remained silent.

"It's not like that, Naomi. That picture doesn't show the depth of despair and turmoil I've been going through since learning Arthur was my father. And I admit I could have handled it better."

"You mean sexing me in my own house and running out like a thief in the night?" Naomi responded.

Lucius visibly winced. "I'm sorry I made you feel like that, Naomi. That wasn't my intent. That night I needed you and you were there for me, and I'm grateful that you were. And I'm sorry that I didn't call you to let you know I was okay, but it was bit much to take in all at once. And Arthur's death has only added to it."

"Don't you think I know that, Lucius?" Naomi folded her arms across her chest. "I wanted to be there for you, but you shut me out."

"I—I recognize that." He spoke slowly, as if he were choosing his words very carefully. "But I needed to handle this alone and in my own way."

"Oh, you weren't alone," Naomi replied, pointing to the tabloid. "You've had several females to keep your bed warm."

Lucius glanced down at the paper and back at her. "I—I'm sure it looks that way, but that wasn't the case."

"What I do know, Lucius," Naomi replied quickly, "is that I never should have trusted you. You're the same player you've always been, bedding women and then tossing them aside when you're done with them. Silly me, I thought I was different—" she laughed scornfully "—but the joke is on me." She rose from the sofa. "I've heard what you had to say and now you can leave."

She started toward the foyer.

"Naomi!" Lucius rose to his full six-foot-two height and blocked her path. "Don't do this. I don't want to leave like this."

"Like what, Lucius?" She glanced up at him. His dark eyes were unfathomable—she couldn't read him any more than she ever could, except maybe when they were filled with lust. "You and I both know this—" she motioned back and forth between them "—was never going anyplace, right? You only wanted Brooks and Johnson, and in the process I caught your eye and you decided you wanted to have sex with me."

Naomi shrugged. "I get it. I really do. Well, you've done both. You took me to bed and Kelsey's ready to sell you her shares. You won! I've nothing left to give you, Lucius. And you sure as hell have nothing to give me."

"Naomi, please." Lucius's arm circled around her waist.

Naomi hated that her traitorous body trembled at his touch. A riot of sensation coursed through her system. That he could still have an effect on her even though she knew he didn't truly care about her. He didn't love her like she loved him.

"Stop!" Naomi pushed at the hard wall of his chest, trying to get distance from him.

"Baby…" He tried to pull her into his embrace, but she pushed him again.

"Stop! Don't *baby* me, Lucius," she cried out. "I told you I loved you. The last time we were together. I admitted how I felt about you. And yet here you stand, not even acknowledging those feelings."

Lucius stared at her. She was right. He'd thought she might be too preoccupied with the tabloid to bring up her declaration of love, but he was wrong. Naomi was a strong woman and she wasn't backing down.

"Nothing to say, slick?" Naomi jeered, calling him by the nickname she'd given him that he disliked. "Cat got your tongue?"

He was torn. He didn't want to hurt her, yet he wasn't ready to say the words it was so clear she needed to hear back. Even though he'd felt the emotion. At times when they were together, Lucius had wondered if he was indeed falling in love with Naomi, but loving someone who had the power to hurt him scared him.

Naomi stared at him wide-eyed, waiting for his response.

"I—I…" He stumbled over his words. It was the first time in his life he was ever unsure of himself, of what to say. He couldn't tell her what she needed to hear, but he could show her.

So he acted instead. He reached for her, pulling her firm against him and then dipped his head. Her lips parted beneath his. He didn't know if her response was because he'd surprised her or because she was submitting to him, but he enjoyed it all the same. He delved into her mouth, gliding his tongue back and forth across hers until he heard her moan. He backed her up, pinning her between the wall and him as he ravaged her mouth.

His blood felt like liquid fire in his veins, and his body pulsed with the need to bury himself inside her. He needed this. It had been days since he'd tasted her. And she tasted the same. No, better than he remembered. Naomi was an unforgettable woman, and the all-consuming passion he felt with her was like nothing else he'd ever known. There was no way he could look at, let alone *be* with another woman. So why couldn't he tell her he loved her?

His fingers began creeping beneath her top, and the jolt of reality must have hit her in the face, because Naomi sprang away from him as if she'd been burned.

Naomi gulped in a breath. "Okay, you've proven that I'm still weak for you, that I have no self-control, but I do have some modicum of self-respect. And I want more, Lucius, but you're just not capable of giving me what I want—what I need. So you have to go."

He stared at her for several long beats. He wanted to wrap her in his arms and take her to her bedroom and remind her how good they were together. But what would that solve?

"Please go, Lucius," she ordered when he hadn't made a move to leave.

"All right, I'll go." Lucius walked to the door and opened it but turned to glance back at her. "But I need you to know that it wasn't just sex for me, Naomi. I do care for you. Perhaps not in the way you need me to right now, but I do care."

He closed the door behind him and quietly walked to the car. Once inside, he glanced back at the craftsman-style house. He knew Naomi was crying inside. He wanted to go in and comfort her, to tell her he loved her, but he couldn't.

So he drove away.

"Lucius, I'm so glad you came to see me," his grandmother said when he stopped by her home later that evening.

He'd had to take some time to get himself together before he dropped by. His visit at Naomi's had been the hardest thing he'd ever had to do. To see her hurting and to be unable to fix it was heart-wrenching and had shaken him to the core. He'd thought about going back to the gentleman's club and drowning his sorrows again, but what would that do?

Instead, he'd stopped by the office to go through the hundreds of emails and calls he'd received while he'd been MIA the last several days. It was there that he'd seen an envelope from a courier sitting on his desk.

When he'd opened it, he'd been shocked to see it was from an attorney's office. After tearing it open, he'd scanned the letter and tossed it down. Inside was his invitation to the reading of Arthur Knight's will. What the hell? The man had never even acknowledged his existence and now all of sudden he'd been invited to the reading of his will? Why? What did it mean? And would he go?

If nothing else, he should to satisfy his curiosity as to what Arthur could possibly have wanted to say in death that he hadn't been able to say in Lucius's thirty-four years of life.

He brought the letter with him to his grandmother's, because if anyone could help him make sense of it all, it was her. He was, however, shocked to see she had a guest when he walked into the living room. "Mother." He regarded Jocelyn quizzically as he sat down. "What's going on, Grandma?"

She followed him into the room. "I figured someone had to get you two together to talk."

"That's not your place, Grandma."

"Like hell, it isn't, boy," she responded hotly and pounded her chest. "I raised you, because she was too afraid to face you. Too afraid to stay and be the mother she should have been. Too afraid to tell you about your father, and now he's gone."

"That's right, Grandma. And it's because of her that I never got to know the man. And he's dead. D-E-A-D." Lucius glared at his mother, whose eyes glistened with unshed tears.

"I know I'm to blame, Lucius," Jocelyn said. "I—I just thought I was doing what was best for you, what was best for everybody."

"By taking away my choices?" Lucius asked. "And leaving me fatherless? Motherless?"

His mother lowered her head. "I'm so sorry, you don't know how much. Sometimes, Mama—" she looked up at her mother "—I think about how different things would have been if I'd told Arthur I was pregnant with Lucius." She shook her head in frustration. "But I didn't. And—and I can't take it back. Instead I'm left out in the cold to grieve for him alone. I can't even go the funeral."

"You're here because of your choices, Jocelyn," Ruby responded. "There's no denying that, but—"

Lucius interrupted her. "She doesn't have the monopoly on grief, Grandma. I didn't get invited, either. Instead all I got is this." He held up the envelope. "An invitation to the reading of the will."

"That's something, Lucius. Perhaps he'll acknowledge you in some way," Jocelyn said hopefully, sitting up straight.

"Because he was too cowardly to do it in person?" Lucius snorted.

"I didn't bring you both here to gripe at each other." His grandmother stepped between them. "I brought you here because you both—" she looked in Lucius's direction "—are grieving. I think you could lean on each other during this time, help each other through it."

Lucius shook his head. "I'm sorry, Grandma, but that's never going to happen. I will never forgive her for denying me my father. Never."

He rose to leave, but his grandmother stopped him. "All this anger you have inside you, Lucius. It isn't good. You have to let it go. You have to forgive. If you don't, it'll eat you alive and taint everything that's good in your life—like that young lady you're in love with."

His mother perked up from her seat. "What young lady?"

Lucius turned to glare at her. "That's no concern of yours."

"Lucius," his grandmother reprimanded.

"Her name's Naomi Brooks. But it doesn't matter anyway. Naomi wants nothing to do with me. Why? Because I have a block of ice where my heart should be," Lucius responded. "And that's because of you." He looked in his mother's direction.

"Baby." His grandmother moved from her chair and cupped both his cheeks in her small, frail hands. "Don't you see? It doesn't have to be. You don't have to be alone anymore. If this girl loves you as much as I suspect she does, then all you have to do is open your heart and allow the love in. Tell her how you feel. I promise you, love will help heal your heart like no other."

"Grandma…"

"Trust me, boy, I've been on this earth a lot longer than you. Tell her you love her 'cause I know you do. I see it." She motioned with her two forefingers between both their eyes. "I saw it the first time you told me about her, but you've been too scared or too blind to see it."

"Mama's right." His mother rose from her seat. "Don't be like me. Don't let love slip through your fingers, Lucius. Otherwise, you'll regret it forever."

Were they right? Lucius thought. Was it possible to have the love he'd always wanted in his life if he just reached out and grabbed it? If he told Naomi he loved her, would she accept him with all his flaws and baggage? Would she be with him always? There was only one way to find out.

Chapter 19

"I had the papers drawn up as you requested," Adam said, sliding the stack across Lucius's desk and stepping back.

"Thank you," Lucius said, looking up from his computer monitor.

"Are you sure you don't want me to take care of this for you?" Adam inquired. "I know you have a lot on your plate."

"No, I want to do it," Lucius replied.

"All right. You know once you do this, you'll own majority interest in Brooks and Johnson."

"I'm aware."

"You know Naomi won't be happy about this. You're going to get a lot of resistance from her on any changes you want to implement."

"I can handle Naomi."

"Famous last words," Adam laughed. "Any man that thinks he can handle a woman has grossly underestimated her. She could cause you real headaches if you're not careful."

Since he'd left his grandmother's nearly a week ago, he'd given serious thought to what she'd said. And had come to a conclusion on what he had to do next. When all was said and done.

"You might be right about that." Lucius closed the folder he'd been working on. "Which is why I'm putting a plan in motion that will ensure I have Naomi on my side."

"That sounds mysterious," Adam replied. "Care to explain?"

Lucius shook his head. "Nope. But you'll see soon enough." He rose from his chair, grabbed the envelope with the papers Adam had drawn up and headed toward the door without another word.

"Daddy, what are you doing here?" Naomi asked when her father found her sitting on her favorite love seat in her parents' backyard, wrapped in a blanket.

"C'mon, baby girl," he said, joining her on the love seat and underneath the blanket. "I know where you go when you have something on your mind. You want to go someplace peaceful, quiet, so you can allow yourself to be introspective. Same as me. Plus, Gemma called and said your car was parked outside the house in the middle of the day."

Naomi smiled. Her sister was always a little too nosy for her own good. Couldn't she start her weekend early if she wanted to? "Yes, I guess I got that gene from you." She bumped her shoulder with his.

"You've always been the most like me," he said. "Tim is like your mother. He's more deliberate, but you and me, we're all heart. Always have been and always will be."

"Yeah, well, wearing my heart on my sleeve has gotten me in the predicament I'm in."

"And what's that?"

"In love with a man who doesn't love me back."

"Lucius."

Naomi nodded. She'd hoped that Kelsey had been right

and that Lucius perhaps was too overwrought or caught up in his emotions to tell her he loved her, but it had been nearly a week since she'd kicked him out of her house and she hadn't heard from him. It had hurt more, because she'd gotten her hopes up that Kelsey had been on to something, but she too had been wrong. Lucius didn't care about Naomi any more than he did the hundreds of other women he'd been with.

Apparently she wasn't so special, even though he *cared* for her.

"I don't believe that," her father said. "Did he say that?"

She turned to him. "No, but it was what he didn't say that made it crystal clear how he feels about me, Daddy."

"Then he's a fool if he doesn't realize what a gem he has in you."

Naomi smiled. "Daddy…"

He circled his arm around her shoulders and gave them a gentle squeeze. "I love you, baby girl. And one day you'll find someone worthy of all the love you have in your heart."

"I know. I just wanted Lucius to be that man."

"I know, pumpkin." He cupped her head to his shoulder. "Just give it some time. Because in time, it'll hurt a little less."

Naomi doubted that was even possible. Lucius was her first love, and she wasn't sure she'd ever find another man that made her feel like he did. He made her feel sexy and alive, bold and daring, as if she could do anything when she was with him. She missed that feeling. Would she ever find it again?

"Lucius, this is a risky move." Kelsey handed Lucius back the pen after she'd signed her shares of Brooks and Johnson over to him later that afternoon.

After receiving the papers from Adam, Lucius had come directly from the office to Kelsey's home in Belmont Shore. He'd known he would have to act quickly, not just for his sake, but before they sold to another buyer. Adam had gotten wind that another of his competitors had made the Johnsons an offer.

"Yes, I know."

"Naomi was on the fence on whether she wanted me to sell to you," Kelsey responded, rubbing her seven-months-pregnant belly. "Owen and I were seriously entertaining another offer to make Naomi's life as easy as possible during this transition."

"Yes, I'd heard about the other group, which is why I had to move."

"But if what you've told me is true and your intentions are honorable, this could end beautifully." Kelsey smiled. "And I want that for my best friend. No, my sister, because Naomi is that important to me."

"I know that, Kelsey," Lucius said. "And I promise you, I won't let you down. I won't betray the trust you have in me. And I will be good to Naomi and good for her."

Kelsey pointed her finger at him. "You'd better. Because if you hurt her, I will come after you after I have this baby."

Lucius laughed as he imagined Kelsey holding a baby in one arm and a toddler in another, chasing him down the street with a bat. "I don't doubt you would, Kelsey, but I have the best intentions." He used his index finger to make a cross over his heart. "Scout's honor."

Now all he had to do over the weekend was get all the pieces in place.

As she drove in to work on Monday morning, Naomi was ready for whatever the day had in store. The talk with her father on Friday had helped. It always did. He had a way of calming her like no one else could. Over the week-end, she'd had time to reflect and realized she would have to face her feelings for Lucius head-on. He'd own a significant share of her company when he purchased Kelsey's stock, and there would be no way around it.

She didn't know how much of a role he wanted to play at Brooks and Johnson and if she'd have to see him every day, but somehow, someway, she would be strong. She wouldn't let him see how much she hurt inside because he didn't share her love. It would take a long time for her to get over him, but she'd done it once before when she'd been a teenager, except this time was different. This wasn't the crush of a young girl longing to date and heal the hot loner bad boy.

She was a grown woman now. And she'd experienced pure bliss in Lucius's arms. With the few lovers she'd had in the past, she'd never felt the way he made her feel. When she was with Lucius, the need and desire to be together was so strong, so potent, she thought she'd die if he didn't touch her again. And when they were just having fun and being normal, it was awesome. But it was over between them, and she would have to go on without being able to kiss him, touch him, make love to him.

Naomi pulled her Audi into the parking space outside her building. She said her hellos and morning greetings to her staff as she made her way to the elevator. She pressed the up button for the top floor and anxiously tapped her foot against the tile. When the doors opened, Naomi stepped out and made her way down the carpeted hall-way to her corner office.

"Naomi." Sophie was waiting for her in the hallway and blocking her path.

"Good morning." Naomi was surprised to see her. She

tried stepping around her, but Sophie took the same two steps, blocking her path.

"Good morning, Naomi," she said, rather loudly in Naomi's opinion.

Naomi stared at her strangely. "Are you okay, Sophie? You're acting weird this morning."

Sophie glanced behind her at Naomi's door. "Oh, I—I'm fine. I'm just so happy to see you," she said again, very loudly.

Naomi smiled. She was glad that she had the kind of relationship with her employees that boasted mutual respect and admiration. "It's good to see you, too. Now, if you don't mind—" She stepped around her swiftly and reached for her door handle. "Hold all my calls, I have to catch up on a few things this morning."

"With pleasure," Sophie said excitedly as Naomi pulled the door lever.

When she opened her door, Naomi was shocked to see hundreds of roses in every shade and color sprinkled throughout her office. The scent was overwhelming, but nothing was more so than seeing Lucius standing in the middle of her office in a silver designer suit with a black tie and a large grin spread across his full lips.

"Lucius?" Naomi was taken aback and stood at the doorway, ready to flee. "Wh-what are you doing here?"

"Isn't it obvious?" he asked, coming toward her with his arms stretched out. "I've come to win you back."

When he reached her, he pulled her inside, enveloping her in his arms. Naomi breathed in the spicy, woodsy scent of his cologne that she loved so much. It was all Lucius. A Lucius she loved with all her heart, but she mustn't get carried away by such a grand gesture. She had to hear him out, find out why he was here.

Reluctantly, she pulled away and looked up at him. "I don't understand."

"Come." He took her hand in his large one and led her over to the sofa. He didn't let go of her hand; instead he followed her movements as she sat down on the edge of the sofa, unsure just how long this conversation would last.

"Naomi," Lucius began. "I'm sorry about last week. How I left things between us."

The memory of the pain of his rejection of her and her love still stung, and she slid her hand out of his. "There's nothing to be sorry about. You don't feel the same way about me, and I'll just have to accept that."

He shook his head. "That's not true, Naomi."

She stared at him, perplexed.

"From the moment you came back into my life, I've known you were someone special. No—" he stopped himself "—I think I knew before, when we were in high school, when you were this awkward teenager with bad acne and hair, who wore baggy clothes and followed me around. I knew then that I liked you. You were different from all the other girls who were just interested in me for my looks or because they wanted to show off to their friends that they were hanging with the bad boy."

"I sensed that you were hurting," Naomi stated.

"I know. And you wanted to be a friend and perhaps more, but I was too blind to see it back then. All I could think about back then was blocking out the pain. And since then I've been doing the same thing. Using sex as a crutch as a way to keep women at arm's length, but what I've come to realize is that all those other girls were just fill-ins for you."

Naomi's heart turned over in her chest at Lucius's words, and tears welled in her eyes. With the pad of his thumb, he wiped an errant tear from her cheek.

"You may not believe this, and I don't think I knew it myself, but I'd been waiting for you my entire life, Naomi. And somehow, despite all the odds, fate brought us back together. When I first learned about your IPO last year and started buying shares, I didn't know why I was drawn to you, to your story. It must have been my gut telling me that it was time I finally acted on those feelings I had for you long ago. When I searched you out in Anaheim, I told myself it was to convince you to sell to me, but deep down I knew better. Deep down I knew it was because I wanted you."

"You did?"

He nodded. "And when we reconnected, I sensed that you were as attracted to me as I was to you. I was overjoyed, and I admit I used my charm to break down your defenses. But imagine my surprise when I discovered heaven in your arms."

The breath caught in Naomi's throat and she didn't know if she could let it out. Could this really be happening? Could Lucius really be pouring out his soul to her?

Lucius could see the shock in Naomi's eyes as he laid his soul bare. He'd thought it would be easy, and he'd tried practicing the speech he'd give and how he'd tell her he loved her. Instead, he was rambling on about the past, but somehow he would get the words out. He would say the three words she longed to hear and that he couldn't wait to say aloud.

"I feel the same way," Naomi said. "Being with you was everything." She touched his cheek with the palm of her hand.

He took her hand in his and bent over it. He pressed his lips against her hot skin. Lucius had never felt this way, this level of intensity with any woman.

"I'm sorry if I ever made you feel this was just about sex for me, because it wasn't."

Naomi nodded. "I know, because you *care* for me."

There it was. The line she'd always remember. He cared for her. Not loved her. Cared for her. He hated that she did and vowed to erase it from her memory. He looked into her eyes, searching for—what? That somehow her love had suddenly vanished? It hadn't. He saw a glittering in her eyes, the sentiment he'd always seen. Love.

"I more than care for you, baby. I love you, Naomi."

"You do?" The hopefulness in her voice stole his heart.

He nodded. "I do. I love you. I think I have for some time, but I was just too afraid to see it, to admit it. When you told me how you felt, I wanted to run in the other direction."

"Why?"

"Because I've never felt worthy or deserving of love. My mother left me and my father never claimed me. If it wasn't for my grandmother, I would have been all alone."

"Oh, Lucius." Naomi threw her hands around his neck and pulled him into her embrace. She clutched him to her chest, and Lucius hugged her back tightly. He could feel his throat constricting, tightening, yet he felt like his heart was expanding at the same time. He hadn't thought it was possible that he'd ever feel love in his life.

Naomi pulled away slightly to cup both his cheeks in her hands. "I love you, too, Lucius. I never stopped. And I'll always love you."

She leaned in slightly, tilted her head and then kissed him. Lucius kissed her back with all the love, pent-up desire and passion he'd been holding in all week. He enjoyed the velvety slide of her tongue, the warmth of her lips.

There was nothing else but him and Naomi. He wove his fingers through her thick curls and held her like that, anchored to him, and kissed her. He both gave and demanded, and Naomi matched him want for want. She arched her body against him as if needing to be closer to him, as close as she could get under the circumstances.

He fell backward on the sofa and she gripped his shoulders as if she needed something to hold her to earth. He palmed her bottom as his mouth left hers. He kissed the tender skin along her jaw until he made it to her neck. His tongue traced the line of collarbone until he came to her ear and suckled.

"Lucius." Naomi's moan caused him to remember their location.

"Baby." Lucius held Naomi in his lap as he lifted them from the sofa. "We have to remember where we are." Naomi always made him feel like a randy teenager in the back of a pickup truck.

Naomi blushed. "Yes. You're right."

"Plus, I didn't tell you everything I had to tell you."

Naomi's brow rose. "There's more?"

"Oh, yes," Lucius said. He set her back on the down on the sofa and reached into his suit pocket. Producing an envelope, he handed it to her.

"What's this?"

"Open it." He couldn't wait for her to see what was inside.

Naomi stared at Lucius for several long beats before she finally slid her index finger under the flap to open the envelope. It was an official-looking legal document. She glanced at him, fearful. Was she going to like this?

"Read," he ordered.

"All right, all right." She began scanning the document. As she continued to read, she was stunned by what she read. He didn't! Surely, this had to be some sort of mistake.

Naomi glanced up at Lucius. "I don't understand."

Lucius smiled broadly. "Yes, you do." His smile showed off his perfect white teeth.

"But—but it says that you bought Kelsey's shares and are signing them over to me?"

"That's right, baby," Lucius said. "It's my gift to you."

"But I thought…"

"You thought wrong. Brooks and Johnson is your baby, and you deserve the right as majority shareholder to lead it into the future. I would like to share it with you and maybe give you a few ideas, since I do own 30 percent of the company."

"Oh, Lucius." Naomi's eyes welled with tears at not only his generosity, but his love. Because that's exactly what this was. He was showing her that he loved her and wanted *only her.* "I would love your help. We can run B and J together."

"Are you sure?" This time he sounded unsure. "I don't want to step on your toes."

She nodded. "I'm sure." She was so touched by his generosity and that he would give up his own ambitions for her. "I can't believe you arranged this and that Kelsey agreed."

"Oh, your bestie told me I was signing my death warrant if I didn't live up to my word."

"You've—"

She never got another word out, because Lucius lowered himself to the ground on one knee.

Lucius plucked a ring box from inside his suit pocket and held it in front of her. "Be my wife? And make me the happiest man alive," he said with a large grin.

"Oh, my God!" Naomi's hand flew to her mouth. In her wildest dreams, she'd never imagined this. That Lucius, the love of her life, would not only love her as much as

she loved him, but wanted to *marry her*? Surely, she had
to be dreaming, so she closed her eyes.

"Oh, no, you don't." Lucius squeezed her hand. "Open
your eyes, baby. 'Cause this isn't a dream, and I don't want
you to miss a single moment."

Slowly, Naomi opened her eyes, and the love she saw
shining in Lucius's eyes was the same she'd seen in her
own that very same morning. "Neither do I. It seems like
I've been waiting my whole life for you, Lucius."

"So is your answer yes?" Lucius asked. His dark eyes
peered into hers. "Because I'm getting kind of anxious
down here."

"The answer is a definitive yes." Naomi wound her
arms around his neck.

When they pulled apart, Lucius slid the round five-carat
halo diamond ring on her finger. "It's beautiful," Naomi
gushed, helping him up onto the couch. "It's just beautiful. Just like you."

"Me? I don't think I've ever been called beautiful."

"How about gorgeous and sexy?" He motioned with
her hand for her to continue praising him. "And handsome, and incredibly intelligent. And I'm going to be the
luckiest woman in the world to have you as my husband."

"No, I'm the lucky one," Lucius said, "because I was
smart enough not to let the best thing that ever happened
to me get away."

Chapter 20

Later that night, after they'd told Naomi's parents the good news and celebrated with champagne, Lucius returned to his penthouse with Naomi. He didn't care if the press was still stalking him, waiting to see his next move. His statement several days ago had been less than forthcoming, and they were all eager to see what the millionaire playboy would do next. Little did they know that he was hanging his player card up for good.

Even Adam had been shocked when Lucius had shared not only his engagement to Naomi, but that he'd gifted her Kelsey's stock. His best friend had called him insane, but when he'd seen how happy Lucius he was, he'd offered his congratulations. And now Lucius could finally do what he'd been dreaming about all day—take Naomi to bed.

Unfortunately, his cell phone rang, interrupting their moment and allowing his fiancée to slip away into his bedroom.

"Hello?" Lucius asked roughly, since he didn't recognize the number on his caller ID.

"Lucius Knight."

The curt and businesslike tone of the male voice on the

other end caused Lucius to stop uncorking the bottle of champagne he held. "Yes?"

"This is Robert Kellogg, Arthur Knight's attorney. I sent you an invitation to the reading of his will several days ago and never heard from you on whether you intended to attend."

Lucius glanced down at his watch. It was well past 8:00 p.m. "Do you always make a habit of calling your former client's family after business hours?"

"If he was a personal friend, yes," Robert answered. "And since the reading of the will is tomorrow, I'd rather know what's ahead, given how your presence could create a volatile situation with the family."

"My presence?" Lucius snorted. "You mean my existence, Mr. Kellogg?"

He ignored the dig. "So will you be attending? I'd like to prepare Charlotte. As I'm sure you're aware, this has been a trying time for the Knight family."

Lucius thought about Arthur's wife screaming at his mother and how she'd called him a bastard for everyone to hear. "I couldn't care less about the family's feelings."

"That may be the case, but you're now a part of it, Mr. Knight and as such, your presence is required."

Lucius's blood boiled. He didn't want or need this aggravation—not today, not when Naomi had agreed to be his wife.

"So can I consider your attendance confirmed?"

He didn't appreciate the haughty or presumptuous nature of the attorney. "No, it's not. And whether I decide to attend or not, it will be *my decision*, Mr. Kellogg. So I guess you, Charlotte and the entire Knight clan will just have to wait and see."

Click.

Lucius relished hanging up on the snobbish lawyer. How

dare he talk down to him like he had the right to? Lucius Knight was no one's pushover.

"Baby...are you coming to bed?" He heard Naomi's voice softly calling from the direction of his bedroom.

Lucius turned to his bedroom door. He would think about the will and his new family tomorrow. Tonight, he wanted to be with his lady love.

He quickly uncorked the bottle and took it along with two flutes to the bedroom. When he arrived, he was greeted with Naomi leaning against the doorway of the master bath with her robe open. She was wearing a sexy red bustier, garter belt and thigh-high stockings. He darn near lost hold of the champagne bottle in his hand and set it on the dresser nearest him while he stood still, mesmerized by her beauty.

"You look hot!"

"That was what I was going for."

"How long have you had that getup?"

Naomi shrugged as she playfully let the robe slip from her shoulders and strolled toward him. "Oh, I don't know... awhile." She twirled a curl between her fingers.

When she reached him, Lucius growled low in his throat and pulled her to him, kissing her, hard and quick. His body was on fire with a need to have her.

She undressed him, first his shoes and then one piece of clothing at a time. As each item fell in a pool at his feet, desire took over. And when she finally reached his waist, she relieved him of his belt, pants and underwear in one fluid movement until he stood naked and completely aroused.

"Is it my turn?" he asked, stepping away from his clothes, unashamed of his erection jutting forward.

She nodded. "Oh, yes, you can unwrap your gift." She

backed away from him and slid onto the satin comforter on his king-size bed.

Lucius moved forward like a panther, sliding onto the bed and over her.

Naomi's body trembled as Lucius unclasped her bustier and garter belt and slid her barely-there thong down her legs. Once he'd relieved her of her ensemble, he made sure she was ready for him by pushing one finger inside her. She was already wet for him. Would always be. She'd always wanted Lucius. And that would never, ever change.

Lucius fished a condom out the drawer of his nightstand and made quick work of rolling it on and rejoined her on the bed.

She wove her hands around his neck and kissed him deeply as he moved back into position over her, poised to take possession of her body, of her soul. She parted her thighs for him, and he glided inside her with one erotic thrust. Naomi focused on the pleasure that was building inside her, but this time it was different between them. It was deeper, more intense because they had confessed their love for one another.

As Lucius kissed her neck, her collarbone, and lowered his head to take one of her nipples into his mouth while his other hand molded the other breast, Naomi arched to meet his thrusts.

"More, Lucius…" she moaned.

He obliged and his thrusts became faster, harder. Naomi wrapped her arms around his neck holding him to her as her orgasm hit her with full force.

"Lucius!" she shouted.

Lucius's control was slipping. His hands moved to Naomi's hips as he tried to slow down his movements, but Naomi was gyrating her hips and taking him deeper and deeper inside. And when her entire body contracted around his shaft, he was lost.

And when she slid her tongue over his jawline, every vestige of control he'd been trying to maintain, to make it last between them, vanished and Lucius's body began to shake. A loud groan escaped his lips.

Pleasure.

Happiness.

That's what Naomi brought to him. And would always bring. He didn't move; he didn't want to extricate himself from being entwined with her body. He could stay like this forever. And now they always would be. Naomi was his forever.

Much later, after they'd succumbed to sleep, Lucius awoke with Naomi's head lying on his chest. He stroked her damp curls and she glanced up at him.

"Hey, sleepyhead," he whispered, looking down at her.

"Hey, you. You've exhausted me."

"I could say the same," Lucius responded.

A wide grin spread across Naomi's face. "Well, I had to get your mind off the reading of the will tomorrow and onto more important things."

Lucius frowned. "You heard?"

Naomi nodded. "I didn't mean to eavesdrop, but when you raised your voice, I was concerned."

"Well, you don't have to worry. I'll deal with it on my own. I'll go there tomorrow and face my new family, who probably wish I'd go back under the rock I crawled out from under."

Naomi slid up toward Lucius. "But you don't have to, honey. Not anymore. You'll never be alone again, because you have me. I'm coming with you."

"You are?"

"Absolutely. We're a family now. You and me." She pointed to his chest.

"I guess I never thought about it like that—because I—I've never been in love before, Naomi. Never been this happy. Never thought I could be."

"Neither did I, but I am so happy and I can't wait to be your wife and your partner. And it's why I will always be here for you, because you're the one for me, Lucius."

"And you're the woman for me."

Epilogue

The next morning, Lucius wasn't nervous about attending the reading of Arthur Knight's will. Why should he be? He hadn't even known the man. Sure, he'd read the dossier Adam had drawn up, but it told him nothing. He was certain that his presence would cause an uproar among the Knight clan. They were a tight bunch, or so he'd read. None of them interested him much except Maximus Xavier Knight, heir to the throne.

Maximus Knight was Lucius's half brother, a brother Lucius had known nothing of until that fateful night at the hospital when Charlotte Knight let the cat out of the bag about Jocelyn's longstanding affair with her husband. But it was Maximus whom Lucius longed to know. He'd always wanted a brother, someone to talk to and, in this case, since Lucius was older, look after.

But that had never happened, thanks to his mother's machinations. Much, he was sure, to Charlotte's disdain, he was here with his mother, Jocelyn, since she too had been named in the will along with him. But he wasn't alone—his fiancée was by his side.

What would he do without his Naomi?

Lucius certainly wouldn't have come here to this mausoleum the Knights called a house, but he also wouldn't have found the love of his life. How could he have known that hearing about that IPO a year ago would cause him to buy up stock in Brooks and Johnson and lead him to this moment? Lucius certainly wouldn't have thought it.

He'd been content with his bachelorhood until a feisty curly-haired beauty had entered his life. Meeting her was the single best thing to ever happen to him, and it was because of her that he would get through this day, no matter how hard.

"Ahem." A loud cough echoed from the front of the room as Robert Kellogg, Arthur's attorney, stood in front of the small gathering in the library of the Knight family home. "Thank you all for coming and attending the reading of the will for the late Arthur Knight, one of my oldest and dearest friends."

Lucius rolled his eyes upward. When he did, he caught sight of Maximus watching him warily from across the room as he sat with his mother, Charlotte, holding her hand. He sat rigidly upright in his chair in a classic suit that spoke of old money.

"Well, let's get right down to it," Robert said. He pulled out the legal document from his briefcase and began reading. "'I, Arthur Knight…'"

From his side, Naomi squeezed Lucius's hand, and he gave her a sideward glance. She mouthed, *You okay?*

He nodded and lowered his head. He wished Kellogg would just get on with it. Lucius couldn't care less about the old man's bequests to charitable organizations or giving away his most prized jewelry, vehicles and horses. Why was he here? What was the purpose? Arthur Knight had never claimed him in life. Why should he claim him in death?

He soon learned.

"When it comes to the disposition of Knight Shipping, I bestow 49 percent equally to my firstborn son, Lucius Knight, and to my youngest, Maximus Xavier Knight, with 2 percent to my dear girl, Tahlia Armstrong, for always listening to an old man."

"What!" Maximus rose to his full height and glared over at Lucius. "What the hell, Robert? He—" he pointed to Lucius "—gets half of Knight Shipping?" He shook his head. "I won't accept this. I've been groomed to run this company since the day I was born."

"He's right." Lucius rose from his chair, shaking off Naomi's pleas to sit down. "This can't be—you must have gotten it wrong. Why would he leave me stock? I don't know anything about the shipping business."

"It's true," Robert advised. "It was your father's wish that *both* his sons run his empire, Lucius. And you'll learn."

"I can't believe this." Stunned, Lucius sat down with his head between his hands. "Why would he do this? What could it possibly accomplish?"

"It was your father's desire that you two—" Robert looked at both men "—learn to work together, to become brothers one day. He felt like he owed you that after keeping you apart."

"And how are we supposed to do that?" Maximus bellowed.

"One day at a time," a feminine voice said from behind them.

Both Lucius and Maximus turned to stare at the quiet

yet stunningly gorgeous woman standing behind them.
"And who the heck are you?"

"I'm Tahlia Armstrong, your partner."

* * * * *

INTERVIEW WITH
A TYCOON

CARA COLTER

To all those readers who come to visit me on
Facebook, thank you!

CHAPTER ONE

STACY MURPHY WALKER's heart was beating way too fast. She wondered, gripping the steering wheel of her compact car tighter, how long a heart could beat this fast before it finally calmed itself out of pure exhaustion.

Or exploded, her mind, with its tendency to be overly imaginative, filled in helpfully.

But, still, she was entirely aware the slipping of her tires on the icy mountain roads was not solely responsible for the too-fast beating of her heart.

No, it was the sheer audacity of what she was doing.

Bearding the lion in his den.

A bronze name plaque, *McAllister*—in other words, the lion—set in a high stone fence, tasteful and easy to miss, told her she had arrived. Now what? She turned into the driveway but stopped before tackling the steep upward incline.

What was she going to say? *I need an interview with Kiernan McAllister to save my career as a business writer, so let me in?*

She'd had two hours to think about this! No, more. It had been three days since a friend, Caroline, from her old job had called and told her, that amidst the rumors that his company was being sold, McAllister had slipped away to his Whistler retreat.

"This story is made for you, Stacy," her friend had whispered. "Landing it will set you up as the most desired business freelancer in all of Vancouver! And you deserve it. What happened to you here was very unfair. This is a story that needs your ability to get to the heart of things." There had been a pause, and then a sigh. "Imagine getting to the heart of *that* man."

Stacy had taken the address Caroline had provided while contemplating, not the heart of *that* man, because she was done with men after all, but the humiliating fact that what had happened to her was obviously the going topic in the coffee room.

But Caroline was right. To scoop the news of the sale of the company would be a career coup for a newly set loose freelancer. To lace that scoop with insight into the increasingly enigmatic McAllister would be icing on the cake.

But more, Stacy felt landing such an important article could be the beginning of her return, not just to professional respect, but to personal self-respect!

What had she thought? That she was just going to waltz up to millionaire Kiernan McAllister's Whistler cottage and knock at his door?

McAllister was the founder and CEO of the highly regarded and wildly successful Vancouver-based company McAllister Enterprises.

And what was her expectation? That he would open his door, personally? And why would he—who had once been the darling of the media and graced the cover of every magazine possible—grant an audience to her?

McAllister had not given a single interview since the death of his best friend and brother-in-law almost exactly a year ago in a skiing accident—in a place accessible only by helicopter—that had made worldwide headlines.

Now, Stacy hoped she could convince him that she was the best person to entrust his story to.

And here was the problem with imagination.

She could imagine the interview going so well, that at the end of it, she would tell him about her charity, and ask him...

She shook herself. "One thing at a time!"

It was a shot in the dark, after all. And speaking of dark, if she did not get her act together soon, she would be driving back down this road in the dark. The thought made her shudder. She had some vague awareness that ice got icier at night!

She inched forward. She was nearly there, and yet one obstacle remained. The driveway had not been plowed of snow, and the incline looked treacherous. It was in much worse shape than the public roads had been in, and those had been the worst roads Stacy had ever faced!

At the steepest part of the hill, just before it crested, her car hesitated. She was sure she heard it groan, or maybe that sound came from her own lips. For an alarming moment, with her car practically at a standstill, Stacy thought she was going to start sliding backward down the hill.

In a moment of pure panic, she pressed down, hard, on the gas pedal. The wheels spun, and in slow motion, her car twisted to one side. But then the tires found purchase, and as her car shot forward, she straightened the wheel. The car acted as if it had been launched from a canon and careened over that final crest of the hill.

"Oh, God," she exclaimed. "Too fast!"

She practically catapulted into the courtyard. The most beautiful house she had ever seen loomed in front of her, and she was a breath away from crashing into it!

She hammered on the brakes and yanked on her steering wheel.

She'd been on a ride at the midway once that felt just like this: the car spun like a top across the icy driveway. She bumped violently over a curb, flattened some shrubs and came to a stop so sudden her head bounced forward and smashed into the steering wheel.

Dazed, she looked up. She had come to rest against a concrete fountain. It tipped dangerously. The snow it was filled with fell with a quiet thump on the hood of her car.

She sat there in shock, the silence embracing her like that white cloud of snow on her hood that was obliterating her view. It was tempting to just sit and mull over her bad luck, but no, that was not in keeping with the "new" Stacy Walker.

"There's lots to be grateful for," she told herself sternly. "I'm warm, for one! And relatively unhurt."

Relatively, because her head ached where she had hit it.

Putting that aside, she shoved her car into Reverse, hoping no one had seen what had just transpired. She put her foot down—gently, this time—on the gas, and pressed, but aside from the wheels making an awful whining noise, nothing happened. When she applied more gas, the whining sound increased to a shriek, but the car did not move.

With an edge of franticness, she tried one more time, but her car was stuck fast and refused to budge.

With a sigh of defeat, she turned the car off, rested her aching head against the steering wheel and gave in to the temptation to mull over her bad luck.

No fiancé.

No job.

Those two events linked in a way that had become fodder for the office gossip mill. And possibly beyond. Maybe she was the laughingstock of the entire business community.

At least she still had her charity work. But the sad fact

was, though the charity was so worthwhile, it limped along, desperately needing someone prominent—*exactly like Kiernan McAllister*—to thrust it to the next level.

So engrossed was she in her mulling that she shrieked with alarm when her car door was yanked open, spilling cold air into it, stealing the one thing she had been grateful for—warmth—instantly. She reared back from the steering wheel.

"Are you all right?"

The voice was deep and masculine and might have been reassuring. Except for the man it was attached to.

No. No. NO.

This was not how she had intended to meet Kiernan McAllister!

"I seem to be stuck," Stacy said with all the dignity she could muster. After the initial glance, she grasped the steering wheel and looked straight ahead, as if she was planning on going somewhere.

She felt her attempt at dignity might have failed, because he said, his voice the calm, steady voice of someone who had found another standing at the precipice, "That's all right. Let's get you out of there, and see what the damage is."

"Mostly to your garden, I'm afraid."

"I'm not worried about my garden." Again, that calm, talking-her-down-from-the-ledge tone of voice.

"Here. Take my hand."

She needed to reclaim her dignity by insisting she was fine. But when she opened her mouth, not a single sound came out.

"Take my hand."

This time, it was a command more than a request. Weakly, it felt like something of a relief to have choice taken away from her!

As if in a dream, Stacy put her hand in his. She felt it close around hers, warm and strong, and found herself pulled, with seemingly effortless might out of the car and straight into a wall of...man.

She should have felt the cold instantly. Instead, she felt like Charlie Chaplin doing a "slipping on a banana peel" routine. Her legs seemed to be shooting out in different directions.

She yanked free of his hands and threw herself against his chest, hugging tight.

And felt the warmth of it. And the shock. Bare skin? It was snowing out. How was it possible he was bare chested?

Who cares? a little voice whispered in accompaniment to the tingle moving up her spine. Given how humiliating her circumstances, she should not be so aware of the steely firmness of silky flesh and the sensation of being intimately close to pure power. She *really* should not be proclaiming the experience *delicious.*

"Whoa." He unglued her from him and put her slightly away, his hands settled on her shoulders. "Neither you nor your car appear properly shod for this weather."

He was right. Her feet were stylishly clad in a ballet slipper style shoe by a famous designer. She had bought the red slippers—à la Dorothy in the *Wizard of Oz*—when she had been more able to afford such whims.

The shoes had no grip on the sole. Stacy was no better prepared for snow than her car had been, and she was inordinately grateful for his steadying hands on her shoulders.

"What have you got on?" he asked, his tone incredulous.

The question really should have been what did he have on—since she was peripherally aware it was not much—but she glanced down at herself, anyway.

The shoes added a light Bohemian touch to an otherwise ultraconservative, just-above-the-knee gray skirt that she had paired with dark tights and a white blouse. At the last moment she had donned a darker gray sweater, which she was glad for now, as the snow fell around her. Nothing about her outfit—not even the shoes—commanded that incredulous tone.

Then, she dared glance fully at her rescuer and realized his question about what she had on was not in the context of her very stylish outfit at all. He was referring to her tires!

"Not even all seasons," he said, squinting past her at the front tire that rested on top of what had been, no doubt, a very expensive shrub. His tone was disapproving. "Summer tires. What were you thinking?"

It was terribly difficult to drag her attention away this unexpectedly delicious encounter with *the* Kiernan McAllister and focus on the question. She felt as if her voice was coming from under water when she answered.

"I've never put winter tires on my car," she confessed. "And if I were going to, it would not occur to me to do it in October. It is the season of falling leaves and pumpkins, not this."

"You could have asked for me to send a car," he said sternly.

Stacy contemplated that. *She* could have asked *the* Kiernan McAllister to send a car? In what universe? Obviously—and sadly—he was expecting someone else.

Or, was there the possibility Caroline had done more than give her an address? Did she have some kind of in with him? Had she set something up for Stacy?

That was her imagination again, because it was not likely he would be so intent on giving an interview he would send a car!

"Were you not prepared at all for mountain driving?"

"Not at all," she admitted. "I was born and raised in Vancouver. You know how often we get snow there."

At his grunt of what she interpreted as disapproval, she felt compelled to rush on. "Though I've always dreamed of a winter holiday. Skating on a frozen pond, learning to ski. That kind of thing. Now, I'm not so sure about that. Winter seems quite a bit more pleasant in movies and pictures and snow globes. Maybe I should just fast-forward to the hot chocolate in front of the fire."

Was she chattering? Oh, God, she was chattering nervously, and it wasn't just her teeth! *Shut up,* she ordered herself, but she had to add, "Humph. Reality and imagination collide, again."

Story of her life: imagining walking down the aisle, her gorgeous white dress flowing out behind her, toward a man who looked at her with such love and such longing...

She did not want to be having those kinds of treacherous thoughts around *this* man.

"I always liked this reality," McAllister said, and he actually reached out his free hand and caught a snowflake with it. Then he yanked his hand back abruptly, and the line around his mouth tightened and Stacy saw something mercurial in his storm-gray eyes.

She realized he had recalled, after the words came out of his mouth, that it was this reality—in the form of an avalanche—that had caused the death of his brother-in-law.

Sympathy clawed at her throat, as did a sense of knowing he was holding something inside that was eating him like acid.

It was a lot to understand from a glimpse of something in his eyes, from the way his mouth had changed, but this was exactly what Caroline had meant about Stacy's ability to get to the heart of a story.

For some reason—probably from the loss of her family when she was a child—she had a superhoned sense of intuition that had left her with an ability to see people with extraordinary clarity and tell their stories deeply and profoundly.

Not that McAllister looked as if he would be willing to have his story told at all, his secrets revealed, his feelings probed.

Stacy had a sudden sense if she did get to the heart of this man, as Caroline had wistfully suggested, she would find it broken.

McAllister's face was closed now, as if he sensed he had let his guard down just for that instant and that it might have revealed too much to her.

"What did you do when you lost control?" he asked her.

Of her life? How on earth could he tell? Was he has intuitive as she herself was?

But, to her relief, his attention was focused, disapprovingly, on her tires. He was still keeping her upright on the slippery ground, his hand now firmly clamped on her elbow, but if he was feeling the same sensation of being singed that she was, it in no way showed in his face. He had the look of a man who was always composed and in control.

"What did I do? I closed my eyes, and held on for dear life, of course!"

"Imagining a good outcome?" he said drily.

She nodded sadly. The collision with reality was more than evident.

He sighed, with seeming long-suffering, though their acquaintance had been extremely brief!

"You might want to keep in mind, for next time, if you lose control on ice, to try and steer into the spin, rather than away from it."

"That doesn't seem right."

"I know, it goes against everyone's first instinct. But

really, that's what you do. You go with it, instead of fighting it."

The sense of being singed increased when Stacy became suddenly and intensely aware that, despite the snow falling in large and chilly flakes all around them, despite the fact the driveway was pure ice, the question really should not have been what she had on for tires—or for clothes! That should not have been the question at all, given what he had on.

Which was next to nothing!

Maybe she had hit her head harder than she thought, and this whole thing was a dream. The scene was surreal after all.

How could it be possible McAllister was out here in his driveway, one hand gripping her firmly, glaring at her tires, when he was dressed in nothing more than a pair of shove-on sandals, a towel cinched around his waist?

The shock of it made her release the arm she clutched, and the wisps of her remaining sympathy were blown away as if before a strong wind. All that remained was awareness of him in a very different way.

She would have staggered back—and probably slipped again—but when she had let go, he had continued to hold on.

His warmth and his strength were like electricity, but not the benign kind that powered the toaster.

No, the furious, unpredictable kind. The lightning-bolt-that-could-tear-open-the-sky kind. The kind that could split apart trees and turn the world to fire.

Stacy realized the hammering of her heart during the slippery trip into the mountains, and after she had bounced over the curb into the fountain, had been but a pale prelude to the speeds her heart could attain!

CHAPTER TWO

KIERNAN MCALLISTER WATCHED the pulse in the woman's throat. The accident had obviously affected her more than she wanted to let on. Her face was very pale and he considered the awful possibility she was going to keel over, either because she was close to fainting or because her shoes were so unsuited to this kind of ground.

As he watched, her hand, tiny and pale, fluttered to her own throat to keep tabs on the wildly beating tattoo of her pulse, and McAllister tightened his grip on her even more.

"Are you okay?" he asked again. He could feel his brow furrow as he looked in her face.

He had told his sister, Adele, not to send assistance. He had told her, in no uncertain terms, that he found it insulting that she thought he needed it. She seemed to have agreed, but he should have guessed she only pretended to acquiesce.

"I think I'm just shaken."

The girl—no, she wasn't a girl, despite her diminutive size—had a voice that was low and husky, a lovely softness to it, unconsciously sexy. She was, in fact, a lovely young woman. Dark curls sprang untamed around a delicate, pale, elfin face. Her eyes were green and huge, her nose a little button, her chin had a certain defiant set to it.

Kiernan's annoyance at his sister grew.

If she had needed to send someone—and in her mind, apparently she had—he would have hoped for someone no-nonsense and practical. Someone who arrived in a car completely outfitted for winter and in sturdy shoes. In other words someone who coped, pragmatically, as a matter of course, with every eventuality. If he was going to picture that someone he would picture someone middle-aged, dowdy and stern enough to intimidate Ivan the Terrible into instant submission.

Now, he felt as if he had two people, other than himself, to be responsible for!

"You're sure you are all right?" He cast a glance at her car. Maybe he could get it unstuck and convince her to disobey his sister's orders, whatever they were, and leave him alone here.

Alone. That was what called to him these days, the seduction of silence, of not being around people. The cabin was perfect. Hard to access, no cell service, spotty internet.

His sister didn't see his quest for solitude as a good thing. "You just go up there and mull over things that can't be changed!" his sister had accused him.

And perhaps that was true. Certainly, the presence of his little nephew did not leave much time for mulling! And perhaps that had been Adele's plan. His sister could be diabolical after all.

But the woman who had just arrived looked more like distraction than heaven-sent helper, so he was going to figure out how to get her unstuck and set her on her way no matter what Adele had to say about it.

For some reason, he did not want the curly-headed, green-eyed, red-shoed woman to make it past the first guard and into his house!

He regarded her thoughtfully, trying to figure out why he felt he did not want to let her in. And then he knew. Despite the fact the accident had left her shaken, she seemed determined to not let it affect her.

Look at the shoes! She was one of those positive, sunny, impractical people and he did not want her invading his space.

When had he come to like the dark of his own misery and loneliness so much?

"Yes, I'm fine," she said, her voice, tremulous with bravery, piercing the darkness of his own thoughts. "More embarrassed than anything."

"And well you should be." The faint sympathy he had felt for her melted. "A person with a grain of sense and so little winter driving experience should not have tackled these roads today. I told her not to send you."

She blinked at that. Opened her mouth, then closed it, looked down at her little red shoes and ineffectually tried to scrape the snow off them.

"I detest stubborn women," he muttered. "Why would you travel today?"

"Perhaps it wasn't my most sensible decision," she said, and he watched the chin that had hinted at a stubborn nature tilt upward a touch, "but I can't guarantee the result would not have been similar, even on the finest summer day."

He lifted an eyebrow at her, intrigued despite himself.

"My second name is Murphy, for my maternal grandfather, and it is very suiting. I am like a poster child for Murphy's Law."

He had the feeling she was trying to keep things light in the face of the deliberate dark judgment in his own features, so he did not respond to the lightness of her tone, just raised his eyebrow even higher at her.

"Murphy's Law?"

"You know," she clarified, trying for a careless grin and missing by a mile. "Anything that can go wrong, will."

He stared at her. For a moment, the crystal clear green of those eyes clouded, and he felt some thread of shared experience, of unspeakable sorrow, trying to bind them together.

His sense of needing to get rid of her strengthened. But then he saw the blood in her hair.

Stacy could have kicked herself! What on earth had made her say that to him? It was not at all in keeping with the new her: strong, composed, sophisticated. You didn't blurt out things like that to a perfect stranger! She had intended it to sound light; instead, it sounded like a pathetic play for sympathy!

And, damn it, sometimes when you opened that door you did not know what was going to come through.

And what came through for her was a powerful vision of the worst moment of *anything that can go wrong will* in her entire life. She was standing outside her high school gym. She closed her eyes against it, but it came anyway.

Standing outside the high school waiting anxiously, just wanting to be anywhere but there. Waiting for the car that never came. A teacher finding her long after everyone else had gone home, wrapping her in her own sweater, because Stacy was shivering. She already knew there was only one reason that her father would not have come. Her whole world gone so terribly and completely wrong in an instant...left craving the one thing she could never have again.

Her family.

She had hit her head harder than she thought! That's what was causing this. Or was it the look she had glimpsed ever so briefly in his own eyes? The look that had given her the sensation that he was a man bereft?

"You actually don't look okay," he decided.

She opened her eyes to see him studying her too intently. Just what every woman—even one newly devoted to independence—wanted to hear from Kiernan McAllister!

"I don't?"

"You're not going to faint, are you?"

"No!" Her denial was vehement, given the fact that she had been contemplating that very possibility—heart implosion—only seconds ago.

"You've gone quite pale." He was looking at her too intensely.

"It's my coloring," she said. "I always look pale."

This was, unfortunately, more than true. Though she had the dark brown hair of her father, she had not inherited his olive complexion. Her mother had been a redhead, and she had her ultrapale, sensitive skin and green eyes.

"You are an unusual combination of light and dark." She squirmed under his gaze, until he tightened his hold.

"Remember Murphy's Law," he warned her. "It's very slippery out here, and those shoes look more suited to a bowling alley than a fresh snowfall."

A bowling alley? "They're Kleinbacks," she insisted on informing him, trying to shore up her quickly disintegrating self-esteem. The shoes, after all proclaimed *arrival,* not disaster.

"Well, you'll be lyin'-on-your-backs if you aren't careful in them. You don't want to add to your injuries."

"Injuries?"

Still holding her one arm firmly, he used his other—he seemed to have his cell phone in it—and whipped off the towel he had around his waist!

Still juggling the towel and the phone, he found a dry corner of it, and pressed it, with amazing gentleness, onto the top of her head. "I didn't see it at first, amongst the chocolate curls—"

Chocolate curls? It was the nicest way her hair had ever been described! Did that mean he was noticing more about her than his sack-of-potatoes hold had indicated?

"—but there's blood in your hair."

His voice was perfection, a silk scarf caressing the sensitive area of her neck.

"There is?" She peeked at him around the edges of the towel.

He dabbed at her hair—again, she was taken with the tenderness of his touch, when he radiated such a powerful aura—and then he turned the towel to her, proof.

It looked like an extremely expensive towel, brilliant white, probably Egyptian cotton, and now it had little speckles of red from her blood. Though for some reason, maybe the knock on the head, the sight of all that blood was not nearly as alarming to her as he was.

Since he had removed the towel, Stacy forced herself not to let her gaze stray from his face. Water was sliding out of the dark silk of his hair and down the utterly and devastatingly attractive lines of his features.

"You aren't naked, are you?" she asked, her voice a squeak of pure dismay.

Something twitched around the sensual line of his mouth as McAllister contemplated Stacy's question, but she couldn't really tell if he was amused or annoyed by it.

His mouth opened, then closed, and then, his eyes never leaving her face, he said evenly, "No, I'm not."

She dared to unglue her eyes from his face. They skittered over the very naked line of his broad shoulders, down the beautiful cut of chest muscles made more beautiful by the snowflakes that melted on them and sent beads of waters sliding down to the ridged muscle of washboard abs. Riding low on his hips…her eyes flew back to the relative safety of his face.

Only that wasn't really safe, either.

"Underwear?" she squeaked.

He regarded her thoughtfully for a moment. She resisted an urge to squirm, again, under the firm hands at her elbow, and his stripping gaze.

"Kleinbacks," he said, straight-faced.

She was pretty sure the designer company did not make men's underwear, and that was confirmed when something very like a smile, however reluctant, played along the hard line of those lips. Stunned, Stacy realized she was being *teased* by Kiernan McAllister.

But the light that appeared for a moment in his eyes was gone almost instantly, making her aware he had caught himself lightening up, and not liked it. Not liked it one little bit.

"Swim trunks." His voice was gravelly, amusement stripped from it.

"Oh!" She sagged with relief, then looked, just to make sure. They were really very nice swim trunks, not the scanty kind that triathletes wore. Still, there was quite a bit more of him uncovered than covered, and she felt herself turn scarlet as she watched a another snow drop melt and slide past the taut muscles of his stomach and into the waistband of his shorts.

"It doesn't really seem like swimming weather," she offered, her voice strangled.

"I was in the hot tub in the back of the house when I heard the commotion out here."

"Oh! Of course." She tried to sound as if she was well acquainted with the kind of people who spent snowy afternoons doing business from their hot tubs—he did have his phone with him, after all—but she was fairly certain she did not pull it off.

Knowing what she did about him, it occurred to her that

perhaps, despite the presence of the phone, he wasn't doing business. One thing she knew from her life interviewing high-powered execs? They were attached to those phones as though they were lifelines!

Kiernan McAllister might be entertaining someone in his hot tub.

"Alone," he said, as if he had read her thoughts.

She didn't like the idea that he might be able to read her thoughts. But there was also something about the way he said *alone* that made her think of icy, windswept mountain peaks and a soul gone cold.

Even though he was the one with no clothes on, in the middle of a snowstorm, it was Stacy who shivered. She tried to tell herself it was from snow melting off her neck and slithering down her back, but she knew that was not the entire truth.

It was pure awareness of the man who stood before her, his complexities both unsettling her and reluctantly intriguing her. His hands resting, warm and strong—dare she consider the thought, protectively—on her. How on earth could he be so completely unselfconscious? And why wasn't he trembling with cold?

Obviously, his skin was heated from the hot tub, not that he was the kind of man who trembled! He was supremely comfortable with himself, radiating a kind of confidence that could not be manufactured.

Plus, Stacy's mind filled in helpfully, he had quite a reputation. He would not be unaccustomed to being in some state of undress in front of a lady.

Impossibly, she could feel her cheeks turning even more crimson, and he showed no inclination to put her out of her misery. He regarding her appraisingly, snow melting on his heated skin, a cloud of steam rising around him.

Finally, he seemed to realize it was very cold out here!

"Let's get in," he suggested. She heard reluctance in his voice. He did not want her in his house!

She was not sure why, though it didn't seem unreasonable. A stranger plows into your fountain. You hardly want to entertain them.

But he was expecting someone. He didn't want to entertain that person, either?

"I'll take a closer look at your head. There's not a whole lot of blood, I'm almost certain it's superficial. We'll get you into Whistler if it's not."

It occurred to her he was a man who would do the right thing even if it was not what he particularly wanted to do.

And that he would not like people who did the wrong thing. She shivered at the thought. He misinterpreted the shiver as cold and strengthened his grip on her, as if he didn't trust her not to keel over or slip badly on his driveway. He turned her away from her car and toward the warmth of his house.

Aside from her car in the garden, the driveway was empty. The household vehicles were no doubt parked in the five-car garage off to one side.

The house inspired awe. If this was a cottage, what on earth did McAllister's main residence look like?

The house was timber framed, the lower portions of it faced in river rock. Gorgeous, golden logs, so large three people holding hands would barely form a circle around them, acted as pillars for the front entryway. The entry doors were hand carved and massive, the windows huge, plentiful and French-paned, the rooflines sweeping and complicated.

Through the softly falling flakes of snow, Stacy was certain she felt exactly how Cinderella must have felt the first time she saw the castle.

Or maybe, she thought, with a small shiver of pure apprehension, more like Beauty when she found Beast's lair.

McAllister let go of her finally when he reached the front door and held it open for her. She was annoyed with herself that she missed the security of his touch instantly, and yet the house seemed to embrace her. The rush of warm air that greeted her was lovely, the house even lovelier.

Stacy's breath caught in her throat as she gaped at her surroundings.

"It's beautiful," she breathed. "Like upscale hunting lodge—very upscale—meets five-star hotel."

"It suits me," he said, and then as an afterthought, "far more than my condo in Vancouver."

Again, her intuition kicked in, and this time the reporter in her went on red alert. Was that a clue that he was going to leave his high-powered life behind him as rumors had been saying for months?

McAllister turned, stepped out of his sandals, expecting her to follow him. Stacy realized she couldn't tromp through the house in her now very wet—and probably ruined—shoes. She scraped them off her feet, dropped her wet sweater beside them, and then she was left scrambling to catch up to his long strides, as it had never even occurred to him that she was not on his heels.

As McAllister led her through his magnificent home, Stacy was further distracted from the confession she should have been formulating about why she was really here, by not just the long length of his naked back but the unexpected beauty of his space and what it said about him.

The design style was breathtaking. Old blended with new seamlessly. Modern met antique. Rustic lines met sleek clean ones and merged.

There were hand-knotted Turkish rugs and bearskins,

side by side, modern art and Western paintings, deer ant-
ler light fixtures and ones that looked to be by the famous
crystal maker, Swarovski. There were ancient woven baskets beside contemporary vases.

The decor style was rugged meets sophisticated, and
Stacy thought it reflected the man with startling accuracy.

"I've never seen floors like this," she murmured.

"Tigerwood. It actually gets richer as it ages."

"Like people," she said softly.

"If they invest properly," he agreed.

"That is not what I meant!"

He cast a look over his shoulder at her, and she saw he
looked irritated.

"People," she said firmly, "become richer because they
accumulate wisdom and life experience."

He snorted derisively. "Or," he countered, "they become
harder. This floor is a hundred and seventy percent harder
than oak. I chose it because I wanted something hard."

And she could see that that was also what he wanted
for himself: a hard, impenetrable surface.

"This floor will last forever," he said with satisfaction.

"Unlike people?" she challenged him.

"You said it, I didn't." She heard the cynicism and yet
contemplated his desire for something lasting. He was an
avowed bachelor and had been even before the accident.
But had the death of his brother-in-law made him even
more cynical about what lasted and what didn't?

Clearly, it had.

They walked across exotic hardwood floors into a
great room. The walls soared upward, at least sixteen
feet high, the ceilings held up by massive timbers. A fireplace, floor to ceiling, constructed of the same river rock
that was on the exterior of the house, anchored one end of
the room.

A huge television was mounted above a solid old barn beam mantel. It was on, with no sound. A football game in process. A wall of glass—the kind that folded back in the summer to make indoor and outdoor space blend perfectly—led out to a vast redwood deck.

Through falling snow, Stacy could see a deep and quiet forest beyond the deck and past that, the silent, jagged walls of the mountains.

To one side of that deck, where it did not impede the sweeping views from the great room, steam escaped from the large hot tub that her arrival had pulled McAllister from.

The tub seemed as if it were made for entertaining large groups of people of the kind she had written about in her former life. She had never attended a gathering worthy of this kind of space. Or been invited to one, either. As reporter, she had been on the outside of that lifestyle looking in.

The room made Stacy uncomfortably and awkwardly aware she was way out of her league here.

What league? she asked herself, annoyed. She wasn't here to marry the man! She just wanted to talk to him.

Besides, it seemed to her that a room like this cried for that thing called family. In fact, she could feel an ache in the back of her throat as she thought of that.

"Are you coming?"

She realized she had stopped and he had kept going. Now he glanced back at her, and she sensed his impatience. She was trying to savor this unexpected glimpse into a different world, and he wanted their enforced time together over!

Given that, it would be foolish to ask him the question that had popped into her mind the moment she had entered the grandeur of this room. But ask she did!

"Do you spend Christmas here?" She could hear the wistfulness in her own voice.

He stopped, those formidable brows lowered. "I don't particularly like Christmas."

"You don't like Christmas?"

"No." He had folded his arms across his chest, and his look did not invite any more questions.

But she could not help herself! "Is it recent? Your aversion to Christmas?" she asked, wondering if his antipathy had something to do with the death of his brother-in-law. From experience, she knew that, after a loss, special occasions could be unbearably hard.

"No," he said flatly. "I have always hated Christmas."

His look was warning her not to pursue it but for a reason she couldn't quite fathom—maybe because this beautiful house begged for a beautiful Christmas, she did not leave it.

"A tree would look phenomenal over there," she said stubbornly.

His eyes narrowed on her. She was pretty sure he was not accustomed to people offering him an opinion he had not asked for!

"We—" He paused at the *we,* and she saw that look in his eyes. Then, he seemed to force himself to go on, his tone stripped of emotion. "We always go away at Christmas, preferably someplace warm. We've never spent Christmas in this house."

Her disappointment felt sharp. She ordered herself to silence, but her voice mutinied. "It's never had a Christmas tree?"

He folded his arms more firmly over his chest, his body language clearly saying *unmovable.* She repeated the order for silence, but she could not seem to stop her voice.

"Think of the size of tree you could put there! And

there's room for kids to ride trikes across the floors, and grandparents to sit by the fire."

He looked extremely annoyed.

She could picture it all. Generations of family sitting in the two huge distressed leather sofas faced each other over a priceless rug, teenagers running in wet from the hot tub, eggnog on the coffee table made out of burled wood. Toys littering the floor.

Over there, in that open-concept kitchen with its industrial-sized stainless-steel fridge, the massive granite-topped island could be full of snacks, the espresso machine pumping out coffee, or maybe you could make hot chocolate in them, she wasn't certain.

"I guess in your line of work," he said gruffly, "you're allowed a certain amount of magical thinking."

What kind of work did he think she did? And why couldn't she just leave it at that?

"It's not magical," she said through clenched teeth. "It's real. It can be real."

He looked annoyed and unconvinced.

Why had she started this? She could feel something like tears stinging the back of her eyes.

"You have that about-to-faint look again," he said, coming back to her. "I think you hit your head harder than we realize."

"I think you're right," she said. She ordered herself to stop speaking. But she didn't.

CHAPTER THREE

"IF I HAD a room like this? That is what I would want to fill it with," the woman said. "The important things. The things that really last. The things that are real. Love. Family."

Real. Kiernan could tell her a thing or two about the reality of love and family that would wipe that dreamy look off her face. But why? Let her have her illusions.

They were no threat to him.

Or maybe they were, because just for a flicker of a moment he felt a whisper of longing sneak along his spine.

He shook it off. He just wanted to have a look at the bump on her head and send her on her way. He did not want to hear about her sugarplum visions of a wonderful world!

"Nothing lasts," he told her, his voice a growl.

Stacy went very still. For a moment she looked as if she might argue, but then his words seemed to hit her, like arrows let loose that had found her heart.

To his dismay, for a moment he glimpsed in her face a sorrow he thought matched his own. He was intrigued but had enough good sense not to follow up! Not to encourage her in any way to share her vision with him.

"Follow me," he said. "I think I've got a first-aid kit in my bathroom."

His bathroom? Didn't he have a first-aid kit somewhere

else? He did, but it was outside and around the back of the
house, where the staging area for outdoor excursions was,
where he stored the outdoor equipment.

No, it was sensible to take her to the closest first-aid kit,
to keep her out of the cold, to not take her through more
snow in those ridiculous shoes.

But through his bedroom? Into his bathroom? It occurred to him that he should have sat her down in the
kitchen and brought the first-aid kit to her.

He was not thinking with his normal razor-sharp pro-
cesses, which was understandable. He told himself it had
nothing to do with the unexpected arrival of a beautiful
woman in his fountain and everything to do with Ivan.

He hesitated at the double doors to his master suite
and then flung them open and watched her closely as she
preceded him. He saw the room through her eyes, which
were wide and awed.

The ceiling soared upward, magnificent and timber
framed. But here the floors, instead of being hardwood,
were carpeted with a thick, plush pile that their feet sank
into. There was a huge bed, the bedding and the abundance
of pillows in a dozen shades of gray.

She was blushing as she looked at the bed, which he
should have found amusing as all get-out. Instead, he found
it reluctantly endearing.

Who blushed anymore?

Something that heightened color in her cheeks, the way
she caught her plump lower lip between her teeth, made
Kiernan's mouth go dry, and so he led her hastily through
to the bathroom. Again, he saw it through her eyes. A wall
of windows opened to the deck and hot tub area.

There was a shower a dozen people could have gotten into, and her blush deepened when she looked at that.
He'd never shared this room with anyone, but let her

think what she wanted. It might keep him safe from this niggling awareness of her that was bugging him the way a single gnat could spoil a perfect summer day on the hammock with a book.

She stared at the deep, stand-alone tub and swallowed hard. While the shower might hold dozens, it was more than evident the tub could only comfortably fit two! Her eyes flitted wildly around the room and then stopped and widened.

Her eyes, he noticed, annoyed with himself, were green as the moss that clung to the stones of the hot spring deep in the mountains behind this cottage.

"That is not a fireplace," she whispered. "In your bathroom?"

"You want it on?" he asked innocently. "Are you cold?"

He was fairly sure it was evident to even her, with her aura of innocence, that a fireplace like that was not about cold but about romance.

And yet he did not like thinking about her in that light. It was evident to him, on a very brief acquaintance, she was not the type of woman who would share his vision of romance.

For him, it was a means to an end, the age-old game of seduction.

The remarks about his floors and the suitability of his room for a Christmas tree were little hints she was not his type. By her own admission, she was the kind of girl who believed in love and things lasting.

Romancing a girl like her would be hard work! He was willing to bet, despite her awe of the room, it would require something a little less superficial than a bathtub and a fireplace. Romancing a girl like her would require time and patience and a willingness to be a better person.

No, he would stick with his type. Because his type required nothing of him but a few baubles and some good times, no real emotional engagement.

He had always been like that, avoiding emotional attachment. He had been like that before his friend Danner had died. Kiernan had a sudden unwelcome memory of Christmas ornaments being smashed. He suspected the memory had erupted out of nowhere because Murphy here had seen Christmas in a room where it had never been. Kiernan's early life had always been threaded through with the tension of unpredictability, Christmas worse than most times of year.

For a while, having survived the minefield of his childhood, Kiernan had enjoyed the illusion of complete control. He had a sense of making not just his world safe and predictable, but that of his sister, Adele, too.

Yup, he had felt like quite the hero. And then Danner had died. Plunging him into a dark place where his real power in the world seemed horribly limited, where hope and dreams seemed like the most dangerous of things.

And none of that fit with a girl like this, who, whether she knew it or not, wore dreams on her sleeves. Who, despite—if her eyes were any indicator—having gone a round or two with life, seemed to still have that inexplicable ability to believe...

"Sure," she said after a moment, startling him out of his thoughts. "Put it on. The fireplace." She giggled. "I may never pass this way again."

"We can only hope," he muttered, and saw her flinch, the smile die, the words striking her like arrows again.

Just a reminder of how she was soft and he was hard, a reason this was never going anywhere, except him standing on the stairs seeing her off as she drove away.

"Nothing personal," he said. "It just wasn't my idea for you to come. I don't need you."

Having done quite enough damage—he really should not be allowed around these sensitive types—Kiernan turned from her and flicked a switch so that the flames within the fireplace licked to life.

"I've changed my mind," she said proudly. "I don't care to have it on."

See? In very short time his abrasive self was managing to hurt her. Not making any effort to hide his impatience, Kiernan flicked the fire back off and gestured at an upholstered chaise.

Once she was settled, he came back, towered over her and studied the top of her head. "I'm just going to clean it first. We'll see what we've got. Ironic, isn't it, that I'm rescuing you?"

"In what way?" she stammered.

"You're supposed to be rescuing me."

Stacy studied Kiernan and realized his tone was deeply sardonic. Despite the glimpses of shadows she had detected in his eyes, she was not sure she had ever seen a man who looked less like he would appreciate rescuing than Kiernan McAllister!

He was bigger in real life than photos had prepared her for, the breadth of his shoulders blocking out the view of the fireplace!

The bathroom was huge, but with him leaning over her, his real-life stature left her feeling shocked. Even though Kiernan McAllister had graced the covers of zillions of magazines, including, eight times, the one she no longer worked for, nothing could have prepared her for him in this kind of proximity.

Pictures, of course, did not have a scent clinging to them. His filled her nostrils: it was as if he had come, not from a hot tub, but from the forest around this amazing house. McAllister smelled richly of pine, as if he had absorbed the essence of the snow-laden trees through his pores!

He was considered not only Vancouver's most successful businessman, but also its most eligible bachelor, and here in the bathroom with him, his scent filling her senses, his hands gentle on her injured head, it was easy to see why!

In each of those photos that Stacy had seen of him, McAllister was breathtakingly handsome and sure of himself. Behind that engaging smile, he had oozed the confidence and self-assurance of the very successful and very wealthy. His grooming had always been perfect: smooth shaven, every dark hair in place, his custom-made clothing hinting at but not showing a perfect male body.

In those pictures, he looked like a man who could handle anything the world tossed at him, smile and toss it right back.

And that's what he had a track record for doing. From daring real estate deals to providing start-up funds for fledgling companies that no one else would take a risk on, McAllister had developed a reputation as being tough, fair and savvy. In the business world, his instincts were considered brilliant.

Not to mention that, with his amazing looks, McAllister was that most eligible bachelor that every unmarried woman dreamed—secretly or openly—of landing.

And McAllister had availed himself to every perk his considerable fortune allowed him. He had squired some of the most beautiful and famous women in the world on that arm that Stacy had just touched.

But, despite having it all, he seemed driven to more, and he had as casually sought danger as some men would sample a fine wine.

And it was that penchant for the adrenaline rush that had led from *that* McAllister to this one.

Being able to watch him while he tended her head, she could see his silver-gray eyes were mesmerizing and yet different in some fundamental way from how he appeared in pictures.

Her mind grappled to figure out what that difference was, but the distraction of his near nakedness, the luxury of the bathroom and his hands on her head were proving formidable.

"Ouch."

"Sorry."

She deliberately looked at the floor instead of up into his face to break the trance she was in. Instead, it felt oddly intimate and totally inappropriate that Stacy could see the naked length of his lower legs. His feet were totally bare.

And, she thought, entirely sexy.

But she didn't find feet sexy. Did she?

Since his feet provided no more reprieve from the terrible war of sensation going on within her, Stacy dragged her gaze away from his toes and back up the length of him. Despite his disheveled appearance—his hair, always perfectly groomed for magazine shoots, was sticking up in a cowlick at the back of his head, and his cheeks and the jut of that formidable chin were shadowed in dark whiskers—when Stacy looked into his face, she had to swallow a gulp of pure intimidation.

Kiernan McAllister radiated a kind of power that could not be tarnished by arriving at the scene of an accident, dripping wet and with a towel around his waist. Even though her job at *Icons of Business* had entailed interviewing dozens of very successful businesspeople, Stacy was not sure she had ever encountered such a prime example of pure of *presence* before.

McAllister's wet hair, the color of just-brewed coffee, was curling at the tips. The stubble on his face accentuated the hard, masculine lines of his features.

The out-of-the-storm look of his hair and being unshaven gave him a distinctly roguish look, and despite his state of undress, he could have been a pirate relishing his next conquest, like a highwayman about to draw his sword.

His eyes were a shade of silver that added to her sense that he could be dangerous in the most tantalizing of ways.

In the pictures she had seen of him, his eyes had intrigued, a faint light at the back of them that she had interpreted as mischievous, as if all his incredible successes in the business world were nothing more than a big game and it was a game that he was winning.

But, of course, that was before the accident where his brother-in-law had been killed.

There was the difference. Now McAllister's eyes had something in them as shattered as glass, cool, a barrier that he did not want penetrated.

By someone looking for a story. In that moment, Stacy knew Caroline had not set up anything for her. And she also knew, without asking, he would turn her down flat if she requested an interview.

He stepped back from her, regarded his handiwork on her head. "I think we're done here," he said, evidently pleased with his first-aid skills.

He once again offered his hand. She took it and he pulled her from the chair. She relished the feeling of his hand, but he let her go as soon as she was standing. She faced herself in the mirror. It was much worse than she thought.

The top of her hair was almost completely covered with a tightly taped down piece of gauze.

Now she really did look and feel like the poster child

for Murphy's Law. Everything that could go wrong, *had*. Who wanted to look like this in the presence of such a devastatingly attractive man?

Even if he was sardonic. And didn't believe in Christmas. Or love.

"That's going to be murder to get off," she said, when she saw he had caught her dismayed expression.

"Isn't it?" he said, apparently pleased that his handiwork was going to be so hard to remove.

She sighed. It was definitely time to set him straight about who she really was and what she wanted. She took a deep breath.

The phone that he had set on the counter began to ring.

Only it was the oddest ring she had ever heard. It sounded exactly like a baby squawking! There was no way a man like McAllister picked a ringtone like that!

In a split second, Kiernan McAllister went from looking relaxed and at ease with himself to a warrior ready to do battle! Stacy watched his face grow cold, remote, underscoring that sense of a solider being ready for whatever came next.

"What on earth?" she whispered, taking in his stance and his hardened facial features. "What's the matter?"

"It's time," he said, his tone terse. "He's awake."

"Who's awake?"

McAllister said nothing, his gaze on the phone, his brow furrowed in consternation. If he were a general, she had the feeling he would be checking his weapons, strapping on his armor, calling out his instructions to his soldiers.

"That isn't a cell phone, is it?" Stacy asked slowly. McAllister was staring at it as if he was a tourist in some exotic place who had discovered a snake under his bed.

The squawking sound escalated, and McAllister took a deep breath, squared his shoulders.

"A phone?" he asked, his voice impatient. "What kind of person has a phone in the hot tub?"

In her career she had met dozens of men who she did not doubt took their phones everywhere with them, including into their hot tubs! Now, she could see clearly he would not be one of them.

"Cell phones don't work up here. The mountains block the signal. I think it's part of what I like about the place." He frowned as if realizing he had told her something about himself he didn't want to.

That he needed a break from the demands of his business. He was no doubt the kind of driven individual who would see some kind of failure in that.

But before she could contemplate that too long, the phone made that squawking sound again, louder.

"What is it then, if it's not your phone?"

"It's the monitor," he said.

"The monitor," she repeated.

"The baby monitor," he said, as if she had not already guessed it.

She stared at it with him, listened to the squawking noises emitting from it. The monitor was small and state-of-the-art, it looked almost exactly like a cell phone.

But if was definitely a monitor, and there was definitely a baby on the other end of it!

CHAPTER FOUR

BABY?

Stacy prided herself on the fact that she had arrived prepared! She knew everything there was to know about Kiernan McAllister.

And he did not have a baby!

McAllister folded his arms across the breadth of his naked chest and raised that dark slash of an eyebrow at her. "I told you, you were rescuing me, not the other way around."

"Excuse me?" Stacy said, dazed by this turn of events.

"Your turn to ride to the rescue, though I must say, you haven't exactly inspired confidence so far." He reached out and turned down the volume on the monitor, inspecting her anew, like a general might inspect a newly enlisted person before sending them into battle.

His voice was hard-edged, and faintly amused as he regarded her, and she was struck again that, despite his words, he was the man least likely to need a rescue of any sort. Even if he did need one, he would never ask for it!

"I'm riding to your rescue?" Stacy asked, just to clarify.

It was a good thing he seemed to be being sarcastic, because it would be terrible to break it to him that she was the least likely person to count on for a rescue, her own life being ample evidence of that.

"Just like the cavalry," he said, and cocked his head at her blank expression. "I'm stranded. The fort is under full attack. I have no bullets left. And in rides the cavalry."

"Me?" she squeaked. "I'm the cavalry?"

He eyed her with doubt that appeared to mirror her own, then sighed again. "You are the nanny Adele insisted on sending, aren't you?"

The nanny!

Stacy realized Caroline had not called and set something up for her. Far from it! *A nanny. Kiernan McAllister was expecting a nanny!* That's who he would have sent a car through the snowy day for!

Fortunately, Stacy was saved from having to answer because he turned and held open the door of the bathroom for her.

"That way," he said. "To the guest room. You can help me temporarily, until I get your car looked after."

In a daze, she turned left and went down the hall ahead of McAllister.

His voice followed her, his tone mulling. "I thought he would sleep longer. He has barely slept since he got here. Who would have thought that one small baby could be so demanding? He doesn't sleep. And he doesn't want to eat. You know what he does?"

Again, he didn't wait for an answer.

"He cries." His voice was lowered, and she thought she detected the slightest admission he might be in over his head. "Not that I couldn't handle it. But, if my sister thinks I need saving, who am I to argue?"

Stacy swallowed hard. What was it about the thought of saving a man like him that made her go almost weak with wanting? But, despite what his sister thought, the look on his face made it very apparent he did not agree!

That was the *old* her that would have liked him to *need*

her, Stacy reminded herself sternly. The old her: naive and romantic, believing in the power of love and hoping for a family gathered in a big room around a Christmas tree.

Obviously, McAllister did not need saving. She had rarely seen a man so self-assured! What man could stand outside dripping wet and barely clothed and act as if nothing was out of the ordinary?

Still, there was that look in his eyes...defiant, daring her to see need in him! Foolishly it made her want to turn toward him, run her hand over the coarse stubble of that jaw and assure him that, yes, she was there to rescue him and that everything would be all right.

Instead, she kept moving forward until she came to an open door and peered inside. There was a playpen set up in the room, and in it was a nest of messy blankets and stuffed toys.

Holding himself up on the bumper, howling with indignation and jumping up and down, was the most beautiful baby she had ever seen. He looked like he was a little over a year, chubby, dark hair every which way, completely adorable in pale blue sleepers that had the snaps done up crooked.

Was he McAllister's baby? While a secret baby would have been the story of the century, her thoughts drifted way too quickly from story potential to far more treacherous territory.

What on earth was Kiernan McAllister doing with a baby when that was what she had always wanted?

It caught her off guard and left her reeling even more than spinning her car into his front garden had!

We want such different things, her ex-boyfriend, Dylan, had said with a sad shake of his head, dismissing her dreams of reclaiming a traditional life like the one she had grown up in as a life sentence of dullness.

Their last night together, the extravagant dinner had made Stacey think he was going to offer her an engagement ring.

Instead, she had been devastated by his invitation to move in with him!

Really, his defection had been the last straw in a life where love had ripped her wide open once too often. To add to the sting of it all, they had worked in the same office, he her direct superior, and she had been let go after their breakup, which she—and everyone else at the office—knew was entirely unfair.

Still, in the wake of her life disasters, Stacy had made up her mind she would be wounded by love and life no more! But now the yearning inside her caused by seeing that Christmas-perfect great room, and now by thinking of this man before her with a baby, only made her realize how much work she had yet to do!

Though why, when she knew how much work she had to do, her eyes would go to McAllister's lips, she could not be certain. McAllister's lips were full and bold, the lower one in particular spine-tinglingly sensual.

Dangerous, she told herself. He was a dangerous kind of man. His lips should be declared the pillars of salt one should never look at for danger of being lost forever. She was stunned by both the peril and intensity of her thoughts.

She was not, after all, who he was expecting, and she was certainly not a qualified nanny.

But she felt as if she *had* to know the story of the baby.

And McAllister—despite the outward appearance of confidence—was obviously desperate for help in this particular situation.

And if she could give him that even temporarily, McAllister might be much more amenable to the real reason she had come!

Gratitude could go a long way, after all.

The baby was startled into silence by her appearance. He regarded her with deep suspicion.

As if he knew she was trying to pass herself off as something she was not.

He seemed to make up his mind about her and began to whimper again.

"Ivan, stop it!" McAllister ordered.

The baby, surprisingly, complied.

"Ivan," she said, and walked over to the baby. "Hello, Ivan."

The baby appeared to reconsider his initial assessment of her. He smiled tentatively and made a little gargling noise in his throat. Her heart was lost instantly and completely.

"You don't know my nephew's name?" McAllister asked, startled. "It's Max."

She glanced back at McAllister. His arms were folded over his chest, and he was regarding her with suspicion identical to the baby's seconds earlier.

His nephew. The blanks were filling in, but all the same it was unraveling already. Stacy was going to find herself tossed unceremoniously out into a snowbank beside her car and, really, wasn't that what she deserved?

"Aren't you his nanny?" McAllister demanded. "That's who I was expecting."

"I'm Stacy," she said, drawing in a deep breath. "Stacy Murphy Walker." Now would be the perfect time to say who she really was and why she was here.

Tell him the rest of it. But her courage was failing her. So much easier to focus on the baby!

"Uppie? Pwweee?"

And it did feel as if this baby—and maybe Kiernan, too—really needed her. And it felt as if she needed to be in this house that cried for a Christmas tree and a family to encircle it.

She reached into the playpen. The baby wound his chubby arms around her neck, and she hoisted his surprisingly heavy weight. He nestled into her and put his thumb in his mouth, slurping contentedly.

"I'm not exactly your nephew's regular nanny," she heard herself saying, "but I'm sure I can help you out. I'm very good with children."

She told herself it wasn't precisely a lie, and it must have been a measure of McAllister's desperation that he seemed willing to accept her words.

He regarded her and apparently decided she was a temp or a substitute for the regular nanny, which would also, conveniently, added to the bad roads, explain the delay in her arrival. After scrutinizing her for a moment, he rolled his broad shoulders, unfolded his arms from across his chest and looked at her with undisguised relief.

"I'm Kiernan McAllister."

"Yes, I know. Of course! Very nice to meet you." She managed to get one arm out from under the baby's rump and extended it, not certain what the protocol would be for the house staff. Did you shake the master's hand?

He crossed the room to her and took her extended hand without a second's hesitation, but she still knew extending hers had been a mistake. She had felt his hand already as he helped her from the chaise in his bathroom.

Despite the fact that his hand was not the soft hand of an office worker or of her comrades in writing, but hard and powerful, taking it felt like a homecoming.

And if she thought the mere sight of his lips had posed a danger to her, she could see his touch was even more potent. A homecoming to some secret part of herself, because something about his hand in hers sizzled and made her aware of herself as smaller than him.

And feminine. Physically weaker. Vulnerable in some way that was not at all distressing, though it should have been to a woman newly declared to total independence and a hard-nosed career as a freelancer.

She yanked her hand out of his and felt desperate not to give him the smallest hint of her reaction to him. "And just to clarify, is your nephew Ivan or Max?"

"Max. I just like to call him Ivan."

Stacy looked askance at him.

"As in Ivan the Terrible," he muttered.

She could feel disapproval scrunch her forehead—a defense against the electric attraction she felt toward him—and something like amusement crossed McAllister's features as he regarded her, as if he was not even a little fooled.

Annoyingly, the light of amusement in his eyes made him look, impossibly, even more attractive than before!

"But his name is really Max." He cocked his head. "I guess that works, too, if you think about it. He's Max everything. Max noisy. Max sleepless. Max filthy, at the moment. He's just over a year. A horrible age, if there ever was one."

"He's adorable," she declared.

"No. He's not in the least."

"Well, he is right now. Except, he might need changing—

"Never mind! If he needs *that,* you *have* arrived in the nick of time. And while you look after it I will do the manly thing, and go look after your car. You can change his nappy and then be on your way."

Well, there was no need to tell him the truth if she was leaving that quickly!

He made the declaration of assigning them duties with such abject relief that Stacy tried to bite her lip to keep from laughing.

It didn't work. It was probably, at least in part, a delayed reaction to her accident, but a little snort of laughter escaped past her clamped lips. And then another one.

McAllister glared, and more laughter slipped out of her. It seemed to her it was the first time since the disintegration of her relationship that she had had anything to laugh about.

The baby chortled, too, and it made her laugh harder.

"Sorry," she said, trying to bite it back. "Really. Sorry."

Here she was, an imposter in a complete stranger's home, so it must be nerves making the laughter bubble within her. Whatever it was, the more she tried to repress it, the more it burbled out of her, free.

"Are you laughing *at* me?" Kiernan McAllister, master of the house, asked her dangerously.

"No," she said, through giggles. "No, of course not."

"I don't believe you."

"All right," she gasped, wiping an amused tear from her eye, "it does strike me as a little funny that you would be afraid of a baby's diaper."

"*Fear* is completely the wrong word."

"Of course. Completely."

"I'm quite capable of doing whatever needs to be done."

"Yes, I can see that."

"I have been doing what needs to be done. And will continue to do so after you've gone back to Vancouver. You can report to my sister that I am more than a match for a baby."

She nodded. A giggle escaped her. The baby chortled. "So, we've settled it," she said, striving to be solemn. "It's not fear."

Kiernan McAllister glared at her, then the baby, then her again.

"*Aversion* is probably a better word. Not to Ivan himself, but to what Ivan can do."

"Do?"

"Doo."

"Oh." She caught his meaning and tried to bite her lip against the deepening of her laughter. It didn't work. A new little snicker escaped her.

"It's Murphy's Law," he said, frowning at her snicker. "In the changing-a-baby department, I learned something very quickly. I've always been a quick study."

That she did not doubt! "And what did you learn?" she asked.

"Anything that can go wrong, will."

She really did laugh then, not even trying to hold back. McAllister glared at her but could not hide his relief that the stinky baby was in her arms and not his.

Still, he squared his shoulders and said firmly, "You can help me with this one thing, and I will look after your car. Then you can leave."

And without another word, casting her one more warning look that said he was without fear, his chin tilted up at a proud angle, he turned on his heel and left the room.

"And that," she explained to Ivan, "is your uncle, the warrior."

CHAPTER FIVE

KIERNAN COULD HEAR the nanny's light laughter follow him out of the room. Despite the fact it was directed at him, the sound was as refreshing as sitting beside a cold brook on a hot afternoon.

And besides, she was right, and it probably was funny. He was a man who had a reputation for not being afraid of anything. From daring business deals to bold adventures, he had always tackled life pretty fearlessly.

At great cost, a voice told him, but he turned it off, savagely.

He went down the hall and into his bedroom to get dressed. The scent of the nanny—like lemon drop candies—tickled his nostrils. Why was he so aware of her?

When she had picked Max up, the look on her face had been completely unguarded. And she had looked radiant. It had been a Madonna-with-child moment, breathtaking in its purity. And it had moved Stacy Murphy Walker from button cute to beautiful in a stunning blink of the eye.

Kiernan had been taken by surprise by how cute the nanny was from the moment he had plucked her out of her car.

Stacy was not what he'd expected from a nanny at all. What he'd expected was someone like that famous nanny on television: stout and practical, certain of her own authority in the baby department, possibly bossy. Or perhaps, he'd expected an older woman with gray hair in a neat bun, and granny glasses.

What he had not been expecting was a young woman with dark chocolate coils of hair, skin as pale as the inside of a white rose petal and astounding green eyes, as deep and moody as the waters of a mountain pond. He had certainly not expected the nanny to show up in a toy car, whimsical red shoes and skirt that, given how conservative it was, made his mouth go dry.

Attractive women in his world were the proverbial dime a dozen. He'd dated models and actresses, as world renowned for their looks and style as he was for his business acumen.

Somehow, next to her, those women didn't seem quite *real*.

It wasn't just that the nanny was smart that set her apart, though it was more than evident she was, because he'd been around and dated plenty of very smart women, too, business associates and CEOs.

Again, in a very short time, the nanny had made them seem not quite real.

It was because of that moment in the great room, when he had watched her look around with such wistfulness, it felt as if he had seen straight to her soul. And then when she had picked up the baby…radiance.

McAllister had experienced many of the wonders of the world. He had frolicked on beaches and conquered mountain slopes, and ridden zip lines through the rain forest. He had seen lions in the jungle and ridden a camel through the desert.

He had been at the premieres of movies and plays, attended symphonies, eaten at some of the best restaurants in the world and sampled some of the most exquisite wines.

He had shared exhilarating adventure and great moments with friends.

And still for all that each of those experiences had given him that incredible feeling—the sensation of being alive tingling along his very skin—McAllister did not feel as if he had ever experienced anything quite as pure as the radiance that lit the nanny's face when she picked up the baby.

Why was he so stunned by his reaction to her? Because, he realized, he *had* reacted. It was the first time in a year that he had felt a stirring of interest in anything.

But worse, he had been totally caught off guard by the way the look in her face, even her mention of how a Christmas tree would be in his great room, had filled him with a sense of yearning.

Yearning.

He had not allowed himself to feel that since he was a child, when every single thing you hoped for just set you up for huge disappointments.

Simple yearnings back then: *normal* topping his list.

Kiernan shook himself. This was *not* him. Of course, the circumstances were no doubt to blame for the lack of discipline he was exercising over his own mind. Twenty-four hours of terror at the hands of his nephew, ending with the crashing sound of the nanny's car, and then having to rescue her from the garden had shaken his well-ordered world ever so slightly.

He had gone into rescue mode, bringing his defenses—already battered by the unexpected tribulations of caring for a baby—down yet another notch.

It seemed impossible that only yesterday, Kiernan had been in a completely different world. He'd been in his boardroom at a presentation being given by one of his top associates.

Mark had been one of his best friends, once. Now, he

could barely look at him, because he had been there that day, a witness to Kiernan's worst moment, a moment of colossal and catastrophic powerlessness.

Mark was talking about a new real estate development, a tower that combined retail outlets, offices and condos on a piece of property Kiernan's company, McAllister Enterprises, had recently acquired in a posh and trendy downtown neighborhood of Vancouver.

Kiernan had willed himself to focus on Mark. To pay attention. Kiernan was, when all the fancy titles were taken away, still the boss. He needed to care.

His attitude was probably why rumors were beginning to swirl that he had put the company up for sale.

His gaze had drifted out the window to the typical fall coastal weather. The skies were leaden, and raindrops slid, like plump drops of mercury, down the floor-to-ceiling glass of the boardroom window. Through a maze of office buildings and a haze of low cloud, he could just see the jutting outlines of the mountains.

A year.

It had been almost a year to the day.

They said time healed all wounds, and for a while, Kiernan had clung to that, like a man lost at sea clinging to a single bobbing piece of wood.

But the truth was that he'd felt the agony as sharply as the day it had happened. There was a dark place within him, contained, but it felt as if it was taking every bit of his strength to keep the lid on it.

If he ever gave up, if he let the lid off what had been in him since the day his friend died, it would ooze out, sticky and black, like melted asphalt. It felt like it would ooze out and fill him, bit by bit, until there was not a bit of light left.

"Mr. McAllister?"

He'd started. His personal assistant, the ever-competent

Miss Harris, had come into the room without him even noticing. Then she'd been at his shoulder, leaning over, whispering something about an urgent matter needing his immediate attention.

"Mr. McAllister?"

Miss Harris had *that* look on her face. It was the same look he saw on his sister's face and on the faces of his business associates, his staff, his colleagues, Mark. Concern, these days tinged with exasperation.

Kiernan interpreted it as: get with it. Wake up. *Come back to us.*

But he was not sure he could, not when it was taking everything he had to keep the lid on the box within him that contained enough darkness to completely obliterate light.

Relieved to be leaving the boardroom, and Mark, who looked at him with sadness he could not stand—he nodded his apologies, got up and followed Miss Harris out the door.

Miss Harris's voice sounded as if it was coming from underwater. *Left him here...were you expecting him...you forgot to tell me.*

They walked down the thickly carpeted hallways of his empire until they came to a smaller boardroom, across the hall from his own office.

He glimpsed inside the slightly ajar door to his domain.

Once, that room, with its priceless art, hand-scraped floors, fireplace and huge TV hidden behind a secret panel, had whispered to him smugly, *You have arrived.*

Now his victories felt hollow.

Miss Harris had opened the boardroom door and stood back to let him by. The smell that tickled his nostrils should have warned him he was not going to like what he found.

Still, his mind was struggling to categorize that smell

against the backdrop of understated posh decor of this room when he passed through the door and froze.

There was a baby in one of those carrier things, the kind with the plump padding and the handle. The carrier thing was dead center of the boardroom table. The baby's furious kicking of his stout limbs seemed to be fanning the aroma into every corner of the room.

All babies looked identical to Kiernan, but he knew exactly who this one was—Max.

His cherubic facial features had nearly disappeared behind a wall of chocolate. At least, given the stench in the air, Kiernan hoped it was chocolate.

A secretary, no doubt pressed into unwilling service, cast a nervous look at Miss Harris, and at Miss Harris's nod, which Kiernan caught out of the corner of his eye, bolted from her seat and scurried past Kiernan with a whispered "Mr. McAllister."

The young secretary had an expression on her face comparable to a peasant woman escaping the hordes of Genghis Khan.

"What the hell?" Kiernan said. "Where's Adele?"

Miss Harris stared at him. "She left him. She said she arranged it with you."

His sister, Adele, could not seriously think he was in any way suited to be a caregiver to her baby!

She had not arranged anything with him! Kiernan realized things slipped his mind these days, but he knew this was not one of those things. He would never agree to take Max, and Adele knew that, too.

But they were approaching that sad anniversary. He did remember Adele saying she needed some time to herself.

He did remember agreeing with her.

"What exactly did she say?"

"Something about you taking him to the cottage in

Whistler," Miss Harris said, consulting her ever-present notepad. "For a week. And not to worry. She's sending a nanny up to meet you there tomorrow."

He suppressed a groan and smelled a rat, as well as the other things in the room. Adele was plotting, using her child to try to get him back to the land of the living.

Her trust in him seemed entirely undeserved, especially when he reacted to the Max's screwed-up face.

"What are you doing?" Kiernan asked Max sternly. *Here,* he added silently.

But in the end, he had packed the baby into the car seat Adele had provided, texted her a stern *no nanny* while he still had cell service and driven to the cottage, because he knew how much he owed Adele and this baby.

It was his fault his sister did not have a husband, his fault the baby did not have a dad.

Still, it was hard to believe he had committed to looking after the baby only twenty-four hours ago.

It felt like a different lifetime.

And he was so exhausted it had made him vulnerable to the radiance in the surprisingly lovely nanny's face.

Now, bending over her car, already disappearing under a heap of white from the heavily falling snow, he brushed at the tires and looked at the tread, annoyed. They weren't even particularly good *summer* tires.

He was annoyed his mind was still on her, despite the fact he was out here and had things to do. He tried to figure out exactly what it was in her face that had triggered something in him.

And then he identified what that something was. When she had been able to visualize a Christmas tree in his great room, when she had lifted that baby?

He had felt hope.

Of course, she would not carry a burden of guilt the

way he did. His fault, entirely, that he and his brother-in-law had been there that day.

And when he relived that moment, which he did often, of that wall of snow sweeping down on them? He was always aware that he could or should have done something different. He was always aware that it *should* have been him instead of the man who had so much more to lose, who had left the world with a fatherless baby.

Somehow, McAllister's genuine and startling enjoyment of a pretty girl's radiant face felt like the worst threat of all.

After all, wasn't hope the most dangerous of all things?

So, here was the question. Did he walk toward the light he had seen in her face? Or did he walk in the other direction as quickly and as firmly as he could?

Away, he decided. He was, above all things, good at making decisions. He made them quickly and decisively, and he never looked back.

He was unsticking her car and sending her on her way. He frowned at the drifting snow on the driveway. It would have to be plowed before anything else happened. The plowing was contracted, and he was surprised they had not been yet.

But they might not know he was in residence, which would make his driveway a low priority. He would call them right away.

Even when it was done, what would await on the public roads?

Okay, *he* would drive the car to Whistler and grab a cab back. Stacy had already shown, in spades, she could not be trusted in these driving conditions. Except what to do with Max during all this? Was the baby seat transferable to her car? Did he want to be out on these roads with Max?

It proved to be a moot point, anyway. After spending more than an hour pitting his strength and wits against the snow and ice and the summer tires, and almost succeeding in banishing the nanny from his mind, he could not get her car unstuck.

At first his irritation was monumental, but then a light went on. No! It was a good thing. After he called the plow company, he could call a tow company and have the car towed all the way to Whistler for her, with her in the cab of the truck with the driver. He could be rid of her—and her sunshiny visions of Christmas trees in *his* great room— and he would not have to feel responsible for her safety.

Kiernan was actually whistling as he went back through the front door of his house and stomped snow off his boots.

He came through to the great room and stopped.

This was exactly what he was protecting himself against! Stacy had spread a blanket on the floor in front of the fireplace. The baby sat here, Buddha-like, his chubby face wreathed in smiles, his attention on the nanny. She was sitting across from him, on the blanket, her legs tucked underneath her, oblivious to the fact the skirt was riding up to reveal even more of those rather delectable legs.

She hadn't even noticed Kiernan's arrival.

Because she had another blanket over her head. As he watched, she lifted up a corner of it, and cried, "Peekaboo."

Max screamed with laughter, rocked back and forth and looked like he was going to fall over. Her hand shot out from under the blanket and supported the baby.

"Aga!" he screamed at her.

Apparently it meant again, because Stacy disappeared back under the blanket. The baby held his breath in anticipation.

"Peekaboo," she cried.

Max went into paroxysms of laughter. Her laughter joined his.

For all the parties Kiernan had held here, filling this room with important people, rare wines and exquisite food prepared by an in-house chef, his house had never once felt like this.

Kiernan stared at them as if in a trance. That weakness whispered along his spine again. That longing.

For normal. For the thing he had never had. Home.

Something made her glance up, and when she saw him standing there, Stacy pulled the blanket off her head and leaped to her feet, yanking down her skirt. Her hair, crackling with static from the blanket, reminded him of dark dandelion fluff.

"Oh," she said, embarrassed, "I didn't realize you were there."

The baby was frowning at him and yelled his indignation that the game had come to an abrupt end.

Easily, as if she had been born to do it, she scooped up Max and put him on her hip. "I was just thinking of seeing what you have for him to eat," she said.

"Don't bother. You aren't staying." This came out sounding quite a bit more harsh than he intended.

"Oh," she said, looking hurt and baffled by his words, just more evidence she had to go. "You got my car unstuck, then?"

"No," he snapped. "I didn't. Not that I would let you drive if I had."

That chin went up. "That is not up to you!"

"I have to arrange for the driveway to be plowed. And then I'm calling a tow truck. He can tow you all the way to Whistler and you can ride with him."

"But—"

He held up a hand. "It's not open for discussion."

Now, as well as her chin sailing upward, her eyes were narrowed, but she had the good sense not to challenge him.

Obviously she knew her driving skills were not up to the steadily worsening conditions outside.

So, that settled, he went to the phone. And picked it up. And closed his eyes against what he heard.

Which was absolutely nothing.

The storm had taken out the phone line. There was going to be no plow. And no tow truck. Not in the foreseeable future, anyway.

In fact, Kiernan's foreseeable future held a form of torment that he was not sure how to defend himself against.

As if to prove it, Max, annoyed at the abrupt end of his game and the nanny's attention not being focused on him, curled a chubby fist in her hair and yanked hard.

"Hey," Stacy said, "don't do that!"

Max yanked harder.

"I told you he was not adorable in the least," Kiernan said, and went to untangle the baby's determined fist from Stacy's hair.

In doing so, he tangled their lives just a little more together.

CHAPTER SIX

"IVAN, LET GO."

Kiernan's voice sent a shiver up and down Stacy's spine—the man could be deliciously masterful—but the baby was not impressed.

Glaring at his uncle, Max wrapped his fist more tightly with her hair.

Kiernan strode forward, and now both their hands were in her hair.

"Don't hurt him," she said.

"I'm not going to hurt him." Kiernan snapped, insulted.

But the dilemma was obvious: without actually forcing the baby to let go of her hair, he was not going to voluntarily give her up.

"Try distracting him," she suggested.

"How?"

"Can you make a funny face?"

"No!"

"A noise?"

"Such as?"

"I don't know. Try a choo-choo train. Or a duck! Maxie, do you like ducks? Quack, quack?"

She was sure the little fist slackened marginally in her hair. Stacy wished she had a camera to catch the look on

Kiernan's face, that he, one of Canada's top CEOs, had just been asked to quack!

Instead of quacking, Kiernan reached into his pocket and took out his keys. He jingled them enticingly toward Max, who let go of her hair instantly and reached for the keys.

"Baby 101," Kiernan said. "Distraction. Do they teach you that in nanny school?"

That brought her other dilemma into sharp focus. It was, of course, the perfect opening to let him know that she was not a nanny. But now that they were snowed in together—trapped really—wouldn't it just make everything worse if she chose now as the time to let Kiernan know she wasn't exactly a nanny?

He didn't even have the option of throwing her out at this point. Nor did she have the option of volunteering to leave!

Her father had always said, *Murphy, my love, when you are given lemons, make lemonade.*

And that was exactly what she intended to do, right here and right now.

"I need to get the baby something to eat," she said. "And then he needs a bath. After that, he'll probably be ready for bed."

"Humph, he's never ready for bed. Let me show you what Adele left for food for him."

It was a turning point, because Kiernan seemed to resign himself to the idea she was staying. The fact that it was out of his control must have made it a little more palatable to him because, while she opened the baby food and prepared a bottle, he threw together some snacks for the adults.

After they had all eaten, she tackled the bath. To her surprise, Kiernan insisted on helping.

"He's bigger than you think," he said of his nephew. "And he's a slippery little character when he's dry, never mind wet."

Stacy found herself in his master bathroom again. This time, Kiernan flipped on the fireplace without being asked.

For her enjoyment, she couldn't help but wonder, or for the warmth of the baby?

Either way, the experience became wonderful. The fireplace glowing softly, Kiernan's strong hands holding the baby upright, Max gurgling and splashing while she scooped water over him with a cup.

She knew that this good working relationship wouldn't be happening if she had admitted her true identity. It would be better, she decided, for the good of the baby, if she just didn't say anything.

After the driveway was cleared, she could light out of there with no one the wiser. And she would drive her own vehicle, too!

By the time they were done, they were all soaked, but the baby was wrapped in a thick white towel and cuddled sleepily against his uncle's chest.

Stacy was not sure she had ever seen a lovelier sight than that little human being nestled so trustingly against one so much bigger and stronger.

Even the normally stern lines of Kiernan's face had softened, and in the warm glow of the fireplace the scene wrenched at her heart.

"What a beautiful father you will make someday," she said softly.

The look was gone instantly, and Kiernan glowered at her. "I do not have any intention of *ever* being a father," he snapped.

"But why?" she asked, even though it clearly fell into the "none of her business" category.

The look he gave her confirmed it was none of her business. "I'll go get your bag out of the car," he said stiffly, obviously not wanting to spend one more second than necessary with a woman who had spotted father potential in him.

Kiernan didn't just go get her bag. He went out and inspected his driveway, listened hopefully for the sound of a coming plow, but the night was silent. It was the kind of deep, deep silence that did not allow a man to escape his own thoughts.

What was going on in his house? He had just bathed a baby in front of the firelight, and enjoyed it, too.

No wonder Stacy was under the false impression he might make a good father someday.

He hated it that those words had triggered that thing in him, again.

Longing.

A yearning for something that would never be. He remembered as a kid getting the odd glance into other people's lives, a friend inviting him home for dinner, the unexpected treat of a ski trip from his best buddy's mom and dad one Christmas.

Swooping down the hill, he had felt freedom from everything. But after? Eating with that family and playing board games with them and watching them talk and tease each other on the long drive home?

He had wanted what they had as much as he had ever wanted anything. He had learned the hopelessness of such feelings at the hand of his own father, who had been furious with him for accepting the gift of the trip, an affront to his pride, and he had screamed at Kiernan.

His father was a man he tried not to think about.

A man whose brutishness he had distanced himself

from with every success, a man whose shadow he had seemed to escape when the rush of adrenaline was filling his every sense and cell.

Kiernan would never be a good father.

He was convinced it was something you learned, a lesson he had most definitely missed in life.

Though, a voice in him whispered, his sister seemed to have overcome those challenges. It could be done. There was hope.

But he hated it that he even wanted there to be hope. Hated it. And it seemed as if it was her fault, and even though they were stuck here together, he vowed to keep his guard up, find his own space, avoid her.

When he came back in the house, Stacy was sitting on his couch, legs tucked up underneath her, flipping through a book. It had gotten dark outside, and she had turned on a light and sat in its golden glow, unaware what a picture she made.

He recalled again the amazing gatherings hosted in this room, beautifully dressed people, swirls of color and motion, tinkling glasses and laughter.

Despite how much he liked it here, and the good memories he had, Kiernan was aware that, like his condo in Vancouver, his cottage lacked that little *something* that made it feel like home.

Apparently, that little something was a woman making herself comfortable on his couch! The scene was one of homecoming.

Stunned, he felt his decision to avoid her completely dissolving like sugar hitting hot water. Well, he did have her overnight bag, which he had found in the backseat of her car. What was he going to do? Drop it at her feet and bolt?

Really, it would be embarrassing for her to figure out she had rattled him.

"I brought in your bag. Are you okay sharing the guest room with Ivan the Tyrant?" At her nod, he said, "I'll put it in there. Where is Ivan the Tyrant?"

He realized it was blessedly quiet in his house. He tried to tell himself that was probably what he had appreciated at a subconscious level, as much as her presence on his sofa.

"Max is sleeping. You might want to leave the bag there for now rather than risk waking him."

He dropped the bag at his feet as though it was burning his hands. "Seriously? He's sleeping?"

"He wasn't awake very long. When I dug through his bag of things I found his soother and a stuffed toy he called Yike-Yike."

"That thing with eyes on it that looks like an overripe banana?"

"That's Yike-Yike."

Kiernan tapped himself with his fist in his forehead and groaned. "I should have figured that out. Where he goes, that thing goes!"

"Exactly! Within minutes of having both in his possession, he was out like a light. It seems early for him to go to bed, but I think he's managed to wear himself out—"

"Not to mention his poor uncle!"

"—and I really think he could make it through the night. All of your problems with him crying and not sleeping and eating properly had to do with his distress over that. Bad enough, in his mind, that Mommy left. But no Yike-Yike?"

"Baby hell," Kiernan murmured.

"Exactly."

He said a word he was pretty sure you weren't allowed to say around babies. Or their nannies.

"Did you get enough to eat?" he asked.

"Yes, thank you."

There. No reason to stay here in this room with her. None at all. He could retreat to his bedroom. But he didn't.

"Does the fireplace in here use real wood?" she asked wistfully.

"Yeah. I didn't want to light it with Ivan on the run." *Get away from her,* Kiernan ordered himself. But the wistfulness in her face stopped him.

It was such a small thing that she wanted. Not like the things he had once wanted. He could give this to her. No one could have ever given his dreams to him.

Could a woman like this? He shook off the thought, more than annoyed with himself. Another reminder to get away from her and the spell she was casting. But now he'd offered to light the fire!

"I'll light it for you, if you want."

"Oh, no," she said, and blushed. "That's way too much trouble."

It was that blush that sealed it for him. "No, no trouble at all." And he found himself opening the damper and crumpling paper and setting kindling, striking the match.

In no time, the fire was crackling cheerfully in the hearth.

Now retreat, he ordered himself. But he didn't. He said, "I've got this contraption that supposedly you can pop corn in the fire. You want to try it?"

"Yes," she breathed with genuine enthusiasm, as if he had offered to put up a Christmas tree.

Well, what the heck? They were stuck here. Together. Entertainment was limited. Why not?

Stacy realized she should have said no to this. She should have wished him a polite good-night and retreated to her room. But she just wasn't that strong.

She joined him at his counter, and they eyed the open-fire popcorn contraption together. They took it to the fire and took turns shaking it vigorously as per the instructions.

Just when it felt as if nothing was ever going to happen,

the popcorn began to pop. First one or two kernels, and then rapidly, like a machine gun going off.

"We put too much in," she said as the hinge sprang free and popcorn began to spill into the fire. It smelled terrible. A few unpopped husks exploded into the room with the briefest whistled warning and more velocity than she could have dreamed possible.

She dropped the popcorn maker, and he took a firm hold of her elbow and shoved her behind the couch, shielding her with his own body, protection of those who were smaller and physically weaker than him coming as naturally to him as breathing.

They tried to muffle their laughter so as not to wake the baby, while the popcorn flew through the air around them.

When they were sure the fireworks had finished, they came out from behind the couch.

He surveyed his living room with shock.

She giggled. "I've heard of popcorn ceilings," she said, "but never popcorn floors."

And then the laughter died. "Thank you for protecting me," she said.

He looked at her, and suddenly it seemed very still. Almost against his will, he reached down, tilted her chin up, scanned her face, looked at her lips.

"Do unexpected things always happen around you?"

"It's the old anything-that-can-go-wrong thing," she said, but her voice was husky and neither of them was laughing.

Awareness sizzled in the air between them. He dropped his head close to hers. He was going to kiss her!

Stunned, she backed away from him. This was a lie. She was living a lie! She couldn't let it get more complicated than it already was.

She turned on her heel and ran down the hall.

"Hey, Cinderella," he called mockingly, "You are leaving your slipper."

But she had more in common with Cinderella than she ever wanted him to know. Both she and Cinderella were both pretending to be people they were not.

Kiernan watched her disappear and gave himself a shake. Had he nearly kissed her? What on earth did that have to do with the strategy of avoidance he had planned?

Crazy things were happening in this house. The popcorn all over the floor was a testament to that. Nearly quacking for her earlier was a testament to that. Crazy things were happening in his head, too, and he didn't like it one little bit.

He was strong.

Stronger than strong.

He always had been. That was why he had survived. That was why Adele had survived.

But all his strength, he reminded himself bitterly, had not been enough to save Danner.

And that's what he needed to remember, before he tangled his life with anyone's. He was not the stuff happy families were made of. And even if he was, all his strength could not do what he would most want to do.

Protect from harm.

Kiernan gave his head one more rueful shake and began to pick up scorched popcorn from his living room floor.

And the fact that he smiled when he remembered huddling behind the couch with her only reminded him he had been weak when he wanted to be strong.

And so, as one day stretched into two and they remained marooned, he made himself be strong.

He was polite. And helpful with the baby. And aloof. If watching her interact with Max and making herself at home in his house gave him pleasure—which it did—he did not let on.

And when the snow finally stopped, he practically raced outside. If he could get her car free before the plow arrived, he was one step closer to being rid of her. And her laughter. And the way she shook her curls to make the baby coo with delight.

It would be good for him to get outside and do the manly thing! But, an hour later, he was no closer to freeing her car.

Though he did have a plan!

"So, how did it go with my car?"

He had promised the manly thing, and he was not going to admit defeat.

"Still stuck, but I think we could get it out together." What did doing anything *together* have to do with avoiding her?

"Well, the baby's napping, so now would be perfect. I'll just grab the monitor."

"I'm pretty sure it's an easy fix. It just needs two people, one to drive and one to push. Despite my desire to hold you captive—"

He realized he had said that to make her blush, too, and she did.

"—because of your gift with Ivan, looking after the car before he wakes up would be good. Because once he wakes up?" McAllister wagged his eyebrows at her. "Guess what? It's all about him."

"Typical male," she muttered.

That made him frown, because he was pretty sure he heard the faint bitterness of one who had been betrayed in there. Was that the shadow he saw in her eyes sometimes?

Well, how could that be anything but a good thing, that she had no illusions about the male half of the species?

"You are so right," he said. "We are a colossally self-centered, hedonistic bunch. You'd be better not to pin your hopes to one of us."

CHAPTER SEVEN

"You don't know the first thing about my hopes," Stacy said quietly. She had given him entirely the wrong impression when she had imagined a big family gathering in this very room. She had given him the wrong impression when she had told him he would make a good father. She had given him the wrong impression when she had leaned toward him that night of the popcorn and nearly accepted his kiss.

He couldn't avoid her, of course, and he hadn't. But she had felt the chilly lack of connection.

But just underneath that, something simmered between them, as if a fuse had been lit and the spark was moving its way toward the explosive.

She was so *aware* of him when he was in the same room. The same house. The same space. She was aware of loving the way he was with Max, loving the way he was willing to do what needed to be done without being asked.

Kiernan McAllister regarded her thoughtfully for a moment, his gaze so stripping she felt as if he could see her soul.

He was dressed in a beautiful down-filled parka, the fur-lined hood framing his face. Beautifully tailored slacks clung to the large muscles of his thighs, the look made less formal by the fact the slacks were tucked into snow boots.

How could a man look every bit as sexy dressed as he was now as he had when he was dressed in nothing but a towel?

But McAllister did. In the parka and the snow boots, he looked ready for anything. Very manly, indeed.

"Unfortunately, Stacy, I think I do know a bit about your hopes."

"And?" she said, bracing herself for his answer.

"Your career choice says quite a bit."

That was a relief. What he assumed was her career choice was telling him about her. Her hopes and dreams, as battered as they were at the moment, weren't really showing on her face.

"Who wants to look after other people's children?" he said. "Except someone who loves children and dreams of having their own? Probably by the bushel."

The truth was she had planned for three, someday.

It would be the perfect time to tell him she was not who he was expecting, that she was not a nanny at all. Instead, she found herself frowning at him. "Are you saying *you* don't love children?"

"I already told you, I don't plan on being a father."

"That doesn't answer my question."

"I don't even like children."

She snorted.

"Ah, indignation. As if I've announced I don't like puppies. Or Santa Claus."

"Actually, it's not indignation, Mr. McAllister—"

"It's a little late for formality."

Oh, boy. "You aren't a very good liar."

"Excuse me?"

"The baby frustrated you, and you were at rope's end, but I could tell you would have protected him with your life, if need be. Maybe that's not *like*. And over the last few days, when you see something that needs to be done, you just step up to the plate and do it. That seems suspiciously like more than that. Like love, perhaps."

He was glaring at her, and then he shrugged a big shoulder dismissively.

"Whatever, Miss Poppins," he said. "We need to look after the car before His Majesty wakes up. Have you got a winter jacket somewhere?"

"Just my sweater."

"I'll find stuff for you."

The "stuff" he found was mostly his and so, a little while later, Stacy was following him out into the darkness of a still-snowing night, dressed in a jacket that came down to her knees and that tickled her nostrils with the pine scent of him. He had found her a hat that that looked like something a turn-of-the-century trapper would wear. It was too large and kept falling over her eyes. Thankfully, his sister had left snow boots here that fit her.

Really, she should have stopped him at *Miss Poppins.*

And confessed to her true identity. For about the hundredth time in three days, she knew she should have, but she just couldn't.

Because, she had the certain knowledge, that as soon as she did it would be over. She was pretty sure she had not banked enough gratitude that he was going to grant her an interview. Especially now that she had seen him so clearly and called him a liar.

She was the liar. And revealing that to him was going to cause terrible tension and they were trapped here. It would not be good for the baby!

Even if, by some miracle, the truth came out and he did grant her an interview, *then* it would be over.

And somehow she did not want this little adventure to be done. What had he said to her earlier?

You might want to keep in mind, for next time, to try and steer into the spin, rather than away from it. It goes against everyone's first instinct. But really, that's what you do. You go with it, instead of fighting it.

So, what if she went with this? Rode the momentum of the spin instead of fighting it? Let go of her need to control, just for a little while? Isn't that what she'd been doing for the past few days?

It seemed to her that since the second she had wound up with her bumper resting against that fountain, her life held something it had not held for some time. Surprise. Spontaneity. The potential for the unexpected.

When unexpected things had happened to her before, it had been so in keeping with Murphy's Law. They were always bad.

Expecting an engagement ring and being invited to shack up being a case in point.

Dylan had guffawed when she had said that, apparently more loudly than she had thought.

Shack up, Stacy, really? What century is that from?

One where people made commitments and took vows and wanted forever things instead of temporary pleasures.

Then, she had done something totally out of character. She had dumped her wine all over his head, and yelled at him, "What century is that from?"

Unfortunately, her worst moment ever in keeping with Murphy's Law, had been recorded by someone in the restaurant with a smartphone, who had been alerted to turn it toward her by her rising tone of voice.

And then that moment had been posted on the web.

But all that was in her past. Now was now. And, as ridiculous as it seemed, Kiernan McAllister, the man who appeared to have everything, seemed to need something from her.

As did that baby. And so Stacy was going to take his advice.

You might want to keep in mind, for next time, to try and steer into the spin, rather than away from it... It goes against everyone's first instinct. But really, that's what you do. You go with it, instead of fighting it.

"Oh, Stacy," she murmured inwardly, "what kind of predicament have you gotten yourself into?"

A dangerous one, because if what she had experienced so far—his nearly naked self, fresh out of the hot tub— wasn't his idea of 100 percent manly, she was in very big trouble, indeed!

"Okay, put it in Reverse," Kiernan shouted from the front of her car.

Stacy sat in the driver's seat of her car, peering out from under her hat at Kiernan. She had the window rolled down so that she could hear instructions from him. She was already glad for the winter clothing, especially the mittens. The baby monitor was on the seat beside her as she clenched on the steering wheel. It was very sensitive. She could hear Max's soft, sleepy purring above the sound of the engine.

She contemplated the delightful if somewhat surreal quality of her life.

One of the most powerful men in the business world was getting her car unstuck from his front garden as she listened to a baby sleep.

After scowling at her summer tires, he had settled right into it.

It had been a very pleasant experience so far watching him wield a shovel, digging out the tires of her car, one by one, spreading gravel underneath.

"Give it some gas."

She did. The tires made that whining noise. Kiernan put his shoulder against the front bumper of her car and pushed.

Manly, indeed!

Kiernan did look 100 percent man. How it was even possible for him to look more manly than he had in his swim trunks baffled her, but he did and heart-stoppingly so. Of course, sharing a house with him had made her superaware of him: his scent, how his hair looked wet from the shower, the shadow of whiskers on his face late in the afternoon.

Now the winter clothes made him look rugged, tough, 100-percent Canadian male, ready for anything. He had long since dispensed with the gloves, which were lying on the ground beside him. His brute strength rocked her car, and for a moment she thought he was going to be able to push it free, but it seemed to settle back in the ruts.

She let off the gas.

"Try rocking it between Forward and Reverse."

Stacy did this, she could tell from the way his arms crossed over his chest and the expression on his face— part aggravated, part amused—that she was doing something wrong.

"Sorry," she called out the open window.

He came and leaned in the window. His breath touched her like a frosty peppermint kiss. "You really aren't great at this, are you?"

She looked at him from under the hat. Great at what? The whole man/woman thing? No, she was not.

"You're a snow virgin!" he declared. "It's a good thing it's not a full moon. We sacrifice snow virgins at the full moon."

He was teasing her.

She had never been good at this kind of banter, but she reminded herself to go with the spin.

"To what end?" she asked breathlessly.

"Appeasing the god, Murphy."

She laughed then, and the smile that she could have lived for—and that she could have told a zillion more lies to see again—tickled the sensual line of his lips.

He leaned in her window, right across her, and took her gearshift. "Put in the clutch."

He was so close his whiskers nearly scraped her cheek. She wasn't even breathing. He snapped her gearshift into Neutral and backed out of her window, leaving her feeling like a snow virgin very close to melting.

He went back around to the front of the car and showed off his manliness by shoving some more but to no avail.

"I have an idea," she called. "You drive. I'll push."

"Sure," he said cynically.

"No, really. I'm stronger than I look."

He looked skeptical, but by now he apparently had figured out she was not going to get the gas or the gears right to rock the car out of the spot it was in.

"Don't push," he instructed. "I'll see if I can get it out without you."

She could see he knew a great deal about cars. He rocked the car back and forth gently, but it would come to the same place in the ever-deepening rut her great winter driving skills had created.

She went around to the front of her car and pushed.

"Hey," he called out the window, laughter in his voice, "you are not helping. It is like an ant pushing on an elephant."

She ignored him and pushed.

"Try just putting some weight on it."

She threw her weight against the bumper, and when that didn't work, she sat on the hood. Apparently that was the ticket, because suddenly the wheels caught and the car rocketed backward.

She fell off the hood and rolled through the snow. Her hat fell off and her mouth filled up with the white stuff.

He got out of the car, raced to her and got down beside her.

"Are you okay?"

"I'm fine." She spit out some snow, and he brushed it from her lips.

"Are you always so accident-prone?"

"Murphy's Law," she reminded him.

"Ah," he said. "And we have failed to appease him." He held out his hand, and she took it—she was becoming too accustomed to this his-hand-in-hers stuff—and he helped her to sitting. He found the hat, shook the snow out of it and clamped it back on her head.

"Your car is unstuck. Let's get in out of the cold."

"I don't feel cold," she said. "You go in if you want to. I'd like to stay out here for a while. Snow virgin that I am, I want to enjoy this for just a bit longer. This might be the closest I ever get to my winter holiday."

He smiled at that.

Boldly she said, "How would you recommend losing snow virginity?"

His smile faded and he stared at her, and if she was not mistaken, his eyes went to her lips. She could feel her heart beating too fast again. She was inordinately pleased that he seemed flummoxed by her question. Then something burned through his eyes that felt too hot for her to handle.

"I will make a snow angel," she decided quickly.

He looked relieved by her choice. Obviously angels and whatever wicked thoughts he was having did not go together.

He was having wicked thoughts about her? It was dismaying…in the most wonderful way.

Still, she lay back down in the snow, splayed her hands over her head and swept the snow with her tights-clad legs.

"How does it look?" she asked.

"Angelic," he said, something dry in his tone.

"How do I get up without wrecking it?"

He seemed to ponder this and then, with a trace of reluctance—a little close to those wicked thoughts to risk touching her—he reached down. She took both his arms, and he swung her up out of the angel she had made in the snow. He let her go instantly.

"It's lovely," she declared. She stood surveying her handiwork with pleasure and leaned down to brush at the snow that clung to her legs.

"Lovely," he murmured, and she shot him a look. Had he been looking at her?

"It would be great to get Max outside tomorrow," she decided. She opened her car door and checked the monitor. The baby was still sleeping soundly. "Maybe we'll build a snowman."

What was she doing talking about tomorrow? She needed to tell McAllister the truth now. But somehow she was not so certain what truth was. Wasn't there a truth in this moment under inky skies in the way he had murmured *lovely* after watching her brush the snow from her legs?

Wasn't there truth in the way their breath was coming out of each of their mouths in little puffs that joined together to make a cloud?

Weren't these truths as profound as any other truth she had ever known?

"The snow will be gone by tomorrow," he said.

"Really?"

"It's stopped snowing, finally, and the weather has warmed. It won't take long."

He was right. When she looked up at the dark sky, wisps of clouds were moving away to reveal a bright sliver of moon and pinpricks of starlight. It was beautiful.

"It's just an early-season storm," he told her. "The snow won't stick. It'll melt by tomorrow."

Tomorrow the magic would be gone. *Then* she would tell him the truth. There would be an escape route. Max didn't have to be affected. But tonight?

"I better build a snowman now, then," she said.

"Seriously?"

"I'm a Vancouver girl. You never know when you might have another chance."

McAllister stooped, picked up a handful of snow and squeezed it. "It is perfect snow for that."

Was he going to help her? Her astonishment must have shown in her face.

"You don't have enough muscle to lift the balls on top of each other," he said, as if he needed an excuse to join her.

"Hey!" She scooped up a handful of snow and formed it into a ball. "I have muscles aplenty! I just got the car unstuck!"

"Single-handedly," he said drily. "No help from me."

"Very little," she said, and then she realized *she* was teasing *him*. In a moment of pure and bold spontaneity, she tossed her snowball at him.

He dodged her missile effortlessly and stood there looking stunned. Something twitched around the line of his mouth. Annoyance? Or amusement? Annoyance. His mouth turned down in a frown.

She thought he would tell her to knock it off or grow up or get real.

He was the CEO of one of the biggest companies in Canada. You didn't throw snowballs at him.

She held her breath, waiting to see what he would do.

Gracefully, he leaned down. She saw he had scooped up a handful of snow of his own. His gloves were still lying in the snow over by where her car had been, but that didn't seem to bother him at all. With his bare hands, not looking at her, he slowly formed the snow into a ball.

Finally, he looked at her, held her gaze.

A smile, not exactly nice, twitched around the line of that beautiful mouth.

She read his intent and, with a shriek, turned away from him and began to run through the mounds of beautiful white snow.

CHAPTER EIGHT

"DON'T!" SHE CRIED. She glanced over her shoulder.

His too-large jacket flapped around Stacy's legs, making it impossible to attain the kind of speed necessary to outrun the missile he let fly.

The snowball caught her in the middle of the back. Even with the padding of the winter coat, it stung.

"I'm taking that as a declaration of war." She laughed, pushing back the sleeves of the jacket and scooping up more snow. She took careful aim, her hat slipping over her eyes, and to his shout of laughter, she pulled the hat back up just in time to see her snowball miss him by a mile.

She scooped up more snow and formed it into a hurried ball. She hurled it at him. He moved his head to one side and it whistled by his ear.

Deliberately, he walked over and retrieved his gloves. He was already tired of the silliness.

No, he wasn't. With his hands protected, it was evident he was just getting started. He stooped and grabbed a mitt full of snow. He began to shape a rather formidable looking snowball.

"There's no need to be mean about it," she told him over her shoulder, already running again.

"You're the one who declared war!"

And then he was running after her, his legs so much

longer than hers that he was gaining ground fast. She was going to have to outmaneuver him. Stacy scooted around the fountain and through the shrubs. She ducked behind her car.

Silence. She peered over the hood.

Sploosh. Right in her face.

"If you surrender now, I'll show you mercy," she shouted at him, wiping off her face and ducking behind the car to pick up more snow.

"Me surrender to you?" he asked incredulously.

"Yes!" she shouted, forming a snowball, her tongue between her teeth.

"Surrender? Lass, I'm of Scottish ancestry. That word is not in my vocabulary."

She peeked out from behind the car, aimed, let fly. She missed.

"Glad I didn't wave the white flag," he said with an evil grin.

"I'm just sucking you deeper into enemy territory."

"You're terrible at this," he told her.

"What's that called, when you play billiards badly to suck the other person in, and then place a bet and show what you can really do?"

"Hustling," he said.

"Maybe that's what I'm doing."

"I'd be more convinced if you knew the word for it."

"All part of the hustle," she assured him. She let fly a snowball that caught his shoulder and exploded with satisfactory violence. She chortled happily. "See?"

A missile flew back at her. She ducked behind her car, and it shattered harmlessly behind her. Silence. She waited. Nothing happened.

She peeked around the front fender. He had been

making ammunition and had a heap of snowballs in front of him.

She reached inside the still-open door of her car, picked up the baby monitor and held it up.

"Be careful," she said, "you don't want to get this wet."

"It's waterproof. You can take it into the bathtub." He let fly with six in a row and, as she peeked over the car, he tucked six more in the crook of his elbow.

She shoved the monitor in her pocket as he came running toward her, and burst out from behind the car at a dead run.

With a whoop he was after her. They chased each other around the circle of his driveway. As he threw snowballs, she ducked behind shrubs and the fountain and her car until they were both breathless with laughter and dripping with snow.

"Okay," she called, laughing, when he had her backed up against the fountain and his arm pulled back to heave a really good one at her, "I surrender. You win."

"What do I win?" He kept his arm up, ready, if she did not offer a good enough prize.

She licked her lips. If she was just a little bolder, she would offer him a kiss from the snow virgin.

Instead, she backed away from the intensity building between them. She pulled the monitor out of her pocket. "This! A completely waterproof baby monitor."

"Thanks, but no thanks."

"Okay, you win an opportunity to build a snowman!" she said.

"Sheesh. I was at least hoping for hot chocolate."

"Take it or leave it," she said.

"Pretty pushy for the loser." He tossed the snowball away. "I'll take it, but only because it's obvious to me you can't be trusted with making a snowman. You can barely make a snowball, and a snowman is the same principle, only multiplied."

"I'm anxious to learn whatever you want to teach me," she said.

For a moment the intensity sizzled again between them, white-hot into the frosty evening. His eyes locked on her lips and hers on his. She felt herself leaning toward him as if he were a magnet and she was steel.

He stepped back from her. "No, you aren't," he said gruffly. "I wouldn't want you to learn from me. There's something innately sweet about you. My cynicism could demolish that in a second."

Of course, he was saying that because he thought she was a nanny.

This was where lying got you.

"Maybe my sweetness could demolish your cynicism," she said.

"It's an age-old question, isn't it? Which is stronger? Light or dark?"

"Light," she said without hesitation.

He snorted but took some snow and squished it into a ball in his hands. Then he set it down, got on his knees and pushed it. Snow began to glue to the ball magically, and it got bigger and bigger.

Her skirt was not made for this kind of activity!

But what the heck? She had tights on. Following his instructions, tongue caught between her teeth, she lowered herself to her knees, too, and began to push her ever-growing snowball across his snowy driveway.

When she glanced over at him, he was straining against a huge snow boulder! It was so big he had his back against it and was pushing backward off his heels.

"That's big enough! Kiernan, it's bigger than me!"

She realized, stunned, his name coming off her lips

felt like an arrival at a place she had always dreamed of being at.

This is not truth, Stacy warned herself of the game she was playing. But she was not sure anything in her life had ever felt truer than this, playing in the snow under a night sky with Kiernan McAllister.

She was just going with the spin, instead of fighting it.

"Just a little bigger," he said. "Come help me push. It'll be just the right size by the time we get it over to the fountain."

He was far more ambitious than she was. It took them pushing together, shoulders touching, to wrestle it into place where her car had rested a few minutes before.

"You're an overachiever," she gasped, stepping back to admire their handiwork and, surreptitiously, him.

"Yes, I am," he said with complete pleasure.

He moved over to the ball of snow she had been working on. "Break is over," he told her, and side by side they pushed that one into place, too.

It took both of them to hoist the second ball on top of the first. There was much panting and laughing and struggling.

The snowman's head was the smallest of the three balls, and by now the snowman was so tall Kiernan had to lift it into place himself.

They stood back. The snowman was a good eight feet tall, but sadly blank faced.

"This is the problem with all that ambition," Stacy said. "He's so big we can't reach his face. He needs a hat. How are we going to get up there?"

"I already have it covered," Kiernan said.

"You're going to go get a ladder?" she asked.

"Ha! I'm going to be the ladder!"

She contemplated that for a moment. That sounded dangerous in the most delicious way. She saw he was moving snow to get at the rocks underneath, and she joined him.

"Do you have a carrot for his nose?" she asked.

"Oh, sure, in my back pocket. That's why I'm digging for stones."

"This one's perfect for the nose," she said, reaching down and picking up a pure black rock that he had exposed. "And these for his eyes! And these for his mouth!"

He was watching her, amused. "I think you have enough." He crouched down on his haunches.

"Here, hop up. Don't drop the rocks."

He tapped his shoulders. *As if dropping the rocks would be the most of her problems!*

She hesitated for only a moment before climbing on.

He lifted her with ease, and she found Kiernan McAllister's rather lovely neck between her legs. He grabbed her boots and held them against his chest. She had been unaware of how soggy and cold her clothing had become until she felt his warmth radiating up through her wet tights.

He pretended to stagger sideways, and she gripped his forehead and giggled when he yelped, "Hey, get your fingers out of my eyes."

She moved her hands and he staggered back in front of the snowman.

"Quick," he said. "I don't know how long I can hold you. You must weigh all of—what—a hundred pounds?"

Trembling, and not just from cold, Stacy put the face on the snowman. The nose rock was perfect, and if the smile was a little crooked, that was understandable. She snatched the hat off her own head and placed it on the snowman's.

"Okay," she called. "We're done."

But he didn't put her down. Instead he galloped around the yard, pretending he was staggering under her weight, ignoring her pounding on his shoulders and demanding to be put down at once.

Finally, he went down on one knee, but her dismount was clumsy, and she caught his shoulder, and they both went to the ground in a tangle of limbs and laughter.

Then the laughter died and the silence overtook them. They lay there in the snow, looking up at the stars.

"I haven't laughed like that for a long time," he said quietly.

"Me, either."

"Why?"

She hesitated, but from sharing the house and the baby duties there was a sense of intimacy between them. "Oh, life has taken some unexpected twists and turns. I've kind of felt just like I felt on your driveway—spinning out of control."

"A man," he guessed, with a knowing shake of his head. "Failed marriage?"

"No."

"Broken engagement?"

She winced.

"Ah."

"We never got that far," she confessed. "I just thought we were going to."

"Ah, that imagination-collides-with-reality thing again," he said, but with such gentleness she felt her heart break open wide.

Suddenly, she wanted to tell him all of it. She felt safe with him. Ironically, though she was posing as someone else, she felt more herself than she ever had. And she wanted him to know the truth about her.

"It wasn't just a man," she said quietly. "I became on orphan at sixteen."

It was terrible to feel this way: that she could trust him

with anything on the basis of a few days trapped in a house with him.

A few wondrous days, where she felt she knew more about him than she had ever known about anyone. Still, could she continue to blame that hit on the head for the removal of the filter for socially acceptable behavior? You did not unload your personal history on the most powerful man you had ever met.

Except he felt like the Kiernan she had seen bathe the baby.

And who had built a fire for her. And protected her from popcorn missiles.

And who had lent a hand whenever he saw something that needed doing. It was ironic that she could not tell him who she really was, and the more she could not tell him that the more she wanted him to know!

"They died. My grandmother, my mother, my father, my little brother. It was a car crash. My entire family," she whispered.

"I'm so sorry," he said. His voice was velvet with sincerity, and he reached out to tuck a strand of hair behind her ear. He touched her cheek for a moment before he let his hand fall away, something in his face telling her he was as surprised by that gesture as she was.

She had been dating Dylan for three months before she had told him any of this. Of course, he had never looked at her like that…

"I'm sorry," she stammered. "I don't even know why it came up."

"Thank you for telling me," he said. "I feel honored."

"And you?" she whispered, needing more from him, needing the intimate way she felt about him—the trust she felt for him to be reciprocated. Even if she did not deserve it.

The snow had stopped. By tomorrow, there was a

chance she would be gone from here. She could not stay once the snow was gone. She needed to take some piece of him with her. "Kiernan, what has kept the laughter from your life?"

He rolled a shoulder uncomfortably but said nothing.

"The death of your brother-in-law?" she asked softly.

He cranked his head and looked at her. "And what do you know about that?"

"Oh, Kiernan, you are a very public figure. The whole world knows about that."

He sighed and looked back up at the stars. "It's been a year. That's why my sister needed some time right now. People say time heals all wounds, but I am waiting for evidence of that."

"I'm so sorry," she said. "It was a terrible tragedy."

"How did you get over it?" he asked.

"I guess I hoped to have again what I once had before," she admitted, and it felt as if her heart was wide-open to him. "After my disaster with Dylan, I've given up on it."

"No, you haven't."

"I have," she said stubbornly.

"Then why can I so clearly see you surrounded by all your beautiful babies, and a man worthy of you? Someday, you'll look back on it, and be glad it happened. You'll see that he was a complete jerk and that you deserved better."

A hopeless feeling came over her. There was that imagination again. Because somehow it seemed Kiernan might be the better man she had waited for. But she knew she did not deserve him.

"As a matter of fact, I've decided to put my wildest imaginings aside," she said stiffly.

"No, you haven't," he said softly. "Because you know what is possible. You know what it is to be part of a family. You aren't imagining that part. And because you're not?

You'll never stop looking. You'll never stop seeing what could be in rooms like my great room. I need to know, step by step, how you got through the loss of your entire family."

She could hear the desperation in his voice, and she knew how vulnerable he had just made himself to her. He was asking her to help him.

Stacy took a deep breath and contemplated the stars. When she spoke, her voice was husky and hesitant.

"At first, I didn't feel as if I would even survive, not that I wanted to. I went from having this wonderful family into foster care. Thankfully, it was only for a year until I finished high school. I'm not sure you get over it. You get through it.

"Eventually, it was being around the kids in foster care that woke me up. Many of them had never had a loving family, or anyone who genuinely cared about them. At the risk of sounding corny?"

"What else would I expect from Miss Poppins?" he teased, but his tone was so gentle it was like a touch.

"Being around those troubled kids showed me what to do. Find somebody to help. That's what saved me. I started to go to university to get a degree in counseling. Unfortunately, I couldn't afford to finish the program. I became involved in starting a charity—Career and College Opportunities for Foster Kids—and I think that has pulled me through my darkest moments."

"I've never heard of that charity," he said.

"Unfortunately, neither has anyone else. We just don't have the know-how, the expertise, to get it really rolling."

"I'll give you the name of someone who will help you."

See? Despite all the evidence to the contrary, sometimes your wildest imaginings could come true.

"How did you get by?" he asked. "After you dropped out?"

"Thankfully, I had another gift that came in handy."

The other gift was writing. Was now the time to tell him? He was offering someone to help the charity under a false impression of who she was, after all.

But to lose this moment of closeness so soon after she had laughed for the first time in such a long time felt like more than she could bear.

"Your gift was with children," he said. "That's how you became a nanny."

Instead of responding to that, Stacy said, "In time, instead of focusing on the loss, I was able to feel gratitude for my family, and for the time I'd had with them. Every gift I have been given comes from the love they gave to me. Maybe you'll feel that, eventually, about your brother-in-law."

The silence was long and comfortable between them. She realized the days of being trapped together had made them friends, had created a bond between them with astonishing swiftness.

"He was more than my brother-in-law," Kiernan said, finally, softly. "We were best friends. Funny, when I first met him, I was prepared to dislike him. When my sister announced she was bringing someone home, I practically met him at the door with my saber drawn, prepared to give all kinds of dire warnings about what would happen to him if he hurt my sister.

"But Danner was just the best guy." A long silence, and then Kiernan said, "I wish it could have been me, instead of him."

CHAPTER NINE

"OH, KIERNAN," SHE said.

That *feeling* she had of experiencing truth at its deepest and finest intensified. She saw that he was a man who would see the protection of those he loved as his highest calling.

And that he had failed in it.

He gave her a look that forbade her sympathy. "He had a wife. And a baby. It would have been better if it was me."

She did not know what to say to that. She thought a deeper truth was that these things were not for mere men to decide, but she felt it would sound trite to say that in the face of the enormous pain he had trusted her with.

And so instead of saying anything, she took off her mitten and slid his glove off and took his bare hand in hers.

She held it.

And he let her. And it felt so good and so right to lie there on their backs in the snow, looking at the stars through the clouds of their own breath and feeling intensely connected by the fact they both knew the burden of intense loss.

Then he let go of her hand.

"You officially have lost your snow virginity."

She knew he was trying to change the subject, to move to lighter ground, but she felt a need to stay in this place of connection just a bit longer.

"I have built a snowman once before," she said. "With my dad. While everyone else was cursing the snow, he was out playing with us. He could make anything fun."

She could feel his hesitation, but then his hand was once again in hers, warm against the cold of the snow around them and the chill of the night.

Warm in a world that was so cold sometimes it could freeze a person's very heart.

"You're lucky for that. I wonder if that's where your dream of having a winter holiday comes from? Wanting to recapture that moment of childhood magic?"

His perception warmed her as much as his hand in hers. "Do you have moments like those, Kiernan, pure magic?"

He snorted. "Not from my childhood."

This was what being a reporter with some counseling background had taught her, that silence was a kind of question in itself. She suspected Kiernan was a man of many barriers, but for some reason, these playful moments, these few days of being snowbound, had lowered them.

"It was probably more like the kind of family kids you ended up in foster care with came from. My dad was a drunk," Kiernan said softly. "He abandoned the family when I was about twelve."

"That's terrible," she said, "and so, so sad."

"Believe me, it was a blessing. Anyway, that's why I was meeting my sister's boyfriend at the door. By default, I was the man of the house."

"Oh, Kiernan," she said softly.

"That's why my sister and I always go away at Christmas. Someplace warm and beachy and non-Christmassy. To outrun the memories of him, I guess. Adele—that's my sister—she says that's why I'm allergic to relationships."

It was a warning if Stacy had ever heard one. But it was also an admission of something deeply private.

Her hand tightened in his despite the warning. She thought he would shake her off now, but he didn't.

"You must be very proud to have accomplished all that you have," she said.

"Proud?" He was silent for a long time. "I used to be."

"And now?"

"Now I feel as if I wasted precious moments on a clock that I did not know was ticking a relentless countdown, pursuing things that did not matter."

In that moment, for the first time, Stacy realized Dylan, her ex, might have been right about her when he'd let her go from her job. It had seemed too coincidental, in light of the fact their relationship had just ended, but now his words came back to her.

Maybe Dylan had been right, Stacy thought. She just didn't have the instincts for this.

"You're a good writer," he'd told her, *"but you're no kind of reporter. You don't have the guts for it. There's no daring in you. And you have to be able to be a bit ruthless in some circumstances."*

A ruthless person—a true reporter—would have asked right now if the rumors of McAllister Enterprises going up for sale were true.

But Stacy could not bring herself to do anything more than be in the silence of his pain and regret with him.

"Your hands are freezing," he said, as if that was why he hung on to them instead of letting go. The warmth of his own hands was absolutely delicious on her icy flesh.

"Don't feel sorry for me," he said dangerously. "I'm sure it is also the reason I'm so driven to be such an over-achiever in everything I do, including building snowmen."

Still, holding her hand, he got up on one elbow and looked down at her, and for one breathless moment she thought he was going to kiss her.

Instead, he seemed to realize who they were—who he was and who she was, and he shook the snow off himself, let go of her hand and stood up.

"Do you always have this effect on people?" he said. "Draw their secrets from them?"

She didn't know what to say, so she said nothing at all.

The things he had told her felt sacred. Her desire to tell his story to get her career on track was leaving her like the wind leaving a sail.

He stared at her for a long time, and she was sure that he was going to recognize the danger of what was happening between them.

And perhaps he did. But instead of walking away from it, he walked right toward it.

His hand tightened on hers. He lifted it to his lips and blew the warmth of his breath into her palm. It spoke—sadly, she thought—of her past relationship with Dylan that Kiernan McAllister warming her hands with his breath was the most romantic thing that had ever happened to her.

He was right. For the first time, she felt grateful for the fact her relationship had gone sideways. In her eagerness to create a family again, she had been able to gloss over the fact her relationship had been missing a certain *something*.

It felt dangerously as if that *something* was in the air between her and Kiernan, more dazzling than the stars in the sky above them.

And then a sound split the night, deep, rumbling, jarring.

"What is that?" she asked, her eyes wide. "An earthquake?"

He pulled his hand from hers and shoved it in his pocket. "It's the snowplow," he said. "He's clearing the driveway."

It was over, she thought. As quickly as it had begun,

it was over. She could already feel the distance gathering between them, could see the distance in his eyes.

He turned quickly away from her and strode toward the house, leaving her behind.

"I bet the phone is working," he said. "I have all kinds of business to catch up on."

He was letting her know it was completely out of character for him to have been frolicking with the nanny in the snow. He knew the intimacy of the past few days was creating a grave danger between them, and he was doing the wisest thing. Backing away from it.

Returning to his world.

And she would be returning to hers.

Kiernan retreated to his master suite. He contemplated the evening: getting her car unstuck, chasing her through the snow pelting her with snowballs, the huge snowman that now graced his front yard.

He did not behave like that.

Nor did he lie on the snowy ground, the cold coming up through his jacket, telling all his secrets, telling a near stranger things he had told no one else.

Exhaustion, he excused himself. He had not slept properly since Max had arrived.

He had never abandoned his company quite so completely as he had in the past twenty-four hours.

Though he knew he had been abandoning it mentally for months. He knew about the rumors that he was selling out. Not true. He probably should contain them, but the company was not publically held, so he had no one to answer to, no stock prices plunging because of the rumors.

Still, he checked his phone. It was working, finally.

He knew Adele would be frantic and despite the fact it was late, he called her. She did not answer, so he left a message saying the phone had been out, a fact he was pretty sure Adele would have determined for herself when she could not get though.

"Everything's fine," he said in his message. He told her Max was thriving and that the nanny had arrived so all was well, despite them having been snowed in.

And then he did something he *never* did.

"Hey, sis, I love you."

He hung up the phone slowly. What did that mean, anyway, that he'd included that? His sister knew, of course, that he loved her. But he rarely said things like that.

He thought about the snowball fight, and the snowman, and lying in the snow, looking at the stars. Had the words been to reassure his sister? Or did it reflect how he really felt? Softer in some way than he had felt a few days ago. More open.

Was it possible he was happy?

Was it possible his happiness was related to the nanny?

"Don't worry," he growled, setting the phone beside his bed, stripping down and climbing between the sheets. "Life has a way of snatching those moments away."

For months—possibly even for a full year, going to sleep had been a torment for Kiernan. Those were the moments he tossed and turned and endlessly relived moments that could not be undone.

But tonight, he fell asleep instantly. In the morning, the phone rang, and it was his sister. When he hung up he knew just how right he had been.

Life *did* snatch those moments away.

CHAPTER TEN

STACY AWOKE AND stretched, luxuriating in her surroundings. Sleeping in the bed had been like sleeping on a cloud. The room was that beautiful seamless mix of elegant and rustic that she had seen in the rest of the house.

Last night, being careful not to disturb the baby, she had dug through her things until she had found the bathing suit she had brought in case she wanted to avail herself to the facilities at the Whistler hotel she had booked.

A moment of searing guilt when she had found the suit: the hotel she had booked to write a story about Kiernan McAllister.

Obviously, after he had shared so deeply last night, writing about him was out of the question now. He had trusted her.

The thought sent a shiver up and down her spine. How many opportunities had she had to set the record straight with Kiernan, to tell him she was not a nanny?

She stared at the bathing suit. It was plain and black, made for swimming, not for sharing a hot tub with the likes of Kiernan McAllister!

She looked out her bedroom window. The clouds had drifted back in, blotting out the stars. It had started to snow again, heavily. She felt Kiernan's prediction of a melt was probably incorrect.

If she put off making her confession for a little longer, she would have an opportunity to play with the baby in the snow.

She was sure she would be able to talk Kiernan into joining them. The picture of them as a happy family unit filled her with bliss.

Getting into her pajamas—no more chosen for an encounter with McAllister than her bathing suit had been, Stacy crawled between the luxurious sheets and felt herself not just looking forward to tomorrow but feeling strangely excited by it.

She slept well and deeply and woke in the morning feeling that tingle of excitement, as well as feeling rested. She rolled over and peeped at the playpen.

It was empty!

The thought that Max might be old enough to get himself over those railings and out of the playpen had not even occurred to her! Would it have occurred to a real nanny?

She scrambled out of bed.

"Max!"

No answer. And no baby under the bed or in the bathroom or hiding behind the curtains. Her door was firmly closed. Surely, he could not have gone out.

Not even taking the time to avail herself of the luxurious housecoat that hung on the back of her bedroom door, Stacy flew down the hallway to the great room of the house.

"Max!" She had to shout over something roaring.

She skidded to a halt when she came into the room. Max was sitting on a blanket on the floor, surrounded by cookies. His uncle, in a housecoat like the one hanging on the back of her bedroom door, was sitting on the couch. He was at the controls of a...

She ducked as a remote control helicopter dive-bombed her.

Max chortled and pointed and stuffed another cookie in his mouth.

It was a happy scene except for one thing. The master of the house looked far from happy.

In fact, his mouth was set in a grim line, and when his eyes rested on her, there was something in them she didn't understand.

Contempt?

She looked down at her pajamas. All right. Surely he was used to something a little sexier than oversize white flannel with cotton-candy-pink kittens in the pattern. He seemed to have things under control—literally, since his hand was on the helicopter controls. She could duck back into her room and get dressed.

But then he would know she wanted to make a good impression on him. Erase that look of scathing judgment.

Come to think of it, there was no way *that* look was being caused by a choice in night wear!

"You should have called me," she said, coming into the room hesitantly, having to speak loudly over the whir of the helicopter. Had she slept right through the baby waking up? That meant Kiernan had come into her room. Had he watched her sleep?

Of course he hadn't. That would imply far more interest than she saw in his closed features this morning.

"I would have got up with him," Stacy said. And certainly she would not have given him cookies for breakfast.

Kiernan's expression only got darker.

"Because that's what nannies do?" he asked, his tone cool.

Stacy felt something inside her flash freeze at his tone. She said nothing, but she could feel herself bracing for the worst, her heart sinking.

"The phone was working last night," he said, his voice

cool and grim. "I left my sister a message right away. Just a brief message. Don't worry. Ivan and I are fine."

Kiernan paused and stared at her so long and hard that she squirmed. "Cavalry has arrived," he finished, his voice full of menace.

Stacy held her breath. Kiernan looked away from her now, frowning at the helicopter, which had gone seriously off course while he stared at her. It was flying dangerously close to his priceless chandelier, and he corrected its flight path while the baby clapped.

"I told her the nanny was here."

Stacy wanted to flee from the look on his face, but instead she moved across the room and sank down on the couch beside him. He seemed to flinch as he moved marginally away from her.

"She never sent a nanny," he said, his voice a growl of subdued anger. "She wanted Max and I to have time together. She thought—" He stopped himself abruptly and shook his head. "Never mind. It doesn't matter what she thought."

"She thought it would be good for you," Stacy guessed.

Kiernan landed the toy helicopter on the coffee table. He put down the controls and flicked something. The whirring sound stopped, and the blades coughed to a halt. He ignored Max's shout of protest.

The silence was more unnerving than the noise had been.

"We're not talking about me right now," he said, and his tone was dangerous. "We're talking about you. So, if my sister didn't send a nanny, that begs a question, doesn't it?"

Stacy nodded, stricken.

"If you aren't the nanny," he asked quietly, his eyes dark with anger and accusation, "who are you?"

He put a very bad word in between *who* and *are.*

I'm the woman you threw snowballs at, and made a snowman for. That's what is true.

But she couldn't bring herself to say it.

"I never actually said I was a nanny," Stacy whispered.

"You implied it."

"Yes, I did," she said woefully.

"And you probably knew that I was desperate enough for help to go along without asking too many questions."

"I *did* want to help you."

He snorted.

"I'm sorry," she whispered.

"You could be arrested, you know."

She leaned her head back on the sofa and closed her eyes. She was trying very hard not to cry. The look on his face was one of utter betrayal.

"That would be just my luck," she said. "Of all the exciting things a person could get arrested for, I get arrested for impersonating a nanny." She was trying to hide the fact she was nearly crying with the attempt at humor, but she was pretty sure it was a fail.

Humor fail it would say on the internet, just as the post of her last evening with Dylan had said *proposal fail.*

"Don't try and charm me with your Murphy's Law talk," he said. "Just tell me who you are, and what you want from me."

"I'm a writer," she whispered.

He snarled, an angry sound from deep in his throat.

She shivered. "That sounds like a mountain cat, right before he attacks."

"Don't try and distract."

"All right. I'm a writer. I recently lost my job at *Icons of Business,* under very unfair circumstances."

"Lack of ethics?" he said silkily.

"No! You were right last night—"

She could tell he did not want to be reminded of last night. "I made the mistake of dating my boss. Then it ended. I lost my job over it."

"If that's a play for sympathy, it's not working."

"I just wanted you to know everything I said has been true. Except for the nanny part. Which I didn't actually *say*."

"Sure. You probably made that up about your family, just to wiggle in here. The pajamas are a nice touch. What's not to trust about pink kittens frolicking?"

She knew he was angry because she had wiggled her way not just into his home but, for a little while last night, right by his rather formidable defenses. That was what he was truly upset about—that he had trusted her and been vulnerable to her—and she did not blame him.

"That part about my family is true," she said, and felt her eyes smarting from the pain of trying to hold back tears. "Who would make up something like that? And everything I said about the charity is true. Please don't hold it against the charity."

He did not look like he believed her, and she realized her chances of him helping her were over. She could never ask him to be the honorary chair now. Even his giving her the name of somebody who would help her was gone.

Everything that could go wrong had, only she wasn't the victim. She had brought it totally on herself this time.

In a rush she said, "The only thing that isn't true is the nanny part. I was fired—"

"Unfairly," he said cuttingly.

"Yes, it was unfairly! My boyfriend was my boss, and when our relationship ended, guess what? I got fired!"

He looked totally uncaring.

She rushed on. "I'm trying to make a go of it as a free-lancer. A friend from my old office phoned and told me where you live. I thought if I could get the story about the possible sale of your company, I could save my career."

"My company is not for sale," he said grimly, then tilted his head at her and smiled tightly. "No, wait. Maybe it is."

She ignored him and continued, her voice a near whisper, "And I guess I thought maybe I could get help for CCOFK at the same time.

"But then when I wound up in your flower bed, and my head was hurt, and the baby was here, I lost that initial opportunity to be up-front with you. It did seem to me you might need me. And that you'd throw me out if you knew who I really was and what I really wanted."

"Your lies were driven by pure altruism," he said cynically. "You thought I needed help with the baby. Very nice of you. And if all kinds of details about my life that I don't want anyone to know show up in print? That's just the price I pay for being helped, right?"

"I didn't actually lie," she said again, but she knew it sounded weak. "But I did misrepresent myself, and for that I am truly sorry. I'll get dressed and leave right away."

She had spoiled everything, even CCOFK's one chance of getting a much-needed boost. Filled with self-loathing, she scrambled up off the couch, but he caught her wrist and held her fast.

She tried to pull free, but he wouldn't let her.

"You're not going anywhere until you've signed a contract saying what you heard here, from me, stays here."

"That goes without saying," she said, tilting her jaw proudly.

"Sure, it does," he said coolly. "I have your word for that."

Well, could she really expect him to trust her? On what basis? That they had built a snowman together? Chased each other with snowballs?

She thought he had *seen* her, but now she could see she had wrecked everything.

"I'll sign whatever you want," she said with stiff pride, holding back tears. "You can get it ready while I go gather up my things."

She paused at the baby.

Max was looking between them anxiously. Now he looked at her and smiled, tentatively. "Upppeee? Pweeee?"

She cast a look at Kiernan's dark features, and then she didn't care what he thought about it. She scooped up that baby and pressed her nose into the sweet curve of his neck.

"Bye, Max," she whispered. The tears she had held back came when Max pressed both sides of her face with his hands and gave her a worried look.

"No bye!" he shouted imperiously. "No bye."

She buried her teary face deeper in Max's sturdy little shoulder.

"You *are* being a little premature in saying goodbye."

She whirled, scrubbing the tears with her pajama sleeve, and looked at Kiernan McAllister.

"You aren't going anywhere." His tone was cool and dangerous.

He stood up and came over to her. His grace was leopardlike and just as lethal. She forced herself not to turn with the baby and run. Instead, she stood her ground, knowing she deserved his censure. She had to crane her neck to see him. He towered over her.

"The roads are a worse mess than they were yesterday. It's on the news. Despite my driveway being plowed, there are accidents everywhere." Then his features hardened as he realized that could be interpreted as concern for her.

"My nephew, in a very short time, seems to have become attached to you. I think he's suffered enough losses. You will stay until I find a replacement for you."

Emotion warred in her. One was relief: obviously Kiernan did not think she was as terrible a person as she herself felt she was at the moment. He would not trust her with his nephew if he felt she was really a criminal.

But the other emotion she felt was pure horror.

How could she stay here under these circumstances, with Kiernan bristling with dislike for her?

"How long will that be?" she asked, her voice barely more than a whisper.

Kiernan checked the date on his watch. "I have no idea. I've never been in the market for a nanny before."

"I can't stay here indefinitely." Under these circumstances? It was impossible. She would rather face roads with a whole winter's worth of uncleared snow on them.

"Don't even act as if you have a choice," he warned her. "You are here until I tell you you may go? Is that clear?

CHAPTER ELEVEN

STACY'S MOUTH OPENED to protest. Of course, Kiernan could not force her to stay here. Still, she recalled her premonition when she had first turned toward his house. That it was not Cinderella's castle, but Beast's lair.

Was that just a few days ago?

It seemed as if it had been a lifetime ago, as if by playing in the snow and exchanging confidences under a starry night, she had changed in some fundamental way. Kiernan McAllister couldn't keep her here against her will!

"You can't—"

She started to say it but then snapped her mouth shut. He was not the one in the wrong here, she was.

And if it was sincere interest in this baby's well-being— and okay, Kiernan's as well—that had prevented her from telling the truth, those were the very things that would keep her here. Not his order that she could not leave but her own sense of decency.

Whether he knew it or not, she had just been given a second chance to do the right thing. Do-overs were rare in life, and she was taking this one.

Kiernan came out of his home office, sniffing the air like a wolf who had caught wind of something he didn't quite understand. He'd managed to hide out in his office all day.

Finding a nanny was a little more difficult than placing a call, Miss Harris had informed him an hour ago.

You had to fill out applications. You had to provide references.

You had to have a criminal record check, for God's sake.

It was one of those rare circumstances where it did not matter how much power, influence or money you had.

Finding a real nanny took time.

Why, he asked himself, did he feel as if he needed a nanny now? He'd insisted to Adele he didn't need one before.

The truth was, for all that he was giving an appearance otherwise, he felt like an emotional wreck, unsure of himself in ways he had never felt before. He felt angry with Stacy and angrier with himself.

And it wasn't just about her *not* being the nanny.

It was about the hope that he had allowed into his life when he knew that was the most dangerous thing of all. He needed her to stay here until his disillusionment was complete. And then he needed a professional nanny to step quietly into her place and look after Max so he could lick his wounds without doing any harm to the baby.

He knew, after all, how harmful adults dealing with things could be on unsuspecting children.

Kieran was used to solving problems quickly and aggressively. He was used to knocking down obstacles that got in his way. He had found there were very few problems money could not solve.

But apparently the nanny agency was not budging from its position. No criminal record check, no nanny.

He had not even looked at the forms Miss Harris had faxed him to fill out so she could forward them to the Royal Canadian Mounted Police. Instead, he had started looking over the plans for that hotel/condo development in downtown Vancouver instead.

Stacy Murphy Walker could be the damned nanny until his sister came back.

And he wasn't hiding from her, either, as if he was scared of her.

Despite her wariness of Kiernan's scowling bad temper, Stacy seemed determined not to let that affect the baby at all.

Despite the horrible tension between them, his house was filled with happy sounds. Laughing. Lots of laughing. And singing. There was lots of baby talk.

Maxie, you are such a smart baby. And so cute. I'm falling in love with you.

Such was his aversion to hearing about Stacy falling in love that he had gone into his bathroom, ripped tissue into thin strips, which he had then rolled and stuffed in his ears.

Ears plugged, Kiernan vowed he was not going to be pulled into her world or her web. He didn't actually want to see Stacy laughing. Or singing. Or winning over that gullible little baby.

But now, just like that wolf, hunger was driving him from the safety of his den.

As soon as he opened his office door, scent smacked him in the face. His house smelled almost unbearably good, but that intensified his need to approach with extreme wariness. Good smells often laced the trap, after all.

He went down the hall stealthily, ready to retreat at the first sign of danger. He paused at his bedroom door. His bed had been stripped of bedding, and he recognized one of the smells that tickled his nostrils.

The washer and dryer, set back in an alcove in the hallway invisible behind doors, were running. Those scents were not of the kind dangerous enough for a manly man to run from, even if he was peripherally aware there was something about those scents—laundry soap and dryer sheets—that made his house a home.

Feeling even warier, he continued down the hall and came into the great room, where he stopped in the shadow of the hall and watched for a moment, undetected, to gauge the danger.

It looked very dangerous, indeed.

Again, his house looked transformed.

Wrecked but transformed. An abundance of toys were scattered hazardously over the floors.

A tent had been made—was that the goose-down duvet off his bed—between the coffee table and the couch. Max was under the shelter, babbling away happily to Yike-Yike.

Max had not entertained himself, not even once, since his arrival. They had gone through six sets of batteries on the helicopter.

Stacy was in the kitchen area of the great room. Kiernan realized how good this design was for parents—the sink faced the seating area, so a mother could be busy in the kitchen and still supervise the kids.

Not that he wanted to be thinking of Stacy as a mom.

And yet there she no denying she somehow suited for that very role. She was flitting from counter to sink, totally unaware of him. She was humming, and she had that disturbing look of radiance about her that Kiernan had first seen when she had picked up Max.

It occurred to him that instead of butting his head up against a wall looking for a new nanny, he should have been checking out her story.

Surely, someone who had experienced the kind of losses she claimed could not look like that?

Maybe what he thought was radiance was just heat. A

stove timer went off, and she put on a pair of oven gloves and opened the oven door. As she turned back from the oven, hot pan in hands, her face was flushed.

Her hair had been pulled back, but a few strands had escaped captivity, and she blew one out of her eyes.

He had not made a sound or moved, but she suddenly went very still, the doe who had realized the wolf watched her, the prey becoming aware of predator. She looked at him.

"Hi," she said tentatively, hopeful, no doubt, that her flurry of activity was moving him toward forgiveness.

When he didn't say anything, she looked disappointed but moved on quickly.

"Can you put hot pans right on this surface?" she asked, giving a worried look to the countertop.

"What the hell are you doing?"

"I'm making things," she said, and then she beamed at him, still foolishly hopeful of his forgiveness. "Double ovens!"

She said that in a tone that most of the women he dated would have reserved for a diamond tennis bracelet.

"You can bake cookies and pizza at the same time," she told him, with the kind of reverence that should be reserved for technological wonders like putting a backup camera in the tailgate of a truck or being able to stream live from the International Space Station.

Now that she had identified what was cooking, his senses insisted on separating the smells and categorizing them in order of their deliciousness.

He could smell chocolate chips melting and cheese bubbling, bread dough crust crisping.

"Are you trying to worm into my good graces?" he asked. Damn it. His mouth was watering. "Put those down, for Pete's sake, before you burn a hole through the oven glove."

"I just wasn't sure if I could set them right on the—"

"Yes!" He didn't expect his voice to be such a roar of complete frustration. She set the sheet down with a startled clatter.

Cookies.

Chocolate chip, just as his nose had told him.

"I had chocolate chips?" he said.

"Actually, an incredibly well stocked pantry."

There had been many chefs and caterers in this kitchen. Someone had set it up. Still, for all the good things that had been cooked in this kitchen, Kiernan was not sure the scents had ever been quite so tantalizing.

She turned back to the other oven and came out with a pizza, and not the kind you got at the deli section of the store, prefabricated, either.

"I didn't think you'd want to eat out of cans two days in a row."

It felt necessary to let her know he was in no way reliant on her domestic diva-ishness. "I usually order take-out. There are several really good restaurants in Whistler that will deliver."

"Oh, well, this is done now, if you're hungry. I'd hate to ask anyone to tackle the roads today."

Compassion for the delivery guy was not really a sign of a devious mind, his own mind insisted on pointing out helpfully.

He hadn't been aware just how hungry he was until she put that pizza on the counter, the crust golden, the cheese brown and bubbling.

He prevented himself, just barely, from running over there and starting to gobble it up like a starving creature.

"What were you doing in my bedroom?" he demanded.

"I just grabbed your sheets. I thought—"

"I don't want you to think. I want you to stay out of my bedroom."

"I'm making amends," she said stubbornly.

"A cleaning service comes in after I leave. I don't like having staff in my houses. And my feelings about having staff are private. And I don't want you poking through my things. You have enough ammunition on me. I don't need the whole world entertaining themselves with insights into how I live."

"I wasn't poking through your things! I took your sheets."

"No snooping through my drawers looking for fascinating insights into my life?"

"What kind of fascinating insights would I find in your drawers, for heaven's sake?"

She seemed to realize that could be taken two ways and the flush in her cheeks deepened.

"I once had a reporter ask me if I wore boxers or briefs."

"Well, that was bad reporting," she said, annoyed. "Because, believe me, big man that you are, your underwear is of absolutely no interest to anyone."

But her voice sounded strangled.

"You don't care to know?" he asked, taking wicked enjoyment in her discomfort, especially after that *big man that you are* crack.

"No!"

"Neither," he said.

She took a sudden interest in the cookies. She started taking them off the cookie sheet and putting them on a rack. They were obviously way too warm to be moved, crumbling as she touched them.

And she seemed totally unaware of it!

Save the cookies or enjoy her discomfort a little more?

He could have both. He moved into the kitchen beside her and removed the utensil she was destroying the cookies with from her hand.

"There, put that in your story."

"There isn't going to be a story," she insisted. She tried to grab the utensil. "Why would I be making amends if I planned to go ahead and write about you?" she said.

He took a cookie off the sheet with his fingers, still holding the flipper out of her reach. He popped the whole thing into his mouth. "You're just trying to lure me into a false sense of security."

She looked annoyed—which was safer for him than the *radiant* look she'd been sporting as she juggled hot pans out of the oven.

But obviously, part of making her amends was biting her tongue, because she didn't voice her annoyance.

In fact, her voice seemed deliberately sweet as she responded to his just-as-deliberate nastiness.

"Well, now you can have nice clean sheets tonight, and while you're lying in them, you can think, *that Stacy is a much nicer girl than I thought. I don't think I will have her arrested for impersonating a nanny, after all. She's trying very hard to make things right. I may just forgive her.*"

In the battle of light and dark, she was not going to win! And she, he reminded himself, was the transgressor. For all that sweetness, she was the one who had behaved without integrity.

Though, he noticed uneasily, he could not bring himself to think of her as representing dark.

He knew that was his lot in life.

"I don't want to be lying in my bed thinking of you in any way," he said. "And I don't think you want me to be thinking of you, either."

She gulped. And blushed.

Which was exactly what he'd intended. No sense her thinking her *amends* were going to batter down his defenses.

Because they weren't.

He was aware he could forgive her—she'd been misguided. It was obvious to him, from the stripped beds to the tent for Max to the cookies coming out of the oven to the concern for the delivery guy trying to tackle the roads, that there was not a malicious bone in her body.

It was obvious to him that she was going to wear herself out proving that to him and that he should put her out of her misery now.

Maybe he could have forgiven her, but it seemed easier not to. It seemed to him she was the kind of girl who dreamed the kind of dreams he could not ever fulfill.

It was doubtful he could have even before the death of his friend.

After?

Not a chance.

"If I'm ever thinking of you in my bed, Stacy Walker? The last thing on my mind will be the clean sheets."

There. That should scare her right out of her annoying domestic efforts to make amends.

He went over to the counter, took a plate from where she had a stack of them and grabbed two. He filled one with pizza and the other with cookies. He had enough food to avoid her until his sister came home, since he had resigned himself to the facts he was not going to find a nanny and that he didn't really want to find one, either.

Some twisted part of him was enjoying this torment! He got in a parting shot.

"And if you are ever in my bed, the last thing you will be thinking about is clean sheets."

Her mouth opened, and closed, a fish gasping for air. But then her eyes narrowed, and she glared at him.

"You are absolutely right," she said in that same sweet tone of voice. "I wouldn't be thinking of sheets. I'd be thinking about the toilet paper in your ears."

They glared at each other. He fought back the compulsion to tell her it wasn't toilet paper and to rip the tissue paper earplugs out of his ears. He wouldn't give her the satisfaction!

CHAPTER TWELVE

KIERNAN HAD ALMOST made good his escape from Stacy when he heard the sound of a vehicle grinding its way up his hill.

Instead of turning toward his bedroom, he approached the front entry and looked out the window.

It was still snowing heavily and a cab was pulling up in front of the house. It slid in the identical spot that Stacy's car had slid in, narrowly missing where hers sat now.

"Are you expecting someone?" he called.

"Yes," she said. "My old boyfriend. I've been expecting him for months. I hoped he would realize the error of his ways, drop down on bended knee and beg me to come back to him."

Kiernan watched his sister get out of the cab.

He turned back toward the kitchen. Adele arriving meant Stacy was leaving. Since it should have been a *yahoo* moment Kiernan was taken a little aback at how he felt.

Protective.

Despite her effort to sound flippant, he realized she really had, in that wild little imagination of hers, played out her boyfriend's return to her and probably in excruciating detail, too.

Stacy Murphy Walker was leaving. What would it hurt to set her straight before she went?

"So, would you take him back?" he asked, juggling his laden plates and leaning his shoulder against the log pillar that separated the kitchen from the hallway.

"In a breath," she said.

"Why? He sounds like he was an ass."

"At least he wore underwear," she muttered.

"I never said I didn't. I just said I didn't wear boxers or briefs."

He could tell she wanted to ask what, but she didn't. She clamped her mouth in a firm line, and said, "Well, it's not as if we're interviewing you to be my boyfriend. There is going to be no boyfriend. I am going to be a dedicated career woman. I am going to devote myself to CCOFK."

"I thought you'd take him back."

"He's not coming back. It's a revenge fantasy."

"If it really was, when he got down on bended knee, you'd say no, not yes."

"Well, he's not coming back, so I have planned my life without him. Or anyone."

"Sounds lonely," he said.

"I'll get a cat."

He walked across the space that separated them. She backed up until she hit the counter with her behind and had no place to go.

"What are you doing?" she stammered.

He couldn't let her go without tasting her. He carefully set down the plates. He lowered his head to hers and took her lips in his.

In that second he knew everything that was true about her.

Every. Single. Thing.

And he knew something about himself, too. He hadn't insisted she stay here because of the roads. He hadn't insisted she stay here because of Max.

It was because of him. It was because she had succeeded, in a few short days, of doing what no one else had
done. Breaking something open inside him. Something
that *wanted* light instead of darkness…

The kiss deepened. Kiernan took his time exploring
her lips as he felt her initial startled resistance melt. It was
followed by a surrender so complete it felt as if she was
dissolving into him, her slender, soft curves melding to
his own harder lines.

Her hands moved from the counter where she had
braced herself and twined around his neck, pulling him
down to her.

There was something in her he had not expected. Sweetness gave way quickly to something more savage, more
hungry.

He heard the front door open.

"Yoo-hoo? Anyone home?"

"Mama!" Max cried.

Kiernan yanked away from Stacy. They stood staring
at each other, chests heaving. Her hair was mussed where
his hands had tangled in it; her lips were swollen and her
cheeks were flushed.

He turned from her and watched as his nephew exploded out from under his tent and headed down the
hall.

"If there's a Triple Crown for babies," he said, raking
a hand through his hair, trying for a casual note so that
Stacy would not see how that kiss had shaken him, "he's
going to win."

"What was that about?" she whispered. He shot her a
glance just in time to see her touching the swollen swell
of her lips with trembling fingertips. She was staring at
him with wide eyes.

If his sister wasn't shaking snow off her coat in the

front hall, he was pretty sure he would finish what he started.

But then he'd known his sister was coming when he had started, a safety net, in case he fell.

And Stacy was the kind of girl who could make a guy fall: straight into the wide pools of her eyes, straight into the softness of that heart. She was the kind of woman who could make a person who had lost hope entirely think that there was a chance. Stacy Murphy Walker had stormed his world, and it felt as if there was only one defense against that. The one he should have taken the minute he found out she was an imposter but hadn't. Stacy had to go.

"It was a gift," he growled.

"A gift? Your kiss was a gift," she stammered, but her eyes were narrowing dangerously. She was incensed, and he deserved it.

"Just letting you know," he said quietly, "you'll never be satisfied with a cat."

She touched her lips again.

"Or the old beau, either," he said.

He heard his sister coming down the hall and sprang back from Stacy just as Adele came into the room, Max riding in the crook of her arm, her cheeks sparkling from the cold.

And her eyes sparkling in a way he had not seen for a long, long time.

Adele looked at him and then at Stacy and back at him. He had the horrible feeling that Stacy's mussed hair and swollen lips—not to mention the glitter in those green eyes—were a dead giveaway. Adele knew exactly what had transpired between them.

"Stacy Walker, my sister, Adele. The reason you can leave now."

"Leave?" Adele said. "No one's going anywhere in that!

The cab could barely make it from Whistler. I thought we were going to wind up in the ditch a dozen times. The roads were littered with vehicles. Your driveway was in the best shape of any road I was on today."

"I'll drive her," he said. He heard an edge of desperation in his voice. He was pretty sure, from the way Adele's head swung toward him, she heard it, too.

When he had kissed Stacy it had been because goodbye was in clear sight.

Adele had a little smile on her face he didn't like one little bit.

"Yes, that's fine," Stacy said, her voice strained. "I'd have to come back for my car, though."

"I can have it delivered."

"That seems like a great deal of trouble," Stacy said, ridiculously formal, given that he had just kissed her. And she had kissed back.

"No trouble at all."

"Quit being so silly," Adele said.

Silly? He glared at his sister just to help her remember who he was, but she wasn't even looking at him.

"You aren't going anywhere," Adele said, offering her hand to Stacy. "I've been looking forward to meeting you. And even more so now that I saw the snowman! He's adorable. I just can't wait to get to know the woman who could convince Kiernan to make a snowman."

"How do you know I made it?" Kiernan demanded.

"It's eight feet tall, for goodness' sake. Who do you think I would think made it? Max?"

Adele put her nose against her baby's and said, "Mommy missed you so much, you adorable little winky-woo. I couldn't stay away from you for another minute."

He was pretty sure it was news of the imposter nanny, whom she was now greeting with the enthusiasm of a just discovered royal relative, that had brought his sister home.

Or maybe not.

When his sister looked at Max, despite all her losses, she had the same look on her face that he had seen on Stacy's. Radiance.

Or was it all because of Max? It had never occurred to him until this very second that maybe his sister had not been alone on her getaway.

"He's not…" he told Adele, stopping just in time from saying *winky-woo,* "an adorable little anything. He's a demanding little tyrant."

"Takes after his uncle, then," Adele said with a nod.

He'd had enough of her. "Look, I'm exhausted and I need—Stacy needs to go." He felt he'd revealed way too much with that one, because Adele looked at him sympathetically.

"The morning is plenty of time to figure out who is going where. I've just been on those roads. I don't want you on them."

In her voice, he heard the thread of real fear, the understanding that life could change in an instant, in one bad decision. He had put that fear and that awareness in his sister; he had done that when he had failed to protect her husband.

"I guess we could figure things out in the morning," he conceded with ill grace, since he could clearly see an argument was going to get him nowhere.

"Good! That will give Stacy and I a chance get to know each other."

Adele and Stacy, these two ever so resilient women, getting to know each other?

He shot his sister a dark look, which didn't perturb her

in the least, retrieved his plates of pizza and cookies and headed down the hall to his room.

If he closed his door with a little more force than was strictly necessary, it was perfectly excusable.

Hours later he gave up on trying to sleep, because even with pillows over his head—he wasn't using toilet paper again—he could still hear them out there giggling away like old school chums.

A tap came on his door.

He quickly turned off his bedside light.

The door opened and Adele came in. "I saw the light from under the door."

He sat up and grudgingly turned the light back on. "What do you want?"

"You don't have to say that as if I'm some kind of traitor!"

"You knew she was an imposter! You're the one who alerted me that you hadn't sent a nanny at all. I'm surrounded by women who lie to me. What is the idea of saying you were sending a nanny when you had no intention of doing that?"

His sister made herself comfy on the edge of his bed.

"It was just hurting me so badly to see how Danner's death was affecting you, Kee. You seemed to be slipping further away every day. And there was something sharp and cynical and angry about you that I had never seen before."

"That doesn't sound like someone anyone in their right mind would leave an infant with!"

"I knew you were in there somewhere. And I thought being around Max would force you to wake up, to be *here*, instead of in that dark place you couldn't seem to come back from."

"You're saying that in past tense, as though I have come back."

"There's a snowman on the front lawn," she said.

"That is hardly the miracle you are looking for, Adele."

"I need to tell you something," she whispered.

"What?" He was not sure he liked her tone of voice.

"Mark and I started seeing each other a while back. At first, it was just comforting each other over Danner. Sometimes, we'd talk about our mutual concern for you. Anyway, that's why I needed some time this weekend. I needed to make a decision."

"About?"

"Mark has asked me to marry him."

Kiernan held his breath.

"I said yes. I love him very much."

He didn't quite know what to say. He was stunned, in a way, that life moved on. Stunned that he had missed the developing relationship between Adele and Mark. Stunned at his sister's ability to say yes to love all over again.

"Congratulations," he said gruffly. He realized he was shaken but glad for her. "I guess maybe you did get the miracle you were looking for. But don't get any ideas about me."

"I have been looking for a miracle for you," she said, "but I was looking in one direction, and it came from another."

"There have been no miracles here," he warned her. "None."

"Hmm."

"Don't say hmm, like that. If you think that lying little chit of an imposter nanny is a miracle, you need a little miracle research."

"I did some research, you know. On her. That's why I

acted as if I knew her when I got here. I kind of did. You can find out the most amazing things on the internet."

He really wanted to pretend he was not interested in this. He wanted his sister to think he was completely indifferent to what she had discovered about Stacy Walker Murphy on the internet.

Instead, in a voice he hoped was stripped of anything that could be interpreted as interest, Kiernan heard himself say, "Like?"

CHAPTER THIRTEEN

"HER WHOLE FAMILY was killed in a car accident when she was sixteen," Adele told him, her voice aching with tenderness.

"I know that already."

"Oh." Adele cocked her head at him. "Did you look her up on the internet, too?"

"No."

"So, she told you that?"

"To try and wangle her way by my defenses!"

"She *has* used her greatest tragedy as a tool, but, as shocking as this will be to you, it doesn't have anything to do with you. She started that group."

"Career and College Opportunities for Orphans."

"Foster kids," his sister corrected him mildly. She twirled some hair around her little finger. "She told you that, too?"

"She mentioned it briefly."

"Ah. You seemed to have known each other quite a short time to have shared so deeply."

He glared at Adele. "I *regret* that. I don't see it as cause for celebration. Look, the facts are the facts. She misrepresented herself on purpose. She's a writer not a nanny."

"She's a good one, too. I read some of her stuff online. She would be a great person to entrust your story to."

"What story?" he asked dangerously. "Look, sis, she needs to go. She does not need to be adopted by you."

"She's always dreamed of a winter holiday," Adele said with a frightening softness, not hearing the danger in his voice at all. "She's had so much go wrong in her life. She expects the worst."

Poster child for Murphy's Law he remembered her introducing herself.

"And I can hardly blame her. There's a video online—" She stopped.

"A video? Of Stacy?"

"I cannot believe you didn't go online yourself when you found out she wasn't a nanny!"

"Well, I didn't. What's the video of?"

"Never mind. It's not important. What's important is that she's worked really hard at giving things to others. I looked up that charity online. For a group with very little money and a low profile, they accomplish quite a bit. They've handed out two dozen scholarships in the past eight years."

"Earth-shattering," he said drily.

"That's twenty-four young people changed forever. For your information, that *is* earth-shattering."

"Okay, so the company will donate some money," he said.

His sister gave him a look that said he was missing the point.

"And provide some people with know-how to get her little group off the ground."

"You're missing the point."

"Which is?"

"She expects the worst."

"It's her karma," he growled. "What do you expect with a middle name like Murphy?"

"Do not hide behind flippancy with me," his sister warned. He really hated it when she took that tone.

But then her voice softened, "What if the best thing ever happened to her? What if good came from this predicament she finds herself in, instead of bad?"

"What would she learn from that?"

"That life is good!"

"Well, it isn't!" But, he thought, though the thought was unwilling as hell, it had been good. It had been unexpectedly good for a few short days with Stacy. Not that he could ever let Adele know that!

His sister looked at him, then shook her head with disappointment. He felt her disappointment in him all the way to his toes.

He had been Adele's hero since they were kids.

Not that he deserved that title now!

"When did you become *this* person?" Adele asked.

"I'm protecting myself."

"Against what?"

"Against life, as if you should have to ask. I became *this* person the day that Danner died."

His sister suddenly looked very, very angry.

"No one," she said, her words angry, "would hate that more than him. That you would make that his legacy to the world is disgraceful. He embraced life. He treated it all like an incredible adventure, and I'm grateful for that. I'm grateful for the person I am because I got to be with him for a short time. I'm grateful for my son."

Kiernan remembered Stacy, too, had made gratitude her legacy from tragedy.

"For God's sake," his sister said, "that girl has lost everything. You are in a position to get out of your big, fat self-pitying self and do something for her."

His big, fat, self-pitying self?

"She lied to me!"

"If you couldn't tell who Stacy Walker was from the minute you laid eyes on her, there is no hope for you, Kiernan McAllister. None at all."

He remembered claiming Stacy's lips earlier.

And knowing, just as his sister had said, the absolute truth about her.

And of course, the danger she posed to him on many levels.

His sister shot him one last meaningful look and flounced off the bed, tossing her hair. She marched from his room, closing his door with a snap behind her.

One of the things that was not good about being very powerful was that people stopped telling you the truth and started telling you what you wanted to hear. One of the people he could trust not to do that was Adele.

Kiernan recognized that this brief encounter with Stacy had rocked his world, that he could not think with his normal discernment and detachment. His sister was trying to steer him in the right direction.

And his sister had never come from any place but love.

He told himself he was not going to look on his computer. He lasted about thirty seconds before he went and retrieved it from his dresser. Sometimes the internet worked up here and mostly it didn't. He was hoping it wouldn't, but he typed in her name anyway.

A video called *Proposal Fail* came up.

Stacy looked gorgeous: her hair and makeup done, in a sexy dress and high heels. He recognized the restaurant as one of Vancouver's best.

But, despite how gorgeous she looked and the fact she was in one of Vancouver's most upscale restaurants, the scene had obviously been captured after she was already angry.

"You want me to what?" she asked, her voice high and shrill.

The guy looked around nervously, twirled his wineglass and wouldn't look at her.

Kiernan found himself looking at the beau critically. She would take *him* back?

Dylan had guffawed when she had said that, apparently more loudly than she had thought.

"I thought you were going to ask me to marry you, and you're asking me to shack up with you?"

"Shack up, Stacy, really? What century is that from?"

Kiernan had the ugly feeling if he could, he would have crawled through the computer screen, picked that guy up by his throat and knocked his teeth out.

He had obviously caused Stacy intense pain…and instead of trying to make it better, he had a sneering look on his face.

She'd go back to him? Really?

Kiernan watched Stacy stand up. Pick up her wine. Take a fortifying sip and then walk over to her beau.

She dumped the whole glass over his head. It was red and it stained his pristine white shirt beyond repair.

"What century is that from?" she yelled for the entertainment of the whole world.

Only Kiernan didn't feel entertained at all. He could clearly see she was crying as she stormed from the room. The guy looked more annoyed about his shirt than the fact his girlfriend had just left him.

Good grief, what kind of bad luck was it to have a moment like that posted?

He had a moment of clarity as he shut off his computer.

What if it wasn't all about him? Adele was so right. Despite a life threaded through with the worst kind of tragedy, Stacy was struggling valiantly to make it a better place.

Even while she claimed her own dreams were in tatters, he knew she really stood on the edge.

Of going to the place where he was, a place of hopelessness and cynicism that he would not wish on anyone, or a place of being returned to faith.

He seemed like the last person who could be entrusted with an assignment like that—a return to faith—but really, it would not take much of a push to get her moving in the right direction.

What if he could, in some small way, get out of his big, fat, self-pitying self to help another human being to believe in dreams again?

His sister, he was pretty sure, was entirely correct about him. There was no hope for him. None at all.

But despite her denials, he had seen in Stacy's face she clung to hope the way a person who had survived a shipwreck clung to the lifeboat.

There was no sense crushing that thing called hope simply because he could not feel it!

What if he could do some small thing that would change her? Give her a much-needed boost? Not just protect her from the return of her boyfriend or a life as a crazy cat lady, but help her believe in the power of her dreams all over again?

He went down the hall to the room his sister preferred. She had moved Max's playpen in there and was sitting on the bed, leafing through a book.

"What would you suggest?" he asked his sister.

She looked up from the book. A light came on in her face. That light almost made the chance he was taking worth it. Of course, he thought she was going to suggest something he could *buy.* An all-expense-paid week or two to a world-class resort. Like Whistler, only that was probably too close to home to seem like a real dream.

Steamboat, Colorado, maybe.

Les Trois Vallées, in the French Alps. Why had he thought of that? Because of Brides-les-Bains, one of those three very famous resorts?

If his mind was making weird jumps in logic like that: from helping her dreams come true to thinking of her in any context with *bride* in it, then the farther away the better.

"I was thinking you should take her up to Last Chance tomorrow," his sister said.

He had to refuse. Last Chance was, in his opinion, one of the most beautiful places on the planet. And Kiernan had been to many beautiful places on the planet.

The humble little cabin named Last Chance, behind his house, way up the mountain in a grove of old, old cedar, as well as having one of the most panoramic views he had ever seen, had its own private natural hot spring.

"Can you think of a better place for the perfect winter getaway?" Adele asked.

No, he couldn't. On the other hand, did he really want to be at a place named Last Chance with Stacy Walker? Last chance to make things right? To be a better man?

Last chance to hope, to live again, to...

As well as being remote and beautiful, it was a place of romance and magic.

"I'll come, too," Adele said, as if she read each of his doubts. "We can put Max in the sled and you can pull it."

The truth? He'd always had trouble saying no to his sister. Since he had killed her husband, the father of her child, his sense of obligation to her, of somehow wanting to make up to her that which could never be made up felt like a boulder sitting on his chest, slowly crushing the life out of him.

He owed his sister big-time, a debt he had no hope of repaying. There was that word again, hope.

And so if Adele wanted to take Stacy Murphy Walker to Last Chance, that was what he would help her do. He was being given an opportunity to get out of his big, fat, self-pitying self long enough to be the better man.

Temporarily.

CHAPTER FOURTEEN

"Last Chance?" Stacy said, dubiously. "What is that?"

Kiernan glared at her. She was looking the proverbial gift horse in the mouth. He was doing her a favor. He was making her dreams come true, for Pete's sake. Did she have to look so reluctant? But things had been awkward between them since he had kissed her.

That kiss in the kitchen was supposed to have been *goodbye.* But she was still here, and the memory of that kiss sizzled in the air between them this morning.

"It's actually the reason I bought this property," he said, striving for patience in the face of her lack of enthusiasm. "Danner found this little cabin to rent one winter. The only way you can reach it once the snow flies is on cross-country skis. There's a natural hot spring right beside it."

He could see the war in her face.

"Perfect winter getaway," he said. "I've been at some of the best resorts in the world, and it beats all of them. And it's a two-hour ski from here."

He'd almost had her, until he'd mentioned the ski part.

"Oh, I've never skied. I'm sure I would make a complete fool of myself. No, really, now that your sister is here, I have to leave."

Her voice was firm, but unless he missed his guess, Stacy looked wistful. Besides, when he saw her fear of making a fool of herself, he thought of that internet video posting, knew she was still suffering the humiliation of it and committed even more to convincing her to go. He hated the thought of her going through life being afraid to do things.

"The roads are worse this morning than they were last night," Kiernan said. Well, since the fear was there anyway, he might as well press it to his advantage. He hoped her fear of driving on the roads would be greater than her fear of making a fool of herself.

"And I still don't think the snow will last," he continued. "This might be your only opportunity to get up there."

"Last chance?" she said, and hazarded a smile.

"Exactly."

He certainly wasn't inviting her back here, ever.

Because she did all sorts of things to him that he wasn't sure he wanted done. Like made him aware, for the first time in a long time, what it felt like to be alive.

To notice what the light looked like kissing chocolate curls and how her laughter, ringing out with the baby's laughter, made everything different.

Who was he kidding?

The moment the shift had happened was when his lips touched hers.

"I don't have any of the right stuff," she said, and now he could hear in her voice, too, that she had capitulated and was wistful to go.

"Don't worry, I have all the right stuff."

And she looked at him as if that could be taken two ways and that maybe she really thought he did have all the right stuff, despite the fact he had been a complete jerk to her.

Well, she had been frantic in her attempts to make amends. He had slept aware it was her hands that had put the sheets on his bed, with a belly satisfyingly full of really good things.

So, he would make amends, too.

Give her that winter holiday she had always wanted, then send her on her way. No more kissing. *Toodle-oo.*

Kieran McAllister frowned. He did not say *toodle-oo.* Maybe one more kiss to cement it in her mind about leaving both cats and the old boyfriend out of her plans for the future.

The thought of that kiss may have flashed through his eyes, because she looked flustered suddenly, too.

He wasn't going to kiss her again. "We're going to be chaperoned!" he recalled, a touch desperately. "Adele and Ivan are coming, too."

"Oh!" Stacy still seemed underenthused.

And he recognized he had to take a risk. He had to tell her the truth.

"And I've behaved badly toward you," he said. "I don't want our time together to end on this note."

And instantly he was aware of the most dangerous thing of all: this really wasn't about her, no matter how he tried to cloak it in altruism.

He did not want their time together to end at all.

Was that why he was really offering her the journey to Last Chance? It was. It was to see if there was any hope at all, and if there was, if he was brave enough to reach for it, to reach for the life rope that had been thrown into the quagmire he had existed in.

The truth was he needed this trip to Last Chance way more than she did.

Something softened in her face, and he knew she had heard the truth. And he knew she was remembering: snowmen and snow angels and dodging popcorn missiles and sharing ordinary moments together that had somehow become extraordinary.

"Yes, all right," Stacy said. "I'd like that."

Thank goodness for chaperones, he thought.

But Adele announced, minutes before they were set to leave, that she wasn't coming. Stacy reacted to the announcement by blushing, Kiernan smelled a rat, the same as he had when Max had been left in his office without warning.

"I think Max is getting a cold," Adele said. "It wouldn't be good for him to be outside all day. Look at his nose."

Kiernan, to his everlasting regret, looked at his nephew's nose. Even his sister could not manufacture something like that!

In light of Stacy's blush of discomfort, he debated canceling. But only for about two seconds.

Because sometime during the night he realized he was looking forward to going up there as much as he had looked forward to anything for a long, long time.

And he knew part of it was he was excited about showing it to her, the nanny imposter.

How could he think that—nanny imposter—and feel only amusement and no anger at all?

He was working at being a better man. He would show her a great day, enjoy her wonder, bring her home.

There would be absolutely no need to reinforce the cat, ex-boyfriend lesson.

With his lips!

Stacy probably needed her head examined, but here she was having a ski lesson from Kieran McAllister

She hadn't even backed out when she heard Adele and Max were not coming.

Because, really, she had played it safe her entire life. And where had that gotten her?

No, if she had learned one thing in her short time here, it was this: when things started spinning out of control, go with it rather than fight it!

And spinning out of control was a very apt description of how she had felt after Kiernan had kissed her in the kitchen.

One kiss, and she was pretty sure she was cured forever of wanting Dylan back. Or a cat.

Though as a point of pride, she could not let Kiernan know that his kiss had cured her of those desires.

What she did desire now, in a way she had never wanted it before, was to embrace it all, including the uncertainty she felt every single time she looked at Kiernan.

She was being offered an adventure. Not just any adventure. A chance to do something she had longed to do ever since she had enjoyed the snow with her beloved father.

Her dad had never called her Stacy. He had always, affectionately, teasingly called her Murphy.

Bur for once something seemed to be going right for her, and she was not saying no to that.

And it was true she was getting in way over her head with this family. Since Kiernan had kissed her, she felt as if she had the shivers, which could not be cured by anything, not even a roaring fire in the hearth in the great room.

But the thing was, she didn't mind feeling that way.

She felt alive. And so, marveling at the unexpected spin her life had taken, she watched Kiernan get ready.

His comfort with the equipment inspired confidence. She watched him waxing the skis, listened to him explaining how the waxes depended on the temperature and the snow.

"You can buy skis that don't need waxing, but I don't," he said. "I'm a purist."

There was a whole section underneath the back deck of his house devoted to outdoor equipment. He could provide skis and snowshoes and skates to about twenty people.

"We always make a skating rink at the back of the house later in the year," he told her.

And Stacy's desire shifted again: to see that. To see him on skates, to have him teach her that, too. But she knew that was taking it too far into the future, and that today was called the present, because that's what it was, a gift.

A gift that did not promise the future.

She vowed to herself she would just enjoy this day without overlaying it with anxiety about what could possibly happen next.

He'd had no trouble at all finding her size of skis and boots. Adele had lent her a jacket that fit, a hat and good mittens.

"Are we getting on a chairlift?" she asked nervously, despite her confidence in him, she had some doubts about herself. *Anything that can go wrong, will.*

He laughed. "No lifts for this. This is cross-country skiing," he said. "It's way different than downhill skiing, which is the chairlift kind."

"In what way is it different?"

"More work. Everything we do, we do under our own power." Satisfied with the wax, he led the way outside and set two pairs of skis on the ground.

"Okay, these are yours. Put your toe in there and step down."

It was difficult to hold one foot up, position it into a very small area and step down. Her foot slid uncooperatively everywhere *but* into the binding.

To her embarrassment, he had to get down in the snow

and guide her foot into the right place, snap the binding down. Then, while he was already on the ground, he did the other one, too.

She looked down at his head. That their acquaintance could be marked in days seemed impossible.

She felt as if she had known Kiernan McAllister forever. *And would know him forever.*

And there went her vow not to spoil any part of this day fretting about the future and what could happen next.

Still, it took all her will to stop herself from reaching out and sliding her hand through the silk of his hair. He glanced up at her, his long lashes over those amazing silver eyes holding speckles of frost. Her heart swooped upward, like a bird that had been freed from a cage.

Was she falling in love with him?

Of course not. She reprimanded herself. She barely knew him.

But she *had* kissed him. And made a snowman with him. And lain on her back beside him, their cold hands intertwined as they looked at the stars and exchanged confidences.

Of course she did not love him. But the air seemed to sparkle with diamond drops of possibility that outshone the diamond drops that sparkled in the pristine snow all around them.

She felt some exquisite awareness tickling along her spine as she watched him expertly step into his skis.

And then, thankfully, the time for thinking was done, because she was swept into a world of movement and laughter, pure physical activity and exertion.

"I'll show you a few basic moves." He showed her the step and glide.

Then she tried it. "Argh! You are pure power and grace. I am a penguin waddling!"

"Relax. It's all just for fun. I'll break trail, you put your skis in my tracks and follow me. Just do what I do and everything will be fine."

And then, amazingly she did relax, because he was in front of her and not witnessing her clumsy efforts to follow his ski tracks. It was fun and easier than she had anticipated.

"See? Everything is fine, isn't it?"

And it was. No, it was more than fine. Seconds from the house, they entered the trees. The silence was broken only by the occasional branch letting go of its load of snow, and her breathing, loud in her own ears.

"You doing okay?" he called.

"It is hard work. But so much fun!"

He glanced over his shoulder at her, his approving smile lit up her world.

She loved being behind him. She could drink her fill of him without him ever knowing how she gloried in his easy strength, his power, his confidence.

The woods were extraordinarily silent and beautiful. They had been making their way up a very gradual slope, and now it steepened.

"Like this," he said. He set his skis like triangles and walked his way up the hill, making a fishbone pattern in the new snow. She tried it. Now this was harder than he had made it look.

Partway up the incline, she could feel herself sliding back instead of going forward. She let out a little shriek of dismay, threw herself forward on her poles and froze leaning heavily on them.

He looked back at her and burst out laughing. He turned and skied back to her, stopping with a swish of snow.

"I'm stuck," she said.

"I can see that," he said with a smile. "I'll get you unstuck."

He regarded her predicament thoughtfully, then pulled in right behind her, his skis forming a sandwich around her own.

She could feel his breath on her neck, and his hands went to the small of her back and he shoved.

"Okay," he said, his breath still warm on her neck and tickling her ears, "pull with your poles and dig in those edges. That's it. Just one small step. Good. And another one."

A lot of things seemed to be coming unstuck, most of them within her.

"I'm sliding back on your skis." She was. She slid right back into him, and for a breathless moment they stood there, glued together, the majesty of the quiet mountains all around them.

His arms folded lightly around her. "You're doing great." And then he let her go and shoved her again.

Huffing and puffing, she managed to inch her way up the steep incline.

"You've got it." And then he left his place behind her and moved ahead of her, with a powerful skating motion that broke the trail.

Of course, what goes up must come down, and as she crested the hill, she saw it was a long downhill run.

He swooped down it, a cry of pure joy coming off his lips. She watched as he invited speed, crouched, played with the hill and the snow and gravity.

He reached the bottom, slid to a sideways stop in an incredible display of agility and spray of snow.

"Come on," he called.

The truth was she was terrified. Her heart was doing that beating-too-fast thing that it had been doing for almost two full days. She stared down the hill. It seemed a long way down. And it seemed very steep.

"You can sidestep it if you want," he called. He climbed partway back up the hill and demonstrated a way she could come down.

But suddenly she didn't want to play it safe. She let out a war whoop and shoved her poles to get going. Then she was swooshing down the hill so fast she could feel her stomach drop. Her eyes got tears in them. Her hat flew off.

She gained speed. She let out another whoop, the pure joy of letting go completely! She raced by him, screaming with laughter.

Except that beyond him, he had not broken the trail. Her skis hit the virgin snow and slowed so abruptly she thought she was going to be tossed right out of her bindings.

As soon as she started to think about what could happen, it did. She caught an edge and could feel herself cartwheeling through the snow.

Only it didn't hurt. It was like tumbling into a cold pillow. After she stopped, she lay there for a moment, staring at the sky.

He skied over and peered down at her. "Are you okay?" he asked.

"Really?" she said. "Never better."

And then they were both laughing.

And it felt as if *really* she had never had a better moment in her whole life.

CHAPTER FIFTEEN

TWO HOURS LATER, coated in generous amounts of sweat, crusted in snow and dazzled by laughter and the sun that had come out on the mountain, they burst into a small clearing.

Stacy was aware that Kiernan was watching her, and from the small smile that played across his lips, her reaction did not disappoint.

She clapped wet, mittened hands over her mouth, but not before a gasp of pure wonder escaped it.

There was a cabin at the far edge of the clearing. It was tiny and humble, the logs long since weathered to gray. And yet, set amongst the drifts of snow, with snow sparkling on its roof and the red curtains showing through the window, it was a homey sight in the middle of the majesty of the mountains. Even the little outhouse that was behind it, a half-moon carved in the door, was adorable.

On the other side of the cabin, a stream trickled down rocks, heavy mist rising off of it.

"What is that smell?" she asked, the only thing not in keeping with the beauty of the scene.

"That stream is a natural hot spring. You're smelling minerals, mostly sulfur. Despite the smell, they are supposed to be very good for you. Tracks show us that even the animals come here. Come on. I'll show you."

He glided forward. After two hours, she felt her abilities had not improved all that much. She still waddled after him.

He skied right to the cabin, kicked off his skis and shrugged off the pack he had carried the entire way. She arrived and he showed her how to release the binding by putting the tip of the pole on it and pushing.

She stepped out of the skis and had to reach for his arm.

"My legs feel wobbly," she said, and then let go of his arm and went to the edge of the water.

"That water will have you feeling back to normal in no time." He had come to stand beside her.

"This must have taken someone hundreds of painstaking hours," she said, regarding the rock pool, complete with an underwater bench that had been built to capture the steaming water from the springs.

"I had the good fortune to get it exactly as it was. You see how the water is seeping out of the rocks on the downhill side? It acts as a natural filtration system. The water is constantly being replaced."

"The rocks are like artwork," she said. The constant flow of water over them turned colors that might have been muted if they were dry to spectacularly jewel like. There were rocks in golds and greens and grays and blues and pinks.

"Are we going to go in that?" she breathed.

"Of course. If you brought a bathing suit."

Her face crumpled. "No. You never said to. I'm not sure I would have believed you if you had. This is pure magic, Kieran, but I didn't bring a suit. I guess I can't go in."

He raised an eyebrow wickedly. "Unless…"

"No!" she said.

"Well, guess what, Murphy?"

"What?"

"Unless somebody has figured out that anything that can go wrong will, and that someone had your back."

Him?

She could feel tears pricking her eyes.

"What's the matter?" he asked softly.

"Nothing. My dad used to call me Murphy. No one has for a long time."

"Ah, Murphy," he said gruffly, put his arm around her shoulders and pulled her hard against his own shoulder. "Adele packed you a bathing suit," he said, his tone gentle as a touch.

"Oh, Adele," she said, not sure if she was disappointed or relieved. Well, maybe relieved. She certainly wouldn't want him packing her a bathing suit. Come to that, did she want to be sharing a very romantic moment with him in a bathing suit she had not even chosen herself?

"She packed us lunch, too. You want to do that first?"

She realized she was ravenous…and that lunch would give her reprieve from donning the bathing suit. It was hard enough to put on a bathing suit you had chosen yourself, after many self-critical moments in front of the mirror. What would Adele have chosen for her?

He laughed at her expression. "Lunch it is. We just burned about a million calories each." He opened the backpack and took out the contents. "Hot dogs and marshmallows. A good thing we burned so many calories."

He rummaged through the pack some more. "Look, she packed a bottle of wine to go with our hot dogs." He shook his head. "Not exactly hot dog wine. It's a rare bottle of ice wine."

"We don't have to drink it," Stacy said. In fact probably better if they did not. "You are probably saving that for a special occasion."

"I was," he said, rummaging again, and then he hesitated at something he found in that pack, "and I can't think of an occasion more special than this one."

"In what way?" she stammered.

"Part of the snow virgin ceremonies," he teased, and pulled something else out of the pack and held it up.

"I'm pretty sure I lost my snow virginity on the night of the snowball fight," she choked out. "Snowball fight. Snow angel. Snowman. Yup. Done."

"I'm pretty sure you're not done until you've been dipped in the waters of Last Chance in this."

She looked at the tiny piece of black-and-white fabric he was waving, not comprehending.

"Adele packed you a bikini!"

Well, that answered the burning question of what kind of bathing suit Adele had packed for her!

"Let's eat," she said, strangled.

"How are you at fire starting?"

"Is this still part of the whole snow virgin thing? Because I'd be about the same at that as I am at snowman building. And skiing."

"All the same," he said, and tossed a package of matches at her. "You can be in charge of the fire pit out here. I'm going to start a fire in stove in the cabin, too, so we have a warm place to get changed."

Into a black-and-white bikini that looked, at a glance, as if it didn't have enough fabric in it to make a good-size handkerchief.

She was probably going to need the wine to find the nerve to put on the bathing suit. Meanwhile, she would distract herself by trying to start a fire.

Kiernan came back outside and helped her. Soon he had turned her little pile of twigs and tiny flame into a roaring blaze and they were toasting hot dogs on sticks over it.

"Oh, my," she said an hour later. "Did I eat three hot dogs?"

"You did."

"Why did it taste like food from the gods?"

"They're pleased about the sacrificing of the snow virgin?" He laughed at her face. It was so good to hear him laugh like that, boyishly, carelessly, mischievously. He could tease her for a hundred years about being a snow virgin, if she just got to hear him laugh.

"I'm getting a little confused," she said. "Am I being sacrificed or deflowered?"

It was her turn to feel richly satisfied when a tide of brick-red worked its way up the strong column of his neck.

"The cabin is probably warm by now, if you want to go put on your suit," he said gruffly, not looking at her. Really, for the first time since she had gotten on those skies, it felt as if she had the upper hand.

The inside of the cabin was rudimentary but darling. She found the bathing suit wrapped in a towel on the bed.

It was definitely the tiniest bathing suit she had ever put on! So much for having the upper hand. Stacy felt like a nervous wreck after donning the bathing suit. There wasn't even a mirror to check how revealing it was. She wrapped herself in a towel and headed outside.

He was already in the hot pool and she gulped at the pure wonder of the moment life had delivered.

She slipped off the towel and felt a surge of fresh wonder at the look in his eyes, stormy with appreciation, on her. Rough stone steps went into the water, and she took them and then waded across to the bench on the opposite side of the pool from him.

After a moment, she closed her eyes and allowed herself to feel the full glory of it: the hot, natural water massaging her exhausted muscles and her many bruises.

"I didn't really realize I hurt all over, until I got in here," she said.

"You took some pretty good tumbles."

"The water feels great on all my aches and pains. I didn't deserve a day like this, Kiernan. Does it mean you have forgiven me?"

She opened her eyes and looked at him. She saw his answer before he said it.

"Yeah," he said, "I suppose that is what it means."

"Thank you." She took a deep breath. "Now you just have to forgive yourself."

He looked across the steam at her, raised an eyebrow. "What do you mean by that, exactly?"

"Your sister and I talked last night."

"That was my fear," he said.

"She's fallen in love."

"Yes, she told me."

"She's worried about you accepting Mark. She's worried you can't get beyond what happened that day."

"Are you giving me some free counseling?" he said.

She could hear the warning in his voice, to back off, to leave it, but she could not.

"Why are you mad at Mark?"

"I'm not mad at him."

"Adele said you seem furious with him. She thinks it's because he lived and Danner died."

Kiernan swore softly. "That's not it. That's not it at all!"

"What is it then?"

"It's that I lived and Danner died."

"And Mark?"

"He was there." The anger faded from him, and he looked dejected. She saw his heart, and it was just as she had always suspected. She saw Kiernan McAllister's heart and it was broken.

She scooted over on the bench beside him and took his hand. "He was there and…?" she whispered.

"He was there for the moment of my greatest failing," Kiernan said. "It's not his fault, but I can barely look at him. Because he knows."

"Knows what?"

Kiernan's sigh was long and followed by a shudder so massive that the water of the pool rippled.

"It was my fault. I killed him."

She was silent, but her hand tightened on his, and her eyes would not leave his face.

"Danner was different than me. I had used adrenaline all my life, like a drug. Flying down a mountain, flat out, there is nothing else. Just that moment."

"I just experienced that myself," Stacy said.

He nodded. "Danner was more like you. Willing to embrace it, but cautious. I introduced him to that world of untouched snow, but he never took leadership. He always trusted me and followed me.

"And that morning, I picked the wrong slope. And I was strong enough and experienced enough to outrun it, and he was not."

He stopped, but she had read it in his voice and his eyes and the heave of his shoulders.

"And I will feel guilty about that for the rest of my life. That I misjudged his ability to cope and it cost him his life. I will feel responsible for that for the rest of my life.

"When I close my eyes, I can still see it and feel it. I glanced back over my shoulder, could see his skies cutting a line out, setting a shelf of snow free. The sound was like a freight train. It was right on top of both of us. I was closer to Mark, and I shoved him hard, and he saw what was going on and managed to kind of squirt out to the side.

"I thought Danner was right on my shoulder. I could feel

the wind being created by that snow coming. But when I skied free of it, he wasn't there. He'd been swept away."

The silence of the mountains felt heavy and sacred.

"But what could you have done differently?" she finally whispered.

"That is what I lay awake at night asking myself. That's why I wish sometimes it would have taken me, too. So that I would not have to live with this ultimate failure, the sense of being powerless when it mattered most. The only time it really ever mattered."

"And Adele would have lost both of you, maybe even all three of you," Stacy said softly. "I don't know that she could have survived that."

"What if we'd had breakfast a little later, or decided not to go out that day, or what if I had asked to take a different trail?"

"That's why it's your fault?" she asked quietly.

"It's part of it. Wrong decisions, from the very beginning of that day." His voice was broken.

"My family dying was my fault, too," she whispered.

His head jerked up.

"I was going to my first high school dance. Oh, Kiernan, I was so excited. I had a new dress, and I'd been allowed to wear makeup, and my mom had done my hair for me. My imagination, of course," she admitted ruefully, "had gone absolutely crazy creating scenarios. I thought Bobby Brighton might notice me and ask me to dance. Or Kenny O'Connell.

"And then I got there, and it wasn't like the middle school dances, where everybody just kind of danced together, and had fun.

"All the boys were on one side of the room, and all the girls on the other, and pretty soon all the popular girls were being asked to dance, and I wasn't. By the halfway intermission, I hadn't been asked to dance, not even once, not even by the science nerds.

"And so I called my Dad. And I was crying.

"And he said my grandma was over visiting, and they had been talking about going out bowling and for iced hot chocolate after, *and Murphy, girl, we wouldn't have had any fun without you, anyway, so I'm coming to get you. And when I get there, I better not be beating off those boys with my shovel.*

"But—" Her voice had become a whisper. "They never got there. A drunk driver ran a red light and it killed them all."

"Stacy," he said, and his voice was a whisper that shared her agony.

"I didn't tell you that because I wanted you to feel sorry for me," she said. "I told you because I always felt I had killed them, too. If I hadn't have called. Was my Dad rushing to get to me? Was he so focused on the fact his little Murphy girl was in distress, he missed something, that flash of motion, or a sound that would have alerted him to the fact that car was coming? I have tormented myself with this question—what if I had called ten minutes later or earlier?"

"Stacy," he said again, and now his powerful arms were wrapped around her, and he pulled her hard against himself.

"Do you think I killed them?" she demanded.

"No! Of course not!"

"I don't think you killed Danner, either."

Beneath his skin, for a moment she thought she felt his heart stop beating. And then it started again and instead of putting her away from him, he drew her closer.

He pushed the tendrils of wet hair from her face, and he

looked down at her, and it felt as if no one had ever seen
her quite so completely before.

"Thank you," he whispered.

And it was a greater gift, even, than being brought to
this incredible place.

CHAPTER SIXTEEN

KIERNAN WAITED FOR it to happen. All his strength had not been enough to hold the lid on the place that contained the grief within him.

The touch of her hand, the look in her eyes, and his strength had abandoned him, and he had told her all of it: his failure and his powerlessness.

Now, sitting beside her, her hand in his, the wetness of her hair resting on his shoulder, he waited for everything to fade: the white-topped mountains that surrounded him, the feel of the hot water against his skin, the way her hand felt in his.

He waited for all that to fade, and for the darkness to take its place, to ooze through him like thick, black sludge freed from a containment pond, blotting out all else.

Instead, astounded, Kiernan became *more* aware of everything around him, as if he was soaking up life through his pores, breathing in glory through his nose, becoming drenched in light instead of darkness.

He started to laugh.

"What?" she asked, a smile playing across the lovely fullness of her lips.

"I just feel alive. For the past few days, I have felt alive. And I don't know if that's a good thing or a bad thing."

"This is what I think," she said, slowly and thoughtfully,

"we are, all of us, vulnerable to love. And when we lose someone, or something that we have cared about, we are like Samson. We think the source of our strength is gone. We have had our hair cut.

"But without our even realizing it, our hair grows back, and our strength returns, and maybe," she finished softly, "just maybe we are even better than we were before."

Her words fell on him, like raindrops hitting a desert that was too long parched.

His awareness shifted to her, and being with her seemed to fill him to overflowing.

He dropped his head over hers and took her lips. He kissed her with warmth and with welcome, a man who had thought he was dead discovering not just that he lived but, astonishingly, that he wanted to live.

Stacy returned his kiss, her lips parting under his, her hands twining around his neck, pulling him in even closer to her.

There was gentle welcome. She had seen all of him, he had bared his weakness and his darkness to her, and still he felt only acceptance from her.

But acceptance was slowly giving way to something else. There was hunger in her, and he sensed an almost savage need in her to go to the place a kiss like this took a man and a woman.

With great reluctance he broke the kiss, cupped her cheeks in his hands and looked down at her.

He felt as if he was memorizing each of her features: the green of those amazing eyes, her dark brown hair curling even more wildly from the steam of the hot spring, the swollen plumpness of her lips, the whiteness of her skin.

"It's too soon for this," he said, his voice hoarse.

"I know," she said, and her voice was raw, too.

And then, despite having said that, they were drawn

together again, into that sensual world of steam and hot water, skin like warmed-through silk touching skin. Peripherally, he was aware of snow shining with diamonds, and mountain peaks soaring to touch sky, and the insistent call of a Whiskey Jack.

He pulled away from her the second time.

It was too soon to kiss her so thoroughly. Their days together had been intense. This feeling of being cracked wide open was something that could make a man do something irrational.

And he could not do that to her. You did not kiss a woman like Stacy Murphy Walker like that unless you knew.

Unless you knew what your feelings were.

And unless you knew the future held some possibility.

He had brought her here as a gift, to help her heal her pain, not to cause her more. But he had come here for himself, too. Maybe mostly for himself. To see if there was hope, and it seemed to him that maybe there was, after all.

And it seemed to him part of hoping, part of breaking open inside was a requirement to have the events of his life to make him better.

Not bitter.

Worthy of the love of a beautiful woman like this one.

That's what Adele had tried to tell him. That's what Danner would have wanted. Danner would have wanted him to embrace *all* of what he was, darkness and light, and let them melt together.

"We need to go," he said, letting go of Stacy reluctantly, knowing he could not push the bounds of his own strength by kissing her a third time.

He stood up, put his hands on the rock edges of the pool and heaved himself out of it. "We don't want to be trying to get home in the dark."

It was an excuse. An excuse to step back from the intensity between them. Because that kind of intensity did not lend itself to rational thought and it seemed to him he owed her at least that.

To make decisions from here on out, as far as she was concerned, based on reason.

And not what he had felt there in the pool with her: the powerful release of something he had been holding on to, followed all too quickly by the ecstasy of her lips on his.

She looked disappointed.

And maybe a touch relieved, too, as if she knew things were going too fast, spinning out of their control.

He grabbed his dry clothes from the toasty warm cabin, leaving it to her to get dressed in privacy. He ducked behind the cabin, hoping the cold air on his heated skin would be sobering.

Instead, being able to feel the cold air prickle across his skin only increased his sense of being alive as totally and completely as he ever had been. He quickly packed up their things, waited for her to come out of the cabin and resisted the temptation to greet her with a kiss, as if they had been separated by weeks instead of minutes.

He schooled himself to be all business as he helped her into her skis. The sun was now warm, and the snow was melting quickly. It made it heavy and hard to ski, despite the fact he had changed waxes. Partway home, they lost the snow completely.

They took off the skis, and he shouldered them. They walked along the forest trail. Stacy slipped at one point, and he reached back and took her hand, and somehow he didn't let it go again until he noticed she was limping.

"Are you okay?"

"I think the ski boots are rubbing."

"Let's have a look."

"It's okay. I can practically see your house from here."

"I think I should have a look."

Cross-country boots were not made for walking. His were custom, so they fit him well, but hers were not.

They sat in the snow, and he took her boots off, and then her socks. She did, indeed, have terrible rubs starting on the back of both heels. One of them was bleeding.

"Why didn't you say something sooner?"

She looked sheepish. "To tell you the truth, I hardly noticed."

And so, she, like him, was in an altered state, one where maybe the best decisions were not made.

With a tenderness he had not known he was capable of, he found a little of the snow that remained in a shaded spot beside the trail and rubbed it on the frayed skin of her heels, aware of how he loved caressing her feet and the look on her face when he did it.

And then, ignoring her protests, feeling stronger than he had ever felt, feeling like Samson who once again had hair, he picked her up and cradled her against his chest.

"I can walk," she protested.

But he didn't want her to. He wanted to carry her. He wanted to protect her and care for her. Maybe he wanted to show her how strong he was.

"What about the skis?" she asked, when it was evident he did not intend to put her down.

"I'll get you there and then I'll come back for them."

She looked as if she was going to protest. But then she didn't. She snuggled deep into his chest, and he strode along the trail that led toward home.

He set her down on the front steps of his house, and still feeling strong and full of energy, he went back up the trail to retrieve their skis.

When he came back to the house, she was waiting at

the door. He could tell by the look on her face something was wrong.

"What is it?"

She passed him the note. In Adele's handwriting it said that Max had gotten worse since they left and had developed a high fever. She had taken him to the hospital in Whistler.

Kiernan stared at the note.

It seemed as if his whole world crashed in around him. While he'd been out playing in the snow, entertaining foolish notions about the nature of love and forever, of hope and of healing, his nephew had been getting sicker and sicker.

Sick enough, apparently, to require a trip to the emergency room.

It was a reminder, stark and brutal, of what was real, of how quickly everything could change and of how what you loved most could be snatched away from you. That was reality.

What was not reality was the way he felt after he had showed his soul to Stacy. It was not the laughter that had entered his life since she had been here.

It was not snowmen and snowball fights, homemade cookies, bikinis in hot springs.

Reality was a man who was not in control of any of the things he wanted to be in control of. The way he had felt, carrying her the last few yards, strong and able to protect her with his life if need be, was the biggest illusion of all.

He was not Samson.

Because he did not have the strength to say yes to any of this again. To be open to the caprice of fate and chance.

That's what love did, in the end—it made a man's life uncertain. It left his heart wide open to the unbearable pain of loss.

He took the note and shoved it in his pocket. He went

through the house and found the phone and dialed Adele's number.

"Everything okay?" he asked when she answered. He was aware he was bracing himself for the worst.

"Everything's fine," she said, and the air went out of him like a man who had dodged a bullet whistling by his ear. "The doctor says Max has an ear infection. They're keeping an eye on him for a bit, but it looks like he'll be released in about an hour."

Relief welled up in him. "That's good," he said in a calm voice that gave away nothing of the precipice he felt he had just stood on. "How did you get to the hospital?"

Better to deal with details and logistics than that uncontrollable helpless feeling that came with loving someone.

"I took a cab. I'm going to rent a car, and go home. I think Max needs to be at home. How was your day?" she asked. "Did you have fun?"

And he heard it in her. Hope for him. And the one thing he did not want to do was give anyone false hopes. Not her.

And certainly not Stacy.

"I'll come get you," he told his sister. "I'll drive you home."

"But what about Stacy?"

He said nothing.

"Oh, Kiernan," she said, her voice part annoyance and part sympathy. "Don't throw this away."

He ended the call without responding to that. Stacy was in the kitchen putting on a kettle. For a moment his resolve wavered. He could picture them sitting together having hot chocolate. Max wasn't here. He could build a fire in the hearth without concerns for the baby's safety.

It felt, for a moment, as if he could picture their whole lives together…for a moment he could see this room the way she had seen it the first time she had entered…full of laughter and family, a big Christmas tree and toys on the floor.

And he steeled himself against the yearning that vision caused in him.

"How is Max?" she asked anxiously.

"It's an ear infection. He's being released in an hour or so. I'm going to go get them."

"All right." She had heard something in his tone. He could see his coolness register on her face. "Do you want me to come with you?"

It felt like that *no* was the hardest thing he'd ever said. But no, there was something harder yet that had to be said, that had to be done.

She had to know there was no hope. Not for them. None.

"I'll go back to the city with them," he said. "I won't be coming back here."

"Oh! I'll get my things, then. And clear out, too."

"I'll need your contact information."

Hope flickered briefly until she registered how he had worded that. Not *I'll call.* Not *I'll be in touch.*

"My lawyer will contact you," he said, struggling to strip all emotion from his voice. "I'll want you to sign something saying the things we have discussed were in strictest confidence."

It did exactly as he had both hoped and dreaded it would do.

It shattered her.

She turned swiftly from him and unplugged the kettle. She went through the drawers until she found a piece of paper and a pen.

She wrote her information down, her curls falling like a curtain in front of her face. He didn't stay to watch. He went to his room and shut the door. He did not come out until he heard the front door close behind her.

He ordered himself not to look, but he went to the front window anyway and watched her drive away.

Then he went and retrieved the information from where she had left it on the counter. He unfolded the piece of paper.

Written on it was not her mailing address or her phone number or her email.

Written on it in unhesitating script, it read, *"Go to hell."*

And despite the pain he was in, he could not help but smile. Because, unlike him, Stacy Murphy Walker had long ago learned to roll with the punches.

He crumpled up the paper and threw it on the counter. He went and looked at the guest room.

There was nothing in there to show she had ever been there. The faint smell of lemons and soap would not be here by the next time he came back. The fountain she had toppled would be righted, eventually, and the shrubs re-planted.

Probably all that would happen before he came back here, because he was not at all sure when that would be.

Wouldn't this place, now, be forever connected in his mind to her?

All he had left of her was a wet bathing suit in his back-pack. A bathing suit Adele might want back.

And then in a moment that he recognized as utter weakness, he went back into the kitchen, picked Stacy's note up off the counter and straightened the crumples out of it with his fist. He folded it carefully and put it in his shirt pocket.

He wanted to keep something of her. Even if it was this.

Maybe especially if it was this. Something that showed him, after all, that she was strong. And spunky. She was going to be fine.

He was just not so sure about himself.

CHAPTER SEVENTEEN

STACY MURPHY WALKER would have been stunned to know that Kiernan McAllister thought she would be fine. She was not fine.

She cried for a week. She screamed into her pillow. She didn't get dressed. Or comb her hair. She didn't brush her teeth or pick up her newspapers from the front door.

She made cookies and ate them all to prove cookies tasted just as good without him in her life. She drank a bucket of hot chocolate just to reassure herself that it was still good.

But the truth was, the cookies tasted like sawdust and the hot chocolate might as well have been bathwater.

A few days with him, and she was reacting like this! With more drama and heartache and grief than the end of her six-month courtship with Dylan. It was shameful! She was lucky it had only been a few days with him! Imagine if it had been longer? Imagine if they had let that kiss get away from them? Then what would she be feeling?

Though, in truth, she wondered if she could possibly be feeling any worse!

This seemed like a preview of her future life: drab and tasteless, unexciting. The potential for it to be something else had shimmered briefly and enticingly, and now that was gone.

At the end of a full week of immersion in her misery, Stacy knew she had to pull herself together. She had bills to pay! Other people might have the luxury of wallowing in a heartbreak but she did not!

Murphy's Law once again: everything that could go wrong, had. Why should she be surprised? It was the story of her life, after all.

And there was a positive side: nothing could steal those moments from her. Nothing could take the memories of her snow angel, and their snowball fight, the snowman that might still be melting in his yard. Nothing could take the ski trip and that beautiful little cabin and those moments in the hot tub, where it had seemed, for one shining instant, as if the events of all her life had led her to *this*.

"Stop it," she ordered herself. It was her imagination, run wild again, that had got her in all this trouble.

Had she actually talked herself into believing a man like Kiernan McAllister could feel anything for her?

She snorted her self-disgust out loud.

Then, newly determined, Stacy went and gathered the newspapers from her front door and went through them, one by one, looking for the lead that would launch her new career as a freelancer.

But nothing in the business section interested her.

In fact, if she was really honest about it, business had *never* interested her. In a moment of desperation, with no funds to complete college, she had taken the first job that had been offered to her. Fallen into it, really.

And if she looked at her failed relationship with Dylan, it had the same hallmarks: the relationship had presented itself to her. She had fallen into it rather than chosen it. She had been flattered by his attention. It had been convenient. It had seemed like the easiest route to what she wanted: to feel that sense of home again.

And then she had made the same mistake with Kiernan, skidded into his life instead of choosing it for herself.

"That's done," she told herself firmly. "Falling into things is done. My life happening by accident is done."

Stacy set down the papers. She got out her laptop.

What did she want to write about? If she was going to steer into the spin instead of away from it, what story would she tell? Asking herself that question seemed to open a floodgate.

A week later she sold the piece to *Pacific Life* magazine for more money than she had ever expected. The article sparked interest in her charity the likes of which she had not seen before.

Some of the kids she worked with had seen the piece, and they wanted to write their stories.

She started a blog for them. *Pacific Life* picked up some of stories.

Speaking invitations began to roll in. Stacy began to have a life she had never dreamed possible.

And if it was missing one thing, she tried not to think about that.

It was only at night, when another hectic day had ended, and her head was on the pillow, that she would let herself think of those fewdays of wonder.

And the newest success story in Vancouver would cry herself to sleep.

Adele walked into Kiernan's apartment as if she owned the place. She looked around as if she was going to set Max down, but what she saw must have made her think better of it.

Kiernan glared at her. The apartment was dark, and he was sitting on the couch, remote control for the TV in his hand. He muted the sound on the television. "What are you doing here? And how did you get in?"

She wagged a key at him. "I got it from the apartment manager. I said I was conducting a well-being check."

"He fell for that?"

"Women with babies are nearly always perceived as trustworthy."

"I'm going to see that he's fired."

Adele made a sucking sound through her teeth. He never liked it when she made that sound. It never boded well for him.

"God, where's your housekeeper?"

"I fired her."

"Well, it smells in here."

"I burned the pizza."

"You tried to make your own pizza?"

She said that as if it told her a deep dark secret about him. And maybe it did. He had tried to cook pizza in an effort to prove to himself he could have the very same life without Stacy that he could have with her. The experiment had been a dismal failure, but apparently, from the look on Adele's face, she already knew that.

"Did you fire your housekeeper before or after you fired Miss Harris?" Adele asked.

"I hired her back! Where did you hear I fired Miss Harris?"

"Mark told me."

"Well, tell him he can be fired, too. What happens at the office stays at the office."

"Look, brother dear, you can fire everyone you come in contact with, but it's obviously not going to make you feel any better."

"It does make me feel better," he insisted, watching her darkly.

"You have to deal with what's at the heart of the matter, Kee."

"And I suppose you know what that is?" he snarled.

"Of course I do!"

He cocked his head at her, raised an eyebrow.

"Your heart," she said. "Your heart is at the heart of that matter."

Her eyes, unfortunately, seemed to be adjusting to the dark in here, because she picked her way through the dirty socks and shirts on the floor and stood over him. Max peeked at him and apparently didn't like what he saw— or feared being left again—because he nuzzled into his mother's shoulder and sucked feverishly on his thumb.

Adele reached down and picked up a magazine off a heap of them on the coffee table.

"What's this?"

"Don't touch that!"

"*Icons of Business.* Haven't you been featured in this?" When he didn't answer, she frowned. "Good grief, Kee, are you ego-surfing through your glory days?"

"You're saying that as if they are in the past," he said, increasingly annoyed at this invasion into his misery, wanting to deflect her from seeing why he was really surrounded by several years of issues of *Icons of Business.*

She was juggling Max, flipping through the magazine, obviously totally looking in the wrong direction, thinking she would find a story about him.

Then, to his chagrin, a light went on in her face. "Oh my God, you are reading all Stacy's stories!"

She said that as if he was being adorable.

"I'm gathering ammunition to help me prepare the lawsuit when she writes the unauthorized story about me!"

It was weak and not credible and he knew it.

"You'll be preparing your own lawsuit, I guess, since you fired Harry last week?"

He didn't even ask her where she had heard that. He hoped his glare balanced out the flimsy explanation of why he was reading Stacy's writing enough to make his sister stop talking and leave. Apparently it didn't.

"She's not going to write about you, silly."

"Silly?"

"I had coffee with her. After I saw the article she wrote in *Pacific Life*."

"You had coffee with Stacy? Last week?" He had to bite his tongue to keep from asking all the questions that wanted to tumble off it. *Was she okay? Was she happy? Did she ask about him?*

Instead he asked, "What was the article about?"

"Not you." She let that sink in, just to let him know the whole world was not about him.

"Is there a point to this visit? Oh, just a sec. Well-being check. You can clearly see I'm alive, so—"

"I brought you a copy to look at." Still juggling the baby, she put down the copy of *Icons of Business* and fished around in a purse enormous enough to hold a Volkswagen. She found what she wanted and put it on top of his mess on the coffee table.

"Why?"

"Oh, quit snarling. Because I love you, and care about you and trust that after you have read it you will still know how to do the right thing."

He decided, stubbornly, even before his sister left, that he was *never* reading the article. He made it for twenty minutes, pretending interest in the football game his sister had so rudely interrupted.

But he was once again, Samson, sans hair. He had no strength.

He picked up the magazine and flipped through it until he found the article that Stacy had written. It was called "Murphy's Law: Confessions of a Foster Child," and it started with the words, *I believed in magic until I was sixteen years old...*

When he finished it, he read it again. He was aware his face was wet with tears.

And he was aware of something else. His sister was right. He still did know how to do the right thing.

And somehow finding his checkbook in this mess he had created of his life and writing a big fatty to CCOFK was not going to cut it.

By the time he had finished reading that story, he knew what he had always known in his heart. He knew exactly who Stacy was.

But he knew something beyond that, too. And it was something that could change his life and lead him out of darkness if he had the courage to embrace it.

CHAPTER EIGHTEEN

STACY WAS BEYOND EXHAUSTED. Her life had taken off in so many unexpected directions in the past few weeks! Though she had sworn her cookie-and-hot-chocolate days were over, it did sound like an easy supper after a long, hard day. And she was putting on her pajamas to eat it, too.

Her doorbell rang and she went to it, in her pajamas, cookies in hand. She peeked out the side window and reeled away, her back against the door.

Her heart was beating too fast.

Just as if it might explode.

She was not opening that door. She was not. She had cookies melting in her hands. She was in her pajamas at seven o'clock at night. Her hair was a mess, and she had already wiped all the makeup off her face.

In her imagination, she had pictured seeing him again, down to the last detail. She had thought maybe their paths would cross at a charity function. And that she would be wearing designer clothes and Kleinback shoes. Her hair would be upswept, her makeup perfect, and she would be sipping very expensive champagne.

Nothing, she thought, a touch sourly, *ever goes the way I plan it.*

He knocked again. She was not going to open that door.

But she could not resist putting her eye to a little slit in the drapery to have one last look at him.

Kiernan McAllister did not look anything like he did in her imaginings. In fact, he looked awful! His face was whisker roughened like it had been the first day she saw him. His hair hadn't been cut recently, and it was touching his collar.

He was not dressed in one of the custom suits that he always wore when he graced the cover of a magazine.

Or in the casuals he had worn at his cottage.

He was in a thin windbreaker that wasn't warm enough for the blustery Vancouver day. His jeans had a hole in the knee.

But it was his eyes that made her fling open the door.

They had dark circles under them. The light in them was haunted.

"Hello," she said. She took a bite of her cookie to make sure he did not have a clue her heart was beating so fast it might explode at any second.

"Hello, Murphy."

Her defenses were down quite enough without him calling her that.

"How have you been?" he asked softly.

As if he really cared.

"All right," she said. She took another bite of the cookie and hoped to hell she wouldn't choke on it. "You?"

It was ludicrous, them standing there asking each other these banal questions as if they had bumped into each other on the street.

"I haven't been doing so good," he said.

She gave up all pretense of eating the cookie and really looked at him. It felt as if her heart were breaking in two.

"Can I come in?" he said. "I really need to talk to you."

Did he have to? Come in? To her space? It wasn't that

it was humble, because it was, and that did not embarrass her in the least.

It was that once he had been in here, some part of him would linger forever. She would never feel the same way about her space again.

Still, she stood back from the door.

He came by her and looked around, a little smile playing around the edge of his mouth.

"What?"

"It's just as I imagined."

"*You* imagined where *I* live?"

"I did," he confessed. He took off his coat and, seeing no place to hang it, put it on the doorknob.

She watched him go and flop down on her couch. He closed his eyes, like a man gathering himself.

Or like a man who had found his way home.

"How did you imagine it?" she asked.

"Like something I saw in a children's book a long time ago—a little rabbit warren, safe and full of color and coziness and those little touches that make a house into a home. Like this." He picked up a doily on her coffee table.

"Why are you here?" she asked, and she could hear something plaintive in her voice that begged him to put her out of her misery.

He patted the spot on the couch beside him.

She hesitated, but she could not say no. She went and sat beside him. The couch was not large enough to leave as much space between them as she would have liked. Her shoulder was nearly brushing his. She could feel the heat and energy pulsating off him. His scent tickled her nostrils, clean and tantalizingly masculine.

"I always thought I was a courageous man," he said, his voice soft. "When I was swooping down mountains where no one had ever skied before, when I was jumping out of airplanes, when I was zip-lining through the jungle, I was always congratulating myself on what a brave guy I was."

She said nothing, but she felt herself move, fractionally, closer to him.

"Of course, I wasn't at all," he said slowly. "I was just filling up all the empty spaces in my life with one adrenaline rush after another. I was outrunning something, even before Danner died."

She shifted again until their shoulders were touching lightly.

"I was outrunning the thing that took the most courage of all. I was terrified of it. I had experienced its treachery, and I couldn't trust it.

"And when Danner died, I took it as proof that I was right."

"Love," she said, her voice choked, her shoulder and his leaning against each other, supporting each other. "It's love that takes the most courage."

"Yes, love."

The way he said the word, love could be taken two ways, one of them as an endearment.

"But the thing I was running hardest from is the thing that will be brought to you again and again. It's like the universe cannot accept no as an answer to that one thing.

"And so love tracks you down. In a baby whose laughter could make a heart of stone come back to life. In a sister who is so brokenhearted and who needs you to man up.

"In a woman who crashes into your fountain, and announces to you, who already knows, that anything that can go wrong will."

"How can you love me?" Stacy whispered.

"I didn't say I loved you."

"Oh," she said, not even trying to hide how crushed that made her feel.

He turned his face to hers, put a finger under her chin and tilted it up to him. "I said I had been brought the opportunity to say yes to love. You see, Murphy, that's why I'm here."

"Why?"

"To see if you can teach me about real courage. You're right. I don't know if I love you. But I have this feeling that I could. And it terrifies me."

"I have nothing to teach you," she whispered.

"Yes, you do." His finger was still under her chin, and he was still gazing into her eyes. After a long time, he said, "I read your article."

"You did?"

"And it's all there. Everything that you are. But maybe, Stacy, writing, at its best and its highest, does not just show who the writer is. Maybe it shows the reader who they are, too. For the first time in a long time, I feel as if I know," he said. "I know exactly who I am."

Stacy looked at him.

And she knew, too. She knew exactly who Kiernan McAllister was. And for the first time in a long, long time, she began to smile, and the smile felt as brilliant and as warm as the sun coming out after a snowstorm.

CHAPTER NINETEEN

WHEN KIERNAN MCALLISTER first began to woo Stacy Murphy Walker, he did it the way he did everything else. He went flat out and over the top. He wanted this woman to know that he meant business.

And so he chartered a chopper and had a white tablecloth dinner for her on a mountaintop, complete with white-gloved, black-suited waiters.

He took her on the company's jet for a weekend of theater and shopping and exploring in New York City.

Kiernan showered Stacy with gifts and baubles and flowers.

He took her to the most select restaurants in Vancouver. He took her to his exclusive fitness club with its climbing wall, indoor pool and steam room.

Her first time downhill skiing was at Steamboat in Colorado, with him by her side.

In other words, he treated her the way he had treated all the other women he had ever dated.

And all those brand-new experiences delighted her, and he enjoyed them more than he ever had, experiencing them anew by running them through the filter of her complete wonder.

But it quickly became apparent to him that Stacy was not like anyone he had ever dated before.

Because while her enjoyment of each of the experiences was genuine, it became more and more apparent to Kiernan that it was when Stacey suggested how they would spend time together that they had the most fun.

Not only had the most fun but really started to get to know each other, on a different level, on a deeper level.

Stacy's idea of a good time was popcorn and a movie in her cozy little Kitsilano basement suite. Stacy's idea of a good time was a long walk, hand in hand along a deserted, windy stretch of beach. Stacy's idea of a good time was a game of Scrabble and a cup of hot chocolate.

One of her favorite things was babysitting Max so that Adele and Mark, who had slipped away quietly to the Bahamas and gotten married, could have some grown-up time together.

Because of that Kiernan got used to eating hamburgers under the Golden Arches and puzzling together the toy that came in the kid's meal. Because of that he got used to visiting the aquarium and going to story time at the library.

"He's not old enough for story time," he had protested when she first suggested it.

And then been proved wrong when the wriggly little Max had sat still as a stone as the librarian read a picture book.

Because of that, he got used to the park, and pushing a stroller, and visiting the pet store and fishing kids' music CDs out of the player in his car. Because of that he knew all about the elf on the shelf, and he knew who Thomas and Dora were.

Stacy's idea of a good time was serving Christmas dinner to her "kids." Her idea of a good time was being able to organize a day of skiing for those foster kids, or a picnic or a day of swimming.

More and more, Kiernan was aware that Stacy's idea

of a good time was often intrinsically intertwined with helping others.

And somehow, he had become involved in that, too. Those kids she introduced him to, the ones in foster care, were so much like his younger self.

But today, Kiernan had chosen what they were doing. He was leading the way to Last Chance. There had been no early snowstorm this year, and so they were hiking up there to what had become one of their favorite places on earth.

"So beautiful," Stacy said, shrugging off her pack.

He was already being distracted by thoughts of what bathing suit she might have brought.

She seemed distracted by food. Getting out the hot dogs, and buns and marshmallows and, as had become their tradition, a very expensive bottle of ice wine.

Later, in the hot pool, with the steam rising around them, he looked at her and thought she was the most beautiful woman he had ever seen.

She was leaning back in the water, her eyes closed, her hair floating around her, her face tranquil.

But he didn't feel tranquil. He was not sure he, who had defied death with countless feats of daring, had ever felt more nervous in his whole life.

"Stacy?"

She turned and looked at him, righted herself. Something in his face must have told her something very, very important was going on. She came over to him and wrapped her arms around him, looked up into his face.

"What is it, Kiernan? Is something wrong?"

Yes, something was wrong. He hadn't planned to do this in the hot pool. The ring was in the backpack inside the cabin.

He swallowed hard. "Do you know what day it is?" he asked her.

She looked puzzled. "October twenty-sixth?"

He nodded, and could not speak past the lump in his throat.

"Oh, no," she whispered. "It's the anniversary of Danner's death, isn't it? Oh, Kiernan."

And then she said, "Oh, gosh, we should be with Adele."

"It's not," he said. "It's not the anniversary of Danner's death."

Though that day was coming, he recognized, a little shocked, it was not the raw, open wound it had been just a year ago.

"Then what day is it?" she asked. "What is wrong with you?"

"It's a year to the day since you chugged up my driveway and slid into my fountain."

"Oh!" she said.

"It's a year to the day since my life began to change forever. For the better. In ways I could not have imagined. I have something I want to tell you."

"What?" she whispered.

"I'm going to leave McAllister Enterprises."

Did she look disappointed? Yes, she did. He could thank his lucky stars, he supposed, that he hadn't cracked open the wine yet, or he might be wearing it!

"With your blessing," he continued, watching her closely, "I want to turn running it completely over to Mark."

Had she been expecting a proposal? If she had, she seemed to be getting over her disappointment a little too quickly.

"But it's your life!" she said. "Your baby. You started that company. You took it to where it is today."

"It was only a step in the road," he said. "It was only to give me the skills I need to do something else."

"But what?"

He took a deep breath. "I feel as if my whole life has been leading me to this," he told her, the person he could tell anything to. "My whole life, every triumph, and every tragedy, too, has led me to this moment, and this decision."

He felt how right this was.

Will you marry me?

But he made himself wait.

"I want take on Career and College Opportunities for Foster Kids. Stacy, that group is getting ready to explode. It's ready to become more than a tiny charity in Vancouver. It needs to go North America wide."

He could tell she was excited, and disappointed, too. He would play her just a little while longer, the anticipation building in him.

"I want to be at the helm when that happens," he told her, having trouble concentrating on what he was saying. "I want to guide it through its infancy. I have an opportunity to do so much for those young people. Working with it has given my life meaning like nothing else, except..."

He looked at her.

She was holding her breath. She knew what was coming. She had to.

He felt his heart swell inside him. He felt the light dancing with any darkness that remained within him, dancing until they all swirled together and became one magnificent, glorious thing.

"...except you," he said quietly. "Stacy, I don't want to take it on by myself. I want you at my side."

"Of course," she whispered, tears running down her beautiful cheeks.

"I don't just want you at my side to take CCOFK to the next level. I want you at my side for everything. Stacy, I want you to marry me. I want you to be my wife."

For a full minute, she tilted back her head and stared at

up him as if she could not comprehend what he had just said, as if maybe she had not expected this after all.

And then she let out a whoop of pure joy that said everything about what she had become in this past year.

Love, he could see, had taken her to the next level.

He was not sure he had ever been in the presence of such pure joy as Stacy radiated an unbelievable enthusiasm for life, an ability to embrace each day as an adventure.

"Will you marry me?"

Kiernan had thought he would be down on one knee, with the ring extended, but he could see that now, as always, when he let go of control just a little bit, life had a better plan for him than anything he could plan for himself.

Because he knew he would remember this moment, in its absolute perfection, forever.

"Yes!" she cried.

And the mountains rang with her joy and echoed that yes back to him as he picked her up and swung her around in the warm steamy water and then kissed her face all over as if he could never, ever get enough of her.

"Yes," she whispered. "Yes, yes, yes."

EPILOGUE

THE MOUNTAIN TRAIL was beautiful in the springtime. The trees were breaking out in tender, lime-green leaves; the grass shoots were young and fragile, and the moss along the path was like velvet under Stacy Murphy Walker's feet.

Kiernan had said he would deliver her by helicopter, but she'd said no. If her life had taught her anything, it was that it was the journey that mattered, not the arrival.

This day was like nothing she had ever imagined, she thought, as she came into the clearing of the little cabin, Last Chance.

The clearing was full of people. The chairs and the pagoda and the tent for the reception festivities afterward had all been delivered by helicopter.

She was in a long white dress, and a cheer went up when people saw her come from the forest. She walked down the aisle, lifted her skirt to let everyone see her hiking boots and was rewarded with laughter.

Waiting, under that pagoda, was Kiernan, his eyes soft on her, a look in them better, so much better, than anything Stacy could have ever imagined.

Oh, everything that could go wrong had. The minister had suffered a bee sting and been airlifted out with one of the supply helicopters. A new official had been found at the last minute—Kiernan's amazing staff, especially Miss Harris, could do anything.

One of the food boxes had been dropped—from a considerable height—and naturally, it was the one that had contained the cake.

Adele had been in charge of the wedding band, and she had turned away from Max for just one second, and turned back to find the jewelry box empty, the ring nowhere to be found and Max looking innocent as could be.

All of those mishaps seemed fairly minor, even comic, to Stacy. One thing about living a life where things tended to go wrong? You developed a certain grace for dealing with it.

Now, as she walked toward the man who would be her husband, all of it faded: the little cabin and the turquoise waters of the spring that bubbled behind it, Max throwing a tantrum because his mother and Mark were at the front and he was not.

All of it faded: the tent that she passed that was as exquisitely set up as if they were having their wedding at the finest hotel instead of in the wilderness; their guests, some of them dabbing at their eyes as she passed them, doing her little heel kick with the hiking boots.

All of it faded, except him.

Her beloved. Kiernan.

She came to a stop before him, and he reached for her, and their hands joined, and their eyes remained on each other, never straying as they exchanged those age-old words:

In sickness and in health,
In good times and in bad,
In joy as well as in sorrow...

It seemed to Stacy that Kiernan's voice rose out of the

mountains themselves, it was so strong and so sure as he spoke the final vow to her.

"Stacy Murphy Walker, I will honor and respect you. I will laugh with you and I will cry with you. I will cherish you, for as long as we both shall live."

When his lips claimed hers, the world, despite the great cheer from the onlookers, went silent.

And when she stepped back and looked into his silvery eyes, Stacy felt a deep truth within herself.

It was the truth that was stated in those simple vows they had just spoken.

There would be moments like this and many of them— moments of genuine and complete bliss.

But even the wedding vows made room for Murphy! In health *and* in sickness, in good times *and* in bad, in joy *and* in sorrow...

And all lightness aside, as she looked into her new husband's eyes, this was the truth that Stacy Murphy Walker McAllister stood in.

It was not the triumphs that shaped the human race. It was not these moments of temporary bliss that were gone in a second or an hour or a day, and that left people in the everlasting pursuit of *more.*

No, these moments were the gift at the end of the long hard climb, like reaching the mountaintop after climbing the long, rocky trail. Only you didn't get to stay there, on top of the world, drinking in the glory and the magnificence forever. No, eventually, you had to eat and sleep and get some clean clothes and brush your teeth. Eventually, you went back down the mountain to the valley that was life.

To the rainy days and the kids crying, to burned cookies and a fender-bender, and maybe a career disappointment or a goal not reached. Eventually you went back down the mountain to a life that was real.

And in that life that was real, Stacy felt it was tragedies that truly shaped people.

It was the breakdown of a relationship.

It was the death of a parent.

It was watching helplessly as someone you loved struggled with an unexpected illness.

It was an able-bodied person becoming disabled.

It was the business decision gone sour.

It was the friendship betrayed.

It was a parent, for reasons real or imagined, cut from a child's life.

These were the things that shaped people forever, what made them who they really were. These were the things that asked them to be stronger, more compassionate and more forgiving than they ever thought they were capable of being.

It was in these moments of utter defeat and utter despair, these moments of absolute blackness, when a person cast their glance heavenward, toward the light.

It was in these moments, where a person found their knees and whispered that plea of one who had been humbled by life and struggled with darkness—*help me.*

And that plea, if you listened carefully and with a heart wide open, was answered with, *how will you handle this?*

How will you use this, your worst moment, your heartbreak, your disappointment, your tragedy—how will you use this in service?

And sometimes if you were very lucky, or very blessed, as Stacy Murphy Walker McAllister had been, as Kiernan had been, you were allowed to stand in the light, in a moment of complete grace, when you could see.

When you could see who you really were.

And when you could see who your beloved really was.

And then you could sigh with contentment and proclaim it all, every single bit of it, light and darkness, and especially love, to be good.

* * * * *

JOIN US ON SOCIAL MEDIA!

Stay up to date with our latest releases, author news and gossip, special offers and discounts, and all the behind-the-scenes action from Mills & Boon...

 @millsandboon

 @millsandboonuk

 facebook.com/millsandboon

 @millsandboonuk

It might just be true love...

MILLS & BOON
Desire

Indulge in secrets and scandal, intense drama and plenty of sizzling hot action with powerful and passionate heroes who have it all: wealth, status, good looks…everything but the right woman.